D1245225

GABRIEL'S STORM

DIEGO HOJRAJ

outskirts
press

To Mona, Hannah and Pooja
who saved me from a boringly simple life

PROLOGUE

August 1983

They took turns at the front door, loosening it from the frame with steel shank kicks. The two tall, dark bodies slick with rain and sweat worked the door with abandon, their stealth uncompromised by the raging storm around them, their kicks subsumed by its roar. They surveyed the street in between strikes, checking for passersby. The front lawn and driveway had dissolved into a thick, tenacious mud that drained in rivulets onto the street, as dark clouds whipped around in an orgiastic swirl above them, and treetops bent and swayed to the wind in feverish and grotesque dances up and down Hope Street. But no one else appeared; the only ones out tonight were madmen and dead men.

Lying in bed at the blurred edge of sleep, he'd missed the first several kicks whose sounds merged with the storm. But he sat upright panting when the door fell in with a loud crash and the intruders invited the howling wind inside.

Two flashlights scoured the area frantically, catching quick snapshots of the various contents of the living room and dining room, working their way to a common objective. Each room appeared empty, having been partially packed into cardboard boxes that were stacked to the celling. Strategically placed pots and pans on the floor captured the endless tears from a leaky ceiling threatening to buckle and break. A long, narrow hallway leading to the back was bare of any photographs or paintings; rugs and runners were rolled up and propped against the walls.

He felt their heavy footfalls getting closer, reverberating along the wooden floorboards under his bed. He lay back down quickly, his bony, arthritic fingers clutching the bed sheet tightly to his face, covering his eyes. Seconds later he loosened his grip and sat back up again.

He saw small bits of light flashing under the bedroom door as they approached. He shifted his legs to the side of the bed so that he would meet them seated. He reached for his eye glasses on the night stand and wrapped the temples around his ears as he blinked out the blurriness from his eyes. He sucked in a deep breath as the two lights stopped outside his bedroom door. Despite the darkness he saw the quarter turn of the doorknob before the click of the latch bolt.

Two large figures burst into the room wet with the storm, steam rising from the heat of their bodies, they approached him purposefully.

He sat upright and adjusted his glasses; he cleared his throat by way of introduction, and began to greet the intruders, but his words were swept away in a rush of air as the one closest to him brought a brick to the side of his face.

His feet dragged two long furrows down the muddy driveway to the car on the street; furrows that quickly filled with water, erasing the only trace of his abduction. He was thrown onto the back on the floor, a blanket on top of him. The gun of the engines and the screech of the tires were lost to the storm as the car sped away.

He awoke partially as his captors half walked - half dragged him up a steep muddy slope. The three fell several times on the slick, wet path and the man's face and mouth filled with a coarse mix of mud and undergrowth, causing him to choke and cough.

As they crested the hill, the two dragged the man toward a small house, the outside details blurred and black in the storm. The man looked up to the candlelight spilling out through the open door, too weak and beaten to mount any protest.

The Calm

1

June 1983

Good morning, and a great morning it is. With projected highs in the mid-seventies, Summer seems like it's already here. So get your suntan oil and a cooler full of Tab and head on over to the beach. And while you're packing your beach bag let's get the party started with something from Def Leppard's recent album, "Rock of Ages..."

And they sat, the three of them, waiting beneath a sun-bleached sky, wasting time, the only commodity they had in abundance, in the back of Great Hope Country Day School. One of the more prominent public schools in the town of Great Hope, Great Hope Country Day School was where they had studied and played years before. But that was a different time. They were older now, their eighteen-year old bodies outpacing their minds, muscles stretching and scarring the taut overlying skin, their childhoods receding sharply as they hurtled forward into the labyrinth of manhood, with no compass to help avoid the many dead ends that life would lead them to.

The arching sun burned a bright hole in the sky overhead. A mid-morning breeze kicked up dust and sent it spiraling around them. The air, as it always did, stank; it stank with an unchanging sameness that all sooner or later got used to, because Great Hope, fetid and fallow, was a place where ideas went to die (or more appropriately "Great Hole," as the sign had been modified soon after the town's inception, thanks to the creative imagination of the first graduating class of juvenile delinquents and several cans of Benjamin Moore paint; and thanks to every subsequent graduating class of juvenile delinquents who unfailingly and unflinchingly carried on the tradition (with more modern methods)). The stench from this fact seeped into those who moved there, whether by choice or circumstance. And it clung stubbornly to those who fought to leave. Though less than sixty minutes from the city, Great Hope was backward and slumbering. This was due in part to highway 495, the main artery connecting the heart of the city to this distal extremity, which shrank from four lanes to just two before Great Hope, bottlenecking all flow. Thus Great Hope remained unchanged, ischemic with its cynical old world prejudices. Dream Boulevard dissected the town into North and South, affluent and struggling; a stone's throw connected the haves and the have-nots. But the divide was much greater, and respected by each side. Both sides agreed that the American Dream was still attainable but not as fervently in South Hope, where struggling to hold onto that dream was the norm.

Achilles leaned his large muscular frame against the school's brick wall next to one of the rear exit doors, one hand shielding his eyes from the wind and sun as he scanned the distant fence. He dug his other hand into the front pocket of his jeans, faded and hanging low on his hips, an old black button-down shirt clung to his damp chest and back.

Johnny sat on the ground a few feet away, cross-legged in his torn jeans, wearing his leather jacket despite the oppressive heat. But his mind was focused less on the heat and more on the hard and short strokes of his jack knife as he whittled the end of a thick branch to a sharp edge, a cigarette hanging from the corner of his mouth, a wisp of smoke curling its way up. An old but well-maintained dirt bike lay beside him, the closest he'd gotten to owning a motorcycle.

Jared sat sprawled on the ground between them, leaning

against the school wall, his long legs splayed out limply, a leather jacket draped over his left shoulder, Ray Ban sunglasses shielding his eyes from the morning glare. He slurred his way through a Pink Floyd tune, pausing at times to remember the lyrics or catch his breath.

He stopped midway through "The Wall" and lifted his shades partway with his right hand turning from Achilles to Johnny. "Hey man, when's Gabriel showing up?"

Johnny kept whittling away as if he hadn't heard him. Achilles looked down at him for a brief contemptuous moment then looked back up, training his eyes on the horizon. "He should be here soon."

Jared groaned and let the shades slip down the front of his eyes again. "It was so painful getting up this morning. Painful. I could have easily slept another couple of hours and avoid this damn hangover." Jared let his head loll to the side. "Hey Johnny, how much did we drink last night?"

Johnny stopped whittling and stared off into the distance as he made the previous night's calculations. "Is that before or after the joint?"

"Both," Jared slurred.

Johnny started whittling again. "Well, I figure we had two six-packs of beer, a pint of SoCo and half a bottle of Jack Daniels at the start of the night. I know Gabe and Achilles shared a six-pack. And by then end of the night there were a couple of shots lefts in the SoCo."

"It must have been the weed that did it then."

"Don't blame the weed; that was some good quality shit." Johnny shook his head. "Truth is, you shoulda paced yourself. And you shoulda drunk the beer at the end. Classic rookie mistake."

Jared struggled to sit up then crashed back against the wall despite the effort. "Well I wasn't about to drink just a couple of beers to celebrate the last day of high school. I wanted to start the summer off right."

"I see him. He's coming," Achilles announced, still shielding his eyes.

The other two turned to look towards the back fence a hundred yards away. They caught site of Gabriel scaling the 10-foot tall fence then drop down to a cat-like crouch. Which never ceased to amaze them on account of his left arm. The blur of his tall body made its way towards them, wading in and out of the heat that rose as if from underneath the blacktop, as if hell were boiling below them.

At six foot two, Gabriel had an imposing presence even from far away. He had the stance of a boxer, and the movements of a dancer. But it was as much his manner and the way he held himself that made the others recognize that there was more to this boy, this man, than his size. He was their leader, a natural conclusion to an unspoken argument. His size, speed, and strength were only part of that which held the others at times in awe. There was also a raw natural instinct that kept them all safe, regardless of whether it was running from the cops, or fighting with one of the other neighborhood gangs.

Gabriel stopped in front of the other three and grabbed a pack of Marlboros that was rolled up in his left sleeve.

Jared lifted two fingers in Gabriel's direction. "Hey man, can I bum a smoke?" he said, his voice hoarse and dry.

Gabriel took out a cigarette and flicked it to Jared. It took a slap-stick bounce off his head and landed on his free hand. Gabriel held the pack out to Achilles who shook his head.

Johnny looked up squinting. "You sure took off early last night, what gives getting us all together so early? Jared's been bitching about how he could have used a little more beauty sleep."

Jared brought his cigarette to his dry lips and fished around in his pockets for a match but found none.

As Gabriel stooped down to light Jared's cigarette, he stared right through the Ray Bans into Jared's slightly dilated pupils. Jared turned away self-consciously. Gabriel then lit his own cigarette in his cupped hand away from the wind, then straightened up and turned to face his friends. The sun blazing behind him framed his silhouette.

"We're going to kill someone this summer," the silhouette responded.

Johnny stopped whittling. Jared shifted his wilted form. All stared quietly at Gabriel as they digested the announcement. It was Achilles who spoke up first, "Who? And why?"

"A pedophile," Gabriel replied, as if that one response was enough for both questions.

Johnny leaned back, his arms propping him up, and looked up suspiciously. "How do you know?"

Gabriel took a long pull off his cigarette and exhaled a steady stream from his nose. "I just do."

Johnny held up his newly whittled stick, admiring the sharpness in the sunlight. "Pedophile. I've done a lot of hunting, but never killed nobody, yet." He looked back at Gabriel. "Pedophile, huh?"

Gabriel nodded. He was not one to joke, and certainly not about this.

"That's enough for me, I'm in." Johnny nodded matter-of-factly.

Jared tried swallowing and found his throat dry. Despite the headache and the hangover, the wheels were still turning in his head, mulling over the prospect of killing. He ran a leathery tongue over his dry lips before answering. "I'm in too," he croaked.

Achilles looked deep into Gabriel's brown, sorrowful eyes before responding; of the three he was the only one who came close to reading his thoughts. He knew they were thinking the same thing. Murder was a long cry from the vandalism and hooliganism they'd been up to these last five years. One thing was damaging private property and smashing someone's face in. Murder was another story. Still, of all the people he could trust to carry out something like murder, Gabriel was it.

"I'm in too," he said finally.

"So what's next?" Johnny asked.

"We wait," Gabriel said turning around squinting at the sun, as if the time for action could be deciphered in the angry yellow star in the distance. "For now we get on with the summer. Hang out. I'll plan everything. I just want to make sure you're all in." He wheeled around suddenly catching them off guard, which was what he was always good at. "This is a pact, see," he said. "We're all in this. If anything happens we don't rat anybody out, we don't turn anyone in to save our own skins. Clear?" He looked challengingly at each of his friends.

And they met his gaze, accepting this challenge, as they'd accepted his other challenges through middle school and high school. But now high school was over and an uncertain future loomed large and fearsome beyond these next summer months, they clung onto this challenge as if it contained within its completion a power to meet this future.

The loud click of the exit door opening drew their attention. A young man roughly ten years older in a slightly tight-fitting button-down shirt and bow tie half stumbled outside. He caught sight of the four large teens, quickly turned around and reached for the door, only to find it locked.

Gabriel caught Achilles' eye and smirked. "Hi Mr. McGregor."

The man turned back to the boys. " Hi guys. You know- uh- you really shouldn't- uh- be back here."

Johnny leaned back on his hands. "We're all alumni of this fine institution," he said, turning to the other three. "I think it's perfectly fine to come back here and reminisce. Don't you, teach?"

Mr. McGregor began to redden, whether from the sun or from embarrassment, the others couldn't decide. "Well it's against school policy, but I guess just this time I'll let you hang out here a little while longer." He turned around and grabbed the doorknob, only to remember too late that it was locked. He dug both his hands in his pockets and began walking around the side of the school.

"Dick," Johnny called out, loud enough for the teacher to hear. But the teacher kept on walking while the others in the group burst out laughing.

"Any of you guys working this summer?" Johnny turned from Gabriel to Achilles.

Gabriel took a long pull off his cigarette and let the smoke leak out as he answered, "Probably will go down back to the library on Monday see about getting my job back."

"I got a job at Rosa's Flower Shop. She said I could start Monday," Achilles said.

"A flower shop?" Johnny feigned a look of shock; even Gabriel raised an eyebrow.

Johnny started laughing and coughing. "What kind of fag-gedyass faggot job is that?"

Achilles pushed himself off the wall and walked up to where Johnny was sitting. He had a good four inches and thirty pounds on him. He'd also looked as if he'd gained more mass recently; the others suspected he was injecting steroids. "Maybe I don't have my daddy lining me up with a nice tidy job for the summer like some people," he said through clenched teeth.

Gabriel was getting ready to put himself in between the two when Johnny brought both hands up, fingers v-shaped in peace signs. "Okay, okay. Truce." He got up slowly. "Alright, I gotta get going. My ole man's got some work for me this morn-ing." He stretched his arms up above his head, groaning with the effort. "Tracy's invited us to a party tonight at a friend's place. Are you guys in?"

"I'm in." Jared sat up, suddenly excited.

Gabriel looked away. Achilles shrugged.

"Aw, come on." Johnny walked over to Gabriel arms out, pleading. "It's not going to hurt you guys to do a little min-gling. Who knows, you guys might even get laid."

Gabriel took a drag off his cigarette and exhaled to the sky. "Maybe."

"What time's it at?" Achilles asked.

"Starts at eight and ends whenever the cops close the party down." Johnny lit up a cigarette and walked over to Jared's sprawled body and gave it a kick with his boot. "Hey dickhead. I'll give you a ride back to your house." He then picked up his dirt bike by the handlebars and started it up. The loud whine of the bike's engine echoed off the walls of the school.

Jared got up rubbing his leg then walked over to the back of the bike and sat down. "See you guys tonight," he said.

Gabriel and Achilles exchanged brief handshakes with the other two on the bike before it took off around the side of the school.

Achilles turned to Gabriel. "Why are we still hanging out with those two idiots?"

Gabriel looked on meditatively at the dust the dirt bike had kicked up.

"What are you doing for the rest of the morning?" Achilles asked.

"Nothing." Gabriel thought for a moment before adding, "I don't feel like going home. I know my mom needs me there right now. But I don't have the heart for it."

Achilles fought the urge to put a hand on Gabriel's shoulder. "It's his anniversary coming up."

Gabriel brushed a tear away, whether from the wind or memories it was hard to say. "It's today."

"Jesus man, I'm sorry." Achilles shook his head.

"It's okay. I should probably hang out a little with my mom this morning." The two high-fived and Gabriel started walking toward the back fence.

"If your home gets too much for you, you can come over to my place and we can hang out."

"Sounds good," Gabriel said over his shoulder.

Achilles waited until his friend had climbed the fence and had disappeared before making his way home.

2

Gabriel's past returned to him in bits and pieces, like float- ing dust particles that appear in and disappear from the fanning rays of the morning sun. Sometimes the memories disappeared as quickly as they appeared. Sometimes they stayed, clinging to the edge of his mind, difficult to shake loose, although the details were never available for immediate recall and he often relied on the accounts of others. At times they were images and faces, four by six snapshots beckoning from under an album's shiny cellophane; many of them were of his brother, or of the two together, the older brother as- sisting with the younger brother's bath, helping with his feed- ing, sometimes both of them sleeping together during nights when a storm's hungry roar could be heard outside the win- dow of Daniel's bedroom. Other times the past came back as a smell- the sweet chemical scent of baby shampoo, the fun and care-free smell of popcorn. There was no linear quality to his past, the way he witnessed it in others, the way he imagined it ought to be. There was no logical order, but random events that intruded his mind. At times he couldn't quite know if they happened or not. Occasionally he questioned his past, his ex- istence from just several years before. He wouldn't realize until much later that much of this was to suppress the pain. There was so much pain to suppress.

He knew from others that his parents had once loved one another, in their own way. That they had plans- big plans with a future that spread out vast and wide, beyond family, home, and career. He himself did not remember the end to the mar- riage, only the pain and anger that tainted the air in the half vacant rooms of his mother's house. Daniel, the eldest by eight years, was a truer witness. He saw the end and then took the brunt of his mother's silent rebuke. He took it quietly, because he was a quiet boy, a quiet son. The scapegoat to the problems she faced, alone. Even now, Gabriel remembered his brother's muted presence, the reflection of a transparent slide projected elsewhere.

Gabriel made his way down Hope Street, oblivious to the stares of other people. He'd grown immune to the way others reacted to him, their circus freak show gawks. But today they no longer existed. Today his thoughts turned to his brother, as they did each year on this day; the poker faced stony silence of the last several weeks of his life. And with each passing year, Gabriel came to see how his brother's quiet inward gaze had masked an unbearably lonely suffering. Since turning sixteen two years before, Gabriel had begun to think a lot about his older brother, beyond the painful anniversaries; he'd begun to recall the many ways about him, the way he talked, the way he moved, and most of all the way he swayed.

June 1973

"Come on boys," she yelled from the bottom of the stairs. "Your father's going to be here any minute."

"Co- co-coming," Daniel said from his room. He put his book in his book bag; he grabbed his inhaler for just in case. What his father called a security blanket, as if to minimize the shortness of breath and wheeze that intermittently struck him, an affectation.

"Coming." Gabriel ran down the stairs.

He entered the kitchen and sat down, eyeing his mother uneasily. "I'm here," he chirped.

Isabelle sat across from her son, one hand gripping a hot mug of coffee, the other a half-smoked cigarette. She stared out the kitchen window through thick dark sunglasses. "Where's your brother?" she asked him in a voice of suppressed hostility.

"You want me to go get him?"

"No." She took another sip from her mug. "Do you have everything?"

"I think so."

"You better. You know how your father is. He won't turn around once he gets onto the highway." She pronounced highway the Israeli way, the way she pronounced Challah, with a strong, guttural H.

Gabriel rummaged around in his mind for any last minute items he would need for the weekend. "I think I'm okay."

She turned her interrogating gaze from the window to her youngest son. "Is he still with that woman?"

"What woman?" Gabriel asked with the eyes of a startled deer.

"What woman, he says." She looked over her shoulder at no one in particular, before turning back to Gabriel. "Don't play dumb with me." Her voice hard, her words surrounded Gabriel, binding him in her accusation against his father, as if he were an accomplice to the crime.

Gabriel sat speechless, unsure how to respond.

Daniel entered the kitchen, breaking the moment of tension and silently sat down next to Gabriel. He gave his brother a half-smile and then stole a glance at his mother. "Are you g-g- going to be okay? Do you wa- wa- want me to st- st- st- stay?"

His mother cast her gaze out the window again. "No, you go," she said with finality. "I need a break from both of you today and- there's your father." She stood up suddenly, half panicked. "Don't keep him waiting." She stubbed her cigarette out and dispelled the last traces of smoke with her hand.

Daniel and Gabriel rose quickly and took turns hugging their mother's stiff frame, she softening in their embrace.

"Go, go, go." She pushed them away gently. "I'll be okay. I'll see you soon."

The two brothers pushed through the side door and made their way to a bright red Mercedes, brighter and more perfect than anything on the block. As they reached the car the driver's side door opened. "Come on, what is it with you two? I've been waiting here for five minutes." A well-dressed middle-aged man with a coif of wavy black hair that seemed suspiciously less and less gray stepped out of the car impatiently. Thick, curly black hair peaked out from the top of his button-down shirt and rolled up shirtsleeves revealed the same hair lining his tanned, muscular arms. Raul walked around to the back and opened the trunk. He was as tall as the older son, though wider, and more solid.

"Hi Daddy." Gabriel wrapped his arms around his father.

"Hu- hi- hi Dad." Daniel went forward to kiss him on the cheek, but his father held him at arms length. "Put your bag in the back here, there's no room up front."

He opened the back door. "Okay, in you go. Say hi to Monica, she's a friend of mine."

The two eyed a beautiful blonde adorning the front seat, smiling and giggling at them. "Hi boys," she greeted with a Spanish accent that was as thick as her makeup.

"Hi," chirped Gabriel happily, hopefully. He knew his father was kinder in the company of women.

"He- he- hello."

Their father got in the car flashing Monica a broad smile "What did I tell you?" he said by way of introduction. "One looks like a freak, and one talks like a freak."

"Oh, Raul you're so mean," laughed Monica.

Daniel blushed and turned away. He looked out the window at his mother's house.

Gabriel reached over to grab his brother's hand for comfort but found it limp. His brother had already withdrawn into himself, something he had been doing more and more lately.

A door seemed to be closing, shutting Gabriel and others out, but only Gabriel sensed it.

Oblivious to the toll of his words in the back, their father continued to charm the woman up front.

"Raul, you didn't tell me you had such handsome sons."

"Well, they got half of my genes, what do you expect?"

Monica giggled in response.

"Okay." Their father slapped the steering wheel sharply. "Are we all in the mood for a good time?" Coming from their father, it seemed as much a threat as it was a question. And a response was required.

"Yeah!" cried Gabriel, silently hoping his exuberance would count for both him and his brother.

His father seemed to accept it, because he shifted the car into gear and sped away. "We'll grab some lunch and then hit a movie."

He turned on the radio and twisted the tuner knob half a dozen turns until he found some lively jazz music.

The car made several turns before merging onto the highway, heading west "out of the barbaric burbs and to the civilized city" as he liked to say. Despite the music, both boys could make out some of the words to a conversation they weren't meant to hear.

"He was born that way," his father was saying, looking into the side mirror.

It was a typical response to a question Gabriel had grown used to hearing, even at the age of eight. Where was his left hand? What had happened to it? He himself didn't know the full account, only that it was some birth defect, all the bones in his wrist fused into one massive block, and that was that. His mother had come to accept it early on. His father continued to deny any culpability, let alone acceptance.

"There certainly isn't anyone on my side of the family with one hand, trust me. At least he doesn't have one of those flippers instead. That would have looked ridiculous," Raul said as he flashed a smile in the rearview mirror at Gabriel. "I would have been forced to cut it off."

"Oh Raul you are so horrible." Monica slapped him gently. "But his arm looks so big and muscular?"

"I don't know, the doctor said something about the mis-wiring to the arm, causing hypertonicity," Raul replied frowning. "They said he'd grow into it; until then he looks like a superhero. And the other one was born perfect. No problems. But now he's got this damn stutter." Raul shook his head. "I've done everything I could: doctors, specialists, therapists- you name it I've done it."

His sons sat in the backseat silently listening to Raul define them according to their deformities, as if the potential for normalcy in their lives ended at the rounded end of Gabriel's carpal bones, and the tip of Daniel's twisted tongue.

"How old are your boys?"

"Sixteen and eight."

"Why the big difference?"

"Who knows? That's how the chips fall," Raul replied, looking off into the distance as if remembering. "Rosie's Diner," he said moments later as they pulled into the parking lot. "There's always something for everyone and no one can complain." He turned off the ignition and turned around to face his sons. "If you boys behave yourselves, there's ice cream for dessert and a movie this afternoon." The spark in his eye suggested the threat of a more ominous alternative if they did not behave.

"Great!" Gabriel punched the air.

Daniel sat sullenly, his eyes on Monica.

"Alright then," their father said opening the car door. "Let's get going. There's a 2 o'clock show. We have a couple of hours to eat and get over to the theater." Raul stepped around briskly to the other side of the car and opened Monica's door with one hand as he fanned his other arm out. "Madam, or should I say mademoiselle."

Monica giggled and took his hand. "Thank you, sir."

He then stepped to the back and opened Gabriel's door. "Young sir." As Gabriel stepped out, his father gave him a swift smack to the side of the head and leaned in close to whisper, "This is for what you are going to do."

Gabriel smiled meekly in response. He'd stopped flinching to his father's slaps a long time before, having grown used to them, anticipating one or two with each meeting, accepting them as an honest part of the relationship.

Daniel stepped out without the same warning. At sixteen he had learned enough from the hard knocks to the head and required no more. But it did not save him from other blows.

"What's that in your hand?"

"A b- b- book."

"We're not going to a library for Pete's sake, we're going to a restaurant."

But Daniel clung his book close to him and walked past his father. Raul flicked his hand dismissively.

They all filed in to the restaurant, Gabriel taking the lead, followed by Monica, then Raul who looked back as he held the door open. "Come on. What's up with you? Let's go." Daniel entered reluctantly.

They all made their way to one of the booths by the window closest to the car, the boys filing in on one side, Raul and Monica on the other.

A stout elderly woman with thick fleshy arms placed menus in the middle of the table. "Can I get you all something to drink?"

Their father looked up and flashed her a bright smile. "Hi Agnes, how are you?"

Agnes blushed under Raul's gaze. "Fine, thank you sir."

"I'll have a cup of coffee, the boys will have Coke's and-"

"Water's fine with me," Monica cut in.

"Agnes, bring this young lady the finest water in the house."

Agnes retreated to the back for the drinks.

Monica giggled. "Oh Raul, you are so funny."

Raul winked back, then turned to his sons. "Well boys, what'll you have?"

Daniel looked at the menu as if to stall his response, forming the words fluently in his head, repeating them over and over for when the waitress came. His stutter was less pronounced in benign company.

"A hot dog," Gabriel replied. "And fries," he quickly added.

His father looked on blandly, a half smile formed on his lips, as if remembering a joke. Then he turned to Daniel. "And you?"

Daniel continued to peruse the menu, pretending to not hear. Hoping the waitress would come soon.

"Yoo hoo. Daniel. Earth to Daniel," his father spoke into his fist, now a small NASA microphone.

Resigned, Daniel looked up from the menu; he knew what he had to say, a burger and fries. Burger. And. Fries. Three simple words. "Bu- bu- bu-." His mouth stretched out around the large uncomfortable syllables, stalling midway. "Bu- bu- bu-."

"Bubbu what?" His father took the menu from Daniel's hand. "I don't see any Bubba on the menu."

Daniel blushed, looking down.

Gabriel, hoping to help his brother, cut in, "He wants a burger, Dad."

"I wasn't talking to you," Raul said, turning to Daniel. "If he wants a burger than he has to learn how to say it. And say it right." He handed Daniel back the menu. "If you want a burger then say it. Bur-ger," he enunciated exaggeratedly slow, as if talking to a mental invalid.

Daniel looked up defiant though the tears betrayed him. "Bu- bu-bu-"

"Come on. Come on. Jesus!" Raul shook his head, turning to Monica. "What did I tell you. Savages, the two of them."

Monica looked on. Being ill equipped to handle these situations she had difficulty restraining nervous laughter.

"So have you decided?" The waitress stopped with the tray of drinks.

"Burger," Daniel almost shouted. "And fries."

Raul laughed out loud. "Danny, you crack me up."

Gabriel looked on smiling from his father to Daniel.

"Well it looks like someone is hungry," Agnes remarked, smiling.

Gabriel looked back to his father, whose laughter was such a wonderful sound, so full and sonorous. To make him laugh had become Gabriel's aim each visit. The more he laughed, the less angry he was, the less angry he was, the less abusive he became.

"Bubbu- burger," he said suddenly, surprised as his own audacity.

His father responded with another laugh, he was turning red from the strength of it. Even Monica had begun to giggle, hiding her precious white teeth behind the cup of her palm.

"I'll get a bubba hot dog," he said, smiling." With bubba fries." He was impressed with his own wit; his father seemed to encourage it.

"Yes, yes," his father prodded. "You got it! You got it!"

His grin widened at the positive response from his captive audience. He was riding the crest of a wave he'd never experienced before, demonstrating a measure of creativity and audacity he had never known he was capable of. Smiling, he turned to Daniel only to find that his brother had turned away from the three of them, escaping his family into the pages of his book.

His father sensed it only partially. "Aw, come on Danny. We're all just kidding. Can't you take a joke?"

But Daniel said nothing. His jaw was tight and his tongue heavy and inert in his mouth.

And then the food came and Raul and Monica's thoughts wandered away from the sons. They ate heartily and resumed a previous conversation.

"It's a small piece of land nearby, bought it with my brother-in-law, my ex-brother-in-law - not one of my smarter moves," he said as an aside. "Anyway, I- we haven't figured out what to do with it. But trust me there're much better prospects on the west coast. I'll show you when we get back." They moved on with talk about their upcoming trip to the south of Spain. "We'll take you boys when you're a little older," Raul said, still looking at Monica in a tone that suggested that day, if ever, was a distant promise sure to be broken.

Gabriel stared at his food, sick to his stomach. He forced his lunch down through the knot of shame in his throat. He stole quick glances at his brother who ate his burger quietly beside him. He longed to turn to his brother but sat unmoving.

Later on in the theater Gabriel leaned in to his brother, whispering, "I'm sorry." He was at a loss for more words. As much as he wanted to express his feelings of remorse and love, about how much his brother meant to him, about how they were both in the same boat and should stick together, he knew how absurd it would sound after today.

"Forget about it," Daniel whispered back, staring vacantly at the screen.

And Gabriel knew he had somehow lost a part of his brother and would never get it back.

"Bye boys." Their father gave them a kiss and hug, oblivious to their response. "I'll see you after my vacation. Enjoy your summer."

Daniel marched away from the car straight to the side door of his mother's home. Gabriel ran behind trying to catch up.

He met the haze of his mother's cigarettes as his brother began climbing the stairs. "How was the movie?" she asked without giving two shits about how the movie was or even if they had seen a movie.

"Oh Mom- it was great- there was this cop- and this gang of robbers..." Gabriel rambled on, describing in full detail the movie he had only half paid attention to, anxious and scared in a way he hadn't felt before, hiding behind his sprawling narrative. Yet this narrative failed to hide him from the crystal clear notion that he had betrayed his brother, his friend, his comrade in arms. Danny was the only person he could turn to for respite from the abusive words, and beatings they both shared. He was the only one who understood. Gabriel wanted desperately to run to his brother's room and beg for his forgiveness, and promise a summer's worth of slave labor to be able to retract his comments, to do this day all over again.

"Why don't you set the table?" his mother interrupted, as she stabbed the remains of her cigarette into the half-filled ashtray. "Dinner will be ready in fifteen minutes."

Gabriel became aware of the two pots on the stove. "What are we having?"

His mother lit up another cigarette, her back to him. "Pasta," she answered, stirring the sauce. She walked over to the cupboard and opened the door. "Here," she took out several boxes, "which pasta do you want?"

"Spaghetti please."

"Okay, set the table." She threw the spaghetti in the boiling water, stirring mechanically, lost in her own thoughts, absent to her son for the moment and unaware of his torment.

Gabriel raced through his chore, glancing periodically at the ceiling for any noise. "I'm done. Should I go get Daniel?"

"Okay, go wash up and get your brother down here."

He walked over to his brother's room and knocked gently on his door.

No answer.

"Danny?" he asked softly outside the door. "Danny?'"

No answer.

He tried the doorknob and was surprised to find it unlocked. He walked in slowly, his eyes adjusting to the dark. The glow of early evening outlined the scant contents of his brother's bedroom. Daniel was nowhere, not in the bed, not at his desk. He saw the open window and for brief moment was afraid Danny had run away. Then he looked up.

The first thing he thought was whether a breeze through

the window caused Danny's swaying; slow, rhythmic, almost hypnotic. Gabriel reached up and held his brother's hand. He closed his eyes and allowed himself to be calmed by Daniel, allowing the world around him to recede. Only to be awakened by his mother's wild shrieks moments later, to be pushed aside, while she grabbed her older son's body, crying into his chest, "No, no, no, no!"

Within days after the "accident," Gabriel's home was invaded by distant relatives (all of them Raul's), who participated in an expertly choreographed frenzy as each strove to outperform the other, be it in the Shiva, the ceremony at Temple Beth El, the cooking, the cleaning, or the organizing of transportation and housing. And then there was the burial. Aunts, uncles, cousins, great aunts, any and all who could travel from all corners of the earth that Gabriel had not even visited, marched in to provide whatever consolation and to share the tears that Gabriel's mother had not stopped shedding. Gabriel sustained a low level of anxiety throughout the events. He had difficulty eating the many banquets prepared; he slept very little and in those moments when he did rest, he had nightmares. With every hug and pat on the back, with every wet kiss on his cheek or sweaty handholding, he felt more and more wretched. A part of him longed to cry out, "It's me. I'm the one. I'm to blame for all this." At the burial he looked into the hole that awaited his brother and shed tears of shame and guilt, tears that were misconstrued by others present as appropriate grief, and was consoled even more, adding to his wretchedness.

Gabriel turned the corner onto Hope Street and made his way to his house. He dreaded this day, this anniversary. His mother decompensated the week before and would not dig herself out of her hole for another week after. He wanted to turn back and walk to Achilles's place and spend the next few days camping out on the bedroom floor.

He opened the unlocked side door and walked in. He met with the stale and hot air, mixed with the rising stink of unwashed dishes piled high in the kitchen sink. The lights were off on the first floor and he was grateful for the bright sunlight streaming in through the sheer curtained windows. The carpeting muffled his steps.

"Mom?" he called out. No answer. He sighed and walked to the bottom of the stairs, steadying himself while holding on to the banister. The stairs creaked under his weight as he slowly made his way up.

He stood outside her room and put his ear to the closed door, but heard nothing.

"Mom?" He knocked lightly on her door, then walked in. Her inhalations and exhalations accompanied the soft whirr of the air conditioning unit. Its weak, cool breath made the room slightly more comfortable than the rest of the house. The shades were pulled down, allowing only the barest traces of light through. He let his eyes adjust to the dark before he made his way to the sleeping form on the bed, then knelt and watched his mother sleep. He'd done this many times since his brother's death; it seemed to be the only time she was at peace. He hesitated waking her, bringing her back to the tragic reality that awaited her. He looked over at the nightstand, frowning at last night's cigarette, left to burn down to the stub, adding another burn mark to the edge.

"Mom," he called out softly. He laid his right hand on her shoulder, letting it rest there a moment. "Mom." She stirred as she rose up from the depths of sleep, before struggling back down again, sinking deeper.

"Mom," he said again, a little louder now, shaking her shoulder gently.

"Huh, what." She lifted herself slightly from the pillow, lost now, somewhere on the somnolent waters between death and life.

"Mom, it's me."

"Dan- no, wait." She shook her head. "Gabriel, sorry." She lay her head back down her eyes closed. "What time is it?" Her tone was one of resignation.

"It's almost twelve." Gabriel paused a moment. "I didn't know if I should wake you."

"Yes, yes," she nodded, her eyes still closed. "I need to get up. We have so much to do- flowers, visit your brother, pick up uncle Leon at the airport-"

"Leon's coming?" Gabriel stood up suddenly upset, and his large frame seemed to take up the entire space of the bedroom. "Why didn't you tell me?"

With some effort his mother pushed her legs to the side of her bed and pushed up to sitting. "I only found out myself yesterday. He said he was taking some time off and wanted to spend it with us." She opened her eyes, looking up at her son. "You've gotten so big, Gabriel. You remind me of Leon when he was your age."

Gabriel hadn't seen Leon since- he ran his hand through his hair. "I'm going downstairs, get something to drink."

His mother stared down at the floor, then her bed, closed her eyes and shook her head. "I'll be down in a minute."

3

Johnny and Jared rode across town, the dirt bike leaving a wake of dust and loose rocks. They crossed Dream Boulevard, leaving behind the dense clutter of small homes that crowded around small streets, and entered a stretch of increasingly larger homes with larger, landscaped lawns that showcased Mercedes and BMWs in long driveways. Johnny turned down Ivory Lane and traveled two more blocks to Jared's, where he rode to the end of the driveway. He killed the ignition and the two got off. "Anybody home?" He turned to Jared.

"Dad's at work probably," Jared responded blandly as he opened the side door.

"On a Saturday?"

Jared continued as if he didn't hear, "My stepmom's at the gym, or shopping."

"So we're alone." Johnny followed him in.

They found the maid busy with the breakfast cleanup. "Hello Jared," she greeted him, a thick Columbian accent laced in and out of her English.

"Hi Maria. Where are my folks?" he asked as he made his way down the hallway leading to his bedroom.

Maria responded as if reciting a list she had committed to memory. "Your father went to work, he said he would not be back until late. And your mom went shopping. She said she would be home late too."

"Okay, thanks Maria," Jared replied over his shoulder.

"Are you hungry?" Maria pressed forward, wringing her arthritic hands, a look of concern brushed across her face.

"You want me to make you something?"

"No thanks, maybe later." Jared led the way into his room and Johnny locked the door behind him.

Jared slumped forward face down into his bed, groaning. His head felt thick and heavy, and his body was weak and sore.

Johnny sat down on the chair next to the desk and lit a cigarette. He took a pull and exhaled a few smoke rings in the air as he looked at Jared with a small measure of disgust. "So are we gonna do this transaction or what?"

Jared turned onto his left side to face Johnny, grunting in pain as he did so. His tall lanky frame had outgrown his bed and his legs now dangled over the side. He bent an elbow and rested his head on his palm. "Okay, let's do it," he said yawning.

Johnny dug a hand into his front pocket and pulled out a rolled up baggy. "An ounce, just like you wanted." He unrolled it and opened it up to show the bright green buds. "You're never going to find anything like this on the East Coast. 100% Columbian Gold. Two fifty."

Jared sighed as he pondered the realization of yet another scam he was being subjected to. As much as he didn't want to lose his only drug connection, he wasn't keen let Johnny off the hook so easily. "I thought you said two hundred."

Johnny hitched his boots up on Jared's desk and took another drag. "Two hundred was for the regular Mexican shit. This stuff will get you high without knocking you out."

"Alright, my wallet's on the desk. Take out the money."

"Let's roll a joint first, then we can talk money. I'll even put in a little of my own."

As Johnny rolled, Jared gathered up whatever strength to get out of bed. He opened the window but drew the blinds down and took a towel out of the closet and pressed it under the door. He turned on his stereo and popped in a Pink Floyd tape. "Don't want Maria freaking out," he said sitting back down on the bed.

Johnny sparked up the joint and took a deep breath in, talking in small bursts as he held his breath. "Aw, she won't mind, she'd probably love to take a hit."

Jared took the joint from Johnny. "Are you kidding, this woman goes to church every Sunday. She'll probably say a dozen Hail Mary's for my corrupt soul."

The two burst out laughing.

"She's probably saying a few prayers for me right now," Jared said in a voice clenched tight with smoke. He exhaled a large plume into the room and held the joint out to Johnny.

"You're beyond god's help," Johnny said cackling.

As the pot began to take effect Jared sat back on his bed resting his head on interlocked fingers that now seemed to be detaching itself from his body. He let the high overtake his brain, letting the margins of his vision blur slightly and rainbow-colored haloes crown all the light entering through the slats of the blinds. He felt a quick release in his mind, as if a door had suddenly opened with a rush of clarity. "Wow, this is some good pot."

"Told you so." Johnny put his dark shades back on and smiled a large Cheshire grin. He held the joint back up to Jared. "You want some more?"

Jared grasped the joint between his thumb and index finger, licked his thumb and snuffed the lit end. "No man, I'm done. Let's save it for later." He held onto the joint for a minute, gathering his scattered thoughts. "You know, there're two main types of marijuana. There's the Sativa and the Indica-"

"Jeezus H Christ," Johnny shook his head in frustration, "why can't you get stoned like a normal person?"

Jared broke into another fit of laughter and turned the volume up on the stereo as the two zoned out for all of side A of The Wall, letting themselves drift on the alternating currents of the music and the mind-numbing high.

When the music stopped, Jared's attention turned back to the room and his friend. He propped himself forward resting on both elbows. "What about the other stuff I asked you about?"

"Like what?" But Johnny never forgot a business proposition; he just liked toying with Jared.

"You know," Jared leaned forward, "the coke."

"Oh that. Don't worry. At the party tonight there's going to be plenty to go around."

"How much?"

"I can get you an eight ball for about four hundred. Deal?"

Jared thought a moment. "Okay, deal. But don't come back with a higher price."

Johnny stood up suddenly. "No problem. I'll pick you up at eight?" He held his hand up in a high five.

Jared got up and clapped Johnny's hand. "Eight o'clock. But hold on a minute." He reached behind the closet door and took out a can of Lysol, spraying the room a half dozen times before tucking the Lysol back in the closet. "I'll walk you out."

As Johnny rode out the driveway Jared turned around to find Maria staring at him with what could only be motherly concern.

"You want me to make you something to eat?" she asked.

"Sure, thanks Maria. Let me take a quick shower and I'll be out in twenty minutes."

He closed the door to his room and went to his desk where he unrolled the baggie and smelled the pot. It sure did smell better than anything he'd had before. He rolled it back up and stuffed it behind his desk. He counted the money in his wallet; there was $260 less. He sighed. What a petty thief his friend was. But better to deal with a petty thief who knew the limits of how much he could get away with than with someone who would rob you of so much more.

Stripping off his clothes, he walked into the bathroom. He reached into the shower stall and turned on the hot water then stood before his medicine cabinet. He looked squarely at himself in the mirror, his tall, lanky frame, straight, dirty blond hair down to his neck, bright blue irises made now brighter still by his pot-injected sclera. He brought a hand up to his chest and caressed it, then brought it down to feel his penis, nothing. He felt no sensation. No stimulation. For a moment he imagined it was Gabriel's hand. He closed his eyes, letting the image take hold, Gabriel's body behind his, his arm reaching around, caressing him. He quickly opened his eyes, shaking his head, mad at himself for even thinking it. It would never happen. As much as he admitted to himself how much he wanted it. No one knew- or could know- his true feelings; at times he felt betrayed by them. He hadn't even revealed them to his therapist. He palmed a tear before it streaked down his face, shaking his head against the recurring thought.

He liked to think they found each other back in the chaos that was Miss Henderson's 2nd grade classroom. With thirty screaming kids wired on soda and hyper-sweetened cereal, it was easy to lose oneself. But Jared's blossoming psychiatric conditions were difficult to stifle and tested the limits of what Miss Henderson (who herself was riding the wave of her first nervous breakdown) was mentally equipped to handle. At an age when any deviation from the mean was viewed with suspicion if not scorn, the horde of emotionally stunted kids found Jared's unable to accept. That his IQ scores were clearly double those of most in the class, where the average floated listlessly somewhere in the unrespectable double digits, seemed to compensate for the many varied digressions his mind took. Yet it also inspired the abusive natures of the three classroom bullies who sat plotting in the back row. Within a few weeks of the school year, Jared had been targeted.

Gabriel with his monstrous left arm, equipped with the (rumored) amputated left hand, also stood out. He too showed a higher level of intelligence and, as a consequence, was the object of harassment from the bullies, yet given their fear of what this arm with the amputated hand could do to them (because everyone knew that to survive an amputation meant you could fight), they stayed clear of physical contact. Unlike the other children who reacted to Jared's unbridled, maniacal energy, and unexplainable interest in astronomy and physics with ridicule, Gabriel seemed engaged, if not mildly amused. The two soon took to eating their lunches together at the corner table, apart from everyone else, discussing the metaphysical potential of *Star Trek* (which they both agreed was the best show on TV), and laughing over the latest *Saturday Night Live* episode, which they were prohibited from watching (the second best). On weekends they had sleepovers during which they stayed up talking, or playing hours of chess late into the night. In a childhood marked by a dearth of good years, Jared recalled the second grade as the best year ever. In Gabriel he had found a trusted fellow inmate in the mind-crushing institution that passed for a school, someone whom he could communicate his precocious theories and fears with. In short he had found a friend, as much an equal as anyone could be for Jared. That Gabriel had a fully-grown left arm with a missing hand only heightened this awareness that the two were individuals set apart, two sentient beings living amongst mindless drones.

Things changed the following summer, what with his brother's death and all. There were no play dates, no sleepovers, no movies, and the occasional phone call was abrupt and unsatisfying. Gabriel had vanished inside the black hole of family tragedy. He surfaced three months later on the first day of school. Though everyone had grown during the summer, as was expected, Gabriel had aged more than anyone else in Miss Brown's third grade class. He had hardened and had become more distant, in the same infuriating way Jared found in adults who spoke to him. Gabriel didn't smile much anymore, and spoke even less. That year Jared tried extra hard to cheer him up, making it his primary mission. And at times Gabriel would forget himself and laugh at a joke or one of Jared's antics, but then he would stop suddenly and his gaze would drop, as if remembering something, and the smile would fade or worse it would turn sad. Everyone in the school knew the story, or at least some version of it (there were no shortage of rumors in the neighborhood, thanks to the attention-grabbing headlines of mass media). But no one knew the absolute truth. The rest of Miss Brown's class gave him a wide berth, not knowing what to say or how to say it. Even the bullies left him alone, whether out of respect or maybe from confused fear. Although they sat together for lunch, they might have been at opposite ends of the cafeteria; Gabriel said very little, answered Jared's questions with no more than two words strung loosely together. But Jared stayed close to him, out of loyalty, out of the hope of pulling him out of whatever dark cellar Gabriel had locked himself up in.

Then Jared was sent to private school and as much as he tried to keep contact, the two lost touch for several years.

They met up again in the final year of middle school, when Jared had amassed a collection of psychiatric diagnoses the way others collected stamps, with a complementary cabinet-full of medications. Gabriel had grown by then, the rest of his body catching up to his left arm, and towered over everyone else, even most of the bullies. And as much as he was not the bullying type, a handful of fights in the yard after school or in the boys bathroom, usually with older kids, two trips to the principal's office and a one-week suspension were all it took to assume a reputation of someone not to be toyed with. Armored in ripped jeans and a black ACDC T-shirt he surprised Jared the first day of classes with a guy-hug and high five, as if the years apart had never happened.

Caught off guard, Jared silently gasped and stood speechless in the short muscular embrace, mustering all the energy inside to respond but could only manage a weak "Hey." Although they had both grown up, Gabriel had bloomed into adolescence in a way that so few children were able to do, with lines and curves that suggested chiseled unblemished marble.

He reminded Jared of Michelangelo's David, the perfect imperfection of a boy halfway towards manhood, made more imperfect still with a block of unfinished marble at the end of his arm, as if the sculptor had left his masterpiece unfinished purposefully, a secret message for the admirers to decode. Jared was in awe of his friend's beauty. And with the rest of his body proportionate now to his left arm, Gabriel could have easily hidden his deformity but chose not to. He laid the stump on top of his desk on display for all to see. And Jared loved him for it, his inner strength. He began to understand what love was that first day back. Upon returning home from school, Jared took out all his nice clothes, the polos and button-down shirts, the khaki pants, the bright colored sweaters, the loafers, and unceremoniously stuffed them in a large black garbage bag that he tossed to the curb with the rest of the trash. He took whatever money he had and bought jeans, T-shirts, and sneakers, shedding the uptight preppie skin of his previous years and metamorphosing into his new self.

Gabriel had other friends by then. One of the second grade bullies had grown as well, evolved into one of Gabriel's henchman. Jared remembered Achilles from his days of elementary school torture. His face was relatively unchanged, though the nose and lips were somewhat coarser, the cheeks and chin brushed with dark brown stubble. Achilles may or may not have remembered Jared but he did not question Gabriel's actions and accepted Jared of one of the gang. Johnny also shared space with Gabriel, but Jared saw in him an independence that suggested ulterior motives for being part of the gang. But Jared felt no threat, they were friends loosely connected to Gabriel in a gang that he would soon outgrow. Yet here they all were, at the end of high school and still together, planning to murder an old man. Jared needed to believe Gabriel's reasons were honest and pure. He could not reconcile his involvement in the killing of another man otherwise.

Jared opened the door to the medicine cabinet and found

the shelves populated with small bottles of the ever-increasing regimen of pills he was prescribed to take for the ever-increasing list of psychological diagnoses. It began in first grade when his acting out was thought to be a manifestation of ADD, and not his parents' imperiled marriage. First there was Ritalin, which was titrated up until his sleep was affected and appetite became profoundly suppressed. Clonidine was added for sleep, but his tolerance developed to its effects and Halcion was introduced. He became a guinea pig for the succession of child psychiatrists who took turns enforcing his or her own diagnostic theory and corresponding brand of pharmacotherapy. His anxiety over the stress of his parents' divorce was treated with an anxiolytic. Depression was likewise managed with an antidepressant. These last five years, during which time his mother had walked out and another woman had walked in and stayed, he became well acquainted with SSRIs, Benzodiazepines, and Stimulants, as many of these were prescribed and pushed to toxic levels in his blood stream and flooded his neuronal synapses. Most recently the idea of Bipolar disorder was proposed and a new class of mood stabilizer would be started this summer. He knew more than he wished to know about all of these medications. He joked about how well he'd do if he went into pharmacology, if not child psychiatry. He closed the cabinet door. "Better living through chemistry," he thought, smirking at his reflection.

He stepped into the hot shower. Tonight he'd forego any pills. He wanted no interference with any of the drugs he'd used already and would be using tonight. The water washed over his body but failed to penetrate his mind numbing high; still it felt good to bathe the sweat and dirt from the previous night. He laughed out loud when he thought of society's misperceptions and misplaced fears of marijuana but saw no problem with psychiatrists prescribing psychotropic drugs that were so much more toxic.

He stepped out of the shower and toweled himself dry.

And his parents? They stood by, abdicating their role in his life as the parade of clinical social workers, psychologists, and psychiatrists stepped in and out. And they, busy with their own lives- his career (managing a famous steakhouse in the city), her need for personal fulfillment- receded into the background. Then the divorce was final and wife number two entered, she at least had an excuse to not give a shit. But for a moment the house became a home. She suggested his father pay for private school and so he was thrust at the torturous age of twelve into a middle school to learn among the privileged and pampered savages. As the second set of marital bonds frayed and tore, the home became a house again from which the father spent longer hours at work, the step-mother fled to the home of her parents, and Jared was back in public school, Great Hope North with kids who were slightly less pampered, but no less savage. And poor Maria, what could she do? The one who knew most what was happening to him, a witness to the crack he seemed to be slipping through. She went to work and prayed, she went home and prayed, she went to church and prayed some more.

Jared opened his drawers and pulled out some clothes. He began to rebel, he let his hair grow, he made friends his parents disapproved of (had they cared enough), he got drunk, high, stoned... Nothing. Nothing made sense. At times he expected to be caught and punished, at times he wished for it, to be yelled at, hit, punched; something, some form of contact; something to validate his membership in the family.

By the time Jared sat down to lunch the high was winding down, the hangover was miraculously gone. But he still had his mind to contend with.

4

"Jared, Jared."

"Yes?" he said hoarsely, stretching out the aches and knots of his shoulder and legs. He found Maria gently rocking him.

"You wanted me to wake you up at seven."

Jared nodded sleepily, his eyes still closed. "Thank you, Maria. I'm getting up."

"Did you want something to drink? Water? Coffee?"

Jared peered into the eyes of his onetime nanny, rediscovering the maternal affections he found so rare in others. "No thank you, Maria. Well, maybe a cup of coffee." He sat up, shrugging off the sleep. "I'll be out in a minute." Still fully clothed he stumbled sleepily to the bathroom and splashed cold water on his face. He looked up and checked the side of his stubbled cheeks and chin for any zits, then dried his face and headed out. He reached behind his dresser and pulled out the bag of weed. He counted the money in his wallet before stuffing it in his back pocket

He was finishing his coffee when the sound of Johnny's motorbike broke into the driveway. "Okay Maria, gotta go. If you see my dad, tell him not to wait up for me."

"Okay," Maria replied somewhat reluctantly.

The searing heat from the day had ebbed to a comfortably warm evening gilded with the occasional breeze.

"Yo what's up?" Johnny sat straddling the dirt bike, arms stretched out against the handlebars, leather boots poised on the ground, the dark red sunset reflected off his sunglasses. He wore a large thick bicycle chain across the chest like a bandolier. "Hop on back and hold tight."

Jared swung a long leg over the side and grabbed Johnny around the waist as the bike surged down the driveway and out onto the street. The houses blurred on either side as Johnny gunned the engine down the many side streets until he hit Dream Boulevard going east.

"Where's the party?" Jared yelled above the chaos of the wind.

Johnny yelled something back, but Jared could make out only a few disjointed words. After a few failed attempts at conversation, Jared gave in and surrendered himself to the ride.

They pulled off Dream Boulevard about twenty minutes later, taking a series of winding roads until they stopped in front of a large Tudor-style house. Cabriolets, Corvettes and Porsches lined the long driveway abutting the house and an incessant bass beat insisted from large half open windows in the front.

The sun had dropped further leaving a slim belt of light westward. Johnny hitched his thumb back. "Get off, I gotta chain her up."

Jared followed Johnny as he walked the bike to a wooded area across from the house and in several yards until they were invisible from the streets and the music was a soft rumble. Johnny leaned the bike against a tree and unslung the chain. He worked quickly and quietly and clicked the padlock in place. Johnny fished his pack of cigarettes from his T-shirt pocket, took out a smoke and lit up.

"Can I get a cigarette?" Jared stretched out a hand.

"Get your own, asshole." Johnny brushed past him and headed to the street.

"Come on, man." Jared followed behind. "If I would have known you weren't going to share I would have asked you to stop at the gas station and bought my own."

Johnny reached back into his pack. "Alright, a buck a cigarette and I'm keeping count." His eyes twinkled mischievously as he handed over a cigarette, leaving Jared to wonder whether he was joking or not. With Johnny it was always hard to tell.

5

They heard Achilles's car long before it circled around the corner, the engine coughing through a partly cracked muffler. Achilles parked in front of Gabriel's house and gave the horn a couple of light taps.

Inside the house Gabriel slowly got up from the table. "That's Achilles."

His mother looked up tiredly. "Where are you going?"

"There's a party," he said as he grabbed his jacket from behind his chair.

Leon got up and embraced him. "Have a fun time." His accent as thick as his beard, he pulled back smiling. "You have a key to get back in, yes?"

"Yes." Gabriel smiled back weakly. So used to guarding his feelings in his mother's home, he now felt unsure of this sudden affection. And yet, since Leon had arrived the house felt different, as if his uncle had filled all the empty rooms and all the silent pauses; there was no space or need to hide. Gabriel's initial disquiet at his uncle's visit was slowly abating.

"Here." Leon reached into his back pocket and pulled out a twenty-dollar bill from his wallet. "No, no," he said waving away his sister's and Gabriel's protests. "Not another word." He tucked it into the left inside pocket of Gabriel's leather jacket. "Enjoy. Go. Go. Your friend is waiting for you." Leon's other arm was wrapped around his older sister in a playful hug, speaking to her in a tone of mock chastisement. "You shoosh now, I can spoil my nephew if I want."

For a brief moment, Gabriel felt reluctant to leave this new dynamic in the house, this newfound sense of belonging. He looked back to the house as he walked down the driveway.

Achilles's car was out front, a black 1969 Chevelle SS he'd bought the year before. Gabriel stepped into the car, shutting the door tightly. "Hey man," he said, lost in thought.

"What's up? Who's that other person in the house?"

Gabriel turned briefly to the two silhouettes huddled in the living room. "My uncle Leon." He settled back in his seat and looked straight ahead, not wanting to get into a conversation about his uncle now.

"The commando?"

"Right," Gabriel said. He shifted slightly so that he could roll the window down and look outside. He took out a pack of cigarettes and pulled one out. "You know where this party's at, right?"

"Yeah, a friend of one of Johnny's rich JAP girlfriend over in Rosedale. He gave me the address and directions."

Gabriel smiled, lighting up a cigarette. "That guy, I don't know how he fools these rich girls."

"That's his schtick. Rich girls like to piss off their parents with a dirt bag like Johnny. Anyway-" Achilles reached under his seat and pulled out a bag of what looked like small sticks of dynamite. "Just in case things get hot there I brought a few M80s and Blockbusters."

"Something tells me you're planning on things getting hot."

Achilles shifted into gear and the car pulled away from the curb, flashing two ghost-like spools of light on a row of houses opposite them, a disconsolate rumble as it rolled down the street. "Never hurts to be prepared."

The car picked up speed once they turned off of Gabriel's street and then several turns later pulled onto the highway. Achilles popped in an AC/DC tape and turned up the volume. As Brian Johnson screeched and Angus Young picked and strummed through "Back in Black" they raced down the highway, weaving in and out of Saturday evening traffic. The wind howled into the car, whipping Achilles and Gabriel's hair back, sending the smoke into violent eddies that mixed with the rock and roll at the edges of the car.

Twenty minutes later they parked behind a line of upscale cars midway down the block and started walking to the party. As the two approached the house, they were met with the unmistakably nauseating sounds of New Wave music.

Gabriel and Achilles exchanged grimaces. "I hope the DJ has some decent tunes," Achilles said, shaking his head. "Otherwise I'm outta here."

Gabriel smiled. "I'm sure you can convince him to put some Sabbath on."

When they reached the front door, two large, meaty looking teenagers who looked like they could second as tackling dummies blocked their path. Though they were a few inches shorter than Gabriel and Achilles, the bouncers were considerably thicker, their arms pushed out from overinflated chests and egos. "It's BYOB or ten bucks to get in." It was obvious this was the longest number of words they'd ever had to string together; but then again, they hadn't been hired for their elocution. Achilles looked down at the two, as if calculating how many punches and kicks he'd get in before they had a chance to respond. He began to push forward but Gabriel pulled his arm out blocking him. "It's on me, man." He reached into his jacket and pulled out his uncle's twenty-dollar bill.

Satisfied, the two bouncers parted. The one who spoke earlier opened the front door, letting out a blast of heat and noise from within. "Go right on in, ladies." He waved his arm in, laughing.

Achilles clenched his jaw as he pushed his way past the two. "Fuck you."

The two entered the dark of a wide foyer, wading through the steamy, eye-watering mix of smoke, stale alcohol, staler vomit, and the pheromonal heat of intent, young bodies that pressed in on either side, 'kids' responding to an ecdysis of youth and basking in their new skin, ready for a chance at some vague notion of adult mischief. All around they danced, drank, smoked or shouted above the music, trying to make themselves heard, making it easy for Gabriel to overhear small pieces of conversations as he pushed his way forward.

"-yeah, the father was finally convicted-"

"-some white collar crime-"

"-I heard fifteen years in the federal pen."

"-who knows where the wife is-"

Large cavernous rooms branched off on either side of the dimly lit hallway, a large stairwell broke off and rose along the right. Gabriel spotted Johnny along the opposite side of the hallway towards the end, his right arm braced against the wall, a cigarette clasped between two fingers, his left hand caressing the arm of a girl pushed up against the wall. Gabriel caught Achilles's eye and motioned with his head. The girl saw the two closing in before Johnny did and whispered something into his ear. Johnny wheeled around smiling. "What up guys?" He raised his hand to high five them. "This is," he quickly ducked his head to exchange murmurs with the sequestered girl before looking back at his friends, "Bonnie."

The two nodded noncommittally to Bonnie before confronting Johnny.

"Where's Tracy?"

"Uh, she couldn't make it." Johnny replied flatly, giving a subtle shake of his head to dissuade further questions.

"And Jared?" Gabriel asked.

Johnny grinned. "He's upstairs in the party room having the time of his life."

Gabriel and Achilles exchanged looks of doubt and concern.

"Hey, don't worry about him; he's in good hands," Johnny reassured unsuccessfully.

"What the fuck's up with the ten dollar cover?" Achilles leaned in menacingly, still pissed off.

"Hey man, what can I say?" Johnny backed away a step.

"But hey, now that you're in all the beer is free so don't sweat it."

"Where's all this 'free' beer?" Achilles looked around, unconvinced.

"There're a few bars set up with beer and some hard liquor." Johnny hitched his thumb back yelling above the din. "You passed one on the way in. And then there's a keg in the back of the house." He turned to Gabriel. "Yo. Lisa's around, she's looking for you."

Gabriel arched back away, looking suddenly annoyed. "Lisa? What's she doing here?"

"I don't know," Johnny replied, averting his eyes.

Gabriel jabbed a finger into Johnny's chest. "You told her I was coming, didn't you!"

Johnny raised both hands in defense. "Hey man, I didn't know you guys weren't talking."

But Gabriel had stormed off, not waiting to hear anymore. Achilles shot Johnny a hard look before following him.

"What's up with your friends?" Bonnie yelled into Johnny's ear.

"They need a drink," he replied, laughing. "Or two."

"Who's Tracy?"

"Who?"

"That girl," Bonnie replied dubiously, "the one your friends were asking about?"

"Oh, her." Johnny took a long thoughtful pull off his cigarette, then exhaled as he spoke. "She's yesterday."

Gabriel and Achilles made their way back and entered into what had been at one point a large dining room, now without the lavish Tuscan dining set and matching china cabinet, the dark green walls stood stripped bare of the large Botticellis that once graced them, and the three full length windows, without the imported silk curtains, exposed the disgrace within to all passersby. The crowd of tittering teens had thinned inside the room somewhat, allowing some space to move around along the walls, concentrating itself around the bar. Gabriel and Achilles used their large size to push themselves quickly to the front of the bar. The bartender, an aging biker with tattoos on both arms, spotted them as two of his own kind (or close enough). "What'll you have, boys?"

Gabriel held up two fingers and the bartender pushed a couple of beer bottles forward. Gabriel reached into his pocket and dropped a dollar into the empty tip jar on the counter and the bartender nodded in appreciation. Grabbing the beers, Gabriel motioned with his head to an opened window at the other side of the room.

A couple of freshmen dressed in Goth stood by the window looking black and depressed talked quietly. They saw Gabriel and Achilles approach and scattered.

Gabriel and Achilles sat down watching the various cliques of people huddled together. "Look at all the fucking preppies," Achilles spat out angrily.

Gabriel followed his gaze and as if to confirm Achilles's summation. Everyone sported one of a bright rainbow of pressed Polo's, Lacoste's, chinos, plaid Bermuda shorts, and standard issue boat shoes or penny loafers. "Like a fucking LL Bean catalogue."

"Rich fucks. Getting a free ride. They won't have to lift a finger." Achilles's face began to cloud over as he white-knuckle gripped his beer like a projectile.

Gabriel eyed his friend sideways, recognizing the mounting violence within. "Boxes, everyone of them."

"What do you mean boxes?" Achilles asked suspiciously. He always pressed Gabriel on these enigmatic comments.

"You see all these people, man, they all live in these boxes. Little boxes, where everything fits the way it should. Where everybody is pretty, and perky, and perfect, and nobody struggles, no one suffers."

"And?" Achilles took a hard swig off his bottle.

"And they're all living in a dream, a lie. You and I are living in the real world, and sometimes it may feel like we're just surviving it. But if these guys ever woke up from their fantasy, their worlds would crumble." Gabriel clinked bottles with his friend. "Here's to living in the real world."

"Real world?"

"Real world," Gabriel confirmed, no longer smiling. He looked at his friend thoughtfully and the two clinked bottles again, as if the words were something to celebrate if not respect; united in a past they had both felt they'd survived, living in a present that offered quickly fading opportunities of escape, and headed towards a future that was both uncharted and uncertain.

"So what's up with you and Lisa?" Achilles asked, as if picking up the thread of a previous conversation.

"Nothing. Not a damn thing." Gabriel took off his leather jacket, draping it over his left shoulder, watching the bar scene in front of them.

Achilles turned to him. "Man, I thought you guys were doing well. She's such a good looking chick and she's got a hot body."

"You can have her." Gabriel took a drink off his beer.

"So what's wrong with her?"

Gabriel paused, trying to sum up all that was wrong with the relationship before responding. "She gives it up too easy."

Achilles took a swig off his beer and thought a moment. "So what's wrong with her?"

The two laughed. Achilles continued, "Okay, okay. I understand."

Gabriel turned to his friend, smiling doubtfully. "What do you understand?"

Achilles returned the look, now serious. "You want someone special. Someone who values each step of the relationship and doesn't feel the need to rush it. People who go to fast get bored too easily."

Gabriel, taken aback, nodded as if Achilles had put into

words what he had felt towards the end of the relationship. "You're right," he said finally.

Achilles turned to Gabriel, suddenly animated. "So listen to this idea."

"Alright, alright, let me get into position here," Gabriel said, grinning. He was so used to Achilles's get rich quick schemes, he could tell one was coming just by the change in his friend's tone. "So what's it this time?"

"This time it's different," Achilles replied earnestly.

"Oh yeah, how so?"

"We form a rock band."

Gabriel laughed. "What are you talking about?"

"Seriously, I figure," Achilles leaned in conspiratorially, "all we need is one really good song to make it big and we'll have it made the rest of our lives."

"Yeah, except for the fact that none of us play any instruments, none of us can sing, and none of us can read music. But aside from that it's a great idea."

"Don't laugh. I'm serious. I say we each choose an instrument, and one of us is the lead vocal. We write up a song and just practice it every day."

"It takes years for any band that already has talent to make it big time. And we don't have talent. Have you heard Jared singing, he sounds like a cow giving birth," Gabriel replied, laughing. "And Johnny, he can't even air guitar right. Not to mention the fact that being and playing in a band takes discipline."

"Alright, alright, I got it. Man, you shoot down all of my ideas," Achilles grumbled into his beer.

"Your ideas have more holes that Lisa's stockings."

The two sat quietly contemplating over their beers. "Oh shit." Gabriel looked at the entrance to the room and looked away.

Achilles followed his gaze. "Speak of the devil."

Lisa had not matured like most girls. For her, adolescence

came early and fiercely. At an age where most girls were secretly fondling their tiny breast buds with some measure of apprehension if not anticipation, Lisa was in full bloom with monstrous D-cup sized breasts that she harnessed with the measliest of lacy bras. And her long-limbed body took on a series of forbidden curves found only on centerfolds and locker room calendars. While most girls were still playing with dolls, Lisa was playing with boys. Of course, to her dolls and boys were one and the same. Both could be toyed with, both were easily manipulated, both had movable parts (though not detachable for the latter - alas). By the time she was thirteen Lisa provoked double-takes from most men, and some women, on the street. By the time she was sixteen, the only ones not turning their heads had pre-existing cervical spine injuries. And the clothes she chose to wear encouraged these jaw-dropping double-takes. Though of average height, she made herself easy to spot and difficult to forget. Fishnet stockings under torn cut off shorts, tight fitting tank tops, and a bushy mane of dirty blond hair, Lisa loved to provoke. Gabriel had been different, though, for the young siren. She'd gravitated to him initially for the novelty of the anchor at the end of his left arm (a special notch in her pink leather belt), but had soon found so much more to him than to any of the other boys before him (and there were other boys before him). Her cold and calculating nature notwithstanding, Lisa found herself becoming emotionally drawn to Gabriel – slightly- and for once in her short sybaritic life pulled away from the relationship, not out of boredom but out of fear of losing herself.

Lisa scanned the room and immediately spotted the two boys with predatory eyes. She slowly tightrope walked towards them on her stiletto heels, drawing the attention of all around her as everything and everyone else faded. "Hi guys," she said without looking at Achilles, in a deep silky voice well beyond her sixteen years.

"Hi," Gabriel replied.

"Hi," Achilles offered, smiling suggestively.

Lisa's cold eyes turned to Achilles. "Hi Achilles, how's the bacne?"

Achilles stood up, looking at Gabriel, his swagger suddenly gone. "I'm uh- going to get us another round of beers. Who wants one?"

Gabriel lifted his half empty bottle in response as Lisa sat down next to him. "No, thank you," she answered. "I just thought I'd chat a little bit. I got to run soon anyway."

Achilles lumbered off.

Lisa turned to face Gabriel. "So. How've you been?"

Gabriel took another sip of his beer before looking back. "Doing well."

"Good," she nodded, prodding conversation. "That's good to hear." She leaned away from him a little appraising him. "You sure look good. Been working out?"

"Some," he said, frowning at the peeling label of his bottle, then exhaling whatever qualms of a confrontation he turned to face her. "Look, Lisa-"

"I'm sorry," Lisa replied preemptively, a breath too early and a tone too impatient to be believable.

"Sorry!" He smiled bitterly.

"Really, sweetie. I'm sorry. I was wrong."

"About what?" Although he already knew the 'what', he refused to let her in on the pain she'd caused him, the increasingly populous club of the deluded and ditched to which she had cast him a couple weeks before over a six-pack of beer and a pack of cigarettes. Being dumped was a rite of passage for all young men, and he passed through it with the typical tear-soaked pillowcase, the endless 'Why me? Why me?'

"About wanting to see other people. I thought opening up our relationship would make it stronger."

"Stronger?" Gabriel shook his head slowly, taking another sip of his beer. "You'll have to explain the logic to me one day but I don't want to hear it now."

"Aw, come on, sweetie. Forgive me?" Lisa leaned into him, simpering, flashing a look that was part cute puppy dog, part slutty playboy bunny. When Gabriel failed to respond she leaned in, mewing now like a mischievous kitty. "Forgive me? Come on." She flashed a bright white smile. "I have a secret to tell you." Her voice was now hushed.

Gabriel didn't respond, refusing to take the bait.

"Alright, I'll tell you." She giggled, whispering, "I don't have any panties on."

Gabriel sprayed his last sip of beer. "Excuse me?"

"Come on," she whispered again, squeezing his arm, "let's go upstairs and find a room." Her voice was dripping wet and seductive into his ear, forming small eddies that made his mind swirl. She flashed her eyes from him towards the ceiling then back to him, as if counting the numerous rooms in which there even more numerous possibilities and positions. Gabriel's mouth and brain went suddenly dry as all his bodily fluids rushed to his groin; so many thoughts spun inside his mind, his current arousal, the pain of the breakup, the fact that he hadn't had sex in the past few weeks. And yet when he looked at her, Gabriel found cold and callous eyes, so incongruous to the heat of her voice, eyes suggesting future, calculated betrayals. Gabriel stood up quickly, stabling his groin and controlling his voice. "Not interested." And made for the bar.

"Hey Gabriel." He heard her voice a little more sharp, the kind she unleashed when she got pissed, when things didn't go her way, which was almost never. But he continued walking, away from the hard edge of her middle finger and a torrent of four-letter words and insults, her form receding as he allowed himself to be swallowed by the bar crowd. He caught up to Achilles who handed him another beer.

"I heard there's a pool table somewhere in this place," Achilles offered.

Gabriel turned around to find Lisa storming out. "Okay,"

he mouthed through the din and the two headed out.

They wove their way through crowd after crowd of conquering heroes of an ill-conceived war, celebrating in what had once been a foyer, den, music room, study, kitchen, and various other rooms and hallways that made up the labyrinth of the excavated mansion. They finally entered the game room, larger, brighter and less crowded than the rest of the first floor. It was comfortably furnished, royal blue with dark oak wainscoting, a minibar in the corner, a retired fireplace on one side, and a framed collection of pool cues on the opposite wall. A large, well maintained pool table inhabited the center of the room. Gabriel sat down on a bench under the cues. Achilles strode towards the table, a game already in play as four sophomores huddled around a table, one of who was calculating his next shot. Achilles laid a large hand on the cue ball. "Who am I playing?" he said, officially ending the match.

The young man with the cue gulped slightly. "We're playing couples," his voice slowly cracking into manhood.

"Alright," Achilles said impatiently. "Who are 'we' playing?"

The young man looked towards his friends, who had already committed themselves to a retreat to the walls. "Me, I guess, and my friend Bif. I'm Chad." He extended a tentative hand to Achilles who dismissed it with a hard look.

Achilles chose a cue stick off the wall and began chalking it. "Alright Chip, wrack 'em up."

"Uh, Chad," the boy offered. "My name is Chad."

Achilles raised a quick eyebrow at the boy's moxy, but extended a hand. "Mike," he said, with a lightly crushing handshake, "nice to meet you. This is Joe." He nodded over to Gabriel.

Gabriel nodded quietly, silently enjoying himself.

Chad, massaging the pain in his right hand, thought better at another potentially crushing handshake and offered a friendly wave. "Hi."

Achilles paused at the head of the table and looked over at

Chad. "House rules, right." It was less of a question and more of an order, to which Chad nodded with a mixture of confusion and trepidation.

Achilles cracked the wracked balls with a sharp cue shot, sending two solids in on the break. Chad and Bif looked on amazed as Achilles and Gabriel proceeded to sink all the balls. Even with his one arm, the left one hidden under the cloak of his leather bomber, Gabriel shot with incredible accuracy, the cue hovering two inches off the table. And within a span of several minutes, the game was over.

Achilles came over to Chad at the end, extending his hand. "Good game," he said, submitting Chad to another crushing handshake. "You owe me twenty bucks."

Chad looked up in wide-eyed shock, his hand trapped in Achilles's large grip. "What?" his voice cracking again.

"House rules." Achilles nodded. "Twenty bucks a game. You're not telling me you came to play pool without any money on you."

"I- I, no, I." Chad started backing away, a look of fear in his eyes. He looked at his friends who had retreated even further, then turned back to Achilles. "I only have ten."

Achilles scowled down at Chad a moment, but then his face softened. "I'll let you off the hook this time. Just give me the ten and we'll call it even."

Chad's hand shook as he counted ten singles out of his wallet.

Achilles pocketed the money. "Alright rematch, wrack 'em up."

Chad looked up fearfully. "I- I don't have any more money."

"What about Bif?" Achilles pointed the cue at the partner's direction. "He's gotta have ten on him. This way you can win your money back."

Bif made some quick calculations with respect to the cost of reconstructive surgery on a potentially busted face and consented to the rematch. Which was over within less time than the first and soon Bif was counting ten dollars out of his wallet.

The boys made their escape as Achilles counted the money. "Nice doing business with you," he called out to them.

Achilles walked over to where Gabriel was seated and offered a high five. But his hand was stuck in midair as Gabriel's attention had been drawn to the other side of the room. Achilles followed his gaze. "Who's that?"

"Here, hold my drink." Gabriel stood up, not taking his eyes off a tall, young dark skinned woman whose long black cascading hair caressed the front of a bright red embroidered shirt, the curve of her hips confined to dark blue jeans. She stood alone next to the fireplace, a mixed drink in her hand, looking as if she'd been dropped off in the middle of nowhere, not lost, but misplaced. It was obvious she knew no one at the party. She stood a few feet away from the small groups of privileged partygoers. Though she was no older than everyone else, she held herself in a way that showed the experience of a different, older world; not aloof, but apart.

Gabriel walked slow, measured steps as if every pace had now become important and carried meaning. The young woman, sensing his approach, turned her deep dark eyes to him, absorbing his intent. He stopped a foot away from her and extended his hand. "Hello, I'm Gabriel," he said in a voice he could not trust as his own and a frankness he did not recognize.

Her hand gripped his and he sensed an imperceptible pause in what he had come to take for granted as the natural order of the world, the earth's rotation, the moon's orbit, the cresting waves before the surf. The world stopped for the two of them, as the rest of the party continued. They stood as immovable stones in a river, breaking the currents of people around them. And just as quickly the earth beneath began to move, as if reset, spinning once again on its axis, and yet different, as if only now corrected and Gabriel knew he'd been misled by shadows up until now.

"I'm Priti," she said finally in slightly accented English, smiling at the eyes that hid partly by his soft curly brown hair. "But I thought your name was Joe."

Confusion crossed his face for a brief moment then his smile broadened sheepishly. "That's my 'pool name'."

"I didn't know there was such a thing." She let go of his hand, grabbing her drink with both hands.

"I'm just kidding. That's really more of my friend's way of keeping our names a secret from the people here at the party." Feeling the loss of her touch, he reflexively grabbed his pack of cigarettes from his jacket and shook two free.

Priti shook her head at the cigarette. "Your friend sounds like he doesn't trust too well. He also appears troubled." She frowned, as if in remembering.

Gabriel dipped his head forward to light his cigarette. "You may be right about that." He exhaled a steady stream of smoke through his nose "Priti," he said her name for the first time, feeling the smooth texture of it as if passed from his lips to his throat then back to his teeth. "A very pretty name. What does it mean?"

"It's Hindi. It means love," Priti replied. "You know, you're the first person who's asked me that since I've been here."

"I'm curious. I love learning about other countries, other cultures. I find them so much more interesting than what I see here." Gabriel found himself talking more than he'd done in a long while. He'd never felt so confident and free.

Priti frowned, looking around. "Most people here can't even point out my country on a map."

Gabriel continued, "When I was younger, I had a globe in my room. I used to give it a spin every day and then abruptly stop it and try to guess the name of the country. I'm pretty sure I could still find India on the map."

Priti laughed. "What a funny way to learn about countries. I like it." She took a sip from her drink, watching him above the rim of her glass. "And your name. Gabriel. What does it mean?"

"In the Jewish religion, Gabriel is an angel of god," he said, adding his ashes to a pile overflowing the ashtray on the table.

"Are you Jewish?"

Gabriel took another drag of his cigarette while he contemplated the question. "My mother and father are Jewish but I don't believe in it."

"Do you not believe in God?"

He resisted the urge to run his fingers through her long beautiful hair and caress her face. "I believe in-"

"Hey buddy, I'm talking to ya." A voice rose above the already loud din of conversation behind him, thick and slurred.

Gabriel didn't turn around immediately. He exhaled another stream of smoke high into the air and registered the vague look of fear in Priti's eyes as she angled them over his shoulder. He predicted the guy behind him to be slightly shorter. "What was I saying?" he continued. "Oh yeah, God-"

"Hey buddy, I'm talking to ya." By now most of the conversations around them had ceased.

Gabriel looked sideways at the other teen. He was shorter, heavier around the middle, with a gut that strained against the front of his button-down shirt. His hair was cut short, exposing more of his fleshy face that drooped with intoxication. Dotted with narrow-set eyes, the teen's face was odd and disorganized, as if the family chromosomes had gotten old and worn out, the genes having divided one too many times, exposing the recessive flaws. "Do I know you?" Gabriel asked.

"I was just saying to my friends here," the young man spanned his arm out behind him to include several people who seemed to have divorced themselves physically, emotionally and spiritually from him, "I thought that Greasers went out with the sixties. And here you are proving me wrong."

Gabriel turned around fully to face him. "Something tells me this happens to you a lot." Gabriel took another drag of his cigarette and exhaled a plume into his face.

"Ha, ha, very fuckin' funny. Why are they lettin' scumbags

like you into a nice place like this, I don't know. Anyway, you know what? I don't like your face."

Gabriel turned around to Priti. "Don't be afraid, it's just some drunk. There're a lot of those around here. They're usually harmless."

Priti stared back at him disbelieving.

"To answer your question, I do believe-"

"Hey, I'm talking to ya. Ya don't belong here. You and your dot-head friend of yours."

Gabriel felt his jacket tugged off his left shoulder and drop to the floor.

Priti spotted the end of Gabriel's left arm and held her breath. All conversation in the room seemed to pause for Gabriel, leaving only the clacking sounds of billiard balls behind him. There was an abrupt halt in the ethereal New Wave music, replaced now by the rhythmic pounding of Bill Ward's bass-drum-introduction to 'Iron Man'. (Was he the only one who heard it? He wasn't sure. He hadn't seen Achilles in the room for a while.) Gabriel slowly picked up his jacket and put it on. He blew on the end of his cigarette and gently stubbed it into the ashtray, slightly pivoting his left foot. Then with a sudden twist and burst of speed, Gabriel's right fist connected hard with his victim's jaw, which gave way with an audible crunch. The teen's legs buckled and he dropped to his knees. He pitched forwarded on all fours, dazed.

Gabriel turned shamefaced to Priti. "I'm sorry. I didn't mean for this to happen."

Priti peered into his eyes, searchingly. "Are you sure, Gabriel? Are you sure you're not troubled as well?"

Gabriel shook his head. "I don't think so, Priti, but trouble always seems to find me."

A sudden commotion drew their attention toward the entrance to the room. Both bouncers, obviously friends of the dazed teen on the floor, were making their way over to Gabriel.

"Now what do we do?" Priti asked, suddenly fearful.

"Put your drink on the table," Gabriel commanded, and turned to face his attackers.

When the two bouncers were several feet away from him, several large explosions shook the room sending everyone panicking for the door. In the few short seconds of mayhem that followed, Gabriel grabbed Priti's hand and pulled her to the side and the two escaped into the stampede. One of the bouncers helped his friend off the floor while the other spotted them and gave chase.

Gabriel and Priti ran into Achilles on the way out. "Go, go." he shoved the car keys into the inside pocket of Gabriel's jacket and urged them on. "I'll meet up with you at the car, just make sure the car's ready." Then Achilles picked up a pool cue and waited, crouching among the mass of legs for the right moment. As the first pursuer passed him, Achilles raised his cue and stopped him with a barrage of vertical sharp strikes to the head and shoulders. The other dropped to the ground under the assault, crying out with arms raised. But Achilles didn't stop. He broke the cue in half against his victim's back, and picked up another cue before the other could respond. By this time the bouncer's partner and the third teen had arrived. Achilles brandished the stick menacingly as he backed away to the exit, then threw it towards them and ran into the hallway.

Several more explosions shook the house as he ran down the hall along with dozens of screaming teenagers, bumping into Johnny. "We gotta go, we gotta go," he yelled.

Johnny smiled in amusement. "What the fuck did you guys do now?" then looked at the bouncers heading down the hallway. "Oh shit!" The two started for the front door.

Achilles waved Johnny outside. "I'm going to get Jared. You get going."

6

SNIFF!!!

"I think space exploration is only at its infancy. Sure we sent men to the moon back in '69, but that only was the beginning. The Pioneer 10 space probe launched three years later was the first to have the power to escape the gravitational pull of our solar system. Only this past week Pioneer 10 crossed Neptune's orbit! Think about it, we have constructed a rocket that has passed the furthermost planet of our solar system! And it's not going to stop." By this point Jared was up in crouching position on the loveseat, as if ready to leap onto the probe itself. "Who know the amount of data we'll obtain from it over the next 10 years! Not only that, I believe in our foreseeable future the likelihood of sending astronauts to Mars. And not only that, we'll be able to send humans to the farthest reaches of our solar system!"

SNIFF!!!

Jared searched the room, bright eyes twinkling, at the teens around him, excited, manic almost, the cocaine feeding his volatile energy as he held court on one of his favorite topics, looking for converts to his cosmology. He looked beyond them and saw the room for the first time, walls painted deep blue with large opened windows, an evening breeze billowed in dark grey curtains. A son's room, a fortress to a young boy's boundless imagination, a son now grown and heir to an indictment, an overseer of a repossessed future. All remnants to the past glory were gone, leaving a sofa, love seat and two fold out chairs huddled around a coffee table. There were four; one was a preppie-looking older teen, Gregory, who seemed to belong

to the seemingly abandoned mansion. The others were gumbas from Brooklyn, the coke dealer and his two "associates,"
the three of them in track suits, their necks weighted down
by large caliber gold chains. There were more of Carl Sagan's
trillion galaxies worth of stars above them than grains of coke
on the mirror, but it was this galaxy that held them captive.
They took their turns around the slowly sinking mound of cocaine on the commandeered bathroom mirror. They bobbed
up and down, like genuflecting supplicants to an enslaving
god, snorting lines of short lived euphoria then reaching their
heads up to capture the few wayward grains. In between lines
they gazed back at him with eyes bright as midnight moons.

SNIFF!!!

"Yeah, but what about the power that's going to be needed
to propel these rockets?"

Jared turned to answer one of his favorite questions, it allowed him to vent his imagination. He smiled at the preppie,
obviously the person in the room closest in intelligence and
education to Jared. "That's a great question. The Pioneer 10
there were four thermonuclear generators. But I believe that
with advances in aerospace engineering there will be concom-
itant advances in extracting and utilizing energy from renew-
able sources, we will be able to harness the solar energy to
propel our rockets to any point in our solar system."

SNIFF!!!

"Maybe we'll run into some Martians," one of the gumbas
said, laughing at his buddies. "I wouldn't mind getting my
hands on one of them space chicks."

Jared laughed as well. "Maybe, but I don't think we will."

"You don't think there's life on other planets?" asked
Gregory.

SNIFF!!!

"I don't discount the possibility that other life forms exist.
But I think we are too limited in our thinking with respect to
how we define life that we may not recognize other life forms

if we encountered them. Think about it, our own galaxy has upwards of hundreds of billions of stars, and more than a hundred billion planets. There can be life forms on any of those planets but they may not have come about in the way life on earth has. There may have been another process completely alien to us. Also, something tells me if another life source were to make it to our edge of the solar system, we wouldn't survive it-"

Two explosions brought their attention towards the door to the bedroom.

"Probably some fireworks," explained Gregory, before bending over a line of cocaine.

SNIFF!!!

He squeezed his nose together tightly, as if it were at the verge of falling off. "What do you mean we wouldn't survive it?"

Jared smiled, another of his favorite questions. "Think about the history of our world, how the weaker species was wiped out when in confrontation with another species that was stronger, faster, or smarter. The weaker species was killed off, either directly or through competition for essential resources. Any life form making it to the edge of our solar system would be light years more advanced than us. What could they possibly gain from having a relationship with us that was anything other than exploitive?" He searched into the eyes of those around him. He found their eyes, inert, dead. "They say that it's the brightest star," he said distractedly, "that burns out the fastest.

"You know somethin', you're really smart," offered the dealer to Jared. "I mean, maybe not street smart or nothin' but you got some brains on you, a genius or something, like those Mensa people, high I.Q. and all," he summed it up, a smug smile as he looked to his partners. "You twos need a little bit of smarts like this guy."

Achilles hid along the wall as dozens of teens ran down the

steps, crab crawling up the stairwell until he reached the second floor. He walked down the hallway looking quickly into all the open rooms as teens poured out. A door at the end of the hall was still shut. He tried the knob but was unsuccessful. He took two paces back then stepped forward with a large kick, almost breaking the door off the hinges. He walked in, quickly scanning the room: a television set hissed snow on the screen. An untold quantity of white powder piled high on a mirror in the middle of the coffee table, five men huddled around it, including Jared rubbing his nose after a line. "Hey man, you want some?"

Achilles hooked his left arm under Jared's armpit. "Come on, let's go," he said in a tone that brooked no argument.

Jared protested, wide-eyed and wired. "But, but."

Achilles looked at the eldest in the group, mid-twenties, thin and raggedy, with a dark facial shadow from several days without shaving. "How much does he owe you?"

The man, uncertain, looked to his friends on either side. "Three hundred," he quoted finally.

"Pay up," he barked at Jared.

Jared pulled out his wallet and gave it to Achilles. Achilles quickly thumbed three large bills and threw it on the table. "Let's go."

The man closest to them, better dressed that the others, hair slicked back, bright pink polo shirt, stood up suddenly. "It's actually four hundred." He positioned himself between Achilles and the door. "And who the fuck are you coming in giving orders."

Achilles didn't smoke, rarely drank to excess, and avoided mind altering substances; his thing was violence. It was his essence and his drug. His parents and teachers had noted early on with increasing alarm this tendency towards violence. Visits to the principal's office, suspensions from school became the norm. Tryouts to sporting teams usually ended after the second or third violent tackle or, at times, a more overt attack, a punch or elbow to the face, a kick to the groin. His Tae Kwon Do sensei, despite his enthusiasm for the young boy's fighting prowess, also noted his penchant for violence. Other students refused to spar with him after injuries during practice and he was usually disqualified during regional tournaments because of prohibited kicks to the head. In the end, sensei had to let him go just shy of his black belt confirmation. "I'm afraid you have missed the art altogether, Achilles. The truth is you have no self-control." But Achilles was not quick to anger, for him anger diluted the experience of violence. Better to control the temper and maintain the focus, so in fact he had learned something from sensei.

The man was too close for a kick. Achilles twisted sharply to the right, his left elbow catching the man in the temple. He twisted sharply to the left, a closed right fist connecting with the man's jaw. In a matter of seconds it was over. Not waiting for any friends around the table to respond, Achilles pulled out an M80, lit it, and tossed it onto the coffee table, sending everyone cursing and scrambling for cover. By the time the explosion had scattered more than a thousand dollars of cocaine, Achilles was running down the stairs with Jared closely following.

Jared looked heartbroken. "Why'd you do that for? I just lost a potential connection."

"I just did you a favor," Achilles yelled over his shoulder.

They ran out the door as the guitar solo to "Iron Man" belted out from the speakers.

Despite the fleeing mob, the bouncers spotted Achilles and Jared as they cut across the front lawn towards the street. They ran down the street after them. The second-floor drug dealers joined the chase, bent on exacting revenge for the explosive loss of cocaine. The Chevelle idled at the corner fifty yards away. Jared slowed down dyspneic from the exertion, he stopped several yards from the car suddenly, doubled over gasping, hands on knees. Achilles had one foot in the car when

7

The Chevelle whipped around half a dozen turns, leaving a wake of dust and screeching tires before Gabriel pulled out onto the main road. It was only then that the four were able to breathe easily and introductions could be made. Gabriel looked over at Priti, her left hand pressed against her chest trying to steady her breath, her right hand tightly gripping the door handle, a pair of disconcerted eyes fixed on him. "Priti," he announced, nodding to the back seat, "Achilles and Jared. Achilles and Jared, Priti."

Achilles reached forward a firm handshake. "Nice to meet you," he said nonchalantly, as if they had been introduced at the party, a half-hour before, not in some getaway car escaping people intent on harming them, her.

Priti looked at him with a look of undisclosed fright, and murmured, "Priti." The only word she could remember, as much a name as an anchor to the present.

Jared waved from the back seat. "Hi," he said glumly.

Priti turned to Jared's dark figure. "Priti," she repeated, still finding it hard to catch up to the events of the previous half hour.

At the start of the evening she hadn't even wanted to go out. She had stood by the doorway of her mother's bedroom, arms crossed, her lips pouting in frustration. "There's no one like me at these parties," she had insisted.

Her mother had shaken her head, clucking her tongue. "Chi, chi. What are you going on about," her Gujarati accentuating the reprimanding tone in her voice. "Why, when I was your age I went to all of the school parties. I was not like any of the other girls either." Her mother had sat by the vanity in a beautiful green sari, brushing her long black hair, admiring a memory in the mirror.

"That's not what I mean, Mom. They all still see me as Indian. They are white and I am not."

"So. What does that matter? You have to show them who you are, that you're just like them. How else are you going to make any friends? Or be popular at the school."

"Maybe I don't want to be popular."

Priti's mother had disregarded the comment; she'd kept combing and talking. "When I was your age I had more friends than any of the other girls at school. I made sure to know about every school function, every dance, every party," she'd said,. "There were dark-skinned Indians, light-skinned Indians, even a few Britishers. Everyone was different. But that didn't stop me from going." She'd swiveled around in her chair with an air of finality. "And that's how I met your father."

Priti's nascent defiance, as well as her own personal fears, had then faltered under her mother's stare. As ludicrous as it sounded to her- meeting her future husband at one of these parties- Priti had seen no argument around her mother's own life experience. They'd been living in this country, on The Island, or as she'd come to refer to it, 'the armpit of the universe', for five years now, and she'd quickly concluded that Americans, most specifically young upper middle class white Americans, were sheltered, ego-centric and spoiled. She's also experienced first-hand the brand of racism that came from going to school with them. It was not like in the pictures or what her friend, Seema, back at home had told- no, warned her- about. There'd been no lynching, or crosses burning, no one had tied Priti up to the back of a BMW and dragged her along a desolate dirt road. The racism here on 'The Island' had been subtler. She hadn't been ostracized so much as shunned. No invites to birthday parties, sleepovers, dates, play dates. Conversation in between classes had been brief, curt almost.

In fact, this was the first party in five years that she'd been invited to by one of her classmates, a Meredith Somethingberg, or stein, someone who had sat next to her for more than a year without saying so much as a word to her until she casually mentioned it. Against her better judgment, she had shown interest. "Oh yeah, where at?" she had asked it in a tone that presumed this to be yet another in a long line of casual invites between friends. The girl, with a bored expression, had reached into her pocketbook and had grabbed a tall stack of five by seven glossy invites, peeled one off and, without even looking at her, handed it to Priti. "Thanks," she'd said, in the same blasé tone, Meredith Somethingberg or stein would have appreciated.

Priti had reported the party offhandedly to her mother, hoping she would agree that it would be a waste of time, but had quickly regretted it.

"But I have nothing to wear," Priti had pleaded.

"Nonsense. You have plenty of nice outfits. Let's go straight to your closet and we'll pick out something that will attract attention." Her mother had stood up dramatically on the last word, to underscore the 'attention' she'd hoped to attract. She'd grabbed Priti's hand and half dragged her across the hall to her room.

"Twelve eleven Love Lane," Priti now managed to get out, still somewhat gasping but a little bit calmer in the breeze that swept her long black hair behind her.

Gabriel caught her eye. "Are you okay?" he asked. His words meant only for her in a tone of voice that was unlike any she had heard since she had arrived in the States five years before, passed the color barrier, and the faint accent. Sweet, comforting, and hopeful, a garland of Marigolds she would wear to bed that evening.

"Yes," she mouthed the word. Looking straight back at him, at his eyes, before he turned to face the road ahead. She felt a sudden urge to put her arm around him, to tell him that she meant it. Despite all the excitement, and the hyperventilating, she still remembered his approaching her earlier, the intent.

The Chevelle rumbled onto her block stirring up the howl of the neighborhood dogs. "This is it." Priti turned to face the darkness of the backseat. "Good night Achilles, good night Jared."

"Good night," the two replied in unison.

She turned to Gabriel. "Good night," she said. She wanted to say more but found all the words that came to her as excessive and foolish. As she stepped out, she turned back again to see Gabriel staring at her. "Will I see you again?" he asked, with that same voice that had caused her chest to flutter earlier.

Priti smiled, resisting the urge to lean forward and kiss him. "Maybe."

Gabriel smiled back as she shut the car door and walked to her house, glancing back over her shoulder at him.

Achilles climbed over the seat into the passenger side. Gabriel set his sights on the road and put the car into drive. Jared moaned in the backseat.

"What's wrong with him?" he peered into the rearview mirror and caught Jared leaning against the door.

"I pulled him away from a pile of drugs and a future drug connection," Achilles answered as he rolled down the window, inviting more of the evening breeze into the car.

The car slowed at a red light Gabriel reached in and pulled out two cigarettes. He stuck both in his mouth and as he lit them he looked into the rearview mirror searching for traces of Jared in the darkness. As much as he wanted to warn his friend he remained silent. Who was he to tell his friend how to live his life? What road to hell to choose? He pulled one of the lit cigarettes out and reached back. "Here," he said. "At least these will take a while before they kill you."

Jared took it gently. "Thanks." His buzz now gone, he felt

nauseous and homesick for the euphoria from an hour before.

The light turned green. Achilles turned to look at Gabriel. "Okay Romeo, where's Johnny?"

Keeping his eyes on the road, Gabriel pointed his chin to a spot through the windshield in front of them. "He said he'd meet us at home."

"Home" was a one-room cabin, tucked away in a wooded area behind the local Getty Station that had been abandoned and forgotten in a time on The Island when it was still possible to abandon and forget a stretch of land. The group had happened upon it five years before as they'd raced away from one of their first of many gang fights, this one at the Circle Hope housing projects (or 'C Hole'). They'd crossed Great Hope Road and had disappeared into the forgotten woods that were easy to miss from the road, though by then the C Hole boys had given up the chase. It was a steep thirty-foot climb, difficult at some points, treacherous in others, through a dense barricade of brambles, large rocks, and felled trees long since dead. Once committed to the climb, however, there was no deterring Gabriel who'd reached the top first. Gabriel had spotted it right away and with the bright flame of his brushed chrome Zippo he'd led the group past the unlocked front door, hanging drunkenly off one hinge. The light had cast small flickering shadows as they'd made their way inside; the hardwood floor was carpeted with a fine layer of dust, mouse droppings and crumpled up newspapers. Gabriel's eyes had shone brighter than the flame that first day. "Home," he'd said, just above a whisper, enough for them to hear, and they'd understood what he'd meant.

They had all gone back to their respective houses that day to grab all manner of cleaning supplies and had spent the better part of that first day cleaning the shack out. They had swept out the dust and debris, cleared out all the old broken furniture, then attacked the three windows painted black from the outside, scraping shards of sunlight onto the floors and walls.

Johnny, with some grumbling, had repaired the front door and installed a lock.

They'd taken their time furnishing the shack, at times with misappropriated items from the many patios in the more affluent North side of town, including chairs, a table, divan fire pit and a gas lamp; at other times they'd financed their furnishing endeavors with the contents of disemboweled parking meters, ones that had strayed too far into the night's shadows.

In the days, months, and years since, each walk up the steep slope had continued to be perilous yet they had never cleared a path to dissuade others from finding their discovery. And no one had come to claim it; there had never been any need to fight for turf. They'd enjoyed total control. It was their home base, or "home."

They met every day, finding more and more excuses. They made more repairs than what would seem necessary, painting the inside walls, staining the floors. As the shack began to assume in all manner a home, their respective houses became to be known as 'my mom's' or 'my dad's' or 'my folks', secondary lodgings filled with people whom they shared less and less kinship with. Sometimes no work was done, sometimes they spent their time lying in meditative silence, appreciating the hard rock and heavy metal that dispersed from a beat up Panasonic RX1450 on the rotted wooden floor, from the orphic wanderings of Led Zeppelin's "Houses of the Holy" or Pink Floyd's "Animal" to Black Sabbath's apocalyptic preaching in "Paranoid."

It was within the walls of their home that they made most of their discoveries of adolescence, that they conducted their unsupervised experiments, successes or failures, but all of their own making, that they smoked their first of many cigarettes, that they ventured into one of a handful of tins of Skoal chewing tobacco (abruptly aborted when one of them inadvertently swallowed), that they investigated porn- flipping through the overworked pages of Playboys, Penthouses, Hustlers- forming inconceivable reference ranges of the various measurements of the female anatomy. It was here that they stroked a sharpened knife along their palms, blood brothers, swearing oaths to kill or die for each other (if not to live), staining the slightly rotting floorboards red with their mingled blood. All four agreed tacitly to put down their differences and accept, if not tolerate, each other despite their various character quirks, like Johnny's penchant for scamming and double dealings, Achilles's violent tendencies, Jared's chemical escapism, and Gabriel's secret demons.

In the early weeks of their new home, all four drew up a short list of rules that they carved into the wall opposite the window (it was as spontaneous as everything else that happened with the four of them). A short list at first but soon lengthened as the need for amendments arose. No Disco was the obvious first, followed closely by No New Wave, New Age was suspect but allowed for certain moments of altered mentation, but clearly No Yanni. No Spiking the Liquor or the Pot (this applied more to Johnny). No Fighting was one of the first amendments added to the list (connected to an unfortunate incident between Achilles and Johnny).

They came in the morning, at times staying late into the night. The walls were porous to the wet summer heat and the winter's freezing cold. To them these were minor tribulations that paled, deserving no mention, when compared with the sense of belonging that this home afforded them, as opposed to the suffocation awaiting them in their own houses, the one they went to bed with and awoke to every morning.

They were in an age of rebellion, but all the revolutions had already been fought and lost. Or worse still, won, then had surrendered to corruption or blind fundamentalism. So they chose to rebel against the older generation, with its outdated prejudices, neuroses, and addictions. They escaped the communal influence, the rites and rituals that defined the older generation. Home was a sanctuary where they escaped to, to redefine themselves.

Gabriel parked the car along a side street and slowly led the way up. Once inside they found Johnny sitting with his back against the wall, kneading pot buds onto a rolling paper over an unfolded newspaper. "What took you guys? I was startin' to get worried."

Gabriel disregarded the question. "No one followed you, right?" he said tiredly.

"Nope. How could they? I slashed all their tires." Johnny smiled as he tightly rolled the joint and lipped both ends. He lit up one end, taking a deep drag before handing it to Jared. "So how'd you luck out, dirt bag?"

Jared sat down next to him, fingering the joint, deflated at the memory of his lost connection. "Still have a little bit." His mind's eye focused on the little baggie of cocaine buried in his front pocket. He took in a drag. "Guess I snorted most of it tonight," he replied tightly, his breath holding the hit.

Johnny's fit of laughter quickly degenerated into a bout of coughing. "That'll happen," he said hoarsely. He looked up at Achilles. "So were you in charge of all the fireworks?"

Achilles sat down leaning against the wall, a hint of a smile. "Somebody had to. Those fucks were getting on my nerves." Who "those fucks" were, no one else questioned. There always seemed to be "fucks," or "assholes," or "jerkoffs" who inspired Achilles's dangerous, if not reckless nature.

"I almost had it made with that chick before your bombs went off. Least I got her number." Johnny reached into his pocket pulling out a thin strip of paper, admiring it, the trophy of the evening.

Jared offered the joint to Achilles and Gabriel who both shook their heads. Gabriel sat down next to Achilles. "No thanks, I have my uncle staying with us. Something tells me he has the nose of a bloodhound."

Johnny opened his jacket and pulled out a quart of Jack Daniels with the self-satisfied air of a host who has forgotten nothing. "How about a drink then?" He tilted his head back and took two burning gulps and passed the bottle to Jared, exchanging it for the joint.

Jared, the hangover from the night before still fresh in his mind, took a small tentative sip. He felt the pleasant welcoming heat of the whiskey in his throat. He took a large swig, feeling the warmth spread throughout his chest and limbs, and passed it to Achilles.

Achilles held the bottle to the light, eyeing the swirling amber suspiciously.

"Don't worry. It's clean." Johnny frowned, insulted.

Achilles shrugged, satisfied at the honesty of the reaction, and took a large swallow. He laughed suddenly. "You should have seen the look on their faces tonight when the M80s started going off." He held the bottle up to Gabriel.

It was only then that Gabriel noticed the blood oozing from the back of Achilles's hand. "Hey man, you're bleeding."

Achilles looked at his wound still fresh with bright red blood, a bit surprised. "Must have been when I punched that fuck's teeth in."

"Here." Gabriel offered, reaching in his back pocket pulling out a black bandana. "Don't worry it's clean," he added with a laugh when he saw the look on Achilles's face.

Achilles wrapped the bandana tightly around his wound. "Thanks." He used his teeth to tighten the knot.

"Did you know I was in trouble?" Gabriel turned to Achilles. "Is that why you did it?

Achilles returned his look. "You were never in trouble with that fat fuck. But I knew he was probably a friend of those two assholes at the front door."

Gabriel took a few drinks off the bottle, thinking about the evening. He relaxed under the numbing influence of the whiskey. So much had happened tonight he found it hard to process. He then realized he had not thought once about Daniel. He tried to suppress the surge of shame at this fact, and on his anniversary. "Thanks," he said finally, looking straight ahead.

Achilles took back the bottle. "You're welcome." He took a swallow then handed it back to Jared.

The four passed the whiskey back and forth, quietly, slowly. The emptying bottle lulling them with its heavy, anesthetizing warmth. No pain. No troubles. No despair.

8

Gabriel walked back to his mother's house, his footsteps echoed heavy and a little unsteady from the booze. He enjoyed the evening heat of early summer, the air was thick with the promise of it. Tonight his thoughts swirled around chaotically in his mind, entering his consciousness momentarily then disappearing: his brother, his uncle, the party, and Priti. She had mesmerized him- so unlike any girl he'd ever met. So much more evolved a person, so solid and grounded. Not that the other girls weren't intelligent, but their interests seemed unadventurous and myopic. Priti's eyes spoke more than any of them did, of other worlds, other lives. Like him she was a traveler, a stranger, stopping only momentarily. Like him she was an outsider, looking in.

His walk home sobered him, the familiar landmarks served to anchor him, so that by the time he arrived at his mother's house his mind was clearer and his gait steadier. The kitchen light fanned out through the window, like a beacon in the dark. He entered quietly through the side entrance into the laundry room, and was met with the smell of fresh brewed coffee and the subdued voices of his mother and uncle, engaged in a conversation that sounded as if it had been going on for some time. He stood there listening for a moment, quiet and unseen.

"Feel. Feel. I don't know what to feel." Leon looked at his mug as if searching for the answer in the serpiginous coffee resin inside, his hands cupped around it as if in prayer. "Betrayed, perhaps, but not just me. I feel like the whole country has been betrayed." He looked up at the ceiling then back down at his mug. "We have lost our way," he said with final-ity, shaking his head. "We are no longer victims and martyrs, but perpetrators and villains. My god!" He looked at his sister distraught. "The things I let happen. Not- not seventy meters away from me."

"What could you do, Leon?" Isabelle reached for a ciga-rette smoldering in an overflowing ashtray and took a drag. She stretched her free hand across the tablet to hold his. And for a brief moment, they were children again- he overwhelmed with childhood fears or pains, and she the older sister, extend-ing a comforting hand to his. "You were just following orders."

"Following orders." He left his hand under hers but turned his face away angry. "Orders I didn't bother to question. Does that absolve me of the crime?"

"You never had to question your orders until now, Leon." Her eyes searched his with a tired concern, for the moment forgetting her own turmoil on this day. "You are a soldier, Leon."

Leon turned back to her, tears forming. "But am I not a human being first? Does becoming a soldier compromise my conscience?"

Gabriel backed away silently, not daring to let his presence be known, then loudly opened the kitchen door and shut it, signaling his arrival.

He took a moment before entering into the kitchen. Both his uncle and mother were standing now, she tidying up the mess around the ashtray, he with his back turned standing by the kitchen counter pouring her coffee.

"Hi," he said, feigning innocence to the conversation sec-onds before.

His mother cast him a welcoming smile. "And how was the party?"

"It was good. But I'm beat," he said stretching his arms toward the ceiling. "I think I'll turn in."

His uncle turned back to him, a small smile on his lips,

his voice slightly hoarse, "Good night, Gabriel. I'll see you tomorrow."

"Good night, uncle."

"None of this uncle nonsense," his uncle waved the idea away as if the term were a burdensome formality. "Leon, please."

"Good night, Leon." Gabriel exited the kitchen and took the short flight two steps at a time back up to his room.

9

July 1973

Isabelle glanced through the dust-stained back window of her kitchen, catching the red glare of her neighbor's tail-light as he pulled out of his driveway. She looked back down at the morning dishes in the sink and began scrubbing furiously. Raul couldn't even bother to buy a house with a decent back-yard. Her comfort was an afterthought- he probably circled the first listing in the morning paper. He would never change; he and his needs first, everyone else came second. And where was she? In the middle of nowhere surrounded by working class Italian and Irish Americans who couldn't even find Israel on a map, let alone spell it. Until they figured out the source of her thick accent, she'd been called a spic; now they had other names for her. A glass slipped from her hand, cracking against the sink. She sighed, tossing the shards in the garbage can.

And the boys? What about them? And their needs? She couldn't do it by herself. He was the one who had wanted a second son. After Daniel, they had tried and failed several times. After the third miscarriage he started blaming her. And the marriage had started to crumble. They had stopped couples counseling when she had become pregnant with Gabriel. She had felt the birth would herald a new beginning, breathe new life into their marriage. But no child saves a marriage, and Gabriel's birth defect had served as more of a wedge. By the time he had turned three they were already separated. One weekend every two weeks was not enough. Had it not been for the opportunities their father would be able to provide for them she would have returned to Israel a long time ago.

She finished rinsing the dishes and turned to the pot on the stove. The boys would be home in a little while, back from some fancy show, or museum, or fancy restaurant, with stories to tell about Raul and his girlfriend du jour- some blond "bimbo" as Americans called them. She yanked open a drawer a pulled out a carton of cigarettes. Raul was the one who started her on smoking. She hadn't had so much as occasional kosher wine on the high holy days. He arrived with his money and bravado, dazzling everyone around him. She was so innocent. A flash of the match lit the frown on her face briefly as she sucked in a harsh breath of smoke. She'd been so duped. She exhaled two steady streams of smoke from her nose as she salted the hot water. No three course meals in this house. It's pasta tonight. "Love it or leave it" as the Americans like to say.

As the water began to boil the side door clicked open and Daniel's silent shadow crossed the kitchen floor. Isabelle turned from the pot to see the back of his heel as he started up the stairs. "Hello?" she called out. No hello, not even a sign of recognition. One weekend alone with Raul and her sons already forgot her. "Remember you have your sessions with Mr. Winter this week."

"Hi mom." Gabriel ran in, slightly out of breath.

Isabelle forced a smile. "Hi Gabe, how was your day?" she asked uninterested.

As Gabriel chattered on about the details, Isabelle became suddenly tired, then irritable. "Why don't you set the table?" she interrupted, as she stabbed the remains of her cigarette into the half-filled ashtray. "Dinner will be ready in fifteen minutes."

"What are we having?"

"We're having pasta." she said and turned to the cupboard, pulling out a few dark blue boxes. "Which one do you want?"

"Spaghetti please."

"Okay. Set the table."

As Gabriel pored through five minutes of play-by-play description of the movie, Isabelle stared and nodded distractedly, intermittently stirring the pasta. The older one seemed quieter after his weekends, the younger one more rattled, chattier. She didn't have time to wonder about what the boys' experiences were with their father. It was enough that they had one; she and Leon had been orphaned when they were very young. Better a bad parent than no parent.

"I'm done. Should I go get Daniel?"

There was something to the timbre in Gabriel's voice she couldn't quite define. "Okay, go wash up and get your brother down here." She drained the pasta and covered the saucepan. Maybe she'd ask him about any problems later on.

She looked out the back window as the sky shed itself of daylight but saw only her reflection. She tucked a strand of grey hair behind her ear. Soon her youth and beauty would fade, and with them her chances with another man. And what man would want an aging mother with two boys. She shook her head. Where were those two? She sighed as she started up the stairs, pausing halfway up, slightly breathless as she noted with a vague unease a silence upstairs, and with every subsequent step the silence became more absolute, complete and deafening. She raced up the last few steps panting, and her heart racing. Rushing into Daniel's room, she discovered the silence torn by piercing shrieks, too busy to notice, holding Daniel's lifeless body as it swayed from the ceiling, his belt cinched tight around his neck, that the shrieks were her own.

A little more than a week after Daniel's death, the number of relatives thinned out, as aunts, uncles, cousins, all of them Raul's, returned to their corners of the world, not to be seen until the next tragedy (or celebration). By the end of the second week, it was just she, Gabriel, and her brother, Leon, who had flown in from Jerusalem, on special leave from the IDF to be home with his only living relatives. Tall, olive skin, with short curly black hair and thick black beard, he had arrived the day after Daniel died, huddling the crumpled form of older sister in his large and powerful arms. He had held her tightly that first day and then, throughout the week, had sought to provide a source of strength and security that she had so desperately lacked and needed. He had helped in organizing and arranging, and had forgone sleep and rest, as there had been so much to do. He had set his jaw tight and fixed at the ceremony and then during the burial, he had shed his tears silently. During this first week he had allowed for a temporary truce with his sister's ex-husband out of respect for her and his dead nephew, his dead godson; this had not been time for animosity, but for prayer and reflection.

He had done what he could for his other nephew whom he had seen suffering alone and detached. He had asked Gabriel more than once if the young boy needed to talk to someone, but his nephew had shaken his head and walked away.

When it was time to return to Israel he pleaded with his sister to come with him, to start a new life in Jerusalem with the boy.

"My home is here," she cut him off. "And so is Gabriel's. He needs his father."

"I'll be back then to visit," he said, giving her a hug and kiss. "Don't hesitate to call me if you need to." He stooped his tall frame over the boy and gave his now only nephew one last hug. "Goodbye Gabriel. Don't forget you are loved." He grabbed his olive-green duffel bag and stood up straight, then walked down the path to the waiting taxi. He threw the bag in and turned to look back at his family before stepping into the car.

10

Once the house was empty again the mother went into freefall. The house fell into disarray, the bills started piling up, the food in the fridge began to spoil, and the plants began to dry up and die.

But Isabelle was not one to lie around feeling sorry for herself. She eventually rose from her bed of mourning and set about to find the guilty. Because this woman, who flew halfway around the world to a new land with a man who would soon betray and abandon her, this former kibbutznik and orphan was also (unknown to her) the descendant of a family of litigators back in Tsarist Russia. It was in her genes, woven into her chromosomes and therefore expressed in body and mind that for every reaction there had been an action, every effect had a cause, and every wrong had a guilty party. She applied for and received the position of receptionist (the very same day) at Cohen & Cohen- previously Cohen, Cohen & Brown, prior to Brown's early retirement amidst a scandalous affair with a certain young plaintive (then again, you can't trust a goy)- a small personal injury law firm that was coming into its own as the country was proving itself to be once again a bright shining beacon, this time for personal injury litigation. A few large trials in the late sixties had placed Cohen, Cohen & Brown on the map, and the two senior partners, both Cohens, had decided to expand and began drafting young law grads, paralegals and receptionists. Did Arthur and his younger brother Samuel know that they had found a true jewel among the waiting room full of ersatz applicants in young Isabelle, Israeli, divorced mother of two- I mean one son? At first no, not really- of course it was obvious she proved to be more intelligent and capable than all the previous receptionists combined in her first few weeks at the firm. Unlike the other secretaries, she had no time for nail filing, no taste for gum chewing, no penchant for solitaire or extra long lunches. She had all dictations done on time, all reports, briefs, and cases ready and in proper order for all the attorneys. The office was flowing more smoothly than anyone could remember.

After one month of Isabelle's eyebrow raising performance, Art and Sam decided (against their better, penny-pinching natures) that a raise was in order. They offered her twenty dollars an hour, and a supervisory role over the other (and more senior) receptionists. She accepted the promotion with the same straight-faced and curt demeanor with which she conducted her work. Were the two brothers a little put off by the seeming ingratitude? But then again she was Jewish, and Israeli at that, and perhaps they had a soft spot for the motherland, and yes they had heard that Israeli Jews were a bit rough around the edges.

Their investment paid off as Isabelle brought all the other receptionists in line, the nail files were put away, the gum was flushed, the cards were re-decked and lunches abridged- a couple of the older receptionists who were unable or unwilling to cooperate were retired under Isabelle's unchallenged recommendation. Her real talent came to be known, however, several months into her job at Cohen & Cohen, when a succession of red marks began to appear on depositions, cases, and briefs that no one could account for. The mysterious marks included, but were not limited to, question marks, exclamation points, cross outs, arrows, asterisks, double question marks. The case of the enigmatic symbols was brought to the attention of the two senior partners. As Art and Sam pored over the marked up documents, they could not help but notice a pattern that made both brothers blink twice. In most of the PI cases during the 'red period' (as it would later be known), inconsistencies in the depositions by the doctors, as reflected in the medical charts, not to mention flaws in the arguments by the defense attorneys, and which had been missed by the junior attorneys at Cohen & Cohen, were recognized and laid bare by the anonymous detective, inconsistencies that could determine the course of the case and the damages awarded. Not being ones to miss an opportunity, the Cohen brothers counseled the younger attorneys as to the nature (and value) of the red marks. As a consequence, cases were won, money came in and Cohen & Cohen soon began to edge out the competition. None of the attorneys or paralegals owned up to the marks or even owned a red pen.

The trail of the red marks soon led the brothers, by process of elimination, to young stone-faced Isabelle. Art and Samuel called her into their office one day. The gothic, oak paneled room with its dim lighting, wall to wall book cases of leather bound texts, intimidated most who entered and inhaled the mannish amalgam of Arabica coffee, old English leather and pipe tobacco, but Isabelle was unfazed. Not wanting to startle or scare the young receptionist sitting in their office (not that anything or anyone could startle her), the two brothers approached her with a healthy measure of praise amidst questions about the astute and insightful red marks. Isabelle patiently thanked her two employers and explained that she had started taking an interest in the testimonies and depositions of the cases that had crossed her desk and when she read the briefs she felt it wrong to not point out the obvious. She apologized that perhaps she gotten carried away with her red pen.

"No, no, no, no need to apologize," both brothers assured and reassured her, and of course no need to stop. They just had questions as to whether this keen insight was the product of some legal education, or exposure perhaps, in the past. Isabelle, blind as she was to the strong penetrance of the litigious gene manifesting in her chromosome, assured them she had never set foot in a law school class or even a law firm before Cohen & Cohen. She herself did not believe her marks reflected anything more than common sense (what she thought of the junior attorneys' inability to pick out the inconsistencies- well, she kept that to herself).

Both Art and Sam nodded with knowing smiles as she gave examples of the law cases she had reviewed and marked up. She was a natural. They had half a mind to pay for her law school, and since two halves make a whole, one of them suggested the obvious. But Isabelle had no desire for any more life changes. For her, the current position and pay was sufficient enough on one condition, that two weeks in the summer during the anniversary of the death of her son, she could be allowed time off to grieve.

The Cohen brothers frowned empathically at this request and offered her unfettered access to as many boxes of red pens as she needed, be they ball point, felt tip, rollerball, perhaps a quill and jar of ink. Was there a brand that she preferred? Bic? Paper mate? Or something higher end perhaps? Parker? Or Mont Blanc? All she had to do was ask. Their obsequiousness was not lost on Isabelle, and had she been at a different stage in her life she would have taken advantage of the brothers' generosity. But she had another objective on her mind, other priorities. She no longer had a wish for money or status. What she searched for was revenge. Her son was dead and no one had paid for it yet. She thanked them curtly and walked out of their office with the same red pen she entered with, leaving them wondering whether or not they had missed something.

But the cases kept coming in, along with the prescient red marks scratched in the margins, and being won (who would have thought pain and suffering could be so lucrative). The two senior partners were kept busy and well fed. Isabelle was a boon to the practice, and they knew it; the young, smart, pretty Jewess was a keeper. That she wanted so little in return was the puzzle they could never quite figure out, in a square peg-round hole sort of way, perhaps she knew more than they did what was at stake. Hers was an old-world, motherland paradigm that upended their western, reform Jewish upbringing. Without even trying she had a direct link to an identity that they could only dream of having. She was the real, Hebrew-speaking deal, and they were but circumcised, bar-mitzvahed, high-holy-day temple going, bagel noshing, non-kosher frauds. She began to occupy and preoccupy the brothers' thoughts. Each sought to connect, commune or identify with Isabelle.

It was a little less than twelve months after she had been hired that the practice hosted its end of the year holiday party. Isabelle arrived early to help organize and stayed late to clean up. At the end of the night all the lawyers and staff had gone home. Sam, being the only one else left, asked Isabelle into his office. She knotted the last of the garbage bags and entered the room, pen and notepad in hand for any instructions. She closed the door shut behind her and turned around to find Samuel Cohen, his unzipped pants now gathered around his ankles, exposing a half erect, and circumcised proposition. The erection was the accumulation of months of obsessive fascination and longing for the young Israeli woman who had captured more than his admiration. That he was married with two school-aged children was well known at Cohen & Cohen. But the annoying, pinch-nosed wife and whiney, spoiled kids were a good thirty-minute drive from the current opportunity, and he was willing to trade the whole nebbish lot for an evening with young Isabelle. He stood, hands on hips, with the same cocksure attitude he affected in the courtroom where he circled predator-like around wayward physicians- "that's all well and good, doctor, but where is the standard of care in your care of your patient? Did you not look at the chart carefully enough before prescribing the medication? Did you not go over the potential side effects? Did you not think it was important?"- quoting standards of care he pulled from dusty textbooks, which were really of no practical use except, of course, in a courtroom, scoffing at the defendant's practice 'style' or use of 'hunches', spinning whirlwinds of confusion into which the poor physicians would trip blindly over their own statements. But what, in the end, did he expect or fantasize Isabelle to do: reciprocate his spiritual sensibilities, or acknowledge his emotional longings? Or maybe did he just want a good fuck? Unfortunately for Sam, fantasy and reality are more than the flipside of the same coin. In the end she did as she always did: she stood back, stone-faced, and observed every detail of him, from head to toe, and Sam felt the power of her penetrating, dissecting gaze. His body, especially the circumcised portion, was soon all marked up in red, castigating ink. With a short, throat clearing cough, the younger Cohen lifted up his pants, as well as whatever was left of his self-respect and bid Isabelle farewell.

Life at Cohen & Cohen continued as before. Samuel resolved never to expose himself to another woman again, or at least not at the office. As for his feelings for Isabelle, they shriveled as quickly as his penis, leaving behind a mild admiration from a healthy distance. And Isabelle, did she think twice about the episode? Did she forgive and forget, or did she catalog it in her burgeoning, mental Rolodex of shortcomings of the opposite sex?

That left the older brother, Art, to make his move on Isabelle, now an office manager, several years after the holiday party incident. He had plenty of opportunity, being somewhat older, with a wife who also kept late hours, Art found himself closing up the practice with Isabelle. One such evening, he called Isabelle into his office. They were the only two people left and she walked in with some hesitation, her raised right eyebrow, and mental red pen un-capped.

Art read the trepidation on Isabelle's face and waved the fear away as if it was an annoying gnat. "Don't worry, I have none of my younger brother's fancies or indiscretions. And also you're not my type."

Isabelle's mind scrolled through her memory bank of images and recalled Art's homely wife, as well as the many late evenings he kept with the same male paralegal from the office, and nodded in understanding.

"I called you in because I think you alone will understand the philosophy behind what it is I- we do here. The junior attorneys are two dimensional and crude. They don't appreciate that there is an art to personal injury litigation; they think it's just a job with the potential for high payouts. In the end it's more, much more. There's a psychology behind what we do here. And I think you know what I'm talking about." Art motioned her to one of the leather chairs opposite the desk. As she sat down he stood up and began to pace, as if giving dictation, but none of this was to be written down. "You see, Isabelle, after twenty-five years in litigation I have come to recognize that there are two types of defendants who receive guilty verdicts. There is the obvious type, the one that has been neglectful or careless. These cases are easy to try, even for the junior attorneys. And most of our cases are these. And don't get me wrong, they do help pay the bills. But it is the second type that makes what we do here an art." Arthur Cohen paused in front of his walled bookcase, touching one of the spines as if remembering. He turned around. "You see, Isabelle, there are many physicians who fall into the second category who are likely innocent of the charge for which they are being sued, the ones who practiced experience-based, common sense medicine, but the patient's disease was the rare one in a million that turned out catastrophic. These physicians are innocent of any real wrongdoing with respect to the case at hand, but they have committed another act for which they are guilty, whether medical or non-medical, and they have carried this guilt for months or even years. They long to be exposed, to exorcise this guilt, and it comes out at the time of the deposition or the trial, this admission of guilt from which they can no longer hide, and that which they can no longer carry, and to some degree they are happy to receive punishment." Art had orbited the whole of his office and now stood behind his chair, grasping it, his eyes boring into Isabelle, as if knowing what she thought, feeling what she felt, and promising what she longed for. "This group, and this group alone makes what we do here an art; this group is why I continue to practice."

Isabelle felt something inside her being pulled by the promise of his words and tears came to her eyes. Finally there was one person who knew what she was looking for; and he alone carried the answer to her prayers. Revenge would come in the form of litigation, and she would make sure that the guilty pay dearly.

Like others who had found their cause, Isabelle devoted her every second, her every cellular function to the endeavors of Cohen & Cohen. But as with others who have found their cause, and have devoted their lives to it, all other aspects of her life suffered, something had to give. She quelled her regret for spending less and less time with Gabriel with the knowledge that she did at least provide the bare minimum for her son, which is more than she ever got. Then again, "bare minimum" presupposes that providing shelter, running water, food on the table and the occasional attempt at dialogue about school, friends are adequate to a boy who'd lost his brother and then his father. But with the passing of time and with his inevitable steps towards manhood, Gabriel's need for her lessened, thankfully, allowing her more time and energy to devote to Cohen & Cohen.

11

The children stood by the bus stop on a damp summer morning, huddled in groups of twos and threes. They talked excitedly all at once, feeding off the clamoring energy of one another. All were freshly bathed and combed perfectly, the girls in pigtails and braids. All wore the same bright yellow summer camp T shirts a size too large. The parents stood apart, talking quietly, occasionally pausing to give patient reminders to their children. All failed to notice the older, greying man sitting alone, quiet and inert, in the deep recesses of the front porch of the corner house. Jack Winter looked on intently at the children in front of him, his arthritic fingers warming themselves around a mug of hot coffee. And as he watched he could picture little Danny running around with the other boys. "Danny," he said conjuring up a memory, his last "session" with the boy.

"Danny, you're getting too old for me," he had told the boy as Daniel had rushed to put his pants back on.

"You're getting too old," he had repeated. "But tell me again how old your brother is. Gabriel, is it?"

Daniel had looked away, out through the bedroom window, as if the answer would be found in the wind-stirred tree branches. He replied inaudibly.

"What was that, Daniel? I didn't hear you." He could not see Daniel's face, hidden in shadows. "Why don't you bring your young brother around?"

"No!" Daniel had turned sharply back to face Mr. Winter. "No," he repeated. "You ca- ca- can't have him. I wo- wo- won't let you."

"Now Daniel," Mr. Winter had said, smiling. "Don't be like that. You know you will. Otherwise I might just have to go to your mother and tell her about what you have been doing here." Mr. Winter had risen from the bed and approached Daniel. He was no longer bigger than the boy. He could no longer use force. He'd had to resort to these threats to keep him coming back. "What would your mother say if she knew what you have been doing here? Or your father?"

"No!" Daniel cried out.

"No, what?" the old man had asked. "No to telling your parents or to bringing Gabriel?"

Daniel walked briskly towards the front of the house with Mr. Winter behind him.

"Remember, Daniel," Mr. Winter had called out to him as the screen door shut, "one or the other. I'll see you next week."

The next week he had stood alone, apart from and unnoticed by the large gathering at the cemetery. He looked on as the casket was slowly lowered into the ground. He had stayed long after everyone had left.

It was the grinding gears of the camp bus pulling away from the corner that broke the spell of the memory, and Jack Winter rose slowly and went inside.

1 2

June 1983

*A cool and cloudy morning will give way to a warm sun-
ny afternoon with highs in the mid-seventies. And now
Sandy with the news. Thanks Phil. Here's a glimpse at our
week-in-review: England's Conservative Party wins a de-
cisive victory allowing Margaret Thatcher a second term
as Prime Minister. Li Xiannian becomes president of the
People's Republic of China. And tensions continue to mount
between Nicaragua and the United States leading to the ex-
pulsion of several US diplomats.*

Leon awoke early the next morning as the soft twilight
glow of the rising sun silhouetted the eastern tree-line. A
dreamless restful sleep; it had been months since he'd slept
so well. He rose nimbly reaching his long muscular arms to
the ceiling, arching his broad back, the muscles tensing and
relaxing. He turned his head left and right, reflexively listening for any movement nearby, and heard none. He crouched
by his olive green duffel bag and picked out a pair of shorts,
T shirt and sneakers. He dressed quietly and tiptoed his way
down the stairs, remembering which creaky steps that needed
stepping over.

He shut the side door gently and stepped outside; the
storm door creaked and hissed behind him. The gravel of the
driveway crunched underfoot as he stretched his legs for several minutes in the absolute quiet of dawn. Again he looked

left and right, anticipating any sudden movement. He set off at a slow pace at first, keeping his breath in time with his step, his body remembering previous runs months before. Initially stiff, his knees began to loosen and soon he had resumed his normal pace, as the lush green lawns and bright white picket fences blurred past. The morning birdsong, a distant car horn, the wheeze of a garbage truck pausing to collect trash; he had missed these isolated, benign sounds, had longed for them the previous several months back in Israel, where any sound suggested danger. But more so he longed for the quiet moments he found here.

His breathing remained steady as he jogged the winding incline of Westminster Avenue. He turned left along the service road, following five-mile run he'd planned the night before, Westminster, then the service road, a left down New Hope Road, then back along Dream Boulevard.

Leon had been sensitized from the war to all loud noises, and though he refused to admit to the assault of sound, he shunned it whenever possible. For him, an increasing number of sounds had become triggers to memories that he preferred to forget. After Beirut he sought asylum in the chaos of Tel Aviv, cloaking himself in the cacophony of the city, and yet he found the noises jarring to his senses and, even more glaring reminders of the war. Nine months home and he resigned from the IDF. His commander of ten years frowned at the letter for several moments before meeting the young lieutenant's eyes. They had fought side by side in the Yom Kippur war almost ten years before. The young paratrooper had shown immense poise and bravery during their successful military operation into Syria. "Great promise," he had remembered saying. He knew Leon's contract was up and had done more than his share for the defense of his country. He also knew what Beirut had done to many other promising soldiers. Morale was low and many battle-weary career soldiers had come by his office with similar letters. He suggested to Leon a one-year leave of absence to 'visit family abroad' as the letter tore down the middle, the two crumpled pieces tossed to the garbage. "Think it over Leon, no need for rash decisions." But then again, he also knew Leon as one who never made rash decisions.

Through the trees separating the service road from the highway, Leon counted very few cars on the road. A sleepy Sunday morning was what he needed to clear his head of ghosts. He kept the brisk pace down New Hope Road; serpiginous tree lined streets and cul-de-sacs branched off in neat clusters of upper-middle class solitude. His breath kept pace with his stride. The initial ache of the run had begun to ease, and he felt the full power of every breath in his chest. His mind was clear. The road widened as it approached Dream Boulevard. He made a left and ran along the sidewalk given the increase in traffic. Halfway back to his street a loud bang jarred him off the sidewalk and he rolled over onto the grass behind a tree, as the idyll of the moment dissolved suddenly, and he crouched low beneath a volley of heavy gunfire. "Ambush," he yelled, but the thunder of RPG fire swallowed his words. He looked left and right, trying to find the rest of his outfit as the whizzing bullets chipped at the trunk and shook the overhead branches. Behind him his commander's tank lay open like a lotus leaf, a thick plume of smoke twisted upwards, escaping the wreckage and bearing witness to the human carnage outside. He knew they were near the coast, several miles at most, as he could smell the salt water. Leon spotted a young private lying face down, frozen in fright, behind a nearby tree to his right. Through the dense, eye-tearing smoke he spotted one or two enemy fighters twenty meters in front.

"Ari," he whispered loudly, but the boy was too scared to move. "Ari," he yelled, but still no response. He had spotted the boy during basic training months before. Ari stood apart from the other recruits, slight and somewhat small for his olive green uniform, thick glasses, protecting large fearful eyes, crowded out the rest of his face. The other officers had joked about Ari's ability to survive basic training, let alone the upcoming war, but Leon took pity on him and spent time helping him. When the war began he made sure to have Ari in his platoon.

He crouched down ready, timing his move after the next rata-tat-tat of gunfire, before hurling a grenade and tumbling to the next tree to help the boy. He put a protective hand on Ari's shoulder. "Don't worry Ari, I'm here, stay down a second," he whispered. He rose to one knee and took several shots at the dark figures receding into the hillside before lying down again. He lifted his head and peered through the haze for any PLO. No one moved, for now. He leaned on his back, exhaling a short sigh of relief as he caught glimpses of the late morning sun. "Looks like they turned and ran." He smiled before turning onto his stomach. "It's okay, they're gone. Ari?" He lifted Ari's shoulder and turned him onto his back to look at his face, only to find behind a cracked lens, a gaping bullet wound where the left eye had been. The boy's blood seeped into the arid Lebanese soil along with nineteen years of what was now a life without meaning, and a death without purpose. Leon took the boy's eyeglasses off his face, carefully folded them and placed them in his front pocket, then closed the boy's right eye. "It's okay," he repeated, frowning. "It's okay."

Leon blinked several times before opening his eyes. He was on his back looking up at the concerned faces of two women, joggers it seemed.

"Are you okay?" they asked.

He sat up quickly, slightly disoriented. "Yes, thank you." He ran a hand through his wet hair. Another loud bang brought his attention to the street and he now recognized the sound as that of a car backfiring.

"Want us to call for help?" One of the women crouched down and offered a hand.

Leon took it and stood up quickly. "No, thank you. I'm fine, really." He offered a smile as proof. "I'm fine- it's been a while since I ran. I'll just walk the rest of the way home."

The two women were still standing by the side of the road when he turned the corner back onto Westminster.

Leon held onto the side door dyspneic and drained, as if he'd run several times more than his five miles that morning. Still gasping he looked up and caught a glimpse of his reflection in the storm door's pane glass. He scratched a palm through his thick beard, turning his face both ways to find a profile that did not seem so disheveled and lost.

13

Gabriel awoke to slow rhythmic scratching sounds next door. He opened the bathroom door and found Leon holding a large knife to his neck. "Uncle Leon don't!" he gasped, lunging forward.

Leon's arm shot out, blocking Gabriel's advancement, as he placed the blade down next to the sink then, still holding onto his nephew, he doubled over laughing. His words came out staccato in between gasps of laughter, "No...Gabriel...I...was...just...shaving."

Gabriel stared back, at first skeptical, then noting the shaving soap and brush by the sink, broke into a smile at the comical scenario he'd helped create. "Sorry uncle. It's just that I saw you with this knife-"

"It's a straight razor." Leon stood up smiling now. He picked up a large melded razor to the bathroom light, screwed at the tang of the blade was an ivory-white handle. "Beautiful, isn't it. Damascus steel, some of the hardest in the world. It was a present from an old friend of mine." Leon looked at the broad side of the blade. "To be honest, other than trimming here and there, I haven't had much use for it until now." He returned to the business at hand in front of the mirror while he spoke, as his beard and mustache disappeared with confident broad strokes, revealing a sharp-edged face at once new and familiar.

"I don't think I've ever seen you without your beard, uncle."

"I've had my beard since I was twenty." Leon put the blade down and ran a towel across his face to wipe off the remaining soap. "Careful," he said. "It's very sharp."

Gabriel held the blade to the light admiring the leafy vine metalwork along the spine and artwork on the handle before putting it back down. "It's beautiful. But why not use a regular shaver?"

Leon picked up the razor and slowly dried and cleaned it with a clean cloth as he spoke. "It's helps me to be mindful and focused. It keeps me from rushing." He looked up at Gabriel. "Sometimes I get caught up in the fast pace of life and I forget that there is beauty in taking things slowly."

Gabriel nodded to the blade. "How does shaving with a straight razor remind you to do that?"

Leon held up his right thumb, a thick scar zippered up the padded middle, ending at the edge of his nail. "This is what happened early on when I forgot to take things slowly." Leon smiled. "Speaking of taking things slowly, I need a jogging partner. Let's you and I go for a jog tomorrow morning, bright and early."

Gabriel looked on as Leon carefully folded the blade back into its handle. "Okay sure," he agreed somewhat reluctantly.

14

*O*ur *mild weather continues as we expect temperatures this afternoon in the mid- seventies. In national news, the unemployment rate reaches twelve million, numbers not seen since the 1940s, with thirty states reporting double digit unemployment rates despite signs of economic recovery after the recent recession. Sally Ride is ready to become the first woman in space as the Space Shuttle Challenger is set for take off later this month...*

The next morning Leon knocked on Gabriel's door several times before walking in. He approached the bed and crouched down. Gabriel had his left arm draped over his eyes, as if needing an extra shield against the light. He placed his arm gently on his nephew's left shoulder and shook it gently. "Gabriel," he said softly.

Gabriel stirred a moment before unraveling himself from sleep and looking up at his uncle then to the window. Dawn was fast approaching. He turned to his bedside clock. It was just shy of six. Gabriel entertained a brief moment of regret at agreeing to get up and jog with his uncle. But he knew he could never say no to his uncle, and he swung his legs over the side of the bed.

Leon tussled his nephew's hair. "I'll meet you downstairs," he said in hushed tones.

Gabriel rubbed the sleep from his eyes then set about looking for shorts and a T-shirt. Moments later he joined his uncle on the gravel driveway. They stretched quietly before setting out on their jog. Leon kept a slow pace until he felt Gabriel pushing forward. They took Leon's route from the day before. As the two warmed up they increased their stride.

Leon looked at his nephew. "How are you feeling?"

"Ok," Gabriel responded, his voice tight. "Guess I'm a little out of shape. I haven't run in a while."

"It's also the cigarettes," Leon added.

Gabriel nodded, smiling. It was one of the things he liked about his uncle, honesty without judgment. He wasn't afraid to point out the embarrassing truth, but he did it in a way that did not provoke.

They turned on Dream Boulevard at its apex, before it sloped downhill a good half mile, much of the town opened up before them. There was some early traffic beginning to congest the road.

"I have something to show you at the bottom down there," Leon said, pointing to an undecipherable spot in the distance.

Gabriel looked to where he was pointing. "What is it?"

"It is a plot of land your father and I bought many years ago. Before... We haven't done anything with it, but I have some ideas. Maybe you can help-"

The slam of a car door at the gas station next to them suddenly caught Leon midstride, and he crouched low fearfully.

Gabriel sensed the sudden movement and stopped jogging. "Uncle Leon. Uncle Leon, are you okay?" He walked to his uncle and extended his hand.

Leon looked up at Gabriel eyes wide, pupils dilated, as if he didn't recognize his nephew, but then took his hand. "Yes, Gabriel. I'm okay. I'm okay." He caught his nephew's worried look. "Really. The sound startled me for a second."

"Maybe we should go home. You can show me the plot of land some other time," Gabriel said.

Leon exhaled forcefully, as if exorcising some demon, then nodded. "Sounds like a good idea."

The two started running again a steady pace down the hill, then turned left onto Westminster. By the time they reached home, they were laughing again, the episode from before put to rest for the moment.

"I think I need to quit smoking," Gabriel admitted, opening the side door. "I was struggling way too much out there."

"If you quit," Leon replied, laughing, "I won't be able to keep up with you."

15

The heavy wooden doors creaked as Gabriel pushed his way into the Great Hope Public Library later on that morning. He was met with the frail, arthritic hug from the ancient librarian and familiar cart full of books ready to be re-filed.

Of all the places Gabriel had sought refuge as a child, he had preferred the unassuming squat square brick structure that took up a quiet corner of Middle Hope Road away from the center of town, partly shaded under a large oak tree, and far enough away from the curb to be easy to miss from the road. It was a place his friends could not connect to and did not associate him with. He could easily disappear. After Daniel's death, Gabriel had spent hours roaming the maze of bookcases, losing himself in the row upon row of titles, his fingers strumming their spines, awaiting the music of their stories. The summertime job had been easy, re-filing the books left scattered from the day before, but more importantly it had allowed him access to its trove of books. He read avidly, consuming books during his breaks and lunch hours. What he didn't read at the library he borrowed, pouring over them under the dim glow of his bedside lamp. Other people who had gone to the library, the regulars, had soon come to associate Gabriel, who disappeared and reappeared from the aisles of books, whose soft foot falls followed behind the creaky push cart, with it. The ancient librarian had recognized in the tall and wounded figure a love of books and had taken to him immediately. She had taught him the necessary tasks of his job, adding more to the list as he mastered them, with the same patience bestowed upon her when she had first started working there fifty years before: maintaining, cataloging and filing books, manuscripts, photographs, newspapers; helping visitors with researching information; suggesting books...

Within the first hour of his return Gabriel assumed his old groove. He worked quietly and methodically, starting at one end of the large room and slowly making his way to the other. He kept his face down, looking up only when shelving the books. In his white button-down shirt and jeans, Gabriel blended in with the regular weekday visitors. He became almost invisible. And so he was surprised when his name was called out. He glanced up and found Rabbi Davidson looking up at him through his thick wire rimmed glasses. "Gabriel," he repeated.

Gabriel forced a smile. "Hello, Rabbi."

"Hello, Gabriel it's nice to see you." Rabbi Davidson grabbed Gabriel's hand with both of his, as he often did, reminding Gabriel of a Tammany Hall politician. Rabbi Davidson smiled through his thick black beard, now with a few strands of gray.

"And how is your mother?" The thick eastern European accent Gabriel remembered from the Rabbi's first weeks at the temple had relented somewhat, he sounded almost American.

Gabriel returned his right hand to the cart, his left arm held a short stack of books to his chest. "Nice to see you too, Rabbi. My mother's fine."

"Good. Good. Nice to hear." Rabbi Davidson nodded vigorously.

He made a move to push forward but the rabbi pressed on with the questions Gabriel knew at some point he'd have to answer. "I know she is very busy, but she still comes on high holy days." Rabbi Davidson shook a scolding finger playfully at Gabriel. "But we don't see you much anymore, Gabriel. Did you forget about us?"

"Sorry, Rabbi. But with school and all, things get very hectic for me. I don't have a lot of time-"

"Tut, tut, tut." Rabbi scolded benignly. "No time for God?"

Gabriel felt his patience receding to anger.

Rabbi continued the interrogation. "So many holidays to come and observe. And I know school is usually closed for some of them." Again with the finger wag. "Tell me the truth, Gabriel, why did you disappear after your Bar Mitzvah? Did you think becoming a man absolves you from your responsibilities to your faith?"

Gabriel began to push the book cart forward but Rabbi Davidson stepped in front and put his hand on Gabriel's again. Rabbi Davidson had taken over the temple several months after Daniel's death. Back then he was younger and more dynamic than the ancient Rabbi Hirsch who had retired. Rabbi Davison seemed a new breed of rabbi, more progressive and forward thinking, more compatible with the times. A strong and passionate orator, he impressed all who attended his weekly sermons. Gabriel recognized the dogged persistence and strength yet again. This little man, who came up only to Gabriel's chest, would not be sidestepped. "Is responsibility to one's faith so much to ask for, Gabriel?"

Gabriel felt himself scowling despite himself. "Perhaps I've lost my faith, Rabbi."

Rabbi Davidson smiled as he shook his head, as if recognizing a weak argument he'd run circles around many times before. "No, no, no Gabriel. I don't agree with that phrase, this idea of losing one's faith. Faith is not some set of keys that can be lost or misplaced. It is not a thoughtless act; it is an active choice that one makes, Gabriel, to believe or not to believe."

Gabriel looked around the library and found it empty. The librarian was at the other end of the room, out of earshot. He leaned forward and pressed his face close to the rabbi. "Choice, huh. You mean like the choice Cantor Shapiro made when he stuck his hand down my pants? Is that the kind of choice you mean?" His words spilled out, having been held in for so long. Rabbi Davidson jolted his head back as if slapped. Gabriel leaned in closer whispering in the rabbi's ear, "Yes,

Cantor Shapiro, the man you assigned to teach me the section of the Torah for my Bar Mitzvah. Cantor Shapiro thought he would teach me something more on our last day of study." Rabbi Davidson shook his head. Gabriel pressed on, "Don't worry, nothing happened. He didn't think I would fight back. Another 'choice' I made."

"So it was you, you're the one who broke his jaw," Rabbi Davidson replied, looking off to the side, as if putting the pieces together to an old puzzle. He quickly looked back to Gabriel. "You must understand I did not know this. I had no idea."

Gabriel straightened up, casting his gaze above the rabbi's head to the window on the opposite wall, catching sight of the cloudless sky outside. "I didn't think you did."

"I am so sorry, Gabriel," Rabbi Davidson said. "Why didn't you tell me? If I would have known I would-"

"Well now you do," Gabriel replied, looking back down at him. "Let's see what 'choice' you make with this information." He pushed the cart forward again, forcefully out of Rabbi Davidson's grip. "I have to return to work," he said gruffly. "Nice talking to you."

He fought off the memory Rabbi Davidson had stirred up and concentrated on the task of re-filing books. He'd found the job meditative, focusing on the books, the reestablishment of order. But certain memories are hard to dismiss.

1978

It had been that day, as he had run down the temple steps holding his left wrist, sore from Cantor Shapiro's jaw, that the past had come to him, yet again- the memory of that night of the suicide was for him an endless wave that struck against the painful recesses of his mind. He had remembered following his brother, racing to catch up to him, as his father's car sped off. But there was something more to that night, a detail that had been swallowed up in the horror of the suicide.

"Don't forget, Daniel, you have your tutoring with Mr. Winter this week," his mother had reminded Daniel, as he had passed through the kitchen to the stairs. And Gabriel had seen the subtle response, even from the side door, his brother's misstep, and the drop in his shoulders. Gabriel had known only peripherally of his brother's weekly tutoring sessions for his stuttering the previous year. Daniel would disappear for an hour a week to his neighbor's home at the end of the block and come back silent and sullen. Daniel's footsteps had paused midway up the stairs, as if absorbing the impact of this message before climbing the rest of the stairs and closing his bedroom door.

And as Gabriel had run home from the temple, his left wrist tingling from the impact with Cantor Shapiro's now cracked jaw, the missing details of that night had returned to him in crystalline clarity. And within these details the underlying truth had revealed itself in a way that had matured him, that had erased his childish view of the world around him. In some ways Cantor Shapiro had showed him the path to manhood more than the Torah scriptures he was to read during his Bar Mitzvah would have allowed. What need did he have for scriptures now? And as he had continued running, his gait had become more purposeful, his movements more fluid. By the time he had arrived at his mother's house he was no longer the scared child with the malformed hand, but a vengeful young man with a weapon. Had his mother been more aware of the goings on in her house she would had recognized the change in him.

After the incident with Cantor Shapiro, Gabriel reentered the seventh grade a different boy. Fully aware of his new power, he set about making a name for himself among his peers. It began in the boys bathroom where two of the well-known eighth grade bullies spent idle hours awaiting younger class-men for their lunch money. Gabriel entered the bathroom that first day back and, dispensing with the formalities, walked right up to them and knocked them both to the ground. He returned to the bathroom the next day and knocked them both to the ground again . The third day Gabriel returned to the bathroom and the two were bullies were gone and Gabriel, with his left limb (which came to be know by as the hammer, south paw, the brick) became famous. Had it not been for his stellar academic performance Gabriel would have faced suspension.

Isabelle was called into the principal's office once to explain her son's fighting, specifically the broken nose of one of the middle school "toughs." She leaned forward in her chair. "My son has straight A's, he does not miss class, he is on time everyday. His teachers have never complained about his behavior. That Gabriel has been forced to defend himself against the anti-Semites in your school only speaks to your inability to protect him. So don't you dare complain to me about my son, tell me what you are going to do to defend him. If I have to come back in here to explain my son's behavior I will come back with so many lawyers you'll be lucky to teach in a daycare center.

Achilles and Johnny gravitated towards Gabriel soon afterwards, and the three took on the gangs of Hope South Middle School. The bathrooms, backyards, and streets became war zones as Gabriel, Achilles and Johnny punched, kicked, kneed, and elbowed their way to the top. By the end of seventh grade they were running the school.

16

June 1983

Thanks for tuning in. Staying in at number ten, The Eurythmics, "Sweet Dreams (Are Made of This)..."

"So you never answered my question the other night."

Gabriel looked up from the spine of the last unfiled book to find Priti leaning against the bookcase. She had a small canvas book bag strung over one shoulder. Her bright smile was the same as he'd remembered from the other night.

"Huh, oh, hi." He looked back at the book, unsure of how long he'd been in the act of re-filing it.

"Looks like I caught you day-dreaming," Priti replied.

Gabriel pushed the book onto the shelf and turned to face her. "I guess you did." He smiled sheepishly. "Are you looking for something in particular? I know where most of the books are." He scanned the shelf.

"Actually, I'm here to do some studying." Priti hugged her bag to her body. "The library here is nice and quiet, better for studying. It's worth the thirty-minute bus ride."

"Studying, what for? Isn't school over?" Gabriel leaned next to her against the bookcase.

"I'm actually taking a couple of summer courses, Calculus and Biology. It'll boost my chances for getting into a good premed program next year." Priti frowned, looking down. "I know you probably think I'm some sort of nerd- taking summer courses and all."

Gabriel smiled caressing the bottom of her chin with the back of his index finger, gently lifting her face up to his. "I don't think that at all. I think you're really cool."

Priti looked up at him, a rapid fluttering in her chest. "You do?"

Gabriel nodded. "I do."

She smiled again "I should probably study, but maybe we can talk later."

"I take lunch in a couple of hours. I'll look for you and we can eat together."

Priti smiled. "Sure." She turned around and headed to a group of tables in the center of the library.

"So the answer to my question?"

The two sat across from each other at the picnic table under the oak tree, the branches overhead hung heavy with bright green leaves, their unwrapped sandwiches from the deli between them.

"What question?" Gabriel asked.

"The question about what you believe in. If you don't believe in God, that is."

"Oh." Gabriel took a bite of his sandwich as he thought about his answer. "I think it depends on what people think God is. I don't believe that there's this white bearded man above the clouds or a red devil below us dictating all our thoughts and actions."

Priti had stopped eating, and was listening intently to Gabriel. "What do you believe then?" she asked finally.

Gabriel put his sandwich down on the table and looked at his left wrist "I think that we live in two worlds. The first world we can see, hear, touch and taste. All the questions have answers, and everything makes sense. The second world exists underneath the first, we have no way to know it exists, we can't see it or feel it but it's all around us. In the second world nothing makes sense, there are no rules; it's complete chaos. Sometimes I think that the second world is real and the first one is just theater."

Gabriel paused and took a bite of his sandwich. He looked at Priti.

She nodded back. "And God?"

His appetite suddenly lost, Gabriel walked to the garbage can and tossed the rest of his sandwich. "People make too much of God and religion here and in many other countries," he answered, walking back to Priti. "Especially the fanatics. They misuse God and religion for their own selfish purposes, leading to war after war. There's so much hypocrisy in religion- people blaming God or Satan for everything." He stopped abruptly, having caught himself rambling. He sat down next to her facing out at the road, his back leaning against the edge of the table, arms crossed. "The truth is we have no one to blame but ourselves for our mistakes," he said heatedly. Talking about God and religion always made him angry, they were subjects he tried to stay away from because it only led to arguments with others. He expected one now.

Priti turned to him. "I agree with you."

"You do?" Gabriel turned to her, at once surprised and relieved.

Priti nodded earnestly. "In India there has been so much blood shed because of religion, so many people have died, and families torn apart. But I don't blame Hinduism or Islam. I blame the people who distort the teachings of their sacred books. In the end, God is the same no matter where you pray. And we are all of God's children; if more people understood that, there wouldn't be as many wars."

Gabriel smiled. "I've never heard anyone say it like that. That's a great way of putting it."

Priti smiled back. "Thank you, but let's not talk about God anymore. I want to know more about you."

"Me? My story is boring." Gabriel laughed. "You're the interesting one."

Priti got up, laughing too, and threw out the rest of the sandwich she was too anxious to enjoy. She walked back and sat down next to Gabriel, facing him. "Come on, if you tell me something about yourself, I'll tell you something about me."

"What do you want to know?"

"Tell me about your family."

Gabriel shrugged, looking out to the cars passing by. "I live with my mom. My father left us when I was young. He hung around for a little bit, but then he took off for the west coast. I don't see him much anymore. I have an uncle. He's visiting us from Israel for a few months. That's where my mom is from. I like my uncle, he's one of the few men who has tried to understand me, or maybe just accept me." He turned to Priti and caught her looking at him.

"What's your mom like?" she asked.

Gabriel exhaled, thinking. "It's hard to know. She works all the time. Whenever she's home she's in a semi-depressed state. I think she's still broken up over my father leaving even though it was more than ten years ago. I don't think she really got over him. That and my bro—" He stopped abruptly and turned to Priti. "Now it's your turn to tell me something about yourself."

Priti nodded "Okay. As you guessed, I'm from India. My parents are engineers. They came to the U.S. when I was six. I was left with my aunt and uncle while my parents worked to make enough money to bring me over as well. When I turned twelve I was finally able to come and join them."

Gabriel looked at Priti as she spoke, she was captivating, high cheekbones rising from a sharp jawline, dimples accentuating her smile, and long braided black hair that hung down to her waist. "It must have been very hard not being with your parents."

Priti looked suddenly sad. "You have no idea. Or maybe you do. Do you miss your father?"

1973

It had been two weeks since the funeral when Raul finally showed up again. He had called earlier that morning to make sure Gabriel would be ready to be picked up by eleven. He arrived at twelve with an angry inpatient series of car honks and Gabriel rushed out of the house, escaping the suffocating weight of sadness inside. His father was good at least for this, a respite from his mother's sorrow.

As he approached the car he made note of the fact that his father was alone. He steeled himself as he opened the back door.

"No, no, get in the front. What am I, a chauffer?" Raul asked.

His father hadn't slept in days it seemed, hadn't shaven, hadn't bathed. He looked smaller, more mortal. Raul hugged his son tightly, tussling his hair, kissing him on the cheek, a sudden disorienting deluge of love and affection after years of so little. "How are you, son? My dear sweet child, my son, my son." Raul looked away for a brief moment, shielding his own eyes with the crook of his elbow, then turned around and embraced Gabriel again, kissing his hair. "How are you, my son?"

Gabriel allowed himself to be swallowed up in his father's strong arms, and bathed in his affection. "I'm okay, Pop," he replied.

"What do you want to do? A movie? Circus? Just tell me, your wish is my command," Raul said, a note of urgency in the question.

"A movie," Gabriel blurted, unsure what to pick, unused to the concept of choice in his father's presence.

"Okay, son, but first let's grab some lunch." Raul tussled Gabriel's hair affectionately again.

"Okay." Gabriel felt whole for the first time in a long time. It felt so good to be with his father, to be his son. With so much going on Gabriel needed this day with him.

It was on the drive back that Raul unveiled his plan, one that Gabriel was not prepared for. His father turned to him, suddenly serious. "Listen, Gabriel. I'm leaving the east coast. It's too hard for me, what with your brother and all. I loved you and your brother- I always did what I thought was best for you. Your brother didn't understand, but what could I do? I'm just one person. I'm sure you understand, right?"

Gabriel nodded, not wanting to disappoint, but he did not understand. This jumble of words was an enigma, one he was ill-equipped to understand let alone solve for himself.

"I'll probably be back every now and again," his father continued, assuming as always that his child could read in between what he was saying. They paused at a red light. "I want you to be strong, Gabriel." Raul turned away from him, and suddenly Gabriel understood his father was leaving him, and would probably not come back. The light turned and Raul sped up, suddenly in a hurry to drop off his one son, to turn the page on this most painful chapter in his life, and begin anew without him.

Gabriel sunk low into his seat, feeling suddenly small. He heard the rest of his father's words but was unable to respond to them. But knowing full well his father wanted no dialogue. He wanted a tacit, unspoken approval to this latest betrayal. "You know I love you, right? This is just something your father has to do."

Gabriel walked up the driveway slowly as his father's car sped away.

17

June 1983

The two held hands as they walked silently along New Hope Road to the bus stop. Their focus slowly coming into clarity on the physical contact, the warm topography of each other's hands, as all other thoughts faded. Gabriel gripped Priti more tightly, suddenly afraid to let go. He looked at her and found her looking back. "I'll ride the bus back with you," he said.

"Okay." Priti smiled back.

They walked towards her house on the corner of the block. Still holding his hand, Priti turned to face him and grabbed his left wrist and felt the hefty weight of it under the coarse callused skin. Worry flashed across her face. "Are you going to be okay?" She looked into his eyes and, finding herself in them, gasped inwardly.

He nodded slowly, not wanting to pull away from her penetrating gaze. "Do you want to go out Friday night?" he asked. "Maybe dinner or something?"

"Sure," she nodded back, smiling. "Just have to ask my mother. But I think she'll be okay with it."

"Good." He bent forward to kiss her on the cheek, his lips grazing hers as he stood back up. "I'll meet you on this corner at eight."

She turned around and walked up the path to her front door. At the door she turned back to look at the corner but he was gone. She brought her fingertips to her mouth, her lips still tingling from the kiss, then turned the knob.

Inside she caught her mother scampering back to the living room couch, the front window curtains dancing back into place. "What are you doing, Mother?"

Her mother thumbed through the day's paper, nonchalant. "Oh nothing sweetie, just cleaning around the house." She quickly dropped the paper and looked up smiling, unable to maintain the pretense or her own excitement. "Who was that boy you were with on the corner?"

Priti closed the door, letting the book bag slide off her shoulder onto the floor. "I'm tired, Mother."

Mrs. Patel pouted expressively, patting the seat next to her on the couch. "I know you are, sweetie. Come here and rest with your mother."

Priti joined her on the couch, letting herself be tended to. She closed her eyes in her mother's embrace but found herself gazing into Gabriel's eyes. "His name is Gabriel. He works at the library."

Her mother hugged her tightly. "Oh, that's so nice. Does he go to Rosedale High?"

"Actually, he lives in Great Hope."

Her mother nodded approvingly. "Then probably goes to North Hope High."

"I think he goes to South Hope, or maybe he recently graduated," Priti responded, her eyes still closed.

"Oh." Her mother responded, a little surprised, South Hope being infamous for its student body of derelicts and ne'er-do-wells. "Is he nice?"

"He is nice," Priti smiled. "He's asked me out to dinner Friday." She opened her eyes and turned to her mother. "Is that okay?"

Mrs. Patel looked down at her daughter's worried frown. A mother's prayers answered. A daughter finally reaching the long-awaited age where she could offer some much needed advice on 'the things that mattered'; a daughter who could start closing all those annoying books of hers and start look-ing to the future, her future. She smoothed Priti's hair back. "But of course, my dear. I don't see anything wrong with a young gentleman calling at your age."

Priti laid her head on her mother's chest. "Thank you, Mother. For a moment I thought there would be a problem."

Mrs. Patel smiled, lost in the memory of her own 'com-ing out' ceremony, with the various suitors, all of course sons of wealthy businessmen. That she chose an engineering stu-dent did not please her parents. Then again, engineering is an honorable, if not lucrative, profession. And despite the initial difficult years during his schooling and training in the States their family was well off now. "No problem at all. Your father and I would be happy to see this young-"

"Gabriel. His name is Gabriel."

"Gabriel? What is the origin of that name?"

"He's Jewish."

"Jewish." Mrs. Patel smiled again, knowingly. Of course, the Jews were very successful businessmen, very business savvy. "We would both be happy to see Gabriel."

18

Leon paused outside Sarah's Middle Eastern Cuisine, contemplating the Help Wanted sign for several minutes before pulling the door open, casting the afternoon sun's reflections inside. At three o'clock the restaurant sat idle and empty except for a few older women huddled around a table in the back near the cash register. The walls were decorated with framed photographs- conspicuous sites in Tel Aviv and Jerusalem: the Wailing Wall, a street bazaar. Interspersed among these were black and white family photographs, in which a large house loomed behind at different angles, a few pictures showed a fruit orchard in back of the same house.

He walked in and made his way to the back. He counted three of them, late sixties to early seventies, involved in a seemingly heated discussion.

"What are you talking about?" The one with her back to Leon had risen from the table, her head crowned by a perm of white-blond hair.

"I'm saying the war was wrong, Rachel, we had no business being there." Her older sister Sarah stayed seated, her voice firm but calm, refusing to get riled up yet again. "It was our Vietnam."

"Right. Right," Rachel nodded her head, "except that Vietnam wasn't sending hundreds of rockets over the border into the United States. How much are we supposed to put up with?"

Ruth also stayed seated, smiling away peacefully despite the argument. For her, these discussions always brought her back to their childhood home in Jaffa, where the three girls ran and laughed, and of course, with Rachel around, argued.

It was Ruth who spotted Leon first. "Girls, girls," she warned as she stood up to smooth out any wrinkles in the front of her dress, "we have a customer."

All arguing frowns turned to sugary smiles as the other two beheld the tall, attractive young man.

"You are a little early for dinner," Rachel said, approaching Leon, appraising him as she would a lamb from the butcher. "But I'm sure we can whip something up if you're hungry."

"I saw the Help Wanted sign up front," Leon said by way of introduction.

"Ohhhh!" the three sisters smiled and exchanged knowing glances, recognizing the accent. Rachel extended her hand. "You're looking for work?"

"My name is Leon, and yes, I am looking for work."

"Hello Leon, I'm Sarah." She approached, eyeing Leon keenly. "Do you have any experience?"

Rachel shushed Sarah, annoyed. "Of course the young man has experience, as anyone can see." She turned back smiling and nodding. "Tell us about your experience."

"I was a cook in Tel Aviv for several years. I also waited tables and worked the register when the owner was away."

Rachel turned to her sisters winking and smiling broadly. "I told you he had experience." Then to Leon, "Of course you'll have to meet my niece, Sarah's daughter. She's our head of 'human resources'. She does the hiring-"

"And firing," Sarah added firmly.

Rachel shot her sister another look.

"And she's single," Ruth chimed in.

"Ruth, please!" Rachel shook her head. "Go get Esther."

Ruth quickly ran to the back of the restaurant, patting her dress down as if it were on fire.

Rachel and Sarah eyed their younger sister until she had disappeared behind the swinging doors then turned back to Leon, resuming their smiling.

"Your accent," Sarah ventured. "You are Israeli."

"I am," he replied, his voice soft and calm.

"What part?" asked Rachel.

"Tel Aviv."

"A beautiful city," said Sarah, adding in retrospect, "We are from Jaffa."

Leon smiled. "I have been there, it is very nice."

The two older smiled even more. "Yes, it is."

"You are here for some time?" Rachel asked.

"Yes. For at least one year. I am staying with my sister."

"How nice," said Sarah. "Family is very important. When I married my late husband, Avram, I brought my two sisters over to be with us." She nodded to a portrait on the wall of a young couple standing under a chuppah, the unmistakable Mediterranean majestic in the background.

Leon stepped forward to look at the photograph. "Beautiful," he said. The two sisters exchanged beaming glances.

The back door swung open and Ruth scrambled forward, almost tugging a pretty woman by the hand. "Here she is," she said ecstatically, "our head of human resources."

The young woman followed, slightly annoyed at the fuss. She looked at her mother and aunt to gauge their intentions, before turning to Leon. "I'm Esther." She stepped forward, hand extended matter-of-factly, with a sliver of an Israeli accent, revealing childhood vacations abroad, and the strong influence of family in her life.

"Leon." He shook her hand. "Nice to meet you."

She looked into his eyes, as was her custom when meeting others. She had a knack for reading people. But his face was closed. "My aunt says you are looking for a job. What experience do you have?"

"Everything!" Rachel interjected. "He can do everything." She stepped forwarded, cradling his face in her hands. "You know you remind me of my boy."

"What boy?" Sarah chastised, arms crossed. "You never

had children."

"Who said anything about children." Rachel turned to her, challengingly. "I said boy, as in *boyfriend*."

"When did you have a boyfriend?" Ruth entered the fray.

Rachel twirled around with arms in the air. "Oh, when I was younger," she stopped mid-twirl, "and my hair was down," she caressed her hands down her sides, "and my boobs were up." She held her hands to her chest, as if holding invisible melons.

All three sisters fell together cackling.

Leon looked down.

Esther shook her head, eyes rolling. "You'll have to forgive my aunts. They can be a bit much." She turned a castigating glance towards them. "Anyway, we are looking for a cook. Our old one picked up and left last week. What is your experience with middle-eastern cooking?"

Leon began to explain when Ruth interrupted. "Let him show us," she said.

"What?" Esther turned to her shocked.

Ruth pressed on. "Let him show us. A taste test, yes like the way the Americans do it. Let's have Leon cook us a dish and we can all try it and if we like it we can hire him."

Sarah turned to Esther nodding in agreement.

"What a great idea," Rachel said, hugging her sister. "You know, Ruth, sometimes you have great ideas. And I'll go in the kitchen to oversee the cooking and make sure everything is Kosher," Rachel continued, winking to her sisters and issuing in another round of cackling laughter.

"I'll go in," Esther said with finality. "Follow me, Leon." And the two went to the back.

Rachel, Ruth and Sarah sat down excitedly, whispering conspiratorially.

Forty-five minutes later, Esther came out with three steaming pasta bowls on a serving tray, and laid them out in front of her mother and two aunts. The bowls were filled with a brownish green mixture of spiced rice and lentils with heaping portions of deep fried onions.

"Mejadra!" Ruth exclaimed happily. Looking from one sister to another. "Mejadra! When was the last time we had that?"

"Years!" Rachel cried, extending her face over the bowl to inhale a deep dose of steam.

Sarah scraped the mixture hesitantly, trying to control the emotions circling a memory of a Mejadra dish shared with her husband during their honeymoon, their first trip alone together. When they were young and poor and found themselves a small hotel room on the coast for several days above a quaint and quiet restaurant that seemed opened just for them.

After a few tentative moments she brought the fork to her mouth, savoring the memory. She pulled out her handkerchief and quickly wiped a tear from her eye before the others could see. She nodded into her bowl. "This is good," she said, struggling to control her voice. "Very good."

The emotion was not lost on Esther who had not seen her mother cry since the death of her father several years before. She laid a hand on her mother's shoulder and spoke to the three of them, "I think we have our new cook."

The three sisters nodded vigorously, their mouths too full to talk.

Leon came in towards the end of their meal, having spent some time cleaning up the kitchen. He stood silently by the door, head bowed.

When the three sisters had finished, they all stood up and walked over to him, smiling victoriously. All took turns holding his face in their soft hands and kissing him on the cheek. "Welcome to the family," Rachel said, giving him a hug.

19

He was unlike any boy, any man she'd ever met. He was strong and tall and muscular, yet there was tenderness to his touch and to his tone, and she felt she was complete within his gaze, as if he appreciated every aspect of her. Her mind wandered all over his body, and came to rest at the end of his left arm. The deformity did not detract from his beauty, but added a depth to it. She could only imagine the process he went through to come to terms with it. Not everyone could go through it and still live as confidently as he seemed to.

The ring of the front doorbell jarred Priti from her reverie, causing her to drop her canary yellow summer dress to the ground, revealing her thin-limbed, semi-clothed figure in her bedroom mirror. "Oh my god he's here," she gasped at her reflection and ran to her bedroom door, peeking out into the hallway. She heard her mother's footsteps slowly making their way to the front door. In a panic, she overlooked the dozen previously rejected outfits on the bed and scooped up her dress and slid hurriedly into it, shaking her hips in to the last bit of it before checking her makeup and hair and running out the door and down the steps, hurrying to be alongside her mother before she opened the front door to prevent any mishaps. First impressions seemed to be her mother's focus with anyone.

Gabriel raised himself up tall, his hair was neatly parted and combed, he wore a dark blue button-down shirt and jeans. He presented a bouquet of flowers to Mrs. Patel as he greeted them with ostensibly rehearsed words. "Good evening, my name is Gabriel. These are for you." He kept his left arm hidden behind his back for the moment. Gazing briefly to Priti, his smile was soft and fragile.

Priti longed to press her fingertips to it, but this meeting was the first act in a play that had to be seen through, and she had her role to play.

Mrs. Patel backed away, smiling with her own set of rehearsed lines. "They are lovely, please do come in. Priti's told me so much about you." She turned around to Priti. "Priti, please show our guest to the living room. I'll go put these in water and get your father."

"Yes, Mother." Priti and Gabriel watcher her mother saunter off to the kitchen then turned to look at each other.

"You look nice." Gabriel smiled again.

"Thank you." Priti resisted the urge to cup Gabriel's smile in her palm. "I'll show you the living room."

They walked into a large, brightly lit room with polished hardwood floors decorated with large Persian rugs. In the center, a large glass coffee table held court to a much larger cream-colored sectional sofa. A piano in the corner basked in the afternoon light streaming in through large windows.

The two sat down on the sofa, their knees touching. Gabriel by now had brought his left arm forward, his wrist wedged into his cupped right hand.

"How am I doing?" he asked anxiously. It had been a while since he'd been nervous about presenting himself to anyone. He'd stopped caring a long time before.

"Great. I think my mother likes you," Priti replied.

"Good." Gabriel looked around the room. "You have a nice house."

"Thanks." Priti smiled again, amazed at finding herself with Gabriel in her home.

The two gazed at each other in the moments that followed, in the silence that grew between them, a shared second skin that embraced them, as they fought the urge to lean forward into each other.

"Ah, here we are." A thunderous voice broke the moment between the two as a large, burly middle-aged man entered the room, Priti's mother following in his shadow. Mr. Patel seemed older than his fifty years, with his greying beard and thinning hair, but he had not lost the booming voice from his younger days, with its thick Gujarati accent, the same one that still rattled the chairs of his undergraduate students for the early morning class. The joke was that with Professor Patel you didn't need coffee to stay alert and in check. But unlike his students, his abdominal girth was unruly and uncontrollable and the seemingly svelte build of his younger days gave way. His abdomen pressed generously against the strained buttons of his light blue shirt. He adjusted the waist of his tan slacks, raising it just over his large gut as he entered the room. It hung there for the briefest of moments before sliding back down.

"Young man." Mr. Patel offered a large paw of a hand, and was pleased to find Gabriel's hand matched his own in size and grip. He met the young man's eyes and found them earnest and sharp. "Very pleased to meet you." If he noticed the disfigured left hand he did not show it, Mr. Patel was not the kind of man who focused on such trifles. More important for him was a man's "character," as was often times revealed by the eyes. The eyes revealed all, even when the tongue lied. "My wife tells me you work at the library," Mr. Patel said as he stroked his beard. "Good job, a good job indeed, to be surrounded by books. Where do you go to school? Please sit down." Mr. Patel ushered Gabriel to the sofa and sat down next to him, leaning forward conspiratorially. "So young man, tell me about yourself."

Gabriel looked back at this imposing presence on the sofa next to him. He caught small fractured images of his father in the distance which he nodded slightly at in recognition. "Tell me about myself?"

Mr. Patel sat upright, stretching his torso up momentarily, then sitting back down he hunched towards Gabriel. "Yes,

yes. Tell me about yourself. Where you come from, what are your dreams?" Here he shook a fist between them, whispering loudly, emphatically. "Your aspirations?"

Had Gabriel been born into another family, he would have been caught off guard with this interrogation. But he'd been schooled in interrogations, the good cop-bad cop routine, except without the good cop. He'd learned to think quickly for suitable, if not wholly honest answers to questions that came out like jabs, questions that he learned to be prepared for at all times and block reflexively. If life was war, his childhood had been boot camp. "I want to do something tangible with my life, I want to never stop learning in order to better myself and the lives of those around me. I want to make a difference." Which was true, except he'd never thought it through before, let alone verbalize it to himself or anyone else. For him life was a day-to-day affair, a struggle. That he'd made it to eighteen was a coup in his family. He'd not had the luxury of thinking he'd make it into adulthood to start planning for it. He had a few wrongs to right first- perhaps then he could think about his having a future to do something with.

"Yes, yes, of course." Professor Patel shook his fist in the air. "But how? How are you going to get there?"

Gabriel caught the answer to the aging professor's question in the gleam of his eyes. Despite his age and ignorance, he had a knack for guessing right. "I have to study hard, go to school."

"Correct!" Professor Patel's finger shot up straight into the air, pulling the rest of his bulk so that the man was now standing excitedly. Gabriel could imagine the force and command the professor had in his classroom. "An education is the key to unlock all these doors that seem closed. And everyone in this country has access to this key." Pleased with the direction this dialectic had taken, Professor Patel sat quickly down changing his tone. "Would you like some tea?"

Gabriel nodded.

Professor Patel turned slightly towards his wife and daughter, both forgotten and standing off to the side in a holding pattern. "Some tea please."

The two women headed off to the kitchen silently.

The professor turned back to Gabriel. "You know," Professor Patel said, "you remind me of myself at your age, ready to conquer the world." He stared off into space wistfully. "So young and strong and full of fantastic dreams." He turned back sharply to Gabriel. "Don't lose your dreams, they are part of the key to a fulfilling life."

Gabriel nodded, wanting to know what part of him or his answers gave such a false impression to this man. Perhaps it was in his silence. The less he talked, the more he became a blackboard onto which the professor could rewrite his own past.

"Ah here we are, some chai." Professor Patel turned as his wife and daughter came back into the room, Priti carrying a large serving tray upon which sat Mrs. Patel's bone china tea set imported from England and a matching plate with Parle G glucose biscuits. "That's 'tea' in Hindi. Tea has an interesting history in India," Professor Patel said as Priti laid the tray on the coffee table. She then backed away as the mother stepped in to serve the tea. "Tea was actually introduced by the British to break the Chinese tea monopoly. Select seeds were brought in and planted and production took off. But it was in this century that tea consumption became part of the Indian identity. Coffee is not as popular in India as it is in this country."

As Mrs. Patel filled the four teacups, she took care to not make too obvious her repulsive curiosity at Gabriel's left wrist. For her, his deformed limb had been the first detail of the young man that she had noticed. What was a trivial detail to her husband was of paramount importance for her, one she could not forget or forgive in another person. Despite her aristocratic upbringing she still harbored provincial prejudices when it came to those with physical defects, as if they represented a flaw in the person's character. Like the family gardener, way back when...with the extra digits on his hands and feet, more than enough to do his work on the house garden, but too lazy or inept to finish his work on time, or even do a halfway decent job of it.

Gabriel tasted the sweet milky tea as the Professor looked on expectantly. It was different from the Lipton his mom had at home. There was a richness and depth of flavor he'd never tasted before. "It's good," he said finally, bringing delight to the professor who slapped his knee happily. "What kind is it?"

"It's homemade chai," the professor said, leaning in closely again. "A family recipe passed on from generation to generation. And I'm glad you like it."

Soon the tea was finished and the professor stood up ceremoniously. "Well young man, it has been delightful meeting you. Where do you two plan to go for dinner? Plenty of fine restaurants in town, you know."

Gabriel stood up. "There's an Israeli restaurant in Great Hope on the corner-"

"Yes, yes, I've been there before, very good food. Run by three Israeli sisters, I believe." Mr. Patel turned to his daughter, reaching his arm out to her. "Okay my dear, don't keep this young man waiting. Have a good time, bring her back early, Gabriel," he said as he ushered the two of them out.

"I will, sir," Gabriel called over his shoulder as the two walked down to the car.

The professor's large bulk filled up the front doorway as the car pulled away, the wife hidden somewhere behind him, and stayed there waving even as the car turned the corner.

Three blocks down, Gabriel pulled to the side and as the motor idled, the two leaned into one another for a second kiss, all the questions circling their minds in the weeks since they first shook hands now answered on their opened mouths. They finally pulled away in a breathless embrace, their foreheads pressed together, their eyes closed. Gabriel grabbed Priti's hand and brought it to his lips, then put the car in gear and pulled away from the curb. "We'll make a quick stop so you can meet my mother, then we'll head over to the restaurant."

"Okay." Priti smiled nervously. She so much wanted to apologize for her mother's gawking. She had watched her mother in horror moments before, knowing full well the way her mother's mind worked. She'd hoped Gabriel had not taken note of it. She turned to look at Gabriel, such a beautiful boy. How different from the man she'd thought she'd wind up with. Some chubby, short, nerdy son of one of her mother's friends, some future MBA or lawyer, someone whose over-indulged, over-coddled opinions she'd have to suffer. How strange to be with this white, Jewish man, strong, muscular. Yet at once also fragile, an eagle with its wing clipped but still felt he could soar.

Gabriel turned to find her staring at him. At the next stop sign he took her hand again and kissed it. As the car picked up speed he sighed. "Please don't take what my mother says to heart. Not that I see any reason for her not to like you, but my mother can be a bit strange."

Priti looked at the road in front of them. "I could say the same about my mother."

Gabriel looked at his side and rearview mirror, checking for police cars, a habit he'd picked up since he'd learned to drive. "Oh that."

"You noticed?" Priti turned to him in horror.

"I'm used to it," Gabriel said casually as he turned the car onto his block. "I don't get hung up about that stuff."

"Then why did you hit that guy at the party?" Priti asked, quickly regretting the question. She bit her lip in self-punishment.

"He deserved it," Gabriel answered coldly as he pulled the car into the driveway. "He insulted you."

Priti smiled inwardly and a bud of warmth flowered in her chest.

Gabriel led Priti to the side door, left open to allow in a cool breeze. He took in a silent breath and stepped in. He found his mother bent over the sink washing her dishes from dinner. "Hi Mom."

Isabelle turned around straightening her dress, offering what seemed a tight lipped smile. "Hi Gabe." She stepped forward to shake hands with Priti. "I'm Isabelle, and you are?"

Priti tried to match the strength in Isabelle's grip but found herself lacking. "Hello, I'm Priti."

"Pretty," Isabelle replied with a slight tilt to her head. "What kind of name is Pretty?"

"Priti," the girl corrected. "It's Hindi."

Isabelle nodded. "Oh, you're Indian." The accusation sat for a moment. "Does Priti stand for anything?"

"It means love."

"Love?" Isabelle nodded back, frowning. "Well, we can sure use a little love around here, right Gabriel?"

Gabriel glared at his mother as the three stood in the uncomfortable silence that followed.

"Excuse me, I am so rude," Isabelle said, laughing. "Would you like something to drink, Priti? I'm sorry I don't have any tea, how about a glass of water?"

"I'm fine, thank you," Priti replied.

"So Gabriel tells me he knows you from the library. Are you taking a summer course?"

"AP Biology," Priti replied, a little more softly than she would have liked.

"AP?" Isabelle made no move to invite anyone to sit down. She stood halfway from the sink as if guarding the kitchen table.

"Advanced placement," Priti explained.

Isabelle nodded. "I see, you want to be a doctor."

Priti smiled. "For now, yes."

Gabriel cut in finally, disappointed in his mother, and at the scene she was making or trying to make, one that did not have to be made. "Well, we're out. Come on Priti," he said, placing his hand on Priti's shoulder, and made to steer her to the open door. "Bye Mom," he said sharply over his shoulder.

"Goodbye Gabriel. Goodbye Priti."

Priti laid a hand on Gabriel's and paused in front of Isabelle. "Goodbye Isabelle, it was nice meeting you."

"Have a good time." Isabelle turned away from the two.

Gabriel and Priti sat down in the car, looking straight ahead, silent for the moment. He shook his head, clearing his anger, then turned to face Priti. "I'm sorry, my mother can be a little difficult sometimes. I-"

Priti laid her hand on his shoulder. "No problem. My mother can be the same way." The earnestness in her eyes set him at ease.

Gabriel leaned in, brushing his lips against Priti's. "Let's go eat?"

She smiled, nodding, unable to speak.

"Welcome, welcome!" Ruth cried gaily, her hands pressed together as if in prayer, as Gabriel and Priti made their way into the restaurant. "Sit anywhere you like."

Gabriel nodded toward a table by the window brushed by the soft evening light. Ruth joined them once they were seated, handing them menus. "My what a handsome couple you are!" she gushed. "Is this your first time?"

Both smiled back, nodding, slightly shy in the face of such exuberant energy. Gabriel looked up at the old woman, had she been informed of their dinner date?

"Take your time, I'll bring some water for you right away," she said.

Rachel met Ruth in the back, hissing, "You're overdoing it."

Ruth shushed her. "Oh come on now, Rachel. I'm just

providing some romantic ambiance," she said, unable to contain herself.

"Fine," Rachel replied in hushed tones as she cast a surreptitious glance at the two teens, then turned square to her sister. "Just remember that you're not the one on the date, okay?"

Ruth rolled her eyes and headed out with the water.

She set the two glasses on the table. "So have you decided what you want?"

Gabriel looked questioningly at Priti who looked up to Ruth. "I don't eat any meat. Do you have anything vegetarian?"

Ruth's eyes crossed as she attempted to register the word before a look of recognition crossed her face. "Oh, yes. We have a number of dips that have no meat. There's also our Mediterranean salad, grape leaves and burekahs which are our puffed pastry filled with spinach, cheese or potato." Leaning in conspiratorially, she added, "And they're quite tasty."

"Wow, so many options." Priti looked at the menu flustered.

"I know," Ruth said, clapping her hands "Why don't I bring a platter of assorted vegemarian foods for both of you to share?"

Both Gabriel and Priti nodded, suppressing a laugh, and handed their menus to her.

Ruth sauntered back victorious to Ruth and Sara. "I fixed it!" she announced proudly.

"Fixed what?" Rachel asked suspiciously.

"She's vegemarian, so I offered a 'vegemarian platter' they can share together. A love platter," Ruth added with a twirl.

"You mean vegetarian, genius," Rachel sighed noisily.

"That's actually a good idea." Sarah nodded, impressed

"A love platter?" Ruth chimed happily.

"No, a vegetarian platter," Rachel said flatly. "Go to the back and tell Leon to get a vegetarian platter together for his nephew and date."

Rachel leaned in toward Sarah after Ruth had left. "She's

more your sister than mine." It was an old joke between the two.

Sarah raised an eyebrow, then turned her attention to the teens. "Handsome nephew, big like Leon."

"Good looking couple, I have to admit," Rachel said.

Sarah nodded in agreement. "Leon said it's their first date." Her face betrayed a trace of a smile. "You can tell by the way they look at each other."

Ruth burst forth through the swinging doors, a large platter teetering on her small, outstretched palm. "Vegem- I mean vegetarian platter coming right up," she announced in a loud sing-song voice. She resisted the urge to twirl and sashay as she made her way to the table.

"Humus, eggplant dip, grapes leaves, bourekahs..." Ruth set the platter on the table. "Enjoy!"

Priti giggled as Ruth walked away. "She's so funny. Must be fun for your uncle to work here."

Gabriel shrugged as he dipped the pita bread into the humus. He hadn't bothered himself with his uncle since he'd arrived. "He doesn't talk much about his work. He did mention three sisters that run the place, more or less."

"Wow this looks delicious."

Gabriel looked up from his plate. "You haven't been here before? I thought your father said he knew the place."

"He does," Priti said, nodding, betraying no emotion, "but I don't. My mother and I don't accompany him when he eats out. It's usually him with other professors in his department or his students."

Gabriel let the unasked questions lay for the moment; some part of him already knew the answers.

"I'm glad you asked me to dinner," Priti said as she leaned in smiling. And for the moment all unasked and unanswered questions lay forgotten as the two reached around their plates for each other.

"Me too, I-" He looked down as Priti caressed his left wrist with both hands.

"What?"

"Nothing," he said. No one had ever touched his left wrist before. Not even his parents. Very few people had even mentioned it except the occasional taunt or ridicule. And now it was a thing disregarded, a phantom limb, even to him. And yet he felt her soft, caressing hands and came to realize how much he had missed the contact to his left arm, how thoroughly starved he had been for it. And it was in these rare moments when he so wished his deformed limb to develop and be normal, to sprout a hand with a full accompaniment of fingers, with which he could caress Priti's sunburst smile. He placed his right hand on top both of hers. "I hope you like the food."

"I'm sure I will," she said, tilting her head slightly, and in that slight gesture Gabriel saw the world's tilt as she saw it, as she knew it, and in that angle the world's secrets were revealed. And in her every gesture, the pursed lips, the arched eyebrows, the smile, he saw more secrets, more locks that only she had the key to.

20

Johnny rode his dirt bike the tortuous five or so miles out of the north end of town. He loved riding through this part of town; he liked the stares, the double takes. He liked making an impression, whether good or bad it didn't matter. It's all about image he'd come to recognize. As a kid, he was nothing; no one respected him. He had striven to create the role he was now living, worked hard at it. And now that he was metamorphosing into it he was recognizing himself more and more. This was who he was. This was who he wanted to be. He was a long haired rebel, a motorcycle riding, drug dealing, rock'n roll renegade, who feared nothing, cared about nothing and lived with no regrets. "Ass, cash or grass, no one rides for free," they say. And he was the one with the ride. Everyone else was a sucker, a born loser who would be taken for a ride. As for Achilles, he was okay, a bit of a psycho sometimes, but great to have in a fight. And Gabriel, the guy had gotten him out of a couple of bad scrapes; he owed him his life. The two of them had been better several years ago, when nights were spent terrorizing the neighborhood, fighting the other gangs, the blacks, the spics... Back then they were creating a name for themselves. But now they seemed to be getting more legitimate, obeying the rules and shit. Had it not been for the plan to ice the old man he would have ditched 'em by the end of the summer. Jared was still good; he'd bring him along if he had to split from the others and join his posse. He certainly had the money to make things interesting.

As he rode further south, the houses steadily shrank, the yards became unruly and disorganized, the cars older and more beat up. Johnny parked his bike in the driveway of a neighbor's house a couple blocks away from home; for a little pot he could store his bike there for free, until his parents warmed to the idea of a two-wheeler. As he walked to his house he pulled out a comb and subconsciously straightened himself out, smoothing his hair down, tucking in his shirt. His parents' house was a small brick 1920s colonial style home (at a time when 'colonial' was used more loosely) that seemed indistinguishable from the other houses crowded in on either side up and down the block. His father's candy-apple red1957 Chevy Bel Air was on full display in front of the house; his father at his usual place, underneath the jacked up front. Johnny caught sight of old man's dusty, oil-stained denims. He approached the car tentatively, unsure of which of the many potentially volatile moods his father, a Vietnam veteran, was in. John O'Connor Sr. had come back from a tour with no apparent physical or mental scars, but there were times when Johnny wasn't quite sure. "Yo Dad."

His father didn't move for a few moments, making sure to finish his current task. Then he slid out slowly from underneath the Bel Air to eye his son, squinting in the afternoon light. "Expected you an hour ago," he said coolly.

"Sorry Dad, I was just helping a friend of mine out, musta lost track of time."

Mr. O'Connor stood up, looking back at his son, silently deciding which part to believe in, or not. He shook his head, upset with himself for not beating his son more when he was younger, when it would have made a difference. "Hair's getting too long. Time for a cut," he said by way of response.

Johnny smiled what he hoped was an ingratiating smile. "Aw, come on Dad. That's the style these days."

"Go on inside," his father said with a sigh. "Your mother's been looking for you."

Johnny headed in quickly, not waiting for his father to think twice and rope him into assisting with the Bel Air, his 'favorite son'.

Beatrice, 'Betty', O'Connor was humming a favorite church hymn in the kitchen as she prepared dinner. Despite her large frame, she moved swiftly about the kitchen. Meal preparation was always an organized affair, thanks to her checklists. In fact the secret to her success at keeping house was her organizational skill. Checklists, all about checklists. She kept an orderly, tidy house. She stopped as she heard Johnny's boot steps. "Oh, Junior, where have you been?" She approached him hurriedly. "Just look at you now," she said, taking off his leather jacket and hanging it in the hallway closet. "You've been all out all morning doing Lord knows what." She used both hands to smooth wayward hairs back into place on his scalp.

"Mom, will you cut it out? I'm eighteen, for Pete's sake."

"Shush now," Betty replied, unperturbed. "I'll have no more cursing out of you." She smoothed out the various wrinkles on his shirt, then caressed his face. "You poor dear, you're all hot and sweaty, and your eyes are so red from all that pollen kicking around outside. You smell of smoke, Junior. You know how I feel about smoking, how it makes your asthma act up."

"Mom, please." Johnny backed away from her heavy hands.

"Some water, sweetie?" Betty asked and turned around to quickly scoop up a glass from the drying rack and fill it with cold water. She pressed it into his hands. "Now go on upstairs and wash up for dinner."

Johnny turned.

"And I tidied up your room."

"Mom, I told you not to go in my room." Johnny's mind ran through all the potentially dangerous discoveries his mother could make if she had half a mind to probe.

"Well I had all your clean clothes to put away. Anyway it was such a mess, you really should keep your room a little more tidy and organized."

Johnny stormed up the stairs, bypassing the twins' room

(the two younger brothers, ten years old, spent their Saturdays glued to their Atari, too busy to notice him or anyone else), and retreating into the cool darkness of his bedroom. He scanned his room for any tampering, but all he could see was a mother's anal-retentive imposition. His bed was made, all the clothes on the floor from earlier that morning had been scooped up, cleaned and put away in his drawers, all the issues of *Easy Riders* and *Iron Horse,* with pictures of scantily clad women dry humping various motorcycles on the covers, were all neatly stacked on his desk (the thought of his mother thumbing through his magazines made him wince). He tested the drawers of his desk and found them all locked, thankfully. Not that his mother would dare open them. The only one he ever really feared was his father. Thankfully John Sr. had his Bel Air, his Mets and his *Daily News* to keep his mind occupied and out of his room.

Johnny sat down on his bed and mulled over Gabriel's proposition again. Murder. He never guessed Gabriel had it in him to plot murder. Johnny was unsure Gabriel would be able to pull the trigger when the time came. Gabriel had never killed anything before. Johnny had gone hunting lots of times. He'd looked into the lifeless eyes of the animals he'd killed and it never spooked him. Johnny aimed his finger like a gun in front of him. When the time came, he would step up if he had to.

21

The late morning sun cast four undulating shadows on the railroad tracks. They stood at the edge facing east for signs of the eleven a.m. local.

The empty track stretched out a good distance, then curved behind a thick patch of maples. The station was quiet and calm, a silent observer to the comings and goings of countless lives.

"Man, I think I might also get me one of them five-inch blades that shoots out the end," Johnny said, flicking an invisible stiletto and jabbing the air in front of him.

Achilles walked back to the bench and sat down, legs stretched out, arms draping over the back. "You should get a butterfly knife. I've seen a Kung Fu master work a pair of them. He was so fast, he'd put your stiletto to shame."

Gabriel walked over to Achilles and sat down next to him. Arms crossed, he eyed Johnny warily. "What do you want a stiletto for anyway? You planning on mugging someone?"

"Protection," Johnny replied. He flicked the imaginary blade back into its handle and walked back to the bench to face them.

"Protection!" Achilles laughed. "You and your ole man have half a dozen rifles, a couple handguns, and a 12-gauge shot gun. How much more protection will a switch blade give you?"

Johnny shrugged. "What can I say? I've got some money to blow."

Gabriel leaned forward, resting his forearms on his knees. "Let's forget about your stiletto and focus on getting a gun today. If there's time afterwards you can get all the knives you want."

"Don't' worry," Johnny said. "I've got it covered. There's guns up and down 42nd street. They're practically shoving them into your pockets. I know how to talk to 'em. I'll get us a great price for it."

Achilles pointed a finger at Johnny. "You fuck this up and you own it. I'm not paying for any piece of shit."

"Don't worry. I got it covered." Johnny lit up a cigarette. "You know something Achilles, you worry to much. And worrying aint good for your health, you know.

Jared grabbed his elbows tightly, hugging himself to stay warm, shifting his weight on his feet trying to steady himself at the edge of the platform. He stared at the inviting, metallic luster of the third rail, lost in a haze to the previous night's drugs that still sizzled at the many borders of his consciousness. He made a brief attempt to recall what they were, or how much he'd ingested of each but soon gave up. A sudden flutter of black wings rising from the third rail frightened him. He shut his eyes against the omen. His friends' voices clutched at passing breezes and drifted toward him in waves. He caught these wisps of their conversation and tried to focus on them, blotting out all other sound, including the whistle of the ten-fifty five express that was fast approaching. The train conductor blew the horn again in warning, but Jared didn't move from the edge, trapped in the image of the black wings. A second before impact Gabriel grabbed Jared by the shoulder, yanked him back and, as the train blurred behind them, yelled angrily into his face.

Jared shook his head alert. "What?" he asked, disoriented.

"Jesus H. Christ! What the fuck are you doing? Are you trying to kill yourself or what?"

Jared looked back at Gabriel in surprise, registering the anger and hurt in his face. He turned from Gabriel to the others. Both eyed him quietly. "Sorry Gabriel- sorry guys- guess I was just nodding off-"

"Sorry nothing! You get it together!" Gabriel checked a rush of violence inside him and walked away.

Achilles shook his head, disgusted. Johnny jabbed his finger in Jared's chest. "Wait until after I get the gun then you can jump onto the tracks." He nodded eastward. "Here comes our train."

The doors pulled open and the four stepped inside, inviting a flush of the morning heat inside the air-conditioned train. Johnny sat down near one of the doors by the window. Jared slouched in the aisle seat next to him. Achilles and Gabriel crouched next to them and peered right and left into the adjoining cars. Gabriel turned to Achilles. "I see him in the other car coming this way." Still crouching , Gabriel opened the door and started to step out.

"Aw, not again," Johnny whined, bringing his hand to his forehead. He reached into his back pocket with the other hand and pulled out his wallet. "Listen, I'll pay for your tickets."

Still crouching, Gabriel and Achilles looked at each other and then at Johnny, shaking their heads with mock disappointment. Achilles sneered, "Only losers and sissies pay." The door shut behind them.

Johnny stayed sitting. "Fuck 'em, I'm not taking any chances."

Jared, too tired or doped or confused to motivate, remained with him.

Outside Achilles and Gabriel waited until the train began pulling away from the station before climbing up unto the roof . They sat together holding tightly as the train picked up speed, kicking up a breeze that tempered the heat from above.

Down below the conductor, a large man with thick tattooed arms and a scowl that suggested he knew more than what he was allowed to let on, cornered Johnny and Jared. "Didn't I see four of you?"

Johnny reached back into his back pocket. "No sir, just me

and my friend here. How much to get to the city?"

The conductor looked at him for a moment before answering. "Seven for both of you."

Johnny pulled out several bills, "Here's my three fifty." He caught Jared's hurt surprise. "I didn't say I was going to pay for you."

Jared pouted a moment before pulling out his wallet.

The conductor gave them two punched tickets and moved on.

Above them Gabriel looked west trying to catch a glimpse of the skyscrapers in the distance, then turned back to Achilles. "Hey man, are you okay?"

Achilles opened his eyes. "I'm alright, just a headache I'm battling right now. Been getting a lot of them lately."

"You should've told me this morning, I would've given you something for it. Maybe we'll get something in the city."

"That's okay." Achilles shook his head. "A little pain doesn't bother me- just weird that they've crept up on me a few weeks ago. Don't seem to be going away."

"Maybe you should see a doctor about it."

Achilles caught Gabriel's concerned look and laughed. "You sound like my mother."

A crack of the train door below caused them to stop. Achilles brought his finger to his mouth and peaked over the edge of the train. He saw the pale blue of the conductor's hat as he walked into the next train car. "We should be able to get back down after the next stop."

The train stopped at Willet's Point, the last stop before the city. The skyscrapers rose up before them like fortresses from a different world.

The train stopped at the station and two teenage girls entered, long blond hair hung loose past their shoulders, with breasts and thighs that pressed against ill-fitting tube tops and mini-skirts. They scissored their long slender legs to the seats across the aisle from Jared and Johnny.

Smelling fresh, young prey, Johnny leaned forward and lifted his sunglasses for a better view. Twins, it appeared. He addressed the girl closest to him. "Hey girlie-girl, my name's Johnny, what's yours?"

The girl turned her head towards him out of boredom, casting him a look that suggested violent apathy. "Fuck off."

Johnny smiled. "Phuckov, is that Russian?"

The twins looked at each other, eyes rolling.

"Come on girls, I'm just making conversation. Make the ride go a little quicker."

The girls let the invitation sit unanswered in the aisle for a long enough moment to no longer warrant a reply. But they turned to Johnny, then to Jared, who seemed asleep at the moment. "We wouldn't mind making conversation with your friend there. He's kinda cute." They smiled mischievously.

Jared grinned behind his sunglasses.

"Him?" Johnny pointed dryly at Jared. "You're not his type." Johnny winked knowingly at Jared.

Jared readjusted himself and pretended to fall asleep.

Gabriel led the way off the train and up the ramp, threading through the crowd of people. Bums collected like trash at the far edges of the large terminal. Gabriel went into a 24-hour convenient store and came out with a small pack of Advil and a bottle of water. "Here." He held out the medicine and water to Achilles.

"Thanks," Achilles said and opened the packet, popping a few pills and flushing them down with the water.

As they turned to leave, an elderly disheveled man with hollow eyes and a long beard rose up from the margins and approached Gabriel. He pointed at Gabriel's left arm and tapped the blunted wrist, speaking in an unknown tongue. Instead of walking away Gabriel allowed the man to talk unopposed. As he rambled on, another man, slightly less disheveled than the first, approached apologetically. Apparently familiar with the elderly man, he tried to coax him back to the wall.

"What's he saying?" Gabriel asked him.

Johnny spoke up behind him, impatiently. "He's just babbling, he's nuts. Let's get going."

The other man shook his head and addressed Gabriel in English thick with accent. "It's Latin," he explained. "In his younger days, this man was a professor of Latin, before..." The younger man looked away a moment, unwilling to finish the thought. "He's explaining to you the right and left hands to you. In ancient Rome, the left hand was called the sinister hand 'sinistre'. You see with the right hand an evil man shakes another's hand, with his left, he stabs him in the back. Being left-handed was a bad omen in ancient times." The man paused, embarrassed. "He says, since you do not have a left hand, you are incapable of doing any wrong. You can only do good."

The elderly man raised an authoritative finger and echoed his friend, "Good."

Gabriel tapped the man's hand. "Thanks." He pulled out a couple of cigarettes from his pack. "Here you go, take care."

The elderly man, suddenly lost, walked back to his spot against the wall accompanied by his friend.

Achilles caught up to Gabriel as they exited the terminal. "What the fuck was that all about?"

"Who knows?"

"'Sinister hand." Johnny chuckled behind them, and elbowed Jared in the ribs. "I know what Jared does with his sinister hand."

Jared, now awake and alert, ignored Johnny. He kept his eyes fixed on Gabriel. What the elderly professor had said he had known their whole friendship. Deep down, his friend was incapable of anything but good. When they had met up again in middle school, Gabriel had seemed the same as before, a kind, sensitive boy who'd showed compassion for others, and yet at times he became a different person. Jared had come to recognize the darkness that clouded over his friend's face; it would surface at any time or place. It was a face Jared understood as one of distress more than malice. And the subsequent violence seemed more of a burden than anything intentional.

The corner of Thirty-fourth Street and Seventh Avenue was chaotic with people despite the heat, moving in the fast pace that's only known to cities. They climbed their way up the famous Seventh Avenue, past the bodegas drenched in loud, fast-clipped Latin music, the porn shop windows crowded with unisexual mannequins posing suggestively in satin and leather, the smoke shops with their mind-numbing assortment of pipes and bongs. The four waded through the sidewalk throng of human realities. If the country was a melting pot, then the City was a hot cauldron, teeming with blacks, Latinos, Asians, gays, hustlers, transvestites and the thousands of others who waved their many multi-colored freak flags proud and high, steaming above the omnipresent fires of the subway system below. Many more submerged themselves in this hot stew- their external, impermeable layers peeling, their old world provincial prejudices shedding- to fuse in creating a new, powerful identity. The four teens stayed outside on the periphery, content enough to feel the heat, to know that it existed.

They made it to Times Square, stopping at the corner to take in the scene. Gabriel turned to Johnny. "Don't go to the first person who comes up to you. Let's just walk over to Ninth Avenue, get a feel for the place and then on the way back you can-"

"No sweat." Johnny brushed past Gabriel walking down Forty Second Street. "We're on my turf now."

Achilles walked up to Gabriel with a raised eyebrow. Gabriel shrugged back. They both followed Johnny several paces back. Jared tailed right behind, his eyes focused on the sidewalk in front of him. The crowd and the shops seemed to extend along Forty-second Street but there were more hustlers here. They congregated in small groups of twos and threes, young black men with dead eyes scanning the street for cops then piercing back toward passing prey, with smooth walks and smoother talks, and endless whispers. "Weed, weed, I got weed- coke, coke, who needs coke- what you want- got it right here- acid, acid..."

Johnny walked with the determined stride of a man with a decision already formed in his head. He looked on casually, brushing past everyone. His eyes connected with an older black man, early thirties, shifty gaze, head always in motion, moving left and right.

The man was tall, thin, a light brown leather jacket and jeans. A thin scar ran down the side of his left cheek. He looked over at Johnny, sizing him up, recognizing instantly the desire, the risk and the potential. He gazed over the boy's shoulder at his three friends behind him, coldly calculating the size and strength of each as well as the seeming disinterest in their eyes.

"What you want white boy?"

"I want a-"

"Come on white boy, I don't got all day. Spit it out."

"I want a gun."

The man scowled. "There's no guns around here, motherfucker. Only drugs and knives."

Johnny turned around to face Jared and Achilles. Both shrugged back at him. He turned back. "Stiletto. Ah. Five inch."

"Italian?"

"Yes."

"Blade pops out the front or from the side?"

The hustler peppered Johnny with questions. Johnny, caught off guard, raced to keep up. "The side, I mean the front."

By this point, several black men had surrounded the two, edging out Gabriel, Achilles and Jared. Achilles made to push back inside, but Gabriel stopped him and shook his head.

"So what is it, the side or the front?"

"The front."

"Ok white boy, 5 inch Italian stiletto, blade comes out the front."

"Right."

"How much you got?"

"How much is it?"

"Hundred."

"I don't have a hundred."

"How much you got?" the hustler asked again, a tone of annoyance and impatience, as Johnny pulled out his wallet.

"I got..." Johnny opened his wallet to search through the bills in his wallet.

Among a bunch of ones, a fifty seemed to poke out. With nimble fingers the hustler quickly eased out the bill. "Got it." He turned to walk.

"Wait. Where are you going?" Johnny shoved the wallet in his front pocket and tentatively reached for the man's shoulder.

The man turned around scowling. "You want the knife, right? Even though it cost a hundred I'm getting it to you for fifty. I'm making you a deal." The man turned once more.

"Where are you going?" Johnny asked again, panicky.

"I don't keep knives on the street. The cops'll bust you and me. I got the knives around the corner. I'll be back in a minute. You stay with my friends." He nodded to the half dozen sullen black men surrounding Johnny.

Johnny pushed his way to Gabriel and Achilles. "Man, I think I've been robbed," he whispered.

"Think?" Achilles replied.

Gabriel looked on saying nothing.

The men looked at the four friends, betraying no emotions.

"What do we do?" Johnny asked Gabriel.

"We wait," Gabriel replied. "The guy said he would be back in a minute."

A patrol car turned off Eighth Avenue and drove down the street. Both groups looked on as the car made its way east.

"Here you go." The hustler reappeared from behind Johnny stuffing a rolled up brown paper bag in his arms. "Don't open it," he hissed as Johnny began to unroll it. "There's cops everywhere. Get the fuck out of here. Go, go, go." And with that, the hustler disappeared. Johnny rushed off in the opposite direction, Gabriel, Achilles and Jared keeping pace behind him. They made their way back to Seventh Avenue and turned back towards the train station.

"Don't you want to open it?" Gabriel caught up with Johnny.

"I'll open it on the train back." Johnny kept up his brisk pace, at times breaking into an unnecessary sprint, an unrepentant smirk tugging at the corners of his mouth.

The doors closed seconds after they jumped on to the train. The four paid their fares and the conductor moved on. They huddled around Johnny's seat as he opened the bag to peek inside.

"Fuck!" He crushed the bag closed in two tight fists. "Fuck, fuck, fuck me."

"What?" Jared asked. "What happened?"

Johnny reached in, at the verge of tears. "It's a Mars bar."

The other three looked at the chocolate bar for a couple seconds before falling over each other in uncontrollable fits of laughter.

"It's a fucking Mars bar," Johnny continued, stuffing the bar back in the bag and whipping it at the opposite window.

"Careful with that," Gabriel said in between coughs of laughter, "that's an expensive piece of chocolate."

The train doors opened up sixty minutes later at Great Hope, and the four friends spilled out onto the platform. The late afternoon sun burned high and bright in the sky, the heat no less oppressive. The others had stopped laughing, but Johnny was still livid. As they made their way down the stairs to home, Johnny took off in the opposite direction.

"Catch you all later," he shouted over his shoulder, not bothering to turn around.

"See ya, Johnny," Achilles called out happily. Then he turned to Gabriel, "This will go down in history as one of my favorite days of all time."

"We'll have to figure out another plan to get the gun." Gabriel smiled back. "For now let's get some beers and go home and cool off."

Achilles stumbled slightly to the door. "Guys, am headin' to my mom's-" His voice was more slurred than what one would expect with the three beers from that afternoon. "Headache's coming back. Think I need some rest."

Gabriel and Jared sat on the floor, beer bottles scattered around their legs. Gabriel sat up concerned, "Hey man, you need some help?"

Achilles struck a 'homeboy' pose, replying, "What do I look like, white boy? Yo grandmother?" Setting off another in a long line of laughs from that day.

Gabriel affected a retort, "Yo, white boy, you's alright." Then in a serious tone, "No really man, you okay to get home?"

Achilles smiled despite the sudden throb in his head, "No problem. Catch you later on."

Jared raised a beer to Achilles, "Goodnight home slice."

Achilles winked back before stepping into the darkening evening.

Jared elbowed Gabriel slightly in the rib. "Yo white boy. I got fifty-dollar M&M's, 20-dollar Babe Ruth and I gotta a special on Reggie bars, one hundred for a limited time only."

Gabriel laughed spraying his beer. "Man, you're a riot."

Jared continued, "But don't go poking anyone with these, you're liable to take someone's eye out."

Gabriel fell to the side laughing. "Stop, stop."

Then just like that Jared was on him, pressing his lips on Gabriel's.

Gabriel pressed his left forearm hard against Jared's chest, pushing him off forcefully. "What the fuck?" He stood up, towering angrily over Jared, who ducked his head and covered his face with both hands. "You're drunk," Gabriel summed it up finally, defusing the moment, throwing Jared a lifeline to their friendship.

And Jared took it. "You're right, man." He spoke into his hands, not wanting to face Gabriel. "I think I've had too much to drink."

Gabriel walked over to the cooler and pulled out a can of soda, then walked it over to Jared. "Here, start drinking this. It'll wake you up."

Jared stared hard at the can, avoiding Gabriel's eyes. "Thanks."

"No problem, I think I'll switch to soda too." Gabriel clinked his can against Jared's and affected the hustler's voice, "Right, white boy?"

Jared laughed. He laughed because he had to laugh, because if he didn't he'd start to cry and wouldn't stop. And he kept on with the joking, employing his best attempts at mimicry for Gabriel, who chuckled at his clowning until the end of the evening when they parted for their respected houses, and the shock of the evening gave way to despair.

22

With the hectic events from yesterday receding into memory the four decided to keep it low key and stay local. Johnny was starting to come around to accepting he'd been swindled and could even joke a little about it over pizza at Tony's.

Tony's was the embodiment of 1970s kitshe pizzeria. Bright, cheery paintings of Venetian gondolas patrolling unnaturally blue waters, alternating with poster-sized photographs of beautifully tanned couples enjoying touristy spots in Italy lined the mostly white stucco walls of Tony's Pizzeria. An eight by ten glossy reproduction of the Italian National Team holding the previous world cup hung by the register. The pizza at Tony's was authentic, made by an aging Italian named Carmine who was a constant and beloved fixture.

"See you later Carmine," Gabriel called out as the four filed out of the pizza shop.

Carmine replied with a thumbs-up sign.

Gabriel closed the door and looked over at Achilles. "Before we go home, I want to swing by the library. I promised Priti we'd give her a ride home."

Achilles shifted the car into gear. "No problem."

"I thought we were going to talk about the plan," Jared pouted in the back.

Gabriel lit up a cigarette and offered the pack to Jared and Johnny. "We will, just as soon we get back."

Priti was waiting at the corner when they pulled up. Gabriel got out. "Hi," he said smiling, wanting so bad to kiss her, but afraid to.

"Hi," Priti said, and got in the front next to Achilles

"You all know Priti, right?" Gabriel climbed in the car next to her.

"Don't believe I've had the pleasure. My name is Johnny," Johnny said, offering his hand.

"Thank you for driving me home," Priti announced to everyone. "I'm sure I'm taking you out of your way."

"Don't worry about it," Achilles replied.

"Yeah, we've got nothing better to do," Johnny laughed.

Jared just scowled in the backseat.

Achilles turned the tuner and caught the climax to "For Those About to Rock." As Brian Johnson's shrieking tribute burst through the speakers Jared leaned forward challengingly from the back seat. "Hey Priti, do you know AC/DC? Do they hear this music in India? Have you heard of Brian Johnson?"

"Don't mind Jared," Gabriel said loudly to Priti as he looked questioningly at his friend. "He can be a bit moody sometimes."

Priti exhaled impatiently and turned around to face Jared. Johnny sat on the other side, smiling. She peered into the shadows, steadying her gaze, her right eyebrow arched, aiming her retort into the dark cloud hiding Jared's face. "I will grant you that Brian Johnson's shrieking was an integral component to Back in Black's success and the band's comeback from an early death. But that is only what it was, shrieking. He has no singing ability whatsoever, let alone one that could compare with that of Bon Scott. He also lacked Bon Scott's charisma and persuasiveness, having to resort to screeches to make up for it. He also didn't write the lyrics to any of the songs in Back in Black, it was all Bon Scott and Malcolm Young's genius. Genius of course, that is if we can disregard the sexual innuendos, and sophomoric, if not misogynistic lyrics. And what has AC/DC done since Back in Black? You want to talk about Flick of the Switch? The albums with Bon Scott were more versatile, and the lyrics were more haunting and dangerous.

So yes, I know Brian Johnson, I'm just not that impressed."

Priti turned around and leaned back, arms crossed, victorious. The four teens around her sat in open-mouthed shock. Priti's high-powered inspection, dissection and, accurate analysis of AC/DC had rendered one of their most beloved bands to little more than a disemboweled cadaver fully exposed on her examination table.

Since early childhood, the big complaint by the many hovering aunts and uncles was that Priti Patel was a bit precocious; the less educated called her a know-it-all. But few were able to appreciate the burgeoning analytical mind, with its powerful perception, able to understand not only the school textbooks that she devoured, but also people, and their intentions. To fall under the scrutiny of her keen mind was to be, in effect, granted a higher state of enlightenment, one that was ultimately a double-edged sword of judgment from which it would be impossible to hide. That Heavy Metal, with its juvenile and manic attention to, among many, many other topics, sex, drugs, violence, death, and lunacy, would become the object of her perceptive powers (as opposed to her pre-med textbooks) seemed undeserved.

Jared blinked furiously in the shadow of the backseat, rummaging through his approximately 151 IQ points- now down several dozen points from the various chemicals (legitimate and illicit) interacting with his neural synapses, to find out how he'd been shown up on one of his favorite subjects.

Achilles grinned mischievously, letting out a long, low whistle. "I think she's won that round."

"Man, she showed you," Johnny taunted in between coughs of Winston smoke trails.

Gabriel gazed at Priti in speechless awe before a long smile tempered his lips. He gave Priti a friendly nudge with his elbow.

Priti smiled back, basking in his radiant attention.

23

Ruth leaned over the table toward her sisters seated opposite, yawning loudly into her fist as Rachel and Sarah went over the day's profits.

"You lick your thumbs too much. Do you think I want your saliva all over the money?" Rachel huffed.

Sarah dared not pause in her counting. This was the fifth interruption by her sisters. The first four times she was forced to start from the beginning. "Six hundred and sixty six, six hundred and sixty seven, six hundred and sixty eight. First of all, that's how I count the money, how I've always counted the money, and I think you have survived my saliva so far." Sarah ran a broad tongue over her thumb for good measure. "Now where was I? Six hundred and sixty nine-"

"I'm so glad you didn't stop at six hundred and sixty six," Ruth chirped happily.

Rachel turned suspiciously to Ruth. "What' so bad about six hundred and sixty six?"

Sarah continued to count, a little more loudly, determined not to be distracted. "Six hundred and seventy one, six hundred and seventy two-"

"You know," Ruth replied, "six, six six, the number of the devil."

"Six, six, six? Devil? Oh, Ruth." Rachel shook her head. "You've been watching too many horror movies." She turned to Sarah. "Did you hear what Ruth was saying about six hundred and sixty six?"

"Six hundred and seventy five," replied Sarah loudly, warningly.

"What time is Esther coming home?" Ruth asked.

Rachel looked at her watch. "Well, she left at six forty-five. Her night class runs for three hours. So she should be back any moment."

"What is she studying again?" Ruth squinted through her glasses.

"Business," Rachel answered, eyeing Sarah's wet thumb.

The chime of the door bells turned their attention to two men in their early to mid-twenties, topped with shaved heads, faded black jeans and white t-shirts, who were making their way towards the back of the restaurant.

"We're closed," Rachel said, approaching them with her hands up apologetically. "We're open tomorrow for lunch starting at twelve."

The young men seemed not to hear and continued to approach.

"Sorry boys." Rachel met them several tables from the back. "If you're hungry I can pack a few treats, but the kitchen is closed."

The man closest to her reached his right hand behind him and pulled out a .38 special, which he quickly jammed against Rachel's temple. His left hand grabbed her shoulder and spun her around so that they both faced her sisters and the cash register. "Where's the money?" he demanded through clenched teeth.

"Oh my god," Ruth cried. Feeling faint, she collapsed on the chair and leaned her head on the table underneath her hands.

"Don't hurt her, don't hurt her!" Sarah yelled, holding up a freshly counted roll of bills. "Here's the money, take it, take it. There's seven hundred dollars here."

The one holding Rachel gripped her shoulder tighter, causing her to wince. "Give me the money from the safe."

Sarah's eyes widened. "What money, what safe?"

The man jammed the gun into Rachel's temple harder.

"Don't fuck with me, you bitch. I know you have a safe in the back room where you keep money for the month."

Suddenly scared, Sarah looked from the man to Rachel, whose eyes were now closed (whether from pain or fear it was hard to tell), then back to the man. "There is no money in the safe, you must believe me. We deposited that money yesterday."

The man blinked several times, and his face flushed bright red. He flashed the gun at Sarah. "I'm giving you one more chance, you stupid kike. If you don't get me that money now I'm going to kill all of you."

Sarah's eyes began to tear, her voice barely above a whisper, "You must believe me, there is no money in the safe."

The man's partner behind him started trembling, the thick scar that traced his left cheekbone twitched wildly. He paced several steps to the front of the store, looked out the window, and then back to his friend. "Come on man, let's do this," he hissed. "Time's running out."

The back door swung open and Leon came in, steering a rolling bucket of water with a wooden handled mop. Whistling as he walked into the scene, seemingly oblivious to what was going on.

The man with the gun aimed it at Leon. "Who the fuck are you?"

Leon answered matter-of-factly, "Just the cleaning man, trying to mop up." He approached them casually, his eyes trained on the floor in front of him, pushing the bucket with the broom. "I promise not to get in your way." He began mopping the front of the restaurant.

The two men exchanged glances then turned back to the women. The man with the gun waved it in the air. "I'm going to count to three, and if I don't see the money in my hand, I'm going to start shooting."

"Okay, okay." Sarah was suddenly angry, forced to contend with these two young "good for nothings." "But the safe is in the back room, how do you expect me to get it?"

The man with the gun turned to his friend. "Joe, take her to the room-"

"What the fuck?" the man hissed back. "I thought the plan was not to use our real names. Jesus Christ!"

"Well they didn't know until now that Joe was your real name until you said it! Just take the woman to the back."

As the two argued, Leon continued to mop his way back to the group, whistling a slow steady tune. He periodically stole quick glances at the two men, taking note of the way the man held the gun, awkwardly like he wasn't familiar with its grip or its weight; how he leaned slightly towards his right, most likely his dominant side; the way he neglected his periphery and kept his eyes only in front; his facial expression, despite his anger, failed to hide fear, he would act hesitantly. The partner was skittish, off balanced, more prone to violent action.

"Fine." Joe brushed forcefully passed him. "Pat!"

Pat shook his head. "Will you just take her to the safe, for Pete's sake!"

Leon had made his way back until he was within five feet of Pat just to his right. He had stopped whistling and had adjusted his grip on the pole, but kept the mopping strokes even and smooth. He eyed the women in the room: Ruth was seated, her head face down on the table wrapped in her hands, Rachel seemed increasingly limp, with more of her weight being supported by the gunman. Sarah was walking back to the group with Joe behind her. She did not have the money, it was clear by their expressions. Leon knew the small window to act was closing fast.

Joe shoved Sarah to the table where Ruth was sitting, making her fall to the ground by her sister's legs. "There's no money, man. What are you gonna do?"

Leon waited for the right moment. It came when Pat reacted. Tightening his grip, Pat lifted the gun slightly away from Rachel, making to aim at Sarah.

With a strong, swift jab Leon buried the end of the pole deep into the front of Pat's neck, collapsing his trachea. The gun clattered on the floor as Pat fell to his knees gasping his last breaths.

Joe's eyes went wild as he saw his friend hit the floor dead. He scrambled for the gun. Leon kicked the gun across the floor and rammed the head of the mop into Joe's face, filling his mouth full of soapy water, causing him to stagger back, sputtering and coughing.

"Are you okay?" Leon put the mop down and rushed to the older women. He knelt down and helped Rachel and Sarah off the floor and seated them next to Ruth.

Sarah seemed to recover the quickest and set about scanning her body for any injuries. "I think so - look out!"

Leon turned around to find Joe with a fully sprung switchblade in his right hand and advancing slowly. Leon took a defensive crouch "You don't want to do this. I don't want to hurt you."

Joe brandished the knife, waving it in front of him, intermittently jabbing it forward as he approached Leon. "I'm not going to jail. You already made me out, I got no choice."

"I don't want to hurt you," Leon repeated, eyeing Joe's movements with the knife. They were rhythmic almost predictable.

Joe committed himself, stepping forward to stab Leon in the chest. Leon stepped to the side, allowing the knife-wielding hand to jab pass him. He quickly wrapped both arms around Joe's forearm and with precise upward and downward movements of his arms, he fractured both forearm bones. As the knife fell to the floor Leon elbowed Joe twice in the abdomen, then turned around to punch him once in the face. Joe fell limp but conscious onto the floor next to Pat's lifeless body.

Sarah was the first of the sisters to recognize that the danger had passed. Brushing a quick tear from her face, she stood up and made for the back room. "I'll call 911," she said firmly.

Leon stepped to the two men and put two fingers on their carotid arteries, noting the presence of a pulse in one and the absence in the other. He then stepped to the two sisters. Rachel sat limply in her seat with both eyes closed; she was pale, the blood drained from her face. Ruth sat shivering next to her, her face buried in her arms on the table. He put his hands gently on their shoulders. "Aunties," he spoke softly so as not to startle them.

Ruth whimpered into her arms, "Are we dead?"

"It's okay." Leon smiled. "You are safe."

Rachel opened one eye. "What?"

"You are safe," Leon repeated.

Rachel opened her other eye and looked around as if seeing the restaurant for the first time. She looked at the two crumpled bodies on the floor, and then at Leon. "Did you do this?" she asked in a soft, curious tone.

Leon looked down at the two men with regret. "Unfortunately, I had no choice."

"Ruth," Rachel called to her sister tapping her on the shoulder. "Ruth look up, we're safe. Leon took care of the Nazis."

Ruth jerked her head up. "He what?"

Rachel laughed with tears in her eyes. "We're saved, Leon saved us from the Nazis."

Ruth laughed in response. "He did?" she asked, looking at Leon.

Rachel stood up hugging Leon. "Our hero, our hero, you did it! I was sure we were going to die."

Ruth rushed to the two of them, hugging both tightly. "Our hero, our hero," she echoed. Leon smiled, slightly embarrassed as the two sisters swarmed around him.

"They're on their way." Sarah walked back to them, stepping around the two men on the floor, giving wide berth as if they carried some horrific infection. She pried the two sisters off Leon. "Let go of him or you'll crush him."

"Nothing can crush this superman," cried Rachel as she

was wrenched from him.

"Thank you, Leon." Sarah walked up to Leon putting both hands on his cheeks, fighting back her tears.

Leon looked down. "You are welcome. I did not have a choice; I had to act quickly. I didn't mean to kill-"

"I know you didn't Leon. You don't have to explain this to me or to any of us."

"What happened?" A shrill voice from the front of the store caught their attention. Quick sharp, click-clacking footsteps rang out as Esther made her way into the restaurant. "Mother, please, what happened?"

Sarah broke off from the group and rushed to her daughter embracing her. "It's okay, Esther, we're safe. Two armed men tried to rob us but Leon fought them and saved us. The police and the ambulance will be here soon."

Esther looked at her visibly shaken aunts sitting at the table and felt a sudden flush of heat climb up her scalp and her knees became wobbly. She pressed a hand to her forehead. "I think I need to sit down."

Leon quickly drew a chair for Esther to sit down in. The older women soon swarmed around her to comfort her. "We're all safe," Rachel said.

Tears had found their way to Esther's eyes as she shook her head. "I can't believe I left tonight of all nights. And all along I thought everyone here was doing fine."

"We are fine." Sarah caressed her daughter's hair.

Ruth remained quiet, holding onto her niece's hand; only now was Ruth beginning to feel fine. So close she- they - had been to getting seriously hurt or killed.

Rachel, finding her strength, stood up and walked to Leon. She reached a tender hand and cupped his cheek. "All thanks to you, Leon."

Soon all the sisters had gone over to shower thanks to the young man who blushed in the face of so much gratitude.

Esther stood up and wove her way through the older

women until she reached Leon. She held his arms and looked into the dark mysteries of his eyes. She found herself at a loss for words for a brief moment. "Thank you," she said finally, embracing him.

Rachel spoke up, breaking the moment, "How did you do it, Leon? How did you take on two men, one with a gun, the other with a knife?" She turned to the other women. "I can't believe it, the most exciting thing happening at Sarah's and my eyes were closed!"

"So were mine!" Ruth chimed in.

The two sisters turned to Sarah, who had, in fact, seen everything, and had guessed at some advanced military training. And more importantly guessed that it was up to Leon to decide to let the others know. "To be honest, it happened so fast and I was so scared I really have no idea what happened."

All eyes turned to Leon, who by now had made his way to the front of the store to open the door for the police outside. It was to them he would have to explain everything.

24

A recent CDC report shows the number of people diagnosed with AIDS has topped more than 1600, of whom 750 have died. These numbers come at the same time that all the national blood banks are making unequivocal reassurances as to the safety of the blood supply, though critics argue no guidelines for screening the donors or testing the blood exist. But on a sunnier side, here's Phil with the weather. That's right Sandy, another gorgeous day today as temperatures will reach seventy-nine and the humidity will remain pleasantly low.

Gabriel stormed into the den and switched on the light, chasing away the evening shadows that had been keeping Isabelle company, shaking her out of her trance, and pointed an accusing finger at her. "Why did you have to insult her? She didn't do anything to you. I finally bring home a girl that I like and all you can do is disrespect her."

They'd rarely fought before, and he found himself in the uncomfortable position of challenging his mother. Yet here they were, squaring off, facing each other in the den, the TV muted, the shades drawn, their faces lit by the bulbous overhead lights, the evening sounds outside distant.

"You did this to me on purpose." Isabelle wasted no time throwing the accusation back at him. "Couldn't you have tried, just a little, to find someone more appropriate?"

"More appropriate? What's that supposed to mean? Do you mean more white? Since when did you become a racist?"

"What about that girl you were dating, Lisa? What

happened to her?"

"Lisa?" Gabriel's eyes widened. "Are you serious? Are you really serious? And what does it matter to you anyway? You don't care about what I do or what happens to me. You never cared, so why now?"

Isabelle lit a cigarette in response, a bright orange flash then a plume of smoke as she hid herself from his interrogation. How often had she really focused on her second son, still second even when he was the only son left? She could not bring herself to answer this, to revisit these past eight years. He had become a foreigner in her home, moving along the periphery, coming into occasional focus to remind her of Daniel and the hollow wound inside her. She was desperate to fill this empty ache but found only loathing, and this loathing would rise and spill over in a torrent that not even Cohen & Cohen could absorb, and she would rage silently at Gabriel. That Gabriel had quietly accepted his role in Daniel's death, that he'd shared in the guilt, that he'd clung to her early on, when all she could do was disappear, had made her more resentful of his presence. Later, when he'd stopped clinging, when he'd stopped sharing, when he'd stopped trying, she'd found it easier to breathe. They became strangers going through the motions of family life. But his real crime, in the end, was that he too could not fill the void.

"But she's not even Jewish," Isabelle blurted, her thoughts scrambled, having run out of arguments.

"Jewish? Since when do you care about being Jewish?" Gabriel counted his fingers. "We don't go to temple. We don't keep kosher. We don't celebrate the high holy days. We don't fast on Yom Kippur. Your idea of unleavened bread on Passover is a bagel."

"Stop it. I don't want to talk about it anymore. You're giving me a headache." Isabelle brought her hands to her head as if to contain the pain inside.

Gabriel walked up to her. Having crossed the threshold he

wasn't stopping now. Eight years of outrage and he needed to exorcise it. "Well I need to say it and you need to hear it." He was inches away from her now, towering above her, his lips trembling from a torrent of emotions that had finally found a breach and were ready to spill forth. "You don't love me, you don't care about me, and I don't know if you ever did. All you ever cared about was Daniel, and that was only after he died. You blamed us for everything while he was alive, for your divorce-"

"Stop it. Stop it." Isabelle held her hands to her ears, shutting her eyes.

"No, I'm not going to stop. Because you need to hear it from me," Gabriel continued. His voice cracked with longing. "I love you, but you don't love me. I care about you but you don't care about me. The only thing I've been for you is a scapegoat for everything that has gone wrong in your life."

But Isabelle was no longer listening. She had shut herself off, too fragile to expose herself to Gabriel's vent. He dried his eyes and looked at his mother as if for the first time. The cruel passage of time was etched in wrinkles and grays, in the body that seemed as if collapsing inward, disappearing.

2 5

"It's for the best dear." Mrs. Patel reached out to comfort her daughter, to dry the tears that came disconcertingly easy, but Priti evaded her mother's contact, and the hand drifted in midair for an uncomfortable moment before dropping.

"The best for whom? For me or for you?"

Both parents sat in the living room, the lights in the room all lit brightly, and both sat rooted to their deep imprints on the couch (his deeper than hers) as if the trap had been planned and set well in advance of her return. But Priti preferred to stand, arms crossed, looking down at the discomfiture on her father's face, the hypocrisy on her mother's.

Professor Patel finally spoke. "I personally have no problem with Gabriel, the boy-"

"And neither do I." Mrs. Patel interjected

Professor Patel continued, "But perhaps your mother has a point."

"Of course I do-," Mrs. Patel said.

"It's best to not settle one's mind on just one boy-"

"You have to keep your options open-" Mrs. Patel interrupted once more.

"Will you shut up!" Professor Patel turned sharply to his wife, daring another comment, before turning back to his daughter, his patience and humor now run dry (he had a shallow well of it) and his voice had lost the sweet persuasive tinge to his otherwise gruff no-nonsense tone. "We're not saying don't go out with Gabriel. We're saying don't go out with just Gabriel."

"So whom do you want me to go out with?" Priti asked,

then regretted giving her parents the opportunity they had steered her to.

"Honey." The mother turned to her husband, having seen the opportunity, and pounced into what smelled like a well-scripted plot. "How about your colleague's son? What is the boy's name?" She looked to the ceiling for inspiration, snapping her fingers, except of course she knew full well the boy's name.

Now Priti knew this was scripted.

"Ankur," the father replied, looking a bit guilty and awkward, regretting having involved himself with the charade.

Both parents were horrible actors.

"Ankur! That's right." Mrs. Patel turned gaily to her husband. "Why don't you call your friend and let's see about arrang- I mean setting up a date with Ankur." Priti could picture a little mouse spinning a running wheel in her mother's mind, but found a more appropriate image of said mouse pressing the tender button of a cash register, popping out a drawer flush with cash.

"You mean the short fat guy whose sole life goal is to go to Wharton Business School? The one with bad body odor?" Priti brought a hand to her head; she could feel a headache coming on.

"Yes that's –I mean no, he does not smell that bad." Mrs. Patel turned to her husband for assistance but found him shrugging in assent at the brief description.

"He's five years older than me." Priti's arms dropped to her sides, fists clenched and found herself perilously close to a preschool tantrum position. "He's in his third year of college."

Here, Professor Patel found some footing and stood up, looming over his daughter. "I'm five years older than your mother. There's nothing wrong with that age difference."

"That's different," Priti shot back. "You two chose each other, nothing was arranged for you."

"Not another word out of you." Her father had had enough

of this charade and insolence. "You are going to go on one date with Ankur and that is final."

"One date," Priti retorted, unable to not get the last word, grabbing for the one detail, the only one she had an option for, before climbing the stairs and dropping onto her bed, letting the pillow soak up her tears.

to visit and push you into doing something you didn't necessarily want to do but said 'hey what the hell'?" Jared didn't bother to respond and Richie didn't wait for a response, he never did. For him, questions seemed less for extracting information and more for filling in the gaps during his story telling; fearing the compromising moments of silence. Jared never believed these stories, these staccato monologues. He couldn't help but see through them for what they were, to see Richie for what he was, a degenerate addict, and Jared always felt he was hitting rock bottom when he came by Eden Park to buy Angel Dust. More specifically the decrepit playground that edged the side street most of the neighborhood addicts used as a drive by for their quick fixes. He'd share a laced joint with Richie and the other PCP addicts. It was a trade off, a monologue for a detached hallucinogenic high. Richie never bought or sold, he leached- a hit here, a toke there- all the while rambling on with his one-man show, as if that would suffice. And as he talked- a barrage of words, rhetorical questions, exclamations, entreaties- Richie's eyes were constantly in motion, a side-to-side, slow paced nystagmic twitch, surveying the area as if he were preparing himself for an escape or an attack. His darting eyes occasionally settled on Jared, and Richie pincered his two fingers together skittishly as he watched, anticipating the next hit. Jared held the joint out limply and Richie, fingers trembling, took it. And the moment became quiet as he sucked in a large drag off the joint, the smoke filling up his lungs, the drug filling up his skull to the point he felt it would crack. As he exhaled he felt the sides of his brain collapsing, his body emptying, and he would pass the joint, reluctantly. And his rambling would resume. "And not ten minutes into the friggin' game I get tackled by both of them- didn't expect it. Not by a couple of kids- though they are pretty big, boy, I think they get that from the other side of the family, certainly not mine- twisted the damn knee hard going down, wound up limping off the field- but they were worried about me- good kids- deep down- I don't think they meant to hurt me- do you have younger cousins?" Jared shook his head. "Had the bag of ice on it all night. And it's been sore this whole friggen' week. Can you believe it? Injured just like that, by a couple of kids- And what am I gonna do? Go to the doctor? What, so he can tell me it's a sprain and not to worry about it? Man, I'm already at the doctor's every freaking month for my arthritis medication. I hate that place- looking at me like I'm some sort of dope fiend. But what can I do? Got this Juvenile Rheumatism, since I was a kid, always with these joint pains. But I was doing good- was even thinking of hitting the gym, doing a little weight lifting and stuff." Richie flexed his biceps but very little happened. His extremities were devoid of any musculature. Every time Jared saw Richie, he found him increasingly emaciated and sickly. Hollowed out from the addiction, from chasing the euphoria from his first hit, one that would never return. Because, in the end, all addicts are jilted lovers. "Hey do you go to the gym? They say it's supposed to be good for you, exercise and all-"

Jared shook his head coughing out another hit.

"And the only thing that really works is Vicodin, man, them Tylenol with codeines are like mints. I was popping those things like Tic-Tacs and they didn't do nothing for me. Just pop a couple of Vike's when the pain hits really bad and I'm able to get out of bed. But now with this bum knee I dunno what I'm gonna do- hey here comes your crew."

Jared looked to the end of the street and caught the Chevelle turning the corner. He looked at the burnt out end of his roach and threw it on the ground, then up at the group of greasy haired burnouts. "See ya," he said, and started walking to the approaching car.

"Hey man." Richie started limping behind him, the familiar edge of desperation surfaced in his voice. "Why not another joint for the road?"

Jared kept walking, not bothering to acknowledge the

question. He looked up towards the car. Achilles was driving, Gabriel was in the passenger seat. And although both of them looked straight ahead, he knew they were talking about him, about this. The car stopped midway down the block and Achilles flicked the lights off and on.

"Hey man." Richie struggled to keep up with Jared's long-limbed strides. "Just one more hit, man, before ya go." The façade of the last forty-five minutes began to crumble, revealing the underlying desperation Richie failed so miserably to hide.

Jared reached the back door to the Chevelle and turned to face Richie. "Have to go, man. See you next time." He reached up a hand for a high five.

Richie mechanically slapped it. "Just one more hit. For the road." He was now pleading.

Jared pulled open the door and got in. "Hi." He looked sheepishly at Gabriel and Achilles, both had turned to look at him with a mixture of pity and revulsion.

Richie approached the car, hugging himself despite the heat of the night, his voice quivering his eyes at the point of tears. "One more hit, man, that's all I'm asking you."

Jared hated these moments; they were as reliable as the monologues. For Richie, there was never just one more hit. And although he was too smart to become violent, he always pushed the boundaries, forcing Jared to be the one to be harder than he wanted to be.

Achilles pointed a finger past Jared. "Get the fuck away from the car, you maggot."

Richie backed off, both hands up, his surrendered form disappearing in the rearview mirror as the car pulled away.

Achilles leaned forward, both arms draped around the steering wheel, frowned over at the group on the picnic benches and shook his head. "What a pathetic group you choose to hang out with."

Gabriel turned in his seat to look hard at Jared, so many unspoken questions in his soft brown eyes. Jared turned away. Achilles kept talking, "Went over to your house to get you. Your maid didn't know where you were. Seems you forgot about us getting together." Achilles looked in the rearview mirror, caught Jared's eye and smiled. "But I thought we'd find you here. Even made a bet with Gabriel. Made a few bucks tonight-"

Gabriel placed a steadying hand on Achilles's shoulder, all the while looking at Jared's face that popped in and out from under the passing street lamps in the backseat. "We were supposed to go over part of the plan tonight," Gabriel said, searching for Jared's eyes. "Can I trust you?" It seemed more of an accusation than a question. "Because if you can't do this, then you back out now."

In the backseat Jared felt the urge to cry. "I can do this." His voice was hoarse.

"You better," Achilles warned as he scanned the streets for cop cars. "Because I don't want to get caught because of your fuckup, am I right?" He turned to Gabriel. "This isn't ring and run, for Pete's sake."

In response Gabriel look back at Jared. "If you're in this then you can't get high anymore, at least not until after this is over. Deal?"

Jared murmured something inaudible.

"I can't hear you, Jared."

"Yes! Yes! Alright, I understand, no drugs. Can I still drink a little alcohol and smoke cigarettes for Chrissakes?"

"Yes, but no more getting drunk. From now on we all have to be with it."

Both Jared and Achilles nodded in agreement.

Satisfied, Gabriel turned to Achilles. "Alright, let's go pick up Johnny. He should be at Tony's."

Johnny leaned back, a hot slice of pizza folded in one

hand, the other arm draped over the back of his chair. "No kidding," he was saying, taking a bite of his pizza. The melted cheese seared the roof of his mouth causing him to sputter and cough. He wiped some tears with the back his free hand. "Jeez, that's friggin' hot!"

The two boys across from him, a few years younger, eyed him doubtfully. They'd been around the neighborhood enough times to know who the braggarts were. The older one leaned back in his chair, continuing the interrogation. "Murder for hire and all that?"

"True as true, just like Murder Inc., though no Italians in the group."

The two boys exchanged glances before looking back at Johnny who took another searing bite of his pizza, holding court with the younger generation. The older one nodded to Johnny. "So how many people have you killed?"

"Can't tell you." Johnny took a gulp of his soda, looking at the two over the rim of his cup. "If I did and then I got caught you'd be accessories after the fact."

"Accessories! But we didn't do anything."

Johnny grinned, satisfied with the pizza, the drink, and the way the conversation had gone. "Yeah, but you'd know, and you'd be obligated to tell the police and if you didn't you'd be just as guilty as I am."

The two were stunned, almost scared. "But we didn't even kill anybody."

"He didn't either." Gabriel kicked Johnny's legs off the chair and put his hand on the table, ending the conversation.

The two boys stared up at the neighborhood hero in speechless amazement.

Johnny recovered his bearings and stood up, making a final attempt to save face. "Alright guys, gotta go. See y'around."

The closing front door signaled Johnny's exit. As the two young boys whispered excitedly, Gabriel approached the counter where Carmine stood hunched over a freshly rolled out pizza dough, his fingers pulled taut by its floured margins. Gabriel reached over the counter and tapped him affectionately on the shoulder. "How's it going, Carmine?"

Carmine smiled back, "Gabriel, howaya? Why don't I see you around here much? You kids used to always fill up these tables talking and laughing, playing the pinball machine."

Gabriel smiled back. "Been busy. Hey, you got a pie for me?"

Carmine dusted his hands on his smock as he turned around to grab a pizza box. "I always got pizza for you, Gabriel. How's your mom?" Carmine had known about Daniel's death, had heard it on the news, and had been one of the few non-relatives to come by and offer condolences, one of the few who did not succumb to gossip.

"She's good, she's good." Gabriel reached in his back pocket for his wallet. "My uncle's visiting."

"The soldier?" Carmine slid the pizza in the box then stretched out a short piece of tape over the front. "He's a good kid. Leon, right?"

"Right, how much do I owe you?"

Carmine smiled and tapped the box with finality. "It's on the house, kid."

Johnny's side door clicked open and Gabriel handed him the pizza box. "Here, hold this," he said, then punched Johnny in the jaw sending him sprawling into Jared. Gabriel loomed over Johnny menacingly. "Don't ever say anything about killing people again," he said, his voice measured and direct. "To anyone, you got that?"

Johnny kept his right hand tight on the box. With the left he grabbed his jaw, checking for broken bones. "I was just kidding around, man. Jesus H!"

Achilles shook his head as they pulled away.

"Alright, so how's it going to go?" Achilles looked at Gabriel expectantly.

The four sat on the floor around the old coffee table, the empty pizza box lay by the door next to a pile of soda cans. The front door was left cracked open to allow in a generous evening breeze. A large candle on the coffee table fed an undulating tenuous flame, exposing only parts of their faces to the surrounding darkness. A covenant of shadows lurked and plotted along the walls behind them.

"The plan is going to be broken down into separate parts, this will make it easier to follow. First is getting the perp. Next is transporting him here-"

"Here?" Achilles broke in. "Why not Eden Park or some other wooded area?"

"Eden Park is crawling with people at all hours of the night. And we don't have enough information about any other wooded area in and around here to know for sure if there won't be someone at the time we bring the perp in."

Achilles nodded, satisfied with the answer.

"Third, the gun."

"I got a good one," Johnny said. "My dad picked up an 1860s US army issue Colt revolver last summer at a gun show down south."

"That's nice and all but, can it shoot?"

"The dealer gave him a handful of bullets and we've tested it out in the woods. The aim's off beyond twenty yards but point blank there's no missing. Best of all, the gun's untraceable."

Gabriel nodded, satisfied. "Okay, so transporting the gun here. I don't think it's a good idea for the perp and the gun to be in the same car in case we get stopped by the cops. We don't want them putting two and two together. Fourth is shooting the perp. I figure I should be the one to pull the trigger; it's my plan, my idea and if anything happens I'll be the one who gets in trouble. We'll need a pillow to muffle the sound. And fifth is disposing the body. Any questions?"

Gabriel looked around at his friends, their faces intermittently painted in small dabs of candlelight, trying to read their minds. All seemed closely listening. He could tell they were all still in. "Okay, so first of all the best time to get the perp is in the late evening. We don't want it too much after midnight as the cops will be suspicious of any activity at that hour. And it should be a weekend night, when there're already a lot of people going out. We'll just blend in with everyone else on the street.

Johnny lit up a cigarette. "How're we going to get the guy to come with us?" he asked, exhaling a stream of smoke to the ceiling.

Gabriel nodded, pleased with the question. "I've been checking out his house. Most evening's at around 11 he's got all the lights out in the house except a small beside lamp. He also leaves a window cracked open in the living room. He has no pets. Two of us can easily get in through the living room window. Once we're in, we can subdue the perp without any neighbors hearing anything. Still, I think it'll be good if we stakeout the place a few nights in the next couple of weeks just to get a good idea about what I'm talking about." Gabriel paused to light a cigarette.

Achilles spoke up, "I suppose you'll want to use my car to transport the perp."

Gabriel looked at Achilles, nodding. "Only if you're okay with it. I mean, you have a large enough trunk to put him in and-"

"No problem with using my car," Achilles replied. "Just was checking. I'll make sure to clean the trunk out to make space just in case we need to use it."

"Okay. Good. Make sure that there's plenty of gas and the car will be good to go for that night. We don't want it breaking down on us. And get two shovels and leave them in the trunk. Now, it should take no more than five minutes to drive home, but I think we should take a roundabout route just in case.

We'll make it a ten-minute ride. I've mapped out the route so we don't pass by any place where people will be hanging out outside."

"I suppose I'll be bringing the gun," Johnny said, taking a drag off his cigarette.

"Right." Gabriel fisted his cigarette, pointing his finger at Johnny. "But make sure you have the gun and the bullets in a secure place a few days before, that way you're not having to sneak them past your dad that night."

"I got it, I got it."

"What do I do?" Jared looked down at his soda can as he asked, not want to look into Gabriel's eyes.

"You'll be driving the car."

"What?" Achilles sat up. "This drug addict, driving my car?" he asked with a healthy mixture of shock and disgust, pointing a dismissive thumb at Jared.

"I'm going to need you to come into the house with me," Gabriel replied. "I don't know what to expect in there so I need you to cover for me. Jared will be in the car at the corner. He'll be driving if we need him, and," Gabriel shot Jared a warning glance, "Jared will be stone-cold sober that night."

Achilles looked suspiciously at Jared, but accepted Gabriel's explanation. "Okay," he said finally.

"Once we get home we have about fifty feet of wooded area to cross to get him inside," Gabriel continued. "There shouldn't be anyone around at that hour, but I want you," Gabriel said, pointing at Johnny, "to get here about twenty minutes before. You stash the gun inside then come out to just before the sidewalk and scope around and wait for us. If the coast is clear you light up a cigarette; that'll be the signal that we can move."

"Got it." Johnny started giggling and rubbing his hands together mischievously. "Man, this sounds like 'Mission Impossible'!"

Gabriel shot him a hard look. "No, this is for real. No mistakes allowed that night."

"When is 'that night'?" Jared asked solemnly, finally daring to look up.

"The third weekend in August." Gabriel looked around the room, gathering consensus. "That gives us almost two months to get our plan down pat."

"One last question." Achilles stood up, his shadow reaching to the ceiling, towering over all of them. "Where are we burying the body?"

Gabriel looked up at him. "I'm still not sure, but I have a couple ideas. I'll let you all know in the next week."

"Alright!" Johnny stood up stretching the ache out of his legs. "I say we call it a wrap, and get some beers to celebrate."

27

Achilles approached his car. The window to the driver's side was down, as it always was. There was nothing really worth stealing, and enough people in the neighborhood knew he owned it, and knew he'd have no qualms about bashing their face in if they even thought about stealing it. Plus, he liked sliding in through the open window feet first into the driver's seat- he liked the idea of himself doing it. Just like in *The Dukes of Hazard* and the General Lee. It was a crappy show otherwise, except for Daisy Duke. She was hot, and she was always wearing those short shorts. Achilles turned the ignition. A loud guttural roar reminded him to take the car to Davey's to get the muffler fixed.

Achilles scanned the street for cops before pulling out onto the road. Not that he had anything to hide, it was just reflex, with all those nights of terrorizing the neighborhood, always looking over his shoulder. Correction: he didn't have anything to hide yet. If and when the time came to kill the old pervert he'd have to be careful, very careful, especially with a drug addict and a scumbag in on the hit. Those boneheads were always fooling around. Why Gabriel had included them in the plan- or even stayed friends with them- he'd never understand. They would be sure to fuck it up and get caught. He'd have to be very careful. Still, as long as Gabriel was running the show he was in. The guy had an edge, a sixth sense about things. He knew when to fight, when to run, where the cops were hiding, how far they should go- and in a fight, there was no one else he'd rather have on his side. No, he didn't usually see Gabriel use his left- "The Hammer"- but Gabriel's right fist came out fast and hard, and he had some high kicks when he needed to use them. No training- they guy was a natural fighting machine.

Achilles pulled up to his mother's apartment complex. A shit hole, not much better than the Circle Hole projects. How he ever wound up in this place he'd never understand. Full of old people! Thank god he lived on the first floor, otherwise he'd be waiting all afternoon for the elevator with all these people with walkers everywhere. And then them uptight queers across the hall with their sissy ass toy dog, trying to pretend they're not queers, but come on you can't be a friggin' grown man living with another friggin' grown man. Not that he has anything against queers- just as long as they don't lay a finger on him. There'd been some kids in the building he'd try to be friends with a few years before, wimps, couldn't fight worth a damn. Before turning the ignition off he revved the engine several times, shattering the serenity of the block, frightening two elderly women seated on one of several benches along the path to the front door of the complex. Satisfied with the response, Achilles pulled himself out of the car through the window. He glanced challengingly to either side before looking at the elderly women. "Good evening ladies," he said. They shot him startled looks he pretended to ignore as he walked by. With their blue dyed hair, they look like freaks.

A petite brunette, hair down to her waist, descended the steps from the front door as he approached. Veronica. She'd always been hot for him, even though she was two years older. Now off to college at the end of the summer, but maybe he'd do her before she left. Probably make the highlight of her friggin' day. She was so hot for him. "Hey Veronica, you're looking good."

"Buzz off, creep." Veronica side-stepped him and rushed towards the curb.

Or maybe not. Achilles shook his head, smiling. Girls were so crazy sometimes. Nuts. One minute they're hot for your jock, the next they're cold fish.

He jammed the key into the lock and opened the door to his mother's cramped one-bedroom apartment. Only one friggin' bedroom in the tiny shit-hole apartment (his mother slept on the pull out sofa in the living room). He cast a quick glance around the living room. Bric-a-brac his mother had chanced upon from her many excursions to the various yard sales all over Great Hope filled every square foot of counter, shelf, and wall space. Sometimes he felt there was no room to breathe. He found his mother glued to the TV set, watching another nutty show, and on a nice evening too. No wonder his dad left her. She was a loser. No goals, no aspirations. He would never wind up like her, no friggin' way.

"Hi honey," she called out. "Want me to make you some dinner? How 'bout a sandwich?"

"No thanks, Ma, I'm not hungry," he said, closing the front door. He made straight for his bedroom, whose four walls had been his sanctuary for the past sixteen years. He looked around his Spartan room: single bed on one side, some free weights in one corner. Several posters populated his otherwise bare walls: Steve McQueen from *Bullitt*, standing tall over his 1968 Mustang GT, a young and angry Muhammad Ali poised over a startled Sonny Liston, an even angrier Bruce Lee ready to do battle in *Fists of Fury*, and his latest acquisition, a snarling Al Pacino from *Scarface* with his M16A1. He idolized these men, their strength, their brute force, their courage- it was to them he had turned for inspiration. But these four walls were now starting to close in on him. He'd outgrown them; he was ready to leave. He clicked the door closed and quickly sought to regain his thread of thought

He himself had drive, ambition, strength, and willpower. He was planning on making it big. No fooling around, no drugs, no TV, no wasting time. All he needed was one great idea. He had a lot of ideas, all the time. That most of them didn't pan out was no big deal. It was just a matter of time before one of them stuck, the details all coming together in a nice package. With Gabriel he knew they would make it big sooner or later. He knew Gabriel was too busy with planning the hit for anything else right now. But afterwards, the world would be theirs for the taking.

28

The doorbell rang downstairs. Priti sat on her bed, her arms sunk between her legs, dreading the next two to three hours.

"Priti," her mother called up. "Your date is here."

Priti planted her feet and stood up, consoling herself to the fact that there would be no more of these. She would make sure to make a firm impression on Ankur.

Her parents were in the foyer, hovering around her "suitor" (their word, not hers). With each step, Priti got an increasingly unflattering view of Ankur. He had dressed up for the occasion, his stout, squat body pressed uncomfortably against an uncharismatic light blue shirt, striped tie, and dark blue suit. It was as if he were dressed for an interview. Perhaps this was an interview, but the position was taken, as far as she was concerned. She had found Gabriel and he fulfilled the job description. Priti found it hard to not compare the two. Gabriel's eyes spoke volumes; he was an unopened epic she knew she could spend her whole life reading. Ankur was a Kaplan review book, a crib note to a prosaic high school textbook. She had already read through him at the previous department summer party and found him lacking.

Ankur had something in his hand, and she suppressed a laugh when she got a good view of it. "A corsage?" she blurted with a mixture of amusement and disgust. "Where's the prom?" she wanted to ask, but thought better of it. She knew her parents had already gathered at his corner and would back him in any exchange. She would have plenty of time to get him when they were alone. "How nice. You shouldn't have," she said unconvincingly.

"You could put it on," Ankur ventured. His voice was just as nasal and pinched as before. Time and maturity had done so little for his vocal cords.

"I'd rather not." Priti snatched the corsage from him. "I'll just put it in water."

In the kitchen, Priti stuffed the flowers upside down in a small glass vase then set it on the windowsill in the kitchen. She hoped her mother would get the not-so-subtle message.

She reentered the foyer, walking straight for the door, ready to get this night underway and over with.

"So where are you two going?" Mrs. Patel asked.

"You two," Priti sighed, her mother already creating the bond, the connection, their definition as a couple. After to-night there would be no "you two," it would be "you" and "that poor boy." So be it, he was no innocent child. She wished and prayed he'd opt for some small out of the way place where no one would notice her. Knowing him, he'd choose a fast-food joint near the community college, four highway exits away. That was fine with her.

Ankur, his glasses having slid down his short nasal bridge to rest on his bulbous nose, pushed them back up. "Well, gee, I'm not sure."

Mrs. Patel cut in quickly. "How about the Mediterranean place, Sarah's?"

"What?" Priti felt faint. "No, not Sarah's."

"Why not? I'm sure Ankur would love to try some Mediterranean." Mrs. Patel was ready to insist.

"But I already ate there last week." Priti crossed her arms.

"Yes, but Ankur hasn't, and you can introduce him to it."

"He doesn't like Mediterranean."

"You don't know that."

"Yes I do."

Ankur followed the volley with some trepidation, glancing back and forth from mother to daughter, and back to mother again. He looked towards Professor Patel, who had wisely stepped away from the exchange.

Ankur interjected nervously. "Ah, sure. Mediterranean sounds fine." He'd actually been hoping for the burger joint near his college, with its signature sixteen-ounce burgers (with all the fixings of course) and hot and crispy fries smothered in cheese. He'd been in withdrawal from meat since the summer began and he'd been forced to hide his carnivorous cravings from his family.

The two women turned to him suddenly, taking note of him as of for the first time, and he squirmed under their scrutiny.

"There, it's settled," Mrs. Patel said finally, ushering them out the door, Priti exiting first, Ankur second. Mrs. Patel grabbed Ankur's arm firmly as he passed her. "And please let me know how you liked it," she added, leaving Priti and Ankur no other choice.

"Are you sure you don't need a sweater, my dear?" Ankur turned to Priti, attempting a tone of concern.

She wasn't sure if the question had been meant for her parents to hear, but it rankled her anyway. "Its more than eighty degrees out, why do I need a sweater?"

"Urr, right. This way to the car." Ankur hurried, trying to save some bit of face with the parents.

A late model BMW waited at the end of the driveway, his father's gift to him at the start of college. For the Shahs, the boy was a source of pride and status, and a BMW was needed to match such status. Ankur bought into the storyline and played his part well. But Priti did not conform to her role, and it left Ankur wanting.

"I'll get that." Ankur opened the passenger car door, a haphazard wave of his free hand by way of introduction.

"Thanks," Priti replied, her voice flat and unimpressed.

Ankur raced around the back and jumped in the driver's seat. He turned the car on and revved the engine. Then, as if remembering, he turned to Priti. "You look beautiful tonight."

"Thanks."

Ankur mistook her sigh for one of enchantment and leaned in.

"What are you doing?" Priti asked, leaning back, a stiff forearm up and at the ready.

"Urr, nothing." Ankur turned in his seat and pulled the car out of the driveway and headed down the street.

Ankur found a spot right out front of the restaurant. Priti looked through the windows, slightly panicky, hoping there was such a thing as an alternate staff for the evening.

As the two headed in Ankur made to grab her elbow or some part of her arm, but found his attempt swatted away.

"Don't touch me," Priti said firmly, and in such a manner as to dissuade any future physical contact.

"Urr, ok." Ankur reached up and loosened the uncomfortably tight tie noosed around his neck.

Rachel greeted the two at the front door. "Welcome to Sarah's, make yourselves at home."

Priti smiled wanly, wishing herself invisible at the moment. Ankur pushed his glasses back up his nose. "Urr thanks.

If Rachel remembered or recognized Priti, she made no mention of it and formed no readable expression. "Sit anywhere you like. I'll be back with some menus and some water."

Priti spotted a dark corner of the restaurant and walked sharply to the table, already wishing the date and her commitment over. Ankur followed puppy dog like.

As Rachel filled up the water glasses, Sarah walked over nonchalantly. "Is that-"

"Yes, it is," Rachel responded, not turning her head, keeping her eyes trained at the couple. "But something tells me the girl's not happy about it."

She walked back to the table, setting the menus and glasses down. "I'll give you two a chance to look at the menu. Please let me know if you have any questions."

"I have a question," Ankur said, raising his hand as if in

class. "Do you have any burgers?"

Rachel raised an eyebrow. "Burgers? No, no burgers. But we do have some meat dishes that you will enjoy."

"Urr, ok." Ankur pouted slightly.

Rachel quickly glanced at Priti, and found the girl blushing madly and attempting to hide behind her opened menu. "I'll be back in a minute."

In the back she met up with Sarah. "I have one word for you: arranged."

Sarah shook her head knowingly. "The poor girl. She seems miserable."

Rachel returned to the table. "So have you two decided?"

"I'll get the lamb kabobs." Ankur closed the menu, handing it back to Rachel.

Rachel turned to Priti. "And you my dear," she spoke softly. "What would you like?"

Priti, on the verge of tears, looked up and met Rachel's eyes. Rachel gave a short quick nod of assent and understanding. "I'm, uh, I'm not hungry really."

"You must have something," Rachel pressed. "How about a salad and some soup. I'll bring the food right away."

Priti nodded back.

"This place isn't too bad." Ankur's nasal voice brought her back. "I'm not sure what kind of food this is, but the place looks nice."

Priti stared back at him, offering no response.

"Urr." Ankur reached down into his pants. "I wrote something for you."

Priti stared back. Hopefully it wasn't a poem.

"It's a poem," he announced, unwrapping a folded paper.

He cleared his throat, ready to orate.

Priti closed her eyes, already irritated.

"How do I love thee, let me count the ways."

Priti opened an eye, incredulous. "Elizabeth Barrett Browning,"

"Huh." Ankur looked up in shock.

Priti, both eyes opened and leaning forward, hissed, "That's Elizabeth Barret Browning, sonnet 43!"

Ankur looked back down, hiding between the words that lined his paper, and continued. "Love is a smoke made with the fume of sighs-"

"Shakespeare!" Priti snapped back.

"Urr. What?" Gleaming beads of sweat began to form on Ankur's forehead.

"William Shakespeare," Priti replied, enunciating clearly every syllable as if she were talking to a buffoon. "The line is from one of his most famous plays, *Romeo and Juliet.*"

Ankur looked at her in disbelief, his open mouth now dry. He looked back down at his paper as if for the first time, then back up to Priti, then back down again. Cornered now, Ankur had no option but to continue, though in his rising panic his voice became reduced to that of an automaton, devoid of emotion and verve, as if he were reading the latest market data from the *New York Times* Business section. "You given me the pleasure of your eyes, face, flesh as we pass, you take my beard, breast, hands, in return-"

Priti shook her head slowly, clucking her tongue. "Walt Whitman, 'To A Stranger'." She sighed loudly to further his embarrassment.

Ankur brought his napkin to his now sweaty brow. He was deep in his self-made hole, but finding no way back out he kept digging. "And it's you are whatever a moon as always meant and whatever a sun will always sing is you-"

"E.E. Cummings, 'I Carry Your Heart With Me'." Priti had begun to pity Ankur, this short, fat, prematurely balding homunculus who'd most likely been cheated by some acquaintance with an English Major for this mishmash of famous poems. She was sure he had paid money, too much money.

Ankur continued reading, for no other reason than to test Priti's impressive knowledge base. It became almost a game for him. "If equal affection cannot be, let the more loving one be me."

"W.H. Auden- Ankur stop, just stop."

"Urr." Ankur raised a feeble hand, desperate for one last chance. "Take my hand, take my whole life too."

"Elvis Presley?" Priti did a double-take, as if she'd been slapped; from the sublime to the ridiculous, actually from the ridiculous to the more ridiculous. "Are you serious? Elvis Presley?"

Ankur's head bent forward sheepishly; he felt nauseous. He folded up "his" poem and tucked it back into the inside pocket of his blazer, wishing himself transported (á la Star Trek) to safety. Still he had to hand it to her, she knew her poetry. Somewhere out there was a game show she'd be able to crush. But for now he awaited punishment as Priti's eyes settled back into their sockets. Her mouth worked through pout and grimace as her mind worked out the scathing rebuke he'd earned.

"I don't know which is worse, your intention to deceive me, or that you thought I was too ignorant and stupid to recognize even one of the famous lines you dumped together into your poem. In any case, Ankur, you've shown me that you're nothing more than a fraud. The little respect I previously had for you is-"

Rachel brought a tray of food and drinks, setting their meals quickly and quietly as she caught bits of Priti's impressive tirade against her dinner date.

"- gone. Actually you're worse than a fraud, you're an unimaginative, uncreative fraud, picking some of the most popular lines in literature. If you're going to plagiarize other people's poetry, why not choose those from an Indian poet? At least that would have impressed me. You could have quoted 'Unending Love' by Rabindrath Tagore, or 'The Piet's Love-Song' by Saronjini Naidu." Ankur saw the feast before his eyes and Priti's voice receded into a background, droning hum as he began tearing into the lamb kabobs. He looked up several times, nodding in agreement to the lost thread of her argument. He was very good at feigning interest, one of his many fortes. It was only when he caught Priti's wide-eyed exasperation that he knew he had missed something. He paused mid-nod. "What?"

"I said, don't you have anything to say for yourself?"

"Urrr. This food is delicious. I'm so glad you chose this place. I'll be sure to tell your mom."

Priti's eyes fluttered behind closed lids. Her head ached. She wished so much to be done with this date.

Now it was Ankur's turn to drone on and on. But Priti had already tuned out, thinking only of the next time she would see Gabriel. She wondered if she should even tell him about this fiasco. Perhaps they would laugh about it.

When the check finally came, Priti breathed a sigh of relief; the end was near.

"Come back soon." Rachel forced a smile.

"Thanks," Ankur replied cheerfully, his belly nice and full. "I will."

Priti could only nod, mortified.

Outside the restaurant the sun hung low and red in the sky and evening had set in. Ankur turned to Priti, moved by the romance of the moment. "I had a great time."

"You're joking."

"What are you doing next week?"

"None of your business."

"I could take you to a nice burger joint I know."

"I don't want to see you again."

"Shall I drive you home?"

"Please."

So engaged was Priti in this exchange that she failed to see Achilles's car at the corner, across the avenue.

Achilles, Gabriel and Johnny sat silently as the car idled at the green light, their faces partly hidden in shadows. Gabriel took a long meditative drag off his cigarette. He let his hand fall outside the front passenger side window, cupping the remainder as a breeze lapped at the smoke winding upward.

Johnny's voice harped from the backseat. "That's what you get when you don't close the deal. G. Some other guy gets a turn."

"Shut the fuck up." Achilles turned around, fist cocked.

Johnny's arms shot up in a feeble defense. "Hey man, I was just saying-"

"Yeah, I know you're always just saying, saying some bone-headed thing." Achilles turned forward, glancing sideways at Gabriel. "What do you want to do?"

Gabriel nodded to Ankur's BMW as it pulled away. "Follow them."

They kept fifty yards behind, enough to avoid suspicion. They parked along the side street, in full view of Priti's house as Ankur raced around the car to open Priti's door, but she was already out and storming back to her house.

"Wait, wait," he called after her as he ran up the walk to the front door.

Priti turned around, scowling at him, making each word to him distinct and final. "What. Do. You. Want?" It was more of a challenge than a question.

Here Ankur, deluded as he was to the success of the evening, leaned in for a kiss. Priti leaned her taller body back and away, causing him to stumble forward and he collided with her stiff forearm.

"Good night, Ankur, and good bye," Priti said with finality. "Don't come back here, or I will let everyone know about your fraudulent 'poem'."

In the car Achilles turned to Gabriel. "You saw that, right?"

Gabriel gave an imperceptible nod. "Yeah, I saw it. Let's get out of here."

2 9

*A*nd coming in at number 1, The Police with "Every Breath You Take." We are 92.3 K-ROCK, your home for the latest hits.

"Oh that's horrible, just horrible. Please let me know if I can do anything."

Priti walked in at the tail end of her mother's telephone conversation. Her mother cupped the mouthpiece for a quick kiss to Priti's cheek, mouthing the words 'good morning'. "Okay, okay, I understand. Let us know any updates." Mrs. Patel hung up the phone clucking her tongue and shaking her head. "Horrible, just horrible."

The kitchen was awash in midmorning sunlight that burned through the three large windows.

Priti poured cereal into her bowl and checked on the tea kettle heating up on the stove. "What's horrible, Mother?"

Mrs. Patel shot her daughter a quick, calculating glance, as if wondering how much she should reveal. She sat down with a dramatic sigh, deciding it would be too difficult to withhold information for too long anyway. "Remember Ankur, whom you went on that date with Saturday night?"

Priti sat down next to her. "Yes, I do remember," she replied, quickly adding, "but I would not call it a date."

Mrs. Patel waved away her daughter's last comment like an annoying gnat. "Well that poor boy was beaten up last night."

Priti's spoon clattered noisily in the bowl as the kettle whistled. Mrs. Patel rushed to the stove and turned off the burner. Distracted by the whistle, she did not register the competing emotions on her daughter's face.

"Is he okay?" Priti asked.

Mrs. Patel poured the steaming water into the teapot; the tea leaves swirled and danced. "No broken bones or internal injuries, thanks to God, but he is in quite a bit of pain. Thankfully, the doctor has informed his parents that all of this will heal with time. Priti, are you okay?" Her mother examined her with a look of concern.

Priti's face had turned the color of her mother's china. She felt the kitchen whirling around her. "Yes, I'm okay." She shut her eyes tightly. "I'm just shaken up about the news."

Her mother draped her arm around her. "I know. I know it's terrible isn't it. But I did not tell you the worst part."

Priti opened her eyes wide. "There's worse? What could be worse?"

"The worst part." Mrs. Patel shook her head and clucked in dismay and disgust before turning to her daughter. "The worst part of it is that he was attacked coming home from a hamburger restaurant." Mrs. Patel's eyes welled up with tears in the recounting. "Imagine, all this time and their son was eating meat. I can't believe I let your father convince me to allow you to go out to eat with that, that- Priti, where are you going?"

Priti raced up the steps, calling over her shoulder, "I have to run to the library, Mother. I just remembered I have a practice exam at the end of the week I have to study for."

"But you haven't finished your breakfast." Mrs. Patel looked down at her daughter's bowl and tea, unsure what to do.

Priti rushed back in to the kitchen, backpack draped over one shoulder. She drank her tea in three throat blistering swallows and kissed her mother on the cheek. "I'll grab something on the way."

"It's just as well. I probably should go over to the Shah's house and pay my respects." She cast Priti a right eyebrow

♦ 188 ♦

arched high above a look of displeasure. "Imagine. The shame of it all."

Priti sat with her books at one of the long row of tables in the center of the library, where she would be in full view. She waited for Gabriel to stop by, making frequent inquiries with the wall clock- nine o'clock, nine thirty, ten o'clock, ten thirty- glancing towards the front door each time it opened, listening for the book cart... There was so much she wanted to ask but so much she did not want to know. Why did she ever agree to going with Ankur? She bit her lip at the idea of Gabriel spotting her with him. Still, he had to know there was nothing going on between the two of them. And she could not believe he was involved. She did not want to believe it. After several hours of staring at the same page, Priti stood up and walked to the librarian.

"You are looking for Gabriel?" The librarian pressed her glasses close to her face, magnifying her eyes to size of one-dollar coins. She appeared very much a wizened owl.

"No, I mean yes." Priti wondered how much the elderly woman who seemed to know everything actually knew. "Is he here?"

The woman smiled. "He's due any moment. He took the morning off- oh here he is." Both women turned to the half open door as Gabriel walked in, white button-down shirt, blue jeans. He looked at both women then paused for an imperceptible moment. He turned around and shut the door gently before turning to face them, the confusion inside him visible to no one. "Hi," he said to the space between them.

"Hello Gabriel." The librarian spoke first, recognizing the tense thread between the two teenagers, and the need to loosen it. "Did you have a restful morning?"

Gabriel bowed slightly. "Yes, thank you for letting me sleep in." He then turned to Priti. "Hi."

"Hi," Priti responded, her mind blank of all that had spiraled around it that morning and, for once, at a loss for more words.

Gabriel bowed slightly again. "I should probably get to work." He walked to the back, leaving the two women to decipher his retreat. Priti lifted her backpack and walked back to her table to gather her books.

In the back, Gabriel heard the front door shut and he peeked from behind a bookcase over to the row of tables to find Priti gone. He fought the impulse to search the library for her. He knew she'd shown up just for him, and then left when he'd not reciprocated the thought. He looked back to the book in his hand and shoved it roughly back onto the shelf. A sudden anger seized him and he looked hard at the bookcase in front of him. All it would take was a good hard kick and he'd knock it down against the next bookcase, and the next, and they'd all fall down like dominoes. Instead he gripped the book cart tightly and closed his eyes until the violent urge passed. Then he resumed his walk up and down the aisle, filing the rest of the books from his cart.

He took long strides from the library as the mid-summer sun sank westward, the sky a palette of pink and orange hues. He sank his hand and wrist into his front pockets and tucked his head in avoiding eye contact with others along the main road. Two blocks behind him, Priti jogged to keep up with his pace, ready to conceal herself in case he turned around. But he never did, and after about ten blocks she realized he was lost in his head and would never even guess he was being followed. By the time they made it to Great Hope Road the sun had set and the night had settled in, making it harder for her to track him. It was on Great Hope Road that she saw him duck into a wooded area and disappear from view. She ran to and hid behind a large tree at the edge of the woods. She spied his dark shadow scale the top of the hill and disappear again. She made her way up the hill, tripping a few times on the uneven surface, at one point falling down on her face and scratching her arms. She stood upright, brushing away the dry leaves and pine needles, and made it to the top of the hill. She took a deep breath and began walking to the small, unlit house in front of her. In the pale moonlight, she guessed the vague outline of the open door leading to a darker shade of black within. She stepped closer, looking to either side, Gabriel was nowhere in sight. She heard the hard-edged guitar opening to Billy Squire's "Lonely is the Night" rattling from a radio inside. Her heart began beating frantically in her chest and a voice inside warned her to run back. She tiptoed up the three steps to the front door, making as little sound as possible. She hesitated, knowing the time for turning back was now. When she reached for the knob a large hand reached out and grabbed her, pulling her inside. She gasped as she was pushed up against the wall. A strong heavy arm pressed against her chest. His face was close to hers. "What are you doing here?" he asked.

Priti was near panic. "I, I, I. Gabriel?"

The arm on her chest suddenly relaxed, as did the grip on her arm and the man stepped back. "Priti?" A spark of flint and the teardrop of candlelight chased away the shadows as Gabriel stepped back from a small coffee table, lighter in hand. Seeing him made all her fears vanish. "What are you doing here?" he said again as he walked up to her. "You're hurt." He reached out to touch the scratch on her neck. Priti reflexively brought her hand to her neck and her fingers found his.

The two stood silently, their hands touching, both unwilling to let go of this touch.

"I came to talk to you." She stepped forward into the light.

"To me? Why- oh Priti you're scratched all over the place." Gabriel grabbed each of her arms, gentler now, inspecting them for the many bruises she'd collected.

Priti continued talking, not wanting to lose her train of

thought. "I wanted to talk to you about this past weekend. You must believe me, I was going to tell you- it was not my idea- never- my mother- she made me go out with Ankur-" Priti's began to cry. "He means nothing to me- absolutely nothing."

Gabriel saw her tears and brushed them off her cheeks with his thumb. She grabbed his hand. "But you didn't have to hurt him."

Gabriel yanked his hand away. "What?"

"I don't know why you did it, Gabriel."

"Did what? I did nothing to him." Gabriel walked to his pack of cigarettes resting on the coffee table next to the candle and pulled one out, lighting it.

"If you didn't, then who did? One of your friends? Did you have them do it?"

Gabriel wheeled around, pointing his two fingers with the lit cigarette at her. "I did no such thing and I would give no such order. I saw you didn't like him, that there was nothing between the two of you and that was enough for me to walk away."

"Then who did?"

"I don't know, but I can tell you this much, if one of my guys did this then it was not under my orders."

"How can I believe you, Gabriel?" Priti pressed on, hoping to hear something real that she could hang on to. She was ready to believe anything, she just wanted to hear him say it.

Gabriel stepped back from her taking a long pull off his cigarette as he narrowed his eyes. He walked to the doorway, exhaling a plume of smoke into the night, then he ground his cigarette into the doorframe and flicked his butt outside. He turned around and in two quick steps was next to Priti, grabbing her by the arm, pulling her to him. "Why are you really here? Are you here to play games with me?"

"No Gabriel. I-"

Gabriel pushed Priti up against the wall, kissing her hard.

Priti turned her head, breaking the kiss. "Gabriel, please, wait."

But there was no time for waiting. He had run out of patience a long time ago. There was chemistry, there was compatibility, not to mention love at first sight. No. No time to wait. You can flip through only so many pages of *Penthouse* and *Hustler*- hot young women in suggestive poses pouting coquettishly at you- not to mention all the physical and emotional manipulations by the infamous Lisa - before your patience runs out.

"Gabriel, I need to tell you-"

But Gabriel had enough of words. Words meant nothing to him. They were but crude inadequate representations of that which went on inside his heart and mind. Gabriel reached under her shirt and pressed his hand over her bra.

Priti gasped at the touch. "Please Gabriel, wait."

Gabriel kissed her hard again as he fondled her breast through the cotton fabric. He released her breast and reached his arm around her waist to draw her body into his. His hand reached the small of her back and his fingertips slid up her taut skin, yet before he could reach the clasp of her bra his fingertips brushed up against a rough fibrous ridge of puckered flesh.

Priti slumped forward against him and wept.

Gabriel deciphered the braille on her back, his fingers reading Priti in a way that his eyes had missed completely. It was the first of a series of linear and crisscrossed markings up and down her back. And he brushed his fingers, now soft and gentle across her scars, unearthing a long buried secret.

"I'm sorry, I'm so sorry," she cried.

The two slid down to the floor to sit, Gabriel's back against the wall with Priti weeping like a child in his embrace.

"I'm sorry, I'm so sorry, I'm sorry..."

3 0

June 1972

"**I**'m sorry Mayaphoi, I'm sorry Mayaphoi!" Priti's cries filtered from behind the slatted closet doors. She knelt on the floor, trembling among the forest of her aunt Maya's hanging Saris.

But the words did nothing to cool her aunt's rage, and the doors shook violently, rattling the doorframe. "Why you worthless child! When I get my hands on you, you will wish you had never come here. Now open this door! Open this door!" Maya became more and more enraged with each passing moment, each violent tug at the closet handles. And again she looked up to the ceiling and made her case to god, how his poor, devoted servant who had given so much and who had asked for so little in this life should not have had to suffer so many injustices. "I ask her to do one thing! One thing! And this ungrateful monkey-" Turning to the door Maya shrieked, "You ruined my beautiful new sari! Now open this door!" The door shook with renewed vigor, as Maya let loose a tight chain of insults and curses.

Priti kept her eyes closed, trying to shut out the present, mouthing a silent prayer her grandmother, Shanti, had taught her six months before, the year her parents had left for America. Even now the prayer brought her back to that time, filled with changes and promises of a new life for the family.

"It will only be for a few months," her mother had promised her as she had dried Priti's tears. "Once we have the house perfect, we will come back for you."

"But I don't need the house, I need you," Priti had challenged, already showing signs of her strong will, one that had worried her mother.

Mrs. Patel had thumbed tears from Priti's cheek, even as she had suppressed her own. "The time will fly, and we will be back for you before you know it. Now just listen to Mayaphoi. She has been gracious enough to take responsibility for you."

Maya had silently observed the exchange, a sliver of a smile pasted on her face, betraying little of the resentment over the responsibility that had been thrust upon her. She too had not believed the timeframe promised to her young niece. She had known her brother and his pregnant wife would take their sweet time to come back for the girl, and the rupees left to her would not come close to covering the cost of this added burden. Never mind she and her husband were childless and had rooms to spare, never mind his good position at the company and their comfortable lives. A burden is a burden, and she could tell this six-year-old girl was going to be difficult to tame, let alone train.

Seeing her granddaughter had been inadequately consoled, Shanti had knelt down and had taken Priti into her arms. "Remember the prayer I taught you," she had whispered into her granddaughter's ear, "and if I can, I will come to take you for a week to my house very soon." Shanti had hugged her granddaughter tightly, as if in response to an omen's sudden whisper, suddenly fearful of the future. As much she had disagreed with the decision her daughter and son-in-law had made, she had known better than to speak out about it now. It had been much too late. Had Shanti known what the future would bring, she would have fought for custody of her granddaughter until her parents had been ready for Priti in the States.

No one had thought about whether Priti and Maya would get along. There were no other options anyway. Mr. (not yet

Professor) Patel was going to be working full time and attend-
ing graduate school, and Mrs. Patel, now three months pregnant, did not have the strength to manage a new home, care
for her husband's needs, stay well for her pregnancy and care
for their daughter. "Maya will be strict with Priti, but nothing
more," Mr. Patel had reassured his wife. And Mrs. Patel had
so much wanted to believe this lie that she had not questioned
the matter further.

Had there been a telephone in Mayaphoi's house Priti
would have been able to report the increasingly hostile and
abusive treatment she was subjected to, and she would have
asked- no, pleaded - to go to them. But back then there had
been no phones, only rumors. And rumors have a way of
spreading; a dark foul liquid that trickled out from the cracks
in the foundation to the Ambawadi neighborhood outside,
exiting through the many gates of Ahmedabad and winding
its way to the various members of the extended family who
still got together for the holy days. True, Maya's kindness rang
false and hollow, especially at the feasts and festivities during her younger brother and sister-in-law's weeklong wedding
celebration seven years before. But that didn't make her a
monster. And who could really trust rumors? Not that anyone
had had the time or energy or inclination to investigate these.
The roads were terrible, fatal accidents happened all the time,
as did thefts and murders by bandits, and even the bus drivers
themselves. Had there been a phone, calls would have been
placed, inquiries into the young girl's welfare, and then what?
Who would take care of her then? And what child did not deserve a good spanking every now and again? No use troubling
the Patels. They were having their own problems, what with
the mother miscarrying several months after their arrival to
the US; the poor dear needed time to mend. And he was sol-
diering on, trying to build a future for the whole family. They
would come back to her soon enough. But Shanti, always the
quiet one, worried, even before the rumors, and she gripped

her sari tightly with bony fingers, wrapping it tightly around her head, shielding her from the sudden cold, as she recited another prayer for her young granddaughter.

"Open this door, by God, or it will be worse for you!" Now the violently rattling doorframe was accompanied by the violent rapping of the wood by Maya's wire hangers. Priti was used to this sound, it was a harbinger of the beating to come.

At first there had been just the words, insults, threats. These had come in response to the kind of mistakes that in another household would have been perceived as innocuous, the honest shortcomings of a child still mastering dexterity: spilled milk on the floor, crumbs on her seat, not making the bed properly.

"Yes auntie, no auntie, sorry auntie..." Priti had strived to improve, but mistakes still happened. That perfection had not been achieved had been inevitable, though the first tight slap to the face two months into Priti's stay had been, in hindsight, also inevitable. Priti had run from the kitchen that first time, hand held to her cheek, straight to the protective arms of her uncle, who had murmured tender words of consolation that proved to be inadequate. And given his congenital lack of a backbone, Rameshphua had soon proven a poor defense to Mayaphoi's assaults. Not that Rameshphua had avoided soothing his niece; in fact, he had been very good at soothing. A born soother, and he had especially liked to soothe his niece, to have her sit on his lap while she had clung to him and her tears had moistened his shirt. And during these embraces his hands had taken on a life of their own, caressing, then caressing some more. Did his wife suspect him of these soothing sessions? Perhaps these were what fed her rage. With each successive beating he became more and more adventurous in his soothing. Caressing, but also poking, prodding, fondling. Even young Priti knew enough to tell the difference between the different touches and soon she sought out other hiding spots within the confines of the Mehta household: the attic, behind the Neem bush in the garden, any of the dozen closets on the three floors of their home, under the bed. Yet one by one these hiding spots were smoked out, forcing the physical confrontations that she came to fear.

Despite the mistakes and resultant beatings, Maya imposed an increasing number of chores and responsibilities on Priti's shoulders. Priti was forced to wake up early so that she could attend to some of these chores before school, stay inside all afternoon to attend to them after school, and then stay up late into the evening. Kesar, who worked for the Mehtas, took pity on the poor girl and helped when she could, when her mistresses prying eyes were focused elsewhere. She prepared the little girl snacks to help keep her strength and spirits up, and when welts cropped up she applied a homemade salve to heal them. But there was no salve for Kesar's own heart when the beatings took place, and the girl's cries and shrieks pierced through the walls, reverberating inside her head, and Kesar, hands pressed tightly to her ears to muffle the sounds, prayed to Lord Krishna that someone would come to save the poor girl.

The light filtering through the slats had faded to a soft blue and the suffocating heat from earlier in the day had cooled somewhat, Priti guessed that it was early evening. Maya had long since abandoned the closet doors and Priti could hear her downstairs in the kitchen berating the servant. Priti emerged from the protection of her aunt's hanging saris and tiptoed quietly to the closet door. Despite the dark she could make out the piece of wood that she had jammed between the two inner doorknobs, preventing the doors from being pulled open from the outside. She took a deep breath and slowly, quietly, lifted it, placing it on the floor beside her. She pushed open both doors and peeked out into the dark expanse of her aunt and uncle's bedroom. No one. She closed the closet doors and tiptoed to the hallway. She trained her ears for the slightest of sounds. She picked out the cacophony of traffic from the street out front, the crickets from the garden in the back, but nothing inside the house. All was stiflingly quiet. She took another deep breath and stepped out into the hallway. Looking left and right she made her way to the banister of the stairs leading down to the first floor. As she peered over the railing to look down, a large hand shot out and seized her by the wrist.

"No Uncle, no," she whispered, shrinking back.

But his grip was too strong and Priti found herself tugged down the stairs. Only once did her uncle turn to look at her, a sad smile beneath pained eyes. He had the look of one who had given up fighting and had resolved to survive according to the dictates of another. At the bottom of the stairs, Priti fell and Rameshphua was forced to drag her, fruitlessly clawing away at the stone floors, down the long hallway to the kitchen in the back.

Two incandescent ceiling bulbs burned brightly above them, reflecting a timeless white glare off the walls and checkered tile floors. Priti used her free hand to cover her eyes.

"Open your eyes," her aunt barked.

Priti peered through slightly opened fingers at her aunt seated at the kitchen table; several wire hangers at arms reach. "I'm sorry Mayaphoi, I won't -"

"Silence!" Maya rose to stand, towering above her niece. She grabbed the hangers next to her, brandishing them in front of Priti's face. Her voice began as a low growl, slow and purposeful, but as always with Maya's pre-beating monologues it rose in tempo and pitch as she worked herself into a frenzied fit. "The time for excuses is over. You had your chance and you decided to hide like a dog. I took you in as a favor to my weak-willed, dim-witted younger brother, who obviously spent the first six years of your life spoiling you. We do so much for you and ask for little in return and you cannot even dedicate an ounce of effort to doing your fair share. Although I cannot fully blame you for the first six years, I can blame you for the last six months. I cannot put up with your insolence any longer. I have been too soft, and you have taken advantage of my fairness and good nature. It seems you do not understand anything but a good beating."

"No Mayaphoi! Please."

"Silence!" Maya looked over at her husband, himself looking down at the floor wordlessly. She nodded. "Ramesh."

"Yes dear," he responded with a servile smile full of bright, small teeth.

"Turn her around and hold her. This," Maya said, waving the metal hangers, "is for your own good."

Ramesh did as he was told. He held his niece's wrists firmly, while his wife raised her right hand above her shoulders, gripping the hangers (which would be the only thing Priti would ever remember her aunt by).

Priti peered into her uncle's eyes, trying to find some meaning to this act through him. But he blushed and averted her gaze.

The first strike of metal against her flesh caught Priti off guard and she yelped, not so much from pain as from the surprise. The second yelp was from pain. And as the strikes rained down on her back her yelps became pleas and then cries and then quiet sobs.

Maya soon become flushed and short of breath, not used to this degree of exertion. Beads of sweat crowned her scalp and dripped down her face, staining her sari.

Feeling his niece become heavy now in his hands Ramesh cried out to his wife, "Stop, stop," less worried of her temper now than of a certain irreversible threshold of abuse that they were fast approaching.

Maya paused, hangers above her head. After a moment she dropped them to the table. "Get Kesar."

Ramesh released his niece and she drooped limply to the floor. Blood from her many open wounds began to seep through and coalesce into a grotesque Rorschach inkblot.

Maya caught her breath and turned to the stove, lighting a gas burner. She put the teakettle on and set about to fix some chai.

Kesar ran into the kitchen and gasped as she saw Priti on the floor, the little girl's shirt splattered with blood. She had stooped over the little girl and had gathered her up carefully, as if she were a fragile doll. She whispered soft comforting words into Priti's ear, all the while her eyes wide with horror and lips trembling with fury. She turned to Maya and met her heavy-lidded gaze with an accusing glance, but said nothing; Maya was, in fact, her employer. Kesar knew her place and so she tempered her rage.

"The girl fell down and scraped her back," Maya replied offhandedly. "You'll need to get some gauze and antiseptic."

"I'll take her to my quarters," Kesar offered, her eyes beseeching. "I have everything I need there. I'll keep her safe until she is better."

Maya's lips twisted into a question at the implications of 'safe'. "Okay, but clean this mess up now. I don't want my floors stained," she said, nodding at the blood-stained floor.

The servant quickly brought Priti to her bed and laid her face down. "I'll be right back, Chaukree." She went back to the kitchen and mopped up the evidence, shaking her head in a silent rebuke to her employer.

Kesar then hurried back to her room and set about cleaning the young girl's wounds. She slowly removed the shirt, choking back a gasp at the bruises, and tossed Priti's clothes into the sink. She wet a clean cloth in lukewarm water, and as she wept, gently dabbed at the little girl's skin. Priti lay flat unmoving, and more than once Kesar put a hand to her nose to reassure herself of the child's breathing. She mixed camphor and ghee and soaked separate sheets of gauze; these she slowly and painstakingly applied to the girl's wounds, taking care not to press too hard and exacerbate the pain. Priti slept fitfully from the pain that first night, whimpering in her sleep, all the while Kesar applied cool compresses to her hot fore-head and whispered soothing prayers to lull the child back to sleep. She repeated the dressing changes hourly until the bleeding ceased. And when she was able to, the old servant wept some more.

The servant kept the child in her room for several days, making changes to the bandages as needed, spoon feeding kichidee, daal, and watered down chai which she brought from the kitchen when Maya and Ramesh were in another part of the house, and when possible she bought sweets and ice cream to boost the child's spirits. Slowly Priti's physical wounds improved.

Within a week she was able to sit up in bed and take a few steps to the bathroom, where Kesar would hold her as she went.

The servant briefed Maya daily as to the progress of the little girl's condition. Maya listened quietly, sipping her morn-ing tea. Kesar knew her mistress' patience would soon run out, and so she offered a mixed record of the child's convalescence, describing the minutest improvements, but also providing de-tailed setbacks and derailments. Each night, after she applied the salve to the healing welts on Priti's back, Kesar prayed to the statue of baby Krishna on her dresser that some form of salvation would arrive for the young girl.

One could argue that there was.

Tired of the rumors coming out of Ahmedabad, or perhaps due to her fear that there may have been some truth to them, Shanti ended her prayers early one Friday evening and pulled out her small valise from the top shelf of her closet, next to the boxes of well-kept dresses and saris she had not warn in years. She set the valise on the floor next to her bed and knelt beside it in contemplation. She blew a fine layer of dust off the brown leather, undid the two metal clasps and opened it up. She then turned to her dresser for what she would need. It would be an eight-hour train ride from Bombay to Ahmedabad. She would most likely spend the night and then take the train back the following morning. She'd confirmed the train schedule the week before when travelling had been a small, impatient seed in her mind. After she re-clasped the valise and set it by the door, she went to bed. She slept poorly that night. It had been years since she had left her neighborhood. She'd given no thought to travel after her husband died. Still, she'd been on plenty of trains in her life and had travelled as far as Delhi with her husband on his many business trips. His company had a branch in downtown Ahmedabad. In fact, Ramesh and his surly wife Maya, owed his current position and their comfortable lifestyle to her late husband. Despite his ignorance of import and export, Ramesh had been offered a mid-level position in the company as a family favor. And though it was never mentioned, it was a card Shanti had kept hidden in her sleeve, and she had no qualms about exposing it if she needed to.

The next day she nibbled on a small breakfast of buttered toast and tea, having no stomach for anything more. She packed a few Rotlis, pakoras and sweets for the trip. She had her young driver take her to Victoria Station soon after breakfast, and had made sure he would not breathe a word of this to anyone. "Don't worry, I'll be back tomorrow night," she replied to his many protests of concern about such an unprecedented trip for a woman, at her age, and alone.

Once on the train her many concerns and fears dissipated. She settled into her seat and looked out the window. Action for her had always been better than inaction. And she missed her granddaughter terribly. The countryside blurred on either side as she kept her focus ahead to the confrontation to come. Despite the heat of summer, the breeze from the windows was cool enough and her fellow travelers seemed friendly and respectful. Each one had some bit of food or beverage that they were willing to share and soon enough a small feast developed and Shanti felt obliged to pull out her tiffins and pass around some of her pakoras and rotlis.

After lunch on the train she set her focus again on the beautiful countryside, and it brought back memories of similar visions years ago, when India had seemed as young as she was, and full of promise. So lost in thought she, that it was only by chance she turned away from the window a moment and found an ancient, slightly disheveled man, supporting his kyphotic frame on a small wooden cane. "Excuse me?" she asked.

"Any money would be appreciated. Food would be even more appreciated."

Shanti reached into her bag and pulled out a tightly wrapped cloth filled with sweet almond cookies.

She placed three large pieces into the beggar's cupped palms.

He bowed deeply in response. "Thank you, thank you, a thousand blessings to you. May your travels be fruitful." Then he backed away, hands together in prayer.

Shanti smiled and nodded politely.

He was but one of a string of vagabonds, minstrels, and trinket sellers that paraded through her car. She had forgotten about this aspect of train travel. But whereas she previously had complained about the many ne'er do wells in her life, she welcomed their interruptions now. She was anxious about the task in front of her, not so much the confrontation with Maya as with taking on the full responsibility for her granddaughter. It had been decades since she had raised her children, and she did not know how much strength she'd have now for it.

She rapped her bony knuckles on the door as the rickshaw driver sped away. She gripped her valise tightly as she heard approaching steps inside the house.

"Shanti? What a surprise," Maya said through a tight-lipped smile.

"Maya, it's been too long, how are you? Are you going to invite me in?" Shanti had rehearsed all her lines a hundred times on the train ride over. She knew that leaving Maya little time to accommodate her thoughts was the best attack. And she left nothing to chance. Better keep the questions going, forcing the other woman to occupy herself with answers.

Maya stepped to the side and allowed the older woman through the door into the foyer. "Shanti, it's so good of you to come. Such a shame we had no idea of your visit, otherwise we would have been better prepared to receive you."

"No need to worry yourself," Shanti replied frankly as she looked around, taking in the living room and dining room. "I'm really here for a short visit. Priti is at school I assume?"

"Er, yes, she is," Maya said. "But we can have some tea and wait for her to return, she should be here within the hour." Maya stood up and walked to the stove, lighting one of the burners.

"Good. That will give me some time to talk to you about my plans for her."

"Your plans?" Maya asked as she set the kettle on the stove lighting the match.

"Yes, my plans. I've decided to take Priti back to stay with me."

"You've decided?" Maya whipped around as if challenging, before correcting herself under the old woman's hard stare.

Shanti was unmoved. "Correct. I believe the burden of raising Priti should be shared amongst relatives."

"But it's been no problem."

Shanti raised a hand. "I know you and Ramesh have done an exceptional job, and I'm sure Priti is all the richer for her time here. But now it's time for her to come with me."

Maya poured the boiling water into the teapot. "The money given to me-"

"Stays with you," Shanti replied, having already read her thoughts. "I have no interest in your brother's money, that is yours to keep. My focus is the girl," she had said firmly.

And the two women sat quietly drinking their tea in the late afternoon heat as an understanding unfolded between them.

The door to the kitchen opened and Kesar walked in followed by Priti.

"Nani!" Priti cried, immersing herself in her grandmother's embrace.

"My dear sweet girl," Shanti replied, planting a soft kiss on Prit's head. "I've missed you so much."

"I missed you too, Nani." Still within the protection of her grandmother's embrace, Priti turned around to Maya with a change in her voice, a muted timbre that was lost on her grandmother. "Good afternoon Mayaphoi," she said mechanically, eyes averted.

"Good afternoon child," Maya replied.

"Priti," Kesar scolded, "let your auntie and grandmother drink their tea in peace. Come, let's get you changed out of your school clothes and I'll get you a snack."

Priti huddled into the protective folds of her grandmother's sari once more before hurrying out of the kitchen.

Maya took a sip from her teacup. "When were you planning on leav- I mean, I hope you plan to stay with us a while."

"First thing after breakfast tomorrow."

Maya nodded, smiling. "I'll have Kesar prepare the guest bedroom."

Shanti stood up suddenly, tired of wasting so many breaths with Maya. "Thank you, Maya, for your hospitality. But now I must take my leave and inform Priti about the change in plans. No need to get up, I'm sure I can find them," Shanti added with a dismissive wave of her hand, and left as the younger woman hurled a silent string of curses at her.

Shanti came upon Kesar and Priti in Kesar's quarters, sitting on the single bed. A small fan whirled frantic gusts of hot air around the room. As Priti drank her milky tea and ate her almond sweets, Kesar applied the daily salve to the child's scars. The angry red had given way to faint cocoa colored strips of raised flesh, darker than the surrounding skin.

The older woman's gasp broke the meditative silence of

the room, and the two turned to her fearfully. Kesar quickly dressed Priti with a bright flowery summer dress, covering the wounds.

But Shanti quickly recovered her bearings, and just as quickly recognized so many things in this one explosive jigsaw of a moment: the need to remain calm for the girl's sake (despite so much boiling inside her), that Kesar had obviously been the child's guardian angel throughout this time, and that she had done the right thing in coming to Ahmedabad to take back her granddaughter.

Priti looked up, a precocious mixture of shame and sadness colored her face in the late afternoon light that peeked in through the small window of Kesar's room.

Shanti approached Priti, her eyes locked with the girl's, all the while resisting the urge to gaze upon her back, marbled with disfigurement. She sat down on the one small chair in the room and positioned herself in front of Priti. Taking the young girl's hands in her own, she spoke softly, "Dear Priti." She suppressed a sudden sob in her chest. "Dear Priti, I- I'm sorry, I just came by to see how you are doing. Did you have a good day at school?"

The little girl nodded quietly as she bit into another almond cookie.

"Do you like the snack and tea that Kesar prepared for you?"

The little girl nodded again.

"You like Kesar, right? I am sure she is treating you well." Shanti looked over at Kesar, whose downcast eyes revealed much more than what she would have been allowed to speak.

"My dear Priti." Shanti smiled lovingly at her granddaughter. "I have a surprise for you."

The little girl looked up and met her gaze with eyes that seemed far older than those she had gazed into six months before. The girl had aged so quickly, it made Shanti want to cry.

"How would you like to come back and live with me in

Ahmedabad? That is to say, of course, until your mama and daddy are ready for you to join them. Would you like that?"

The little girl turned back to Kesar, not so much for permission but in a silent goodbye to the only person she would miss from this short painful chapter in her life. The old servant nodded in assent. Then Priti dove into her grandmother's arms, lest she rescind the invitation. And as the little girl nuzzled into the folds of Shanti's sari, the grandmother shut her eyes tightly to fight off the tears.

Kesar, crying, got down on her knees and kissed the old woman's feet. "Thank you, thank you, thank you."

"That's enough." Shanti patted Kesar's shoulder with a free hand. "Up now, up, up." She looked into the other woman's tear streaked face. "I need you to pack the girl's bags and prepare some food for our travel tomorrow. We are leaving bright and early so I want no more delays."

Kesar stood up as if possessed and hurried out of the room to carry out the old woman's orders.

"Nani?" the girl whimpered within the folds of her grandmother's sari. Shanti held her granddaughter in front of her. "Did I do something wrong?" she asked meekly.

Shanti, startled at the question, shook her head emphatically. "No, no, no. How could you possibly think that?" Children are so forgiving of the wrongs done to them. She longed to take her granddaughter in her arms and undo the last six months. "Don't ever think that you did something wrong." She brushed a wayward strand of hair from Priti's face and smiled. "I just missed you and want you to be with me. Would you like that?"

Priti nodded briskly.

Shanti caressed her granddaughter's face. "Good. I'm sure Kesar," she said, nodding to the empty hallway, "will get everything packed for our trip tomorrow." Shanti leaned in and whispered conspiratorially, "And tonight you sleep with me."

"But Mayaphoi-"

Shanti stood up straight and tall and right then and there she seemed years younger and stronger. "You don't need to worry about Mayaphoi anymore. Now go your room and help Kesar pack your things and I will see you in a moment."

Shanti took precise, sharp steps that echoed down the hall as she stormed the kitchen to confront Maya's corrupt smile. "You!" She pointed a dagger of a finger at the younger woman's face, not allowing the remotest of chances to respond. "Not a word from you. Not a sound," she hissed. "I do not need to remind you of who I am and what you are." And in front of Maya, Shanti stood erect, becoming tall and youthful, like the omnipotent Durga, with her many powerful arms brandishing all manner of weaponry with which to destroy her. "Tomorrow morning you will not come down until we have left. And as far as Priti is concerned, you and your husband are dead. If I ever hear of any attempt to contact my granddaughter, I will come down on you like acid rain."

Maya remained mute, her lips pressed together into a thin flat sliver, unable to neither smile nor frown in the presence of this powerful goddess.

Her message clear, Shanti turned around sharply and left Maya to her silence.

It was not until the train had left the station that Shanti could allow her emotions to show and she hugged her granddaughter close to her. "You poor, poor child," she murmured. "You poor, poor child."

She pushed Priti away so that she could look into her eyes. "Does it hurt, my dear?"

Priti looked back at her grandmother with a profound earnestness and shook her head slowly.

Shanti combed her granddaughter's hair with her fingers. "Do you want to talk about it?"

Again, Priti shook her head.

"That is fine, we do not have to talk about it." Shanti looked out the window as Ahmedabad receded into the past. "We do not have to talk about it ever. It can be your secret."

Priti looked up at her grandmother, who had now turned to the window, and understood for the first time, the power of secrets.

Priti stayed with her grandmother for the next several years; none of the family suspected anything of this sudden change, or if they did, they didn't want to know. Priti's wounds slowly healed into painless scars that were easily hidden by the dresses her grandmother bought for her. That first year, she was plagued by nightmares and would wake up shouting in her grandmother's arms. But with time and with her grandmother's patience and love, Priti's inner wounds healed as well. By the second year, she was able to sleep in her own bedroom, next to Shanti's. Despite her age and her failing heart, Shanti devoted her strength and energy to raising young Priti, providing a stable home environment, a good education at one of the city's top English-medium schools, and a spiritual upbringing through Hindu ritual and prayer at the neighborhood temple. And Priti blossomed under her grandmother's care, earning top marks at school, proving herself useful with house chores and understanding harmony and peace through worship. She fretted less and less about her parents not coming back for her with each passing year.

It was only when Shanti became too ill to her care for Priti that she drafted the reluctant letter to her daughter and son-in law. Priti wept by her grandmother's bedside as Shanti, between apneic pauses, placed a gentle hand over her granddaughter's head.

Priti left with her parents the day after the funeral.

31

July 1983

Gabriel held Priti as they lay on the floor of the cabin for a long time, letting the sobs die down until he spoke. Thumbing the tears from her face, he peered into her eyes. "We're survivors, you and I," he told her. "We've spent so much time and energy surviving our past, so much time trying to convince ourselves that we are valued, that we are good, that we are whole."

Priti pressed her face into Gabriel's chest as he spoke, squeezing her eyes tight so that she could listen closely to his words, words that she would have died to hear before, and drank them in now as if they were drops of water in the desert.

"I know what you go through," Gabriel continued. "You deserve better than what you've had. You deserve parents who love you and dote on you and would love to spoil you. You deserve to be put first before anyone else in your home. You deserve to be able to have family you can trust. As I do." Gabriel looked up to the rafters, as if searching for someone. "Sometimes I feel I could be so much more, and accomplish so much more if I wasn't devoting so much of my energy to just break even, just to make it to the next day. But maybe we can start from this moment," he said, hugging her tightly, kissing her head. "Maybe we can start from this moment believing in each other, and seeing the goodness in one another."

They held hands in the dark empty bus that wound its way towards Rosedale, gazing straight ahead toward the starlit expanse that broadened before them. He walked her to the corner and bent down to kiss her. "Let's start from this moment," Gabriel repeated in a whisper. "Even if it's just the two of us. Let's be what we need to each other."

Priti nodded, smiling, her tears streaks now dried. "Yes, let's," she whispered back.

3 2

Achilles stumbled down the slope from home, catching his fall against the trunk of an aging dogwood. He cursed himself and his sudden awkwardness. Didn't think he'd drunk enough to be this clumsy. He had been so uncoordinated these past couple weeks, and he felt his legs giving way at times. Then there were the unexplainable bruises that seemed to flower overnight. He cursed his body, the one he'd treated so well - he no longer smoked, he never drank to excess, he could count on one hand the times he smoked weed. And now that body was betraying him. He stepped down hard onto the sidewalk, straightened himself up, and began the trek to his mother's place. Jagged pains to the back of his head stopped him several times on his way back, causing him to double over, struggling to catch his breath. Neighbors out that evening gave the large seemingly drunk teen wide berth. "Fuck!" He grabbed his head as his vision blurred- he'd beat the piss out of Johnny if he found out he'd spiked the beers- it slowly came back to him and he made it to his building.

His mother sat in the den, as she did every evening from eight to eleven. Doris Collins loved watching her primetime sitcoms, ones that boasted normal families with healthy relationships, stern but patient mothers and fathers, well behaved (and smart) children getting into well contained mischief, living quirky yet stable lives. Sitting in her easy chair in the dimly lit theater of her TV room, her own world was blotted out, forgotten, and she became a part of her TV family. She had dinner with them, drank her after dinner herbal tea with them, and bid good night to 'the kids' and the family dog. She tested their usual phrases, quips, jokes, in her voice, laughing along with the laugh meter.

Before he died her father had told her she could be on TV. He'd always remarked how pretty she was and had a beautiful voice to go with "such a pretty face." And he'd called her laugh a "movie-star laugh;" the crystalline, infectious, sing-song laugh so common to movie starlets in his day. Such a gentle, soft-spoke loving father he'd been to her, such a good husband to her mother; such emptiness in the home when he'd died, taken away from them by a weak heart. That was so long ago, when she was just about to finish high school and enter a world that was not so generous with soft-spoken compliments. Her mother withered soon after, fading to an imperceptible, gossamer thin shade of herself. More than once the pallbearers suspected the coffin they lay next to her father's grave was empty. The vacuum created by her parents' death was suffocating; she ran quickly to anyone who was willing to fill it.

Another metered laugh brought her back to the show. She loved watching it, the husband didn't greet his wife with a list of complaints. There were no insults or caustic comments, no coming home drunk, smelling of other women, and where was the occasional violent slap to the wife's face? The parents were always smiling, the children always smiling, the dog always wagging it's tail.

She startled at the sound of the front door to their apartment bursting open. "Is that you, Achilles?" she called out in her sitcom voice.

Achilles. It was her husband's idea. For her, David or Tom would have sufficed. But he chose Achilles as he laid eyes on his son. And she accepted it as she accepted all of his mandates. He was the smart one, with the PhD in Classics, and the track for tenure at the local college. Who was she to argue? But that was back then, when he was still involved, when he kept his drinking under control and still had his job.

Achilles struggled inside and leaned back heavily against the front door, closing it with a thud. He walked passed the den to the bathroom, disregarding his mother's question, and closed the door.

Comforted by Achilles's expected, if not normal behavior, his mother tuned back to her program.

Inside the claustrophobic-sized bathroom Achilles peered into the mirror, trying to identify any physical signs to explain his symptoms. There were none. He sighed and splashed some cold water on his face. He didn't know how long he'd be able to keep his deterioration from his friends. He opened the bathroom door quietly and staggered drunkenly to his bedroom. Not bothering to disrobe he fell backward onto his bed. With what little energy he had he let his head fall to the side to survey the contents of his room. His weights lay in the corner idle and untouched for the past couple of weeks. It had been ages since he'd worked out. Despite his drive, he didn't seem to have the strength, and he cursed himself again.

"Achilles, are you okay?" his mother called out from the other side of his bedroom door.

"Yeah, just a little tired. I'm going to bed," he replied, ending the typical mother and son chat for the night. He had no patience for her, she and her mouse-like scampering around the apartment. How his father ever tolerated her, he had no idea. Not that the old man had any tolerance for anyone. Maybe that's why he left.

"Remember you have work tomorrow," his mother said, venturing at some more dialogue.

"Yeah, I know," he called out again through the door, despite the pain in his head. "I'm going to sleep. Wake me up at seven."

He cast another guilty glance at his free weights. He forced out the negative thoughts with a shake of his head. The change would have to start from within, right here, right now. He turned to the alarm clock on his nightstand and set the alarm to wake up two hours earlier the next day, to put in a good workout before work, to get back on track with things, fitness, work, success. Push hard, fight hard, that's what makes a winner. He glanced at the posters of Bruce Lee and Muhammad Ali. These were men who tested their limits, and pushed them. Winners. Fighting past the pain and fatigue. If his father's beatings had etched one thing into his mind, it was that the life was a battle filled with conquerors and the vanquished, and if you don't fight prepare to get walked on. Too many kids had it easy - nice house, nice car, summer homes, holiday vacations. They didn't know the meaning of the word struggle. Take them out of their comfortable lives and they would crumble. His thoughts slurred and he succumbed to a deep sleep.

It wasn't the alarm clock's harsh buzzer going off in his ear, or his mother's frantic pounding at the door that woke him up at seven thirty. It was the need to escape his dream, treading in a lake of blood as multiple arms reached out to pull him under. He lifted his head off the pillow, at first unable to recognize the red stains, his blood on his pillow. He sat up with a jerk putting his hands to his scalp then to his face. The blood was everywhere. He opened the door and ran past his mother to the bathroom. He washed his face multiple times and then looked up. It was his nose. Two semi-dried clots of blood hung down to his upper lip. Shit. Suddenly exhausted and lightheaded, Achilles crumpled onto the bathroom floor, barely registering his mother's screams.

He woke up on a rattling stretcher in the back of an ambulance, an IV line fed his left arm the contents of an overhanging bag, and an oxygen mask wrapped around his face. He lifted his right arm to tug the mask off, but a heavy arm forced it down.

"Whoa, whoa." An older, uncomfortably obese man in a crisp EMT uniform sat next to him on the opposite stretcher, eyeing him intently. "You're in an ambulance." As if the obvious needed to be said. "You blacked out. We're taking you to the hospital," the EMT continued with short bursts of the obvious to which Achilles nodded in acceptance, or perhaps exasperation. The man pointed to the figure sitting next to him. "Your mother's here."

Achilles looked at his mother. Her face was strained with worry and her eyes were red from crying. She seemed so shrunken sitting next to the EMT, as if the little energy that she had for the day had been used up in the first forty minutes. For a brief moment Achilles wanted to reach out and comfort her; but their relationship was never good after his father left. There was a pattern to their relationship and Achilles didn't feel the energy to change it now. He closed his eyes momentarily to rest.

When he opened them he was on a hospital gurney in the emergency room. He lay shivering, naked but for a faded, over-washed hospital gown and a thin sheet to cover him, his clothes now stripped away and packed in a plastic bag somewhere. The room was a sickly green, slightly larger than a jail cell; a large tan curtain blocked the doorway.

A young man in a long white coat pulled back the curtain quietly and walked in. He turned to face Achilles. "Ah you're awake," he said and came by the bedside. "Achilles Collins?"

"That's me," Achilles muffled through his oxygen mask.

"How are you feeling?"

"Like shit," Achilles muffled again.

"I'm sure." The man in the white coat continued talking as he lifted a clipboard off the end of the bed and scanned the vital signs. "Your blood pressure seemed a bit low when you got here. That may help explain why you passed out, but you've already had a liter of IV fluid and your pressure is going up. Still we have to figure out what caused all this, so we've drawn some blood and we're just waiting for the test results to come back." After an insultingly long period he finally looked up. "I'm Dr. Marks. Maybe you can tell me how you've been feeling these past few weeks."

Achilles looked back at the young handsome doctor standing over him wrapped in his professional smugness and confidence, with his expensive sharply pressed shirt and slacks and polished wingtips. Despite his nausea and fatigue, Achilles swelled with the familiar urge for violence, to wrap the stethoscope tightly around the young doctor's neck until his head turned red, then purple then black. He shook these thoughts from his mind. "Tired and achy, not myself. I'm used to working out every day and haven't been able to, even though my body feels like it's been through a grueling workout. Don't feel hungry any more either, and I'm sleeping all the time."

The young doctor sat down on a plastic hospital chair next to the bed listening to the teen's history, avoiding eye contact dismissively as he perused the chart. It wasn't until Achilles stopped that he noticed a woman sitting in the corner, having made herself very small and insignificant. "I'm sorry, are you the mother?"

Achilles looked to the corner suddenly, wondering how long she'd been there.

"Yes I am, doctor," she said in a feeble though hopeful voice. "Can you tell me what's wrong with my son?"

"Not sure yet, just waiting on some lab results to get a better sense of the cause to all this. Ah, here they are now." Dr. Marks stood up as a young, somewhat worried nurse entered the room tightly clutching a handful of papers. He took the lab reports and scanned the results. "Hmm," the doctor said brusquely, a puzzled expression crossed his face for a moment as the differential diagnosis quickly thinned out. "Hmm," he repeated now disconcertedly. He looked up from the lab report to the nurse who met his gaze, nodding slightly, almost imperceptibly. He turned his gaze to both the patient and the mother. At a loss for words he left the room, leaving Achilles and his mother trapped together in a space much too confined for both of them to endure together. If Achilles sensed a change in the doctor he didn't show it. He closed his eyes, succumbing to another bout of restless sleep, as the present dissolved to a point somewhere in the future.

Achilles awoke to find an older man in a long white lab coat sitting at the foot of the bed talking in soft comforting tones with his mother. His short hair and closely cropped beard bore streaks of grey. His mother was in tears but smiling entreatingly as she always did with anyone who gave her half a moment. Achilles crossed his arms, waiting for the doctor to turn to him.

"Hi Achilles," the doctor said finally as if they were old friends meeting for the first time in years. "My name is Dr. Stevens. I'm one of the oncologists here," he said, leaning back as he spoke, fingers intertwined around his crisscrossed legs. He gave off a comforting energy and Achilles allowed himself to be lulled. "Dr. Marks asked me to come by and talk with you and your mother. Has he explained the labs results to you?"

Achilles shook his head groggily.

"It seems as though there is a significant elevation in the white cells floating around in your blood."

Achilles eyed the older physician warily. "What does that mean? And what's an oncologist?"

Dr. Stevens nodded. "To answer your first question, white cells are part of your immune system's way of fighting off infections. There is a range in the number of white cells that occurs normally; during an infection the number of white cells increases to fight off an infection. Sometimes however the number of white cells increases in the absence of infection. And sometimes it gets high enough to start crowding out the other cells in the body, causing problems." Dr. Stevens lifted the lab results. "Your white count is very high, and probably explains why you've been feeling the way you have. You expressed to the other doctor how tired you were-"

"He's been exhausted, doctor." Achilles's mother pressed her body forward anxiously on the chair, her face strained, her tear streaks still visible. "Some mornings it's impossible to wake him."

Achilles shot her a look, stifling any more commentary, then turned to Dr. Stevens, sighing impatiently at this didactic presentation. "Tell it to me straight, doc. What do I have?"

"A white count at the level in your blood stream indicates Leukemia," Dr. Stevens replied.

"Leukemia?" Achilles turned from the doctor to his mother, who had begun to dissolve in her own tears in the corner. "You mean like Jerry's kids?"

Dr. Stevens almost lost his balance on the bed. "No, no, that's Muscular Dystrophy," he said, shaking his head vigorously.

Achilles sat back momentarily mollified.

Dr. Stevens leaned in, looking at Achilles intently. "Leukemia is a type of cancer of the blood stream. To answer your second question, an oncologist is a doctor who treats people with cancer."

"Cancer?" Achilles looked again to his mother, but now as if for the first time. He looked back to Dr. Stevens, swallowing hard. "I have cancer?" he asked, then, "I have cancer." He nodded at the revelation, the explanation to how he was feeling. He caught himself sinking into panic and became angry at his sudden weakness. He grasped for a braver response to this blow, one that Muhammad Ali and Bruce Lee would have come up with. They would have faced this fearlessly, like any other opponent who sought to harm them. It was too early for reconciliation with the diagnosis. He scowled at the doctor sitting in front of him with his air of self-satisfaction and smugness, one he'd love to wipe off. "Tell me what I have to do."

"Good," Dr. Stevens said, slapping the boy's thigh. "First, let's get you to a hospital room. Then I will outline the plan for you."

When the older physician had left the room, Achilles turned to his mother who was doubled over broken. "Mom," he said. "Mom."

His mother looked up with eyes streaming with tears, eyes hopeful for some guidance from her ailing son. "Yes, Achilles. Tell me."

"Mom," he repeated more softly now, lying back onto the gurney, suddenly enervated. "Don't tell anyone about this, not Dad, not my friends, no one." He drifted off to sleep as his mother wept alone, quietly in the corner.

Achilles roller-coasted through the next several days of bone marrow aspiration, lumbar puncture, repeat blood draws and transfusions, as the elderly Dr. Stevens sought to identify the leukemia devouring his body. Achilles fought to be fully conscious and aware, needing the intensity of the moment. He deferred medications for sleep, and he minimized his pain to the staff, all to fulfill the need to feel everything. He listened in on the lightening rounds that took place at his bedside by the team of oncologists, pediatricians, ID specialists and all who washed up along the shore of his bedside. He strove to catch, store and understand the bits of medical pigeon speech repeated in his presence. He asked all the questions, stupid and otherwise, that came to him. The well-dressed, polished members of the various teams listened to these with smiles and winks of condescension. He came to recognize and understand the patterns of medical talk, the jargon of treatment protocol, chemotherapy, induction, toxicity remission and relapse. Despite his efforts he drifted in and out of awareness. Life became disjointed, a haphazard connection of experiences with a wide array of characters in their well-worn roles, connected only by the white sterile background of the hospital room, and the cacophony of bedside monitors. Yet as disjointed as his life had become, there was still some awareness of routine, and logic to the procession of blood draws, temperature checks, meals, IV bag changes, rounds.

Dr. Stevens came to him alone from time to time just to check in. He provided Achilles with updates on the various lab tests run up until that point. Achilles learned the white cell that decided to take over his body was a T cell, and though T-cell type leukemia was more difficult to treat, further testing showed that the barrier to the brain and spine had not been breached. On the night before Achilles was to start chemotherapy, Dr. Stevens came in and sat down on the bed and discussed the protocol, as he promised he would. Despite the late hour, the doctor appeared fresh, with a crisp white dress shirt, polished wingtips, pressed slacks; it was as if he'd just gotten dressed for the occasion. He listed the chemo agents Achilles would start the next day: Vincristine, Prednisone, Doxorubicin - they sounded like mighty Ancient Greek warriors. He also listed the numerous adverse effects from these agents. Achilles dozed off to the growing list of expected assaults on his body. He slept soundly that night, denying himself the panic that others in his place had felt. He would not capitulate to fear. Achilles braced himself for the worst, as he would expect the heroes on his wall at home to, ready to face all the worst this enemy had to offer, preparing to do battle with his cancer and his cure.

33

"Looks who's here." Doris Collins appeared suddenly from one side of Achilles's abridged visual field, smiling imploringly as she turned to someone in the void behind her. Achilles had awoken that morning to find his world constricted, his periphery not only blurred but absent, horse-blinded, forcing him to rotate his neck to compensate. But he'd found the task of moving his head difficult, due as much from the searing pain radiating down his spine as to the vertiginous rocking of his hospital room. A week had passed since he'd been hospitalized and already several days out from his first round of chemotherapy, the effects of which were making themselves known: neuropathy, vertigo, nausea, vomiting, fatigue. With no small effort he turned to the doorway to find distorted versions of Gabriel, Johnny and Jared. Alternate friends from another universe conjured through the mind-bending effects of the chemo. They filed in slowly, carefully, as if in fear of damaging the delicate crystalline order in the room. Despite his hallucinogenic state and his pain, he could sense their fear and it enraged him to see his friends behave like strangers now. He refrained from cursing at his mother for the moment- she was making a quick exit anyway- that would wait until later. He forced a smile, and hoped it formed convincingly. "Hey guys." He caressed his arm outward, stretching his fingers to the limits of his white hospital room, stretching the IV line taut from its pole. "Welcome to my palace."

Gabriel was the first to approach, the only one. He leaned over the bed, bent forward at the waist, gently hugging Achilles.

"Hey man," he said, and then more softly into Achilles's ear, "why didn't you tell us?"

"Didn't want you to worry. It's my battle," Achilles whispered back, then more loudly, "What's up?" for the others to hear.

Gabriel stepped back to let Achilles see the rest of them.

Jared leaned heavily against the opposite wall, adrift behind his sunglasses. Johnny rocked back and forth, on heels and toes, restlessly by the doorway, unsure if committed to entering or ready to escape. Both of them showed their discomfort. The hospital was unknown territory, and disease and decay were foreign enemies, known only peripherally in others. To have either hit so close appalled them, shaking them out of their comfort zone. It was as if a veil had been lifted, exposing them to a world beyond the simple shadows and illusions of childhood, before they had stopped being children. Reality without the veil is horrifying. And no rock and roll lyric, no posturing or swagger, no additional pipe hit, or line of coke or swig off a bottle of SoCo could reconcile it, or protect them from it.

Johnny snickered by the doorway. "So did you get any hot nurse to give you a sponge bath yet?"

"Not yet," boomed a voice from behind him. Johnny jumped to the side as an obese black woman stuffed into extra-large pink scrubs brushed passed him and walked over to the IV pole. "First I got to check the IV, see what's making all this noise." She shared a quick wink with Achilles. "Hi sugar. How you doing?"

"Hi Judith."

Judith had been the nurse who'd met Achilles when transport had first wheeled him into the room, adopting him as her third son. He reminded her so much of her first two sons - one who'd played ball in Notre Dame, one who'd enlisted in the army - that she'd cried that first night on the N21 bus home.

"Bags empty. Looks like you're done for now." She

disconnected the IV line from his picc line and draped it over the pole. She paused at the door. "Be back later to give you that," she said, giving Johnny a hard look before turning to Achilles, "sponge bath."

The other three laughed as she walked out. But the sound of laughter is brief in hospitals, and all four soon quieted for a long, uncomfortable moment.

"What do you have? What's going on with you?" Gabriel sat down on the chair next to Achilles's bed.

Johnny stepped forward, laughing. "You don't have that 'gay plague' do you. I knew there was something funny about you."

The others laughed hesitantly.

"No, really," Gabriel persisted.

"I have leukemia," Achilles responded, turning his head away, not wanting to see the concern on his friends' faces.

"Like Jerry's Kids?" Johnny asked, backing up to the doorway.

Achilles smiled. "No that's muscular dystro-something or other."

"Good cause you don't wanna be sitting on Jerry's lap." Johnny twitched his head nervously to the door. "That guy's a pervert."

"What type of leukemia do you have?"

Everyone turned to Jared, still leaning uncomfortably against the wall, hands now dug deep into his pockets, his skin pale and diaphoretic behind his shades. He appeared to be in the throws of some withdrawal or intoxication, or both.

"What do you know about leukemia?" Achilles scowled.

"I had a cousin with it," Jared responded, suspending the information in the empty space of silence between them, to be absorbed and accepted.

"T-cell," Achilles said, sighing, feeling his energy draining.

Jared nodded. "He had T-cell too."

"What happened to him?" Gabriel turned back to Jared.

"He's okay, he's in remission."

Gabriel nodded approvingly. He turned to Achilles, smiling. "You see, man, you're going to make it. You're a fighter. I know you'll walk out of here on your own two feet."

The two high-fived.

"I'm going to walk out of here," Achilles echoed. "I got too much to do."

"You need to make that million dollars before you're thirty, right?" Gabriel sat on the bed, looking at Achilles.

"Right, I finally know what's going to make me rich."

"What?" Gabriel smiled encouragingly.

"I'm going to be a doctor." Suddenly more animated, propping himself forward on his elbows despite the weight of fatigue around his neck. "You have to see these docs coming in and out of here, dressed to the nines."

"I'm sure."

The two high-fived again.

The effort of entertaining had worn Achilles out, and he soon leaned back, his eyes closed, defeated.

The other three exchanged glances, an unspoken understanding. Johnny and Jared made for the door.

"Thanks for coming, guys," Achilles called out weakly.

The other two reluctantly approached the bed, high-fiving him, hesitant to touch him.

"See ya soon, man," Johnny said, then backed away, both hands in V shape.

"Get better, Achilles." Jared turned away quickly and followed Johnny out the door.

Gabriel leaned in finally, whispering in Achilles's ear, "I'm not letting you off the hook. You're still with us, right?"

Achilles smiled, whispering back, "Right. When's it happening?"

Gabriel stood up fully, looming over Achilles's bed. "Just get better, okay? Once you know when you're getting out, let me know."

Achilles nodded, his eyes closing as sleep overcame him.

Gabriel stood at the door a moment looking at the slumbering form in the bed, his jaw clenched tight.

He met the others in front of the hospital. They were attracting angry glares from hospital personnel as they fed cigarette smoke to the entranceway.

"Let me grab one of those." Gabriel reached over as Johnny shook a cigarette loose from his pack. "Let's walk a bit"

The three set off down the path to the street. Gabriel led the way, deep in thought.

"Man, he looks bad," Johnny said, exhaling a few rings of smoke into the air.

"He's fine," Gabriel replied defensively. "Just like Jared said, he'll be in remission after a few rounds of chemo. He's a fighter. He can make it." Gabriel turned around, nodding to Jared. "Tell him."

Jared looked off to the side, dejected. A soft murmur escaped his lips to the road, to be swept up like dust from a passing car.

The two turned to him. "What?"

"I said I lied." Jared ran a cold clammy hand through his hair.

"What the fuck do you mean, you lied?" Gabriel had stopped walking and turned now to Jared, incensed. "Are you saying you don't have a cousin with leukemia?"

Jared looked away from Gabriel's glare. "I'm saying he died."

But Gabriel wasn't letting him off the hook. "Why even say it? Why even mention it? Why not just stay quiet?" He stepped closer and closer with each question until his face was inches from Jared's.

"I thought I was giving him hope." Jared continued to look away.

Gabriel stared through Jared's Ray Bans, searching his eyes. His right hand curled into a fist, his knuckles clicking closed. The two were more or less the same height, but Gabriel was considerably stronger. Despite all the violence in Gabriel's history, he had never hit Jared. Still, Jared closed his eyes, preparing himself for the blow. But Gabriel turned around, giving a hard front kick to the corner garbage can, upending it onto the street, the refuse within spread out in a chaotic sprawl, then stormed off.

"Hey, where're you going?" Johnny called out.

"Back to work," Gabriel said over his shoulder. A few paces out he turned around to his friends as he continued to walk backwards. "Meet you home tomorrow morning." He spun back around and made his way away from them.

Johnny shook his head, flicking his cigarette butt into the street where it met with the rest of the garbage. "Let's get home and roll one up."

"What about Gabriel?"

The two looked at their leader's form as it rapidly disappeared down Communal Drive. Johnny spoke up when Gabriel was but a speck of dust dissolved into the heat. "He just needs to cool down. We'll see him tomorrow. Let's get stoned."

3 4

"Are you okay?"

Gabriel looked up distractedly from the cart of books he'd been pushing forward since returning from the hospital to find Priti in front of him. She wore a summer dress, vivid with yellows, pinks and reds.

He looked back down and realized that he'd shelved none of the books from the morning; that he'd walked around the maze of bookcases aimlessly, his cart full. "Hi Priti," he said, his voice burdened with the weight of his friend's illness. When he looked up again he found Priti next to him, a hand on his left arm, a look of concern on her face. He ran his hand through his hair. "I'm not sure really- I guess I'm okay- just so many things have happened in the last couple of days that have thrown me a bit." He suddenly felt aged and worn. He pressed his right hand over the front of his wrinkled shirt, tucking it in tightly into his black work pants.

Priti took Gabriel by the arm and led him to the corner of a table off to the side of the main reading room. They both sat down sharing the corner. "What's going on?"

Gabriel leaned forward his forearms on the table, staring absently as he clenched and unclenched his hand. "My buddy, Achilles- you met him at the party a couple weeks ago- we've been friends for years." Gabriel rotated his neck stretching the knots in his muscles. "Well I just found out he's very sick."

Priti leaned in reading the strain on his face. "What does he have?"

Gabriel massaged his forehead with his right hand, then his eyes, which he found wet with tears. He let his fingers linger, talking into his palm. "Leukemia," he answered. "And I don't think he's going to make it."

Priti wrapped her arms around his shoulders, touching her head to his. "My god. I'm so sorry."

The two stayed there at the corner of the table, in the deepening shadow of the library, as the afternoon light faded. The older librarian carried on with her work at the other end, casting casual glances across the great room. Concerned as she was for Gabriel, she smiled furtively at the two friends who'd found each other.

"See you Monday, Gabriel," the librarian called to him from her desk, as he lifted his leather jacket off the hook by the office and slipped it over his left shoulder.

"See you Monday," Gabriel replied softly as he paused at the front door. "Sorry about the books, I'll file them-"

"Don't worry." She waved away the apology. "I can easily file them this evening before I go. Enjoy your weekend." She aimed her glance at Priti. "You take care now. And take care of our young friend."

"Thank you. I will." Priti nodded, grabbing Gabriel's hand.

They walked out of the library into the dense heat of the late summer afternoon, and made their way to Achilles's car. Gabriel pulled out his keys distractedly, his mood fragile. "I'll drive you home," he said.

"Where will you go?"

"Probably grab some pizza and head home."

"I'll come with you," Priti offered, grasping his hand more tightly.

"You don't have to, I know you have your studying to do."

"I know I don't have to, Gabriel," Priti said, pressing herself against him and resting her head against his chest. "I want to."

Gabriel hugged her tightly. "Okay," he whispered, bending his neck forward, his face in her hair.

The two drove to Tony's and grabbed a small pizza and a

couple cans of soda then headed home. As they climbed the hill Priti held the food and Gabriel held her hand, helping her up the steep slope. They walked to the front porch where they were met with a flock of swallows shooting upwards over the roof of the shack and into the deep azure sky before diving down into the woods on the other side and shooting up again in a ritual meditative dance that continued into the night.

The two ate on the front steps in silence, listening to the distant hum of the traffic below, and the wild clamor of cicadas clinging to tree branches above. As the sun burned its fiery glow westward their images faded in the hazy twilight.

They sat against the door looking out as darkness settled around them, breached here and there by the lightshow of a troupe of lightning bugs that had come to life. And as the summer breeze conversed softly with the leaves overhead, Priti turned to Gabriel in the darkness and saw a tear's shimmering trail down his cheek. She rose to her knees, caressing his face dry, then straddled his legs facing him, staring into his eyes, partially hidden in the evening's darkness. She wrapped her arms around him as she pulled his head to her breast, hugging him as he wept for the loss of his friend, perhaps for the loss of others as well.

Then she pulled away and stared at his eyes once again; so much painful innocence reflected back. She kissed one cheek, then the other, and then his lips. She stood up and held out her hand and led him inside where he lit a candle, bathing the room in soft candlelight. He walked to her and held her to him. She arched her neck and their lips met again, then grabbed his hand and pressed it to her breast, her breathing fast and shallow. She raised her arms and her sundress rose with a flash of color, revealing her brown lithe body underneath. Her hands reached out to his neck and then slid down, unbuttoning his shirt, caressing his chest and abdomen. He pulled off his shirt and embraced her, feeling the heat of her body against his. Once again he felt the rough childhood scars etched on her

3 5

Gabriel loved Priti's fondness of B-movie Martial Arts flicks, which they rented from the local Blockbuster almost every night. He loved the way she used her hands to eat, (how she'd learned to eat in India). He loved how she drank water, her head tilted back, holding the cup an inch above her mouth, cascading the water inside (to avoid germs). He loved how she splashed Sriracha hot sauce on everything (she kept a small bottle of it in her book bag). He loved her smile, how her lips would part and the world would disappear around it. But most of all he loved how she'd come to paint his world. His life until her had been a series of broad, rough strokes of increasingly dark greys. Priti brought a palette of bright colors to his life. With a fine brush, she added the details that gave meaning to the canvas. He lost himself in these details, relishing them, wondering at times if they meant he'd missed something before, as if the broad strokes from the past had only served to conceal. At times, he felt an essential part of his past had been whitewashed, leaving him handicapped to face the present.

The next three weeks Gabriel and Priti spent every spare moment together. They disregarded their mothers' arguments, deaf and blind to their pleas, and disappeared from those around them, submerged within this new feeling neither of them recognized, occasionally surfacing for air, and always together.

In those three weeks, for the first time in a long time, Gabriel thought less and less of the plan to kill Mr. Winter, of the revenge that had taken root inside. For once, the storm of thoughts and images that had whirled violently around his mind settled down until it was a distant rumble that was easy to disregard. For once, Gabriel felt free and unburdened. And feeling free and unburdened, Gabriel unlocked the energy with which he adapted to the routines of his new life easily. Rising early with Leon, Gabriel would jog the five-mile loop (he'd stopped smoking), then shower and dress quickly. He'd catch the N21 to Rosedale and wait for Priti at her corner then ride with her to the library. For lunch, they would eat food she'd prepared the night before. After work, they would spend a brief moment by Achilles's hospital bed; at times Achilles was awake and could engage for several minutes, other times Gabriel sat at the foot of his bed, his eyes closed and his head bowed as if in silent prayer. The evenings they would spend together, either at his mother's house (his mother was usually working late), or at home (as long as Johnny and Jared weren't around). He'd ride the N21 with her back to Rosedale and walk her home before her ten o'clock curfew, then catch the bus back to New Hope.

On the weekends, the world, or at least a small corner of it, was theirs. They shed themselves of their families and ventured out. Taking Achilles's car, they explored the Island, the one they'd both lived in and knew nothing of, unearthing its hidden treasures together, taking more pleasure in the sharing of these discoveries than the discoveries themselves. From each shared adventure they returned with a stronger love for each other.

But the past can be suppressed for only so long, and slowly it crept back into Gabriel's mind, regaining foothold, first in his deepest recesses, then gaining strength, setting traps for him to slip into, and laying in ambush for him. After three weeks Daniel began to sway again.

He resisted at first, seeing this return of his obsession as disloyal to his time with Priti. But there was a wrong that needed to be righted, a victim who had perished, a perpetrator who had gone free, and a wave of pain so great that it threatened to wash over all of them.

36

How's the weather, Phil? Well Sandy, yesterday's thunderstorm cut short the Diana Ross concert at Central Park as rain, wind and lightning took control of center stage, trapping hundreds of thousands of fans. But officials report that the concert will go on tonight. And it looks like the weather will behave today with bright blue cloudless skies and miles of sunshine. Tonight temperatures will stay in the low 80s.

"Did you ever kill anyone before?"

Leon looked up from the grill, startled at the forwardness of the question. "Excuse me?"

Johnny smiled guiltily. "I mean in battle," he corrected. "Did you ever kill anyone in battle? We heard about how you took down those skin heads and all, even killed one of them."

Leon looked back down at the grill lined with skewers, chunks of lamb wedged in between bell peppers and coarsely cut red onions, the fat crackling and splitting onto the coals below. He rotated the kabobs, causing another round of angry hissing, taking the time to explore the intent behind the question. When Gabriel had suggested a barbecue with his friends Leon had assumed an innocent get together for Gabriel's small family to meet them (there seemed so few opportunities for Gabriel and his mother to know about one another), and he enthusiastically agreed. In light of Achilles's unfortunate diagnosis, the boys needed an evening to relax.

Leon had been explaining his preference for lamb over beef, and the subtle difference between grilling the two - the cut has to be somewhat thinner for the lamb for proper grilling. Johnny's question came as a surprise, and the look on his face was not one of curiosity, but that of purpose, the goal of which was still unclear. In his ripped jeans, leather jacket and long hair, Johnny looked like a derelict capable of anything. But then again, all three boys were dressed like this; Leon suspected this to be one of the styles of the times.

He looked back up to find both Johnny and Gabriel intently watching and waiting for his answer. He cast a casual glance at the foldout picnic table they'd set up for dinner in the side yard where Jared, head hung low, silently and meekly followed Isabelle's sharp instructions for setting the table. Above them all the red sun was sinking low in the evening sky. "Since joining the army I was involved in several battles," he admitted finally. "It was during these times I was forced to kill the enemy."

"How far away were they?" Johnny asked.

Leon eyed him warily. He shrugged. "It is hard to say. When you are in battle, you do not have the luxury of time to calculate. You make a guess and then you fire- perhaps thirty-fifty yards."

"Was there any hand to hand combat?" Johnny pressed on.

Leon reflexively thought back to a middle of the night raid by a dozen PLO fighters that he and his company had thwarted. "No," he lied.

"Where's the best place to aim when you want to kill someone?"

Leon narrowed his eyes despite his calm demeanor. "Depends on how far away your attacker is. What's with all the questions about killing people?" he asked, eying both Johnny and Gabriel.

Both averted his gaze for a brief pause. He knew they were hiding something, but he did not know what.

"Nothing," they both replied.

"We're interested in you being a solider, that's all," Gabriel explained. "It must be very exciting."

"And fun," Johnny added.

Leon accepted the response. It seemed plausible enough. "There's more to being a solider than killing," he cautioned them. "It's not all fun. Not," Leon looked off to the side in search of the right phrase, "cowboys and Indians. Killing is not something you do casually. It is a big responsibility. When you kill a man, you are robbing him of the rest of his days, you are robbing his family of his help and counsel. When you kill a man, you become a thief, forever indebted to his lost legacy. You have to be able to accept such consequences when taking another's life," he said, with the unwavering gaze of one who had seen more than his share of death.

The two nodded, helplessly under his reprimanding gaze.

"Thank you, uncle," Gabriel said.

Leon smiled. "Forget the uncle. I told you Leon, okay?" He reached an arm around Gabriel's neck and brought him in for a hug.

Leon brought the lamb kabobs to the table as the boys sat down. He fought to suppress his sixth sense, one that could detect a nefarious purpose behind Johnny's questions, the answers to which Gabriel also seemed interested. But they were boys, he ultimately reasoned, and he could appreciate a boy's appetite for battles, the bloodless, sterile ones full of valor and glory, those that could only be found in a boy's imagination.

Isabelle spooned dollops of mashed potatoes onto everyone's plate. There was a bottle of red wine that no one could remember bringing out, and although Gabriel and his friends didn't normally gravitate towards wine they wouldn't turn it down either. The conversation at the grill had turned evolved to other subjects as conversations often do, and Leon spoke to them about his time before the army. "I lived in the kibbutz right up until a few months before my mandatory service," he said as he poured the wine into each of their glasses. "Spent some time with friends in Tel Aviv, working odd jobs."

"What's a kibbutz?" Johnny asked. "Is that like one of them communes?"

"More or less," Isabelle replied blandly.

"What was it like to live in a kibbutz?" Gabriel directed his question to Leon. He had stopped bothering with his mother; there were so many unanswered questions between the two of them over the years.

Leon paused a moment before answering. "It's hard to compare it with anything. We really had no choice. A toast!" He lifted his glass, clinking it with the others. "To friends and family and a beautiful summer's night."

They all looked around as if for the first time, past the shrubs encircling the patio, past the trees lining the streets, the stately elms, the honey-scented Linden blossoms, at the pink aftermath of the setting sun towards the west, at the moon rising small and cold towards the east, and at the stars blinking brightly overhead. They looked around as night descended, as if searching in the uncloaked vastness of the universe to find something worth toasting.

"Really, I want to know," Gabriel urged his uncle.

Leon smiled with a shrug. "I can't imagine I can add much to what your mother has already told you. I was very young when our parents died." He caught the look in Gabriel's eyes. "What? She never told you anything?" He shot a quick glance at Isabelle who sat at the far corner of their conversation, gazing off at the night sky. "Well, sure I can tell you about life on the kibbutz," he said, recovering quickly. "What can I say, it was a blessing for us. After our parents died, everyone in the community stepped in to help raise us. We grew up in the nursery with the rest of the children, and as we got older we were taught how to be active members in the community. We helped take care of the animals, and with planting and harvesting the fruits and vegetables. We never lacked for food, shelter or friendship. It was a great learning experience for me."

Isabelle had turned her gaze back to the table as Leon explained his version of their shared history. It was not for her to argue with him or contradict his telling of it. He had his experience and she had hers. Although he came to eventually know the air raid drills, the nights hiding in the bunkers, the constant fear of attacks from Palestinian or Jordanian militants across the border, Leon was only one at the time when a well-aimed mortar, one of countless, orphaned them. And he did not know of the days after that day; to his toddler eyes there were two less faces peeking in at the nursery. But she remembered that evening. Even at the age of five she understood the sense of loss, which only grew which each passing day, each passing milestone, or success or fall. The elders had sat her down in the kibbutz office; Leon had already been put to bed. She had stayed passive on the chair mutely facing them. With tears in their eyes they explained to her the most recent bombings during which her parents had died and would not be coming back. They hurriedly promised that she and Leon would be well taken care of. As they continued to speak their words became incomprehensible, the meaning becoming blurred as if another language. Their images somewhat blurry, soft at the edges. And her world became suddenly tactile, as her other senses dulled. She felt the hard edge of the wooden chair bracing her, the oppressive dry heat as it wrapped its fingers around her throat, the pleasant rush of air as they opened the door, finally. Isabelle remembered the woman's hard callused grip as she led Isabelle back to the nursery where many of the younger children were already sleeping. She remembered that night lying awake, unable to fall asleep, fretting about what tomorrow would bring. She lay awake looking over at the children in the other beds, comparing herself and her lot to theirs. But tomorrow brought a new sun, the earth still spun on its axis and life continued, minus the two faces she had glimpsed at every evening at the end of their days in the field, along with the soft kisses, and the weary smiles that accompanied the warm embraces. The other children in the nursery knew nothing of her loss; they were too young to understand. For many nights afterward, she lay awake in her bed, watching the other children sleep easily. She could not help comparing herself to them. These nightly comparisons became almost an obsession the older she became, her life and theirs. In reality, all the children in the nursery grew up more or less the same, being cared for by the collective parenting of the kibbutz, the spirit of which was present since a generation before, when the first spade dug the first hole in the ground to plant whatever miracles would grow. All the kids in the nursery rarely saw their parents during the day, catching only brief moments with them in the evening when they returned exhausted from the fields; a brief kiss, a brief hug, a brief wish good night. But in those briefest of moments to Isabelle there existed a vast divide between her and the rest of them. And in those briefest of moments, she realized her life would never be the same. And in this realization an idea crystalized in her mind of the need to be free. Leon, the big baby, became the big boy, became the big young man and found himself an integral part of the community he called his home. But she saw herself as apart. And with each passing year the idea grew, and she recognized the need to learn all that would be necessary to gain her independence from this collective home. In addition to learning Hebrew, she took on the English language, it's impetuousness, it's rebelliousness, it's flagrant disregard for rules. When she was old enough she left for Tel Aviv and stayed with former nursery mates until she found a job as an interpreter. She interpreted for commercial transactions, British, American businesses mostly, ready to invest in the young country. It was during one of these jobs that she met Raul Dayan. Young, flamboyant Raul, carefree with his words, carefree with his money and his arrogance-she was immediately taken with him, overwhelmed. He was a Jew from New York, a place she could not imagine beyond the powerful black and white images she'd gasped at years before. It seemed almost fitting that he would be from New York. A junior partner from an international construction company, he was in Tel Aviv looking at properties. In the end, he lost interest in doing business in that city, but he had not lost interest in the young pretty interpreter, so much smarter than the other people in the room. He courted her strongly and before she knew it she was on an El Al jet crossing the Atlantic. It was in New York, pregnant with Daniel, that she heard from her younger brother of his interest in staying on in the army after his mandatory service.

Leon was at the sink cleaning the dishes from dinner. Gabriel brought in the glasses. "That's the last of the stuff from the table. Jared's wiping everything down." Gabriel leaned against the kitchen counter looking at his uncle. "Thanks for the dinner, un- Leon."

Leon smiled back. "My pleasure."

A sharp burst of a woman's laughter startled them. They both peeked through the open side door to catch an incredulous glimpse of Isabelle smoking a cigarette with Johnny. Leon raised an eyebrow at Gabriel, who shrugged in response. What Johnny could have said or how Isabelle could have interpreted it left them wondering.

"Thanks also for telling me about the kibbutz," Gabriel said, breaking the spell.

"Sure."

"I know so little about my past," Gabriel added, looking down, suddenly despondent. "Sometimes I don't know who I am."

Leon opened his mouth to speak but at first found no words to respond. He too had felt a need for lineage, for a line to look back upon to anchor to. His parents' histories were buried with them, and with them the rich collection of stories parents bond with their children through, the oral histories that are told and retold, changing subtly in the detail but never in the substance, forever maintaining the identity. "I know how you feel," he said finally. "I too have lived feeling like there were many missing pieces to my past. And although I was fortunate to have had a loving community to take care of me, I often feel the emptiness of not having been raised by my mother and father."

"I guess I shouldn't really complain." Gabriel said. "At least I have my parents."

"Don't ever feel you are complaining to me. You are my nephew and I love you and I want you to know that I am here for you." He put a hand on Gabriel's shoulder. "I now regret not staying here longer after Daniel's funeral. I know you were the first to see Daniel after he died. You must have suffered a lot afterwards. I'm sorry you did not have the guidance you needed. There is no way to get used to seeing another person die, even as a soldier I never became used to it. Killing that young man was not easy for me, I had no other choice."

"Thank you," Gabriel said and turned away, wiping the tears from his eyes so that his uncle wouldn't see.

37

In international news, White House officials are calling on Israel to adhere to a timetable for withdrawal from Lebanon in the hopes that Syria will withdraw forces from the area as well. A recent poll reveals the ignorance of Americans in US-Central American Policy. Less than one third of respondents knew of the Administration's support of the Government in El Salvador, less than one fifth knew of its support for the anti-Sandanista rebels in Nicaragua, and less than one in ten were aware of the administration's stance in both countries. Exciting stuff Sandy, but let's move onto something that people really care about, the weather. You said it, Phil...

Gabriel and Achilles walked out of Achilles's apartment complex the morning after his discharge. Achilles was unrecognizable. The chemo had scalped him, leaving patches of stubble sprouting unevenly from his bald head. It had emaciated him as well. Achilles looked thirty pounds lighter, thirty pounds that he couldn't afford to lose. His clothes hung loosely on his wire-like frame. Sunken eyes, hollowed out face, he seemed decades older.

Johnny elbowed Jared. "They're coming- Jesus!" he muttered under his breath. "The poor guy looks like death warmed over."

Jared looked past Johnny out the side window. "Cancer," he answered, as if the one word could suffice to define the losing battle their friend was waging.

Achilles dropped weakly into the front passenger seat,

winded by the short walk to the car. He turned around with some effort. His death-like eyes scanned the back seat. "Hey guys." He greeted his friends with an equally death-like voice and offered his hand.

Johnny shot a hand up front, high-fiving Achilles. "Hey man, what's up? You look like shit."

Achilles smiled appreciably at the honesty; he needed it, he'd been exposed to so much bullshit in the past month. He turned back to the front and leaned back heavily against his seat. "Feel like shit," he answered, eyeing his reflection in the side mirror.

"Hi Achilles." Jared tapped Achilles shoulder. "Glad you're out."

"Me too. Thanks."

Gabriel stepped in behind the wheel. "Thanks for taking care of my car. You can drive it 'til I'm back on my feet," Achilles said.

"No problem and thanks." Gabriel shifted the car into drive and pulled away from the curb. "How long are you going to be out for?"

The car picked up speed and they sped along the back roads towards home.

Achilles looked out the window, reflecting back to the conversation with the oncologist the day before. He could no longer remember the doctor's face- a blur in a white coat. "Doc said some results aren't back yet. Gotta meet him at the end of the week, then they'll tell me whether or not I responded to the chemo this past month. But I'm going to continue with the same poison for I don't know how many cycles, then check again. Chances are I may be able to get some of the chemo as an outpatient." Achilles looked at the road in front, focused on the short bit of freedom he'd been allowed, suddenly realizing the worth of this freedom, how much he'd taken breathing the air outside for granted. He sucked in a deep breath, relishing in the sweet richness of it. "Doc said they may be able to get me into remission," he added, stressing "remission" as much for himself as for his friends.

Gabriel looked from the road to Achilles, nodding triumphantly. "That's great news, man. You'll be as good as new in no time. But for now, we need this week for our plan, make sure we get it down pat."

As they climbed the hill, Gabriel had to grab onto Achilles's hand. With his free hand Achilles grasped at branches to keep from falling. The climb was proving more difficult than he had anticipated. He stumbled a few times and felt breathless for much of the second half. Johnny hung back a few paces in case Achilles fell and Jared took up the rear. At the top they walked over to the side of the cabin and Achilles sat down hard on the ground outside, his back leaning against the side while the others crouched around him. It took a good ten minutes for him to catch his breath. He cursed his deconditioned state.

"Cut yourself a break." Gabriel sat down next to him. "You've been lying in bed for the past month."

Achilles picked up a rock next to him and flung it to the edge of the woods, scattering a small company of grackles and starlings. "Yeah, I know. Never thought I'd be this fucking weak, though."

Gabriel walked to the edge of the hill and picked up a small branch from the ground, clearing it of leaves. He came back to the others and crouched down. "Okay, let's get started. Huddle in." He caught everyone's eye with a look of such earnest intent it chastised them all to pay attention. "Let's break down the plan. One: getting the old man here. Achilles and I are going to park on the corner opposite the house, midnight." With his stick he etched a rough outline of the neighborhood into the ground as he spoke. "Achilles stays in the car, I enter and subdue the guy. We dump him into the trunk and take a roundabout route parking on these side streets 'til we make it here." He turned to Achilles. "I'll be too busy dragging the perp up the hill to help you. I'm counting on you to get your strength back so you can get your ass up on your own." Gabriel winked encouragingly at Achilles.

Achilles nodded in response.

"Two: getting the gun. Johnny," he pointed a finger, "you have to get the gun out of your dad's gun cabinet and have it ready the day before, that way there's no delay that night. Put it somewhere no one will think to look or check. Once the night comes we need to have the gun at home, no later than eleven o'clock, with bullets outside the chamber. Once we bring the old man in we'll load the bullets."

"Got it," Johnny replied, lighting a cigarette.

Achilles raised a weak hand. "Do we need to get rid of the gun?"

Johnny exhaled a hot stream of smoke and shook his head. "There was no bill of sale, nothing was written down. It was just money changing hands. Even if they were to track the gun to the dealer, he wouldn't know who the fuck he sold it to."

Gabriel nodded at the exchange. "Good question, good answer. No need to get rid of the gun." He turned to Johnny. "But you have to wipe it down and put it back in your dad's cabinet the very next day, or that night if possible. Three: things we're going to need. Jared, I need you to bring duct tape, rope, floor cleaning soap, a couple of working flashlights, a pillow to muffle the sound of the gunshot, some rags, and two large trash bags, heavy duty. Put everything in a duffel bag. Johnny, you'll pick Jared up at ten the night of and make your way here. Take a roundabout route as well, and make sure you're not followed. Four: burying the body." Gabriel turned to everyone. "Not everyone should go. It should be two of us only. Johnny, you're going to be taking the gun back; you'll have your bike. Jared, you're going to clean up around here. Once Achilles and I are done disposing of the body we'll come back for you and take you home." He looked up at Jared. "Now I don't expect to get caught, but if we're not back in ninety minutes, you get the fuck out of here and go straight to your place.

We'll meet two nights later at the pizza shop, if all goes well."

Jared nodded through his dark sunglasses at the last four words, comprehending now the riskiness of what they were all about to embark on.

Gabriel looked up at the others. "Any questions?"

"Yeah, when's this thing going down?" Achilles asked, tiredly.

"In two to three weeks, we're talking mid to late August," Gabriel replied. "This will give us time for a couple dry runs and make sure we figure out any possible snags and deal with them beforehand. Any other questions?"

"When do you want me to get everything?" Jared asked.

"This week, and stash it all in a duffle bag in your closet and ready to go. We're doing a run through next Saturday-start to finish. Everyone clear on the plan?" Gabriel looked from one man to the other.

All nodded. All were clear on the plan, or at least with their own version of the plan. And for Gabriel, it was as good as it was going to get.

Johnny stood up, dusting off his jeans. "Alright boys, I gotta burn." He turned to Jared. "Come on bro, I'll take you home."

Jared stood up mechanically. He leaned in for a high-five with his two friends on the ground and then followed Johnny to the edge of the woods and down the hill.

38

"Come on." Gabriel jumped up as if inspired, his body partially shading Achilles from the late morning sun, and held out his hand.

"Where are we going?" Achilles hoisted himself up, grunting with the effort.

Gabriel smiled back. "It's a surprise. Let's go. I'll drive."

Several blocks later they stopped at the corner where Priti stood waiting, her brown limbs stretched long and slender from her khaki shorts and white button-down shirt.

Achilles made to climb into the back but Gabriel steadied him, his right hand on Achilles shoulder and Priti jumped into the backseat.

"Hi Achilles," she said, lightly squeezing his other shoulder with the ease and comfort of a close friend that almost made him cry. "How are you feeling?"

"I'm good," Achilles said, smiling back. "A little tired."

Priti stretched forward, kissing Gabriel on the cheek. "Hi," she whispered and smiled, revealing bright white teeth.

"Hey," Gabriel said, then put the car in gear. "Let's get going."

The car raced down the highway going east as Gabriel stepped hard on the accelerator, pushing the Chevelle past seventy, eighty, ninety, seeking the breathless exhilaration of speed. Hot air flooded through all four open windows, filling the cabin with the roar of the road, drowning out the rock and roll from the stereo. Achilles closed his eyes and breathed in the moment.

Gabriel squinted against the glare of the arching sun as he

scanned the road for undercover cop cars.

Achilles opened his eyes as the car slowed down and veered toward the exit. "The beach?" he asked, looking at Gabriel.

"Why not?" Gabriel answered back.

"Why not," Achilles reaffirmed, his eyes smiling. "Man, I haven't been to the beach in-" but the sound of the waves crashing against the surf drowned out his musings.

Gabriel opened the trunk and pulled out a long maroon and white striped umbrella.

"Where'd you get that?" Achilles eyed it suspiciously, searching his memory for a similar vision within the previous years, before locating it with the mischievous smile that matched Gabriel's. "That's from our patio!" 'Our' meaning Achilles's apartment complex patio which he and his mother never bothered to enjoy with the other tenants.

"I borrowed it," Gabriel replied, adding, "I'll return it."

"You can keep it." Achilles laughed for the first time that day, that month. "Let that crummy landlord fork over some money for a new one."

The sun reflected brightly off the white sand, the ocean beyond beckoned like a promise, and white seagulls sang and plunged half crazed into green water in a well-choreographed dance. Achilles bent down, undid his laces, kicked off his Pumas and socks, and thread his toes into the hot sand. The breeze off the water tempered the sun's hot rays overhead, but he could still feel his head burning, the part that had been scalped by the chemo.

Gabriel motioned to Priti who pulled out a light blue, weather-beaten sun hat. "Here, put this on." Gabriel placed the hat on Achilles's head.

"Wow! You guys came prepared," Achilles said, arranging the hat.

"It's Priti, she's the one who thought of it," Gabriel said.

"Thanks, Priti."

"Sure." She smiled at both of them.

Gabriel and Priti interlocked fingers and walked onto the beach, their bodies falling into each other with each step. Achilles walked several steps behind, his pace slower and labored.

Priti turned around concerned. "Are you okay, Achilles?"

"Yeah, we can wait," Gabriel said.

But Achilles waved them off. "I'm doing great. Are you kidding? I'm just soaking it all in. You two find us a spot. I'll catch up."

The couple gave him an extra look to confirm before continuing on.

Despite his joint and muscle pains and fatigue, he enjoyed walking on the beach. It had been so long.

He met up with them as Gabriel stabbed the umbrella pole into the sand and Priti laid out three large beach towels for them. Achilles sat down, exhausted. "I just need to rest. I'll be all right," he said breathlessly. Gabriel and Priti sat down next to him under the shade and Priti pulled out sandwiches and cans of soda, distributing them to the boys.

"Thanks," Achilles said, opening up his can. He tilted his head back and drank it in several long swallows. "Man, I haven't had soda in ages."

"Sandwich is good too." Gabriel offered him one.

"Good, 'cause I finally got my appetite back."

Gabriel turned to the water and bit into his sandwich.

All ate their lunch in meditative silence, held sway by the rhythmic crash and retreat of the waves.

"I'm going in the water," Priti announced, getting up. She removed her shirt and shorts revealing a bright yellow one-piece bathing suit that Gabriel could not help but notice covered up her back. With her cinnamon skin and bright yellow bathing suit, she seemed out of place with the boys in their ripped blue jean shorts and black t shirts, whose pale skin would quickly redden under the sun. "Coming?" She smiled playfully at Gabriel.

Gabriel took a hard pull off his cigarette, exhaling a burst of smoke that scattered in the breeze swept off the Atlantic. "You go in, I'll join you in a minute. Let me finish my smoke first."

"Okay." Priti frowned slightly. "But can you apply some sunscreen on me?"

"Sure." Gabriel pressed his cigarette between his lips, and reached his hand out to her.

She passed the tube to Gabriel and sat down in front of him, peering off into the water. Gabriel placed his stump along her side and slowly worked the sunscreen into her skin, massaging her neck, shoulders and arms. The intimacy of the moment wrapped itself around the two as each sought each other out through touch. She felt a thrill in the gentleness of Gabriel's otherwise rough and strong fingers. More than once she resisted the urge to grab his hand and kiss the palm and press it to her face. Gabriel felt Priti's smooth, hot skin under his hand, and he too fought to temper his own urges. If Achilles noticed anything between his two companions, he didn't show it. He seemed entranced by the ocean's mighty roar, it's vastness, it's lost horizon.

Gabriel planted a kiss at the base of Priti's neck. "All done," he whispered in her ear.

"Hurry up and join me in the water." Priti hid her fluttering heart behind the smile. She stood up and ran to the shoreline, her chest so full and light she felt she could fly.

"Huh?" Gabriel turned to Achilles, half dazed.

"I said congrats," Achilles replied. He held up a hand to shield the sun as he looked on at Priti. "She's a good chick, different from the others. And I think she really digs you."

Gabriel looked at Priti enter into the warm shallow water, her shoulders hunched with mild trepidation. She glanced back, a white flash of a smile before turning to the water. "I don't know how to describe it. She's something special. It's like I hit the jackpot. It's been – what, a month- and sometimes I think I've known her my whole life. And since I've met her I think about a future, with her. I never used to think about the future. I never really thought I had one." He turned back to Achilles. "We all just have to finish this one thing. Wipe the slate clean. And then we can move on."

Achilles looked from Gabriel to the surf. He spoke softly, his words nearly drowned out by the roar of the crashing waves.

"Do you think so?"

Gabriel took in a drag of his cigarette, exhaling as he spoke. "Sure I think so. This old pedophile's ruined lives, man. And unless we stop him, he'll probably ruin more. I mean, what are we on this earth for, if not to stop monsters like him."

"Why not go to the police?" Achilles asked, his voice tired.

"Police!" Gabriel spit the word out like a curse, looking off to the side to catch his anger before turning back to Achilles. "The police can't even catch a bunch of juvenile delinquents. Plus, there's no hard evidence to use against him. And even if there were, he'd be out on the street after a few years."

Achilles exhaled sharply. "But what if nothing changes? Should we still kill him?"

"What do you mean if nothing changes? The old man is a deviant. A pedophile. He deserves to be killed." Gabriel shot him a sideways glance.

Achilles leaned back into the shade of the umbrella, resting against his forearms, hiding from the sun's glare. "I don't doubt it, man. I'm just asking once we kill him, then what?"

Gabriel took a drag from his cigarette. "I don't understand what you're talking about. We kill him because it's the right thing to do. Period. I'm not expecting more. I'm not looking for a medal." Gabriel pressed his cigarette butt hard into the sand as smoke escaped through his words. "And I hope you're not backing out of this."

"I'm not backing out. I'm in this all the way," Achilles replied. "I'm saying sometimes I wonder what the point of it all is."

"What?" Gabriel turned surprised. "What do you mean?"

Achilles nodded to the water. "She's calling for you."

Gabriel looked up to find Priti knee deep in the dark green water. Brilliant shards of light reflected off the choppy waves that lapped against the shore. She beckoned to him as she drew water up against her shoulders and arms.

Gabriel stood up stretching himself to full height before turning with a note of warning. "This conversation isn't over."

Achilles nodded tiredly. "Go to her."

As Gabriel walked the short stretch of beach to Priti, Achilles recalled a memory of the two of them the summer after they'd found their home. They had both been alone on the floor together smoking cigarettes, listening to a scratchy tape of Van Halen's Diver Down. Gabriel had just shot down one of his get-rich-quick schemes, but he had spoken undeterred. "Alright, alright," he'd said. "But it's just a matter of time, then we'll leave our mark on the world."

Gabriel had turned onto his shoulder, away from his. "I don't know."

"What do you mean you don't know."

"Is that really the point?" Gabriel had asked.

"It's gotta be the point, man," Achilles had replied, looking up at the dark wooden planks lining their ceiling. "Make it big, make our mark on the world. If it isn't that, then what the hell are we on this friggin' earth for?"

"Maybe we're here just to make it to the next day," Gabriel had replied.

"I disagree, man. I disagree. Making it to the next day is not enough for me. I want to do more. I want to be remembered," Achilles had said finally, and the conversation had lapsed into silence and was soon forgotten.

Achilles lay under the shade of the umbrella as the memory faded, and he began to think about memories themselves, how in death there are no memories. Memories are a luxury of the living, offering depth and play. The vertigo from his hospitalization returned and he lay supine and closed his eyes, waiting for the moment to pass. When the spinning had settled he opened his eyes and willed himself to sit. The sand stretched out for miles all around, nothing but white, hot sand; the ocean but a thin slash of green on the horizon. He felt his body shrink under the light blue sky that towered above him, until he was no more than a grain of sand lost in a desert. He closed his eyes and steadied his breath. At some point during his hospitalization he'd recalled the meditative breathing his sensei had tried to teach him years before. And though he had disregarded it then, Achilles clung to it during the many moments of chaos in his hospital bed, just as he clung to it now.

3 9

A *nd now for the weather... Phil? Well Sandy, we are entering what promises to be a typical August heat wave,
with temperatures approaching one hundred degrees, and
the humidity in the low nineties. Get ready for the dog days
of summer. What's going on with that tropical depression
in the Caribbean? Well Sandy, that tropical depression has
gotten much stronger as it moved eastward. With winds of
up to eighty miles per hour Category 1 Hurricane Frederick
crossed over Hispaniola overnight, dumping more than two
feet of rain and leaving a path of destruction on the island,
with untold number dead. At this point the direction is due
east. Let's cross our fingers Frederick does not make any
northward turns. Back to you, Sandy. I'll keep them crossed,
thanks Phil. And now back...*

The side screen door slapped shut as Gabriel walked outside into the dense soupy heat. It was almost reflex, this impulse to leave his house, to the impatient tapping sound of a
car horn. His father stood next to the open car door of a late
model Porsche, candy apple red, some wisps of grey in his
thick head of black curly hair. Shirt unbuttoned part way down
the neck revealing even less grey. Life had treated him well, an
uncovered bowl filled with sweet offerings. He was otherwise
unchanged, un-aged. Superman, impervious even to the heat
around him, not even a drop of sweat on his brown. No impatient scowl, but a large flashy smile this time "Gabe, look at
you. You've grown so much." Raul held his hand out as much
in greeting as in appraisal of his cautiously approaching son.

The convertible roof was down, an unknown young woman sat in the front passenger seat eyeing the rearview mirror, applying the last touches of makeup.

Gabriel allowed himself to be hugged, his hair tussled. This was, in fact, his father. Leaving a hand on Gabriel's shoulder, Raul turned to the car. By now the woman had finished preparing herself and was facing them, a smile suggesting how little she knew of their relationship. "Sharon, this is my son Gabriel, the one I've been telling you about."

"Wow," she replied as she scanned Gabriel from head to toe. "By the way you were talking, I expected a little boy. Not a handsome young man." Raul in response reappraised his Gabriel; the boy had caught up to him in height, though not nearly as thick or meaty. His left arm seemed proportionate to the rest of him.

"He's grown up, huh." Raul clapped Gabriel loudly on the back. "Can't believe it, must be two years now. Can't believe how time flies," he said apologetically, as if time flying was to blame for Raul's absence in his son's life. He reached along the front seat and pushed it forward. "Come on son, get in. Let's have some lunch."

Gabriel glanced back at the house, expecting some deterring response, then stepped in to the back and sat quietly.

Raul and Sharon picked up their previous conversation, talking loudly so as to include Gabriel in their circle of conversation, but the car picked up speed and the wind began jostling their words, and Gabriel heard less and less. He lifted his face up to the bright sun, losing himself to the loud riotous wind that whipped his hair. At times he caught his father glancing at him in the rearview mirror, at times he caught his own reflection.

They pulled off the road and parked at a diner Gabriel remembered, but was not quite sure from where or when.

Raul stepped out of the car and pulled the front seat forward for Gabriel. "Come on out, son." Gabriel exited and his father again grabbed him, squeezing his arms tightly. Proudly. "My boy, my boy." He wrapped one arm around Gabriel and one arm around Sharon and led them into the cool air-conditioned diner.

"Son," Raul announced as he put down his fork. It had been a relatively passive meal for Gabriel who sat across from him father and Sharon, his sandwich untouched. He watched his father expounding philosophically about life throughout lunch; the latter mistook Gabriel's lack of appetite and silence for rapt attention. "The market has been very good to me these past few years- my investments, my properties- I have been able to earn more than enough for my expenses and have been able to set aside some money." Here Raul winked at Sharon who smiled back quietly, suggesting complicity in this surprise announcement. "And as you are already well aware, life can be difficult if you do not have a firm foundation on which to start from. Education is very important in this regard," Raul waved his fork, "but where you go to school is even more important. And so I have set aside enough money these past few years to pay for you to attend a good college. A private college," he said pointing his forkful of extra rare steak towards Gabriel. "Now I know you have made friends that will be going to the community college nearby your mother's place, but let's be honest, you have to think about your future and those boys are only going to hold you back. I mean, come on Gabe, you don't want to be pumping gas or shining shoes or waiting tables all your life." Here he stuffed the meat in his mouth to allow for moment of silence to help Gabriel process these various futures. "There is a very expensive and elite college not too far from my home. No, no. No need to worry." He shot up his hands to ward off any objections, which never came. "Money is no object, and the dean is a friend of mine so your spot for the coming semester is assured." Gabriel continued to look passively at his father, remembering all of his facial expressions, the jaw clenching, the pursing of the lips when thinking, the dramatic gestures with his hands. These affectations, they all came back now, only more practiced, polished to the point that they seemed natural. And given his large build, his coif of perfect hair, they only added to his imposing presence. "Now this is important." His father jabbed a forkful of steak and brandished it. "In this life, Gabriel, there are two kinds of people, two kinds: masters and slaves. If you are not one, then you are the other. Follow my instructions and no one will ever mistake you for a slave." His father finally sat back and chewed his steak with his familiar air of self-confidence.

Gabriel counted the seconds tick away, unsure if his father expected an answer or some expression of gratitude. That was his father, poker faced to a fault. He finally stood up tossing his napkin on his seat. "Thanks for your words of wisdom, but I hope to God I never follow your instructions, or your example, or you. You live in the smallest of boxes where people can be defined so simply and brutally and be treated as such. But not me, I plan to live my life completely outside your deluded box, to be neither slave nor master. In fact, it'll be my main goal in life. But most important, I plan to live my life in open rebellion to yours, to serve as a contrast, even if it means I wind up in a life of struggle. Because at the end of that life I will recognize it for what it truly was, successful." But Gabriel didn't say this as much as he thought it, and wanted to say it. Instead he asked, "Which one was Danny?" And walked out of the restaurant as the thin fragile façade of their relationship, of loving father and dutiful son, fell apart into small tinkling shards.

Father and son were silent the ride back, the vacuum filled by the sounds of traffic and the roar of the wind. Gabriel kept his eyes shut, refusing to meet his father's gaze. This whole visit was a joke; their relationship was a joke; his father's investment in his life was a joke. His father would drive off again and not show up for another several years

Raul ventured conversation as Gabriel stepped outside the

car. "I'd stay longer but I want to make it out of New York be-fore the storm hits." His son stiffened up within his embrace.

"Son," Raul called out as Gabriel took the twenty steps back to the house. "Son, I love-."

Gabriel let the door crash behind him as the Porsche pulled away.

40

It's been brutal out there these past couple of days, Phil. Hope you have some better weather for us to look forward to today. Unfortunately not Sandy, today plans to be even hotter and more humid. Yesterday's temperature approached record highs. The city reported multiple deaths among the elderly all throughout the five boroughs. So keep grandma and grandpa inside today. How's hurricane Frederick, Phil? Well Sandy, Frederick has continued to pick up speed as it moved eastward in the Caribbean. Mass evacuations from coastal areas took place overnight in Cuba, Jamaica and the Bahamas as drenching downpours and gusty winds destroyed an untold...

Doris Collins wrung her hands nervously, keeping time to the wall clock's ticking hand in Dr. Stevens' waiting room. She'd dressed up for the occasion, as if today was her son's graduation, for both of them really. And to some degree it was. She and Achilles had learned more than they had ever cared to know about his condition the past four weeks, and here they were expecting a diploma of a different sort, one that would guarantee the rest of his long and natural life. She wanted to be done with all this, the needles, the medications and their horrific effects on her son, the interminable beeps and buzzers, the overhead pages. But most of all she wanted her son back home. She looked sideways at him. He'd dressed up for today as well, wearing pressed khaki's and an ironed white button-down shirt she'd bought the week before. But she'd not factored in how much weight he'd lost and his clothes hung limp and baggy. Achilles slouched back in his chair resting, his legs stretched out in front of him.

The door suddenly opened, startling her. Achilles opened one eye as Dr. Stevens stuck his head out of the office to usher them in.

Dr. Stevens' office was smaller than Achilles had expected, but it allowed for a large mahogany desk, a large bookcase behind Dr. Stevens' chair and two chairs in front for Achilles and his mother. The room also offered a view of the parking lot in the back and the highway beyond.

Dr. Stevens opened up Achilles's chart to pull out the results of the last bone marrow aspirate and blood draw. But all this was a formality. He'd obviously looked at them before and had recognized the dim prognosis spelled out in the findings.

Though he'd never gotten higher than a B in school, Achilles was no fool. He could tell when someone was stalling. "So doc, what's the good word?" His calm voice betrayed neither his pounding heart nor the invading dread.

Dr. Stevens nodded at the question. "More important than these lab results is how you're feeling today."

Achilles could sense the falsehood in the question, in the direction his oncologist was leading them. "I've been better and I've been worse."

Dr. Stevens looked intently at Achilles for a moment. "That's good, I suppose," he said as he shuffled the papers in his hands. "So as you know, the first step in chemotherapy for your leukemia is induction which usually lasts a month. At the end of that month we do testing of your blood and bone marrow to see how well you responded to treatment-"

"You told me this already," Achilles interrupted, impatient and angry at what he had already guessed the lab results would show. "Just tell me about my blood and bone marrow, doc, tell me what my chances are."

Dr. Stevens nodded again. "Your bone marrow showed blast cells, Achilles. In fact roughly thirty percent of the cells were blast cells when there should have been none."

"What do these numbers mean, Dr. Stevens?" Achilles's mother pressed anxiously, suddenly finding her voice.

"The thirty percent blasts in Achilles's bone marrow tell us that the chemotherapy did not rid him of the cancer."

Doris reflexively covered her mouth with her hand, as her eyes began to well up with tears. She looked at her son then back to the doctor. "What do we do now?"

Achilles looked away from the scene unfolding in front of him to the one outside the window. A white sun-bleached sky exposed a pallid, washed out scene; a colorless, hopeless world gazed back at him.

"We will continue the chemotherapy for a few more weeks and repeat the testing."

"Then what are we doing here?" Achilles asked, his voice edgy with irritation. "Why didn't you just treat me for six weeks to begin with and then do the testing?"

"The testing we did Friday is a standard gauge for us with regard to how you are going to do with the leukemia, and that your chances of long term remission and survival are."

"And what are they?" Achilles asked, regretting the question, having already guessed the answer.

The ensuing silence answered for him. "Given what we know to date about this type of leukemia and-"

"What the fuck, man? You lied to me." Achilles sat forward, pointing his finger accusingly at the doctor.

Dr. Stevens sighed, shaking his head slowly. "Nobody lied to you."

"You led me on." Achilles rose from his chair despite the unrelenting weakness. "You made me believe I could make it. What the fuck!" Achilles slumped back into his chair.

"At the start of chemotherapy we all want to have hope for the best possible outcomes and we usually do. There's still a chance for remission."

"Well I don't want any more of your chemo." The fuse, lit

long before, had finally burned through, igniting, detonating. Achilles leaned forward again, yelling back, "Look at me, man. Look at what your drugs have done to me." Achilles spread his arms out revealing his cachectic frame. "And for what? So that you can sit there in your big leather chair, wearing your expensive clothes, and that fucking smug look on your face." And as the endlessly dividing lymphoblasts phagocytized the inside of his body, Achilles rallied the little life left within him and rebelled against the prognosis he'd been sentenced to, unleashing the bitterness and anger that had been simmering for so long, and now boiled over, spilling out, at the oncologist, at the chemo, at the cancer, at the short, brutal life he'd been born into, with so little to show for it. He yelled until he was breathless and collapsed back in his chair.

Dr. Stevens waited patiently. When at last he spoke to Achilles, he directed his measured response to his mother as well. "With chemotherapy you still have a chance at life, no matter how small. Without it, you face almost certain death."

Achilles fought the urge to cry, but he had very little fight left in him. He looked away from the physician.

Dr. Stevens assumed the formal, professional tone that he'd met Achilles with that first day in the emergency room. "We are going to have you admitted today and resume the induction phase of your treatment," he said, closing the file.

His mother, always willing to please, nodded approvingly. "Thank you, doctor. We will do as you say," she said, wondering at that moment if she'd seen this very situation played out on one of her television programs, and felt comforted by this.

4 1

So Phil how's the weather today? Well it's official, we are in the middle of one of the decade's worst heat waves with today making it ten straight days with the tempera-ture breaking the 100 degree mark. If you don't need to go anywhere stay indoors where it's cool. Sounds like some good advice, Phil. What's the latest on Hurricane Frederick? Unfortunately, Hurricane Frederick has only gotten stron-ger, now a category 3 hurricane with reports that it could soon strengthen to category 4. With a diameter of five hun-dred miles, Sandy, this is a monster. Since early yesterday it has pounded the eastern seaboard with coastal flooding al-ready reported from South Carolina all the way to Virginia. Governors in all coastal states, including our own governor, have declared a state of emergency. By most predictions, we should be facing the worse of Frederick by tomorrow eve-ning. Should I get my umbrella out Phil? (Light chuckle) I think you'll need more than an umbrella, Sandy...

Johnny and Jared struggled to keep up with Gabriel's pace as they climbed the hill to home. "Yo, where's Achilles?" Johnny called out in between gasps of air. "Man, it's friggin' hot, I feel like I'm in a Turkish bath."

Gabriel didn't bother turning his head. "He's back in the hospital starting his chemo again. Not sure what the hell's go-ing on."

Jared brought up the rear; he too struggled to keep up with Gabriel's pace, stopping several times along his climb up, dys-pneic in the heat and humidity. Gabriel was halfway to the shack when Jared reached the top of the hill; he was several yards behind when Gabriel reached the door.

Gabriel stopped to inspect a notice nailed on the front. "Fuck!" he cried suddenly, startling the other two. He scratched at the notice, kicking and punching the door until it rattled on its hinges.

Johnny turned to Jared questioningly; Jared shrugged back. He approached Gabriel cautiously. "What's going on, man?"

Gabriel, nostrils flared and wild eyed, ripped off the notice and held it for the others to see.

Johnny leaned in, skimming as he read. "In compliance with the Building Act, section 80- We, Jones Contracting firm- Order of intent to demolish on the date August 15." Johnny looked up at Gabriel. "August 15! That's Monday! What are we going to do?"

Gabriel crumpled up the notice and threw it against the door. "I knew this wouldn't last. I knew it was too good to be true. Shit. Shit. Shit." He sat down hard on the steps, staring off into space. "I knew it. I knew it. I knew it," he whispered to himself.

The others sat down next to him, eyeing him expectantly. All was quiet under the scorching midday sun. "We don't have a choice," he said finally, running his hand through his sweat-drenched hair. "It has to go down tomorrow." Gabriel turned to Jared and Johnny. "Would've been nice to get in a dry run or two...but we've already gone over the plan a bunch of times. I know we can do this."

"What about Achilles?" Johnny asked.

"I'll head over to the hospital today and let him know about the change in plans."

"What about our home?" Jared asked, verbalizing the ache that each felt as the shock of the news faded and the reality of the imminent loss of their home set in.

Gabriel shook his head, unwilling or unable to delve into

the subject. "Let's just go over the plan one more time," he said, his voice subdued.

And as the three crouched down on the ground Gabriel discussed the last minute changes in the plan, all three silently shivering in anticipation of the moment that they'd all thought might never come.

42

2008

Philip McGregor peered through the blinds of his office at the half dozen tractors tearing up the back lot of his school. Workers with neon yellow reflective vests dotted the landscape. As principal of Great Hope Country Day School, he felt entirely responsible for the renovations being done. How hard he had fought for the funding for this project. And now all his efforts were coming to fruition. He sat down, leaning back in his chair, resting his head back on crisscrossed fingers. He immediately stood up and returned to the window, peering out again; he was at once happy and anxious at the thought of so much activity at the school- his school. Finally, after so many years, this much needed facelift- new playground for the elementary school, new sports fields for the middle school- would put his school on the map. If this crew could just get the work done before the end of summer break.

"Principal McGregor." A jarring, impatient knock at the door. "Principal McGregor."

The foreman's large bulk filled up the doorframe, sweat stains darkened the front and sides of his light blue shirt, strained at the front by a thick and heavy paunch. "Yes, Mr. Stanych, what is it this time?"

The foreman mopped a bandana over his forehead, his face betraying a new worry. "Principal McGregor, sir, I think we have a problem."

The school principal sighed audibly, a bit perturbed at

the thought of an unforeseen delay in what was to be the biggest project of this school, his school, and followed the foreman outside. They navigated their way around crater like dirt holes of the back lot, then came to the far corner of the school grounds and nudged their way through a group of workers that had collected around the mouth of a recently excavated hole.

"What did your men dig up this time- Oh my god!" Philip McGregor backed away nauseous.

Mr. Stanych looked into the hole as he passed the bandana across his sweaty forehead. A collection of bones lay strewn about the bottom of the hole; the vacuous eyeless sockets of a human skull in the center looked out as if in greeting, waiting to be discovered.

43

Johnny caught the last few rays of sunlight peeking through the thick green eastern Pennsylvania pines. His motorcycle rumbled along the curve of route 1, a blur of dark green on either side. He flicked his wrist to check the time; 8pm. It would be pitch black within twenty minutes, more or less the same amount to bike it home. Sandra would be waiting for him, pissed as usual.

Up ahead on the right the lights of the local roadhouse shined bright and beckoning. As he approached he recognized an old Eagles song blasting on the speakers. He looked again at his watch. Fuck it. He rode his bike up to the door, parking it alongside a long row of bikes- Harleys, Hondas, Suzuki-hogs and rice rockets, a revolutionary mixing that would not have been tolerated thirty years before.

He pushed the doors and walked through. A long dark wood bar stretched along the left, hugged by a row of stools, a full-length mirror behind the bar reflecting back the countless sad, dribbling stories. A pool table took up a chunk of space on the right, a few dartboards and old photographs decorated the walls. He made out the dozen or so usual aging, long-haired drunks, some flitted around the bar, rehashing old memories, others circled around the jukebox, as if seeing the same list of songs for the first time. A few scantily clad women sat strategically along the bar, eyeing would be customers for action in one of a couple discreet rooms in the back.

Johnny leaned over the bar summoning the bartender with a quick nod. "Shot of bourbon." He turned to his right and winked at one of the women. "Hey Jackie, how you feeling?"

The woman, mid-thirties, a mane of wavy red hair, her twisted her lips in a wry coy smile. "Feeling a bit better now that you're here," she answered, her voice silky and deep. "Buy me a drink?"

Johnny turned to the bartender pouring the bourbon. "Give the young lady another of what she's having."

The bartender, a large muscular man who was as handy with mixed drinks as he was with rowdy drunks, nodded quietly.

Johnny looked at his bourbon a moment, as if in contemplation, then extended his head back, his hair caressing the collar of his leather jacket, and downed the amber in two sharp swallows. The harsh burn in his chest eased into a mellowing warmth that spread out to his limbs. Then as if suddenly remembering, Johnny turned to the woman nursing her drink and sidled up to her. "How's the action tonight, doll face?"

Jackie stirred her drink with a thin red straw. Up close she looked older, late thirties perhaps, unable to hide the wrinkles around her eyes and at the corners of her mouth with makeup without seeming garish, a few strands of grey hair, having escaped the magic of the red dye, peaked through. As tired and bored as she was she mustered a smile. "It's been slow until you came, hon."

Johnny smiled. "Aww come on Jackie, you're the hottest gal in this joint. I bet you're fighting 'em off every night." He turned back to the bartender and whirled his finger a few times. "Another round please."

"So any plans tonight, sugar?"

Johnny grabbed his drink, raised it as if to toast the aging whore, a woman pulling at the end of the string of all her life's bad choices. He downed it quickly and smacked the counter with the glass. "Perhaps, perhaps, perhaps. I may be back, Jackie, so don't go anywhere."

Jackie raised an eyebrow at the idea that she even had a choice. "Here, hon," she said, reaching into her black satin

purse dangling from her bare shoulder and pulling out a casino chip.

"What'd you do, rob a casino?" Johnny chuckled at his
own witticism.

Jackie smiled. "This is what I call a freebie," she said as she
stood up, pressing the chip in his palm. "If you come back tonight it'll be worth something." She hitched the purse back on
her shoulder and walked to the back to watch the pool game.

Johnny pulled out a wallet shackled by a chain to his belt,
took a few bills and tossed them on the bar, raised a parting
salute to the bartender, and walked out.

The backfiring roar of his Harley breached the last few
lines of an old Lynerd Skynerd tune then faded.

Sandra kept her eyes trained on the doorknob. She took
a sharp drag of her cigarette then stabbed it deep into the
mounting pile of ruby red, pinched cigarette butts that by now
had overtaken the ashtray on the kitchen table. She sighed
a steady exhale of smoke as she let her gaze wander around
their home- his home really. She recalled the tireless effort at
the beginning to establish her presence in his life, in his little
ranch house in the middle of nowhere- 'my shotgun shack' he
had liked to joke. Pictures, flowers rugs, little knickknacks to
measure and remember their months, years together. She had
taken his lack of resistance for the carefree, 'Rambling Man'
ways- part of what drew her to him. But eventually she had
come to realize he just didn't care about the changes she'd imposed, had come and gone as he pleased, acknowledging them
and her less and less. And soon enough she had stopped pressing, stopped trying, recognizing herself less and less. And after
five years there was so little of her left. Another five years and
she would disappear. The end of her cigarette smoldered in
the ashtray, marking the passage of time, time waiting, time
passing, time-. The familiar sound of his motorcycle jolted her
awake. She quickly tossed the ashtray's contents in the trash
and sat down, lighting up a cigarette, her last, hopefully, in

this house. She waited.

A jangle of keys, a familiar whistle and now Johnny stepped into the crosshairs of his girlfriend's acrimony. He quickly surveyed the room, taking in the one piece of luggage that stood at attention by the table, a quickly folded jacket draped on top. "What's up, baby doll? Sorry about the holdup. Lot's of traffic, some construction on I80, bumper to bumper most of the way. Planning a trip?" He walked into the kitchen, opened the refrigerator and grabbed a can of beer, then sat down, eyeing her expectantly, with the look of a poker player who's holding a good hand.

Sandra followed Johnny with her eyes; she didn't reply, not at first. She knew better than to engage him in his banter. She stood up, hovering over him, staring at the bright ember end of her cigarette as if remembering something that had burned out long ago. She stabbed it into the ashtray and picked up her jacket and suitcase. She then looked back at Johnny one last time. "I'm leaving you." Her voice was deep with resentment and sorrow.

"Aw, honey, wait a second." Johnny stood, making a half-hearted attempt at stopping her with an even less than half-hearted attempt at embracing her. "Why are you so angry? Come on, you don't want to go anywhere."

Sandra, refusing to engage or respond, set her bag down within his embrace but only to take off her engagement ring. "Here." She placed the ring on the table. "You can keep it." She pushed forward towards the door, knocking Johnny slightly off balance.

"Come on, Sandra." Johnny turned to the door as it slammed shut.

A few moments later, Johnny heard the sound of her Ford come to life then slowly fade. He picked up the ring and looked at the inscription, caught a few words of some meaningless drizzle he'd made up at the jewelry store several years before.

He placed the ring on the table and stared at it. Then he

remembered the chip in his pocket. He spun the chip and the ring on the table, watching the two rotate around an invisible sun, waiting to see which would stop first, allowing fate to decide his next move. He finished his beer and smoked a cigarette. He looked around outside the kitchen at the living room. All the lights were out, and house was pitch black. No light. No sounds. Nothing.

He stood up, pocketing the ring and the chip in the inside of his leather bomber jacket, and made for the door. Outside, silence succumbed to the deep rumble of Johnny's Harley, but only for a moment.

44

Dr. Gabriel Dayan sat across from the patient at a loss for words as the man crumpled under the weight of his death sentence, of his body's sudden betrayal.

Late thirties, a pregnant wife at home waiting for the new life inside her to join them on the next chapter in their journey together, the young man sat leaning forward, rocking, his head cradled in his hands. "Why? Why? Why? I'd been living clean for more than fifteen years now, eating right, exercise. You name it, doc, I did it."

He'd entered Dr. Dayan's office a few years before, back when his exam was normal, when all the labs looked good. 'You're too healthy,' Gabriel had joked with him. 'Come back in a few years.'

But those few years had passed and they sat together now as the present circled the drain. "I'm sorry," Dr. Dayan replied, shaking his head. "I didn't know about the IV drug use. I should have asked, I would have done more testing earlier."

"It's not your fault, doc, it was me. All those drugs way back when. When I got clean, I counted myself lucky I never overdosed or got HIV." The patient covered his eyes with his palms as he cried into them. "I should have come clean with you and told you everything. But I thought, I thought- to be honest I don't know what I thought - maybe that I was like everybody else, that my past didn't matter. I should have come sooner, doc, when I first started feeling off. I guess I was lying to myself."

He showed up the week before, fatigued and out of breath. Lab showed liver inflammation but very little else. Further testing revealed positive hepatitis C. A subsequent CT scan showed a large mass consuming the right side of his liver with the malignancy spreading to neighboring lymph nodes.

"Of course we have to run some more tests to confirm the diagnosis," Gabriel found himself saying, as much to console the patient as to justify the need to provide such false hope. But he lost the strength of his conviction, and his voice dropped to just above a whisper, "I will refer you to the best specialists, to give you the best opportunity to beat this."

Despite nodding at everything Dr. Dayan said, the patient was no longer listening; he was beyond consoling. His thoughts were of his wife and unborn child at home, of all his future plans, sand castles that were now washing away with the tide. "Our past, doc," he said, numbly looking at the tips of his interlocking fingers, "it always seems to catch up with us in the end."

He walked the patient to the front desk where a pleasant heavyset woman stood up and took the chart. He shook the man's hand, but in doing so felt the inadequacy of the gesture. It was in these moments when the patient had reached the sharp boundaries of what medical care could provide, that Dr. Dayan found himself lost in his role. "Maggie here will set you up with referrals for the oncologist and gastroenterologist."

He walked back to his office, defeated, his thoughts reflexively spiraling down the path of self-recrimination, slipping into his addictive habit of self-blame, revisiting every encounter with the young man in search of the "screw up", the missed question, or the faulty exam. He would search the deepest recesses of his mind, his haystack for the needle of blame and then torture himself with it for days. It was an exercise he engaged in almost regularly, and could not remember the first time. But there always is a first time. Eventually the patient and this episode would fade. But it would never disappear, it would be added to his file of failures and would appear easily at the next screw up. He wondered during these times how his father would respond. Raul would probably brush it off as one of the calculated casualties of working in medicine. But then again, the arrogance of the father is matched only by the humility of the son.

He knew there were more patients to see this morning, but what he needed most now was to sit in his room to reflect and process. Yet time for reflection and processing was a luxury not afforded to those in his profession; he had a full panel of patients for the morning and he was already behind. A wisp of a medical assistant with her hair tied tightly back and her name scripted on her neck passed him in the hallway "Doctor, there's someone in your office to see you," she warned in thick Bensonhurstese.

His sadness gave way to annoyance. "It better not be a drug rep. I thought I told Maggie not to let any more of those guys back here." He walked briskly to the door.

"What's up doc?" He sat back comfortably in Gabriel's chair, fingers interlocked behind his head, motorcycle boots crisscrossed on the edge of the desk. Johnny had grown older, like everyone else, a paunch hung from his otherwise wiry frame, some greying in his wavy shoulder length mullet. But the eyes plotting mischief and mayhem were unchanged. He quickly stood up and presented Gabriel his chair with a flourishing wave of the hand. "Your seat, captain."

Gabriel sat down as Johnny took up a chair across the desk. He eyed him for a few moments. Twenty-five years had passed, and yet this was not the meeting of parted friends. To Gabriel there were certain bonds that were better left broken, certain memories that were better left forgotten, locked away in the past. "What are you doing here?" It was as much a question as a warning.

Johnny reached into his shirt pocket for his pack of cigarettes. "I'm having issues getting my Johnson up for the ladies. I heard they've got this new little blue pill that'll make me fuck just like John Holmes." His laughter degenerated into a hacking throat clearing cough.

Gabriel looked back at him blankly. "What are you doing here?" he repeated, his tone cool and unwelcoming.

"Oh, just thought I'd check in on my ole pal from the neighborhood." Johnny lipped a cigarette out of the box and offered it to Gabriel.

"I don't smoke," Gabriel said, reaching across the desk and snatching the cigarette out of Johnny's mouth, "and this is a smoke free facility. Now, what are you doing here?" His voice was steadily rising.

Johnny grinned, tucking the cigarettes back in his pocket. "You don't come around much any more, do you." Gabriel stayed silent. "You probably don't even remember what it's like." Johnny shook his head. "I always told you, don't forget where you came from- not that your memory was ever that good." Johnny flicked his Zippo lighter open and closed repeatedly against his jeans. "Then again, with all the Koreans moving into the neighborhood, I can hardly recognize it myself."

Gabriel had trudged halfway through his patient panel with several patients left, and felt his patience running out. "I know exactly where I came from, I lived in it. And as soon as I could, I got out of it." He rose from his chair, preparing to kick this ghost from his past out the door. "And I don't need you coming around here and telling me-"

"They found him," Johnny said, finally playing his trump card; he seemed to have a sleeve full of them.

For a brief moment Gabriel wondered "who" but then of course there was only one person who was never meant to be found. He sat down. "How do you know?" His tone was now cautious.

Johnny, finding himself with a captive audience continued, "Seems like the new principal had big plans for renovating the back lot of the school – you remember that piece of shit block of cement? I don't know how any of us got away without cracking our skulls on that thing." Johnny shook his head, smiling. "What a joke that school was. Well anyway, they were tearing everything up, the cement, the back field, and at some point they came upon a skull and a pile of bones."

Gabriel ran his fingers through his hair, greying now and receding. He thought he had banished his past, and here it was now coming back to haunt him. "How do you know all this?"

"I'm on the construction crew for this project. I was hoping they wouldn't find it. But this new principal's got his butt clenched for a major overhaul. Got the funding and everything."

"And now?"

"Now it's a police investigation, with yellow tape all over the friggin' place. But I got my ears and eyes open every day, cause they're letting us work around the spot for now. They don't know anything."

"Eventually they'll find out who it is," Gabriel said distractedly.

"Yeah but that's all they'll know. It's been twenty-five years."

Gabriel thought for a few moments more, letting the revelation sink in, and all of its potential risks. He stood up finally, abruptly. "Thanks for telling me. But I've got patients to see."

"Hold on a second," Johnny said, blocking Gabriel's path. He was several inches shorter and still quite a bit lighter, so he knew he was taking a chance with Gabriel. He poked his index finger into Gabriel's chest threateningly. "Reason why I'm here is to make sure we all keep our part of the bargain. What'd you call it? A pact."

"Are you honestly scared about me talking, Johnny?"

"I don't know, that's why I'm here."

Gabriel swiftly grabbed Johnny's finger and twisted it sharply, causing Johnny's knees to buckle, and leaned in. "A pact is a pact, right Johnny? So you can go back to the hood and rest easy."

Johnny backed away, suddenly scared. "Okay. Okay. And Jared? Maybe he don't have the same respect for pacts."

Gabriel let go of Johnny's finger and made for the door. "I've got patients to see."

"Wait. I promise never to come back," Johnny said, massaging his finger, "unless of course there's some news from the cops, if you promise to check things out with Jared. Deal?"

Gabriel looked down at Johnny and weighed the options. He knew all about Johnny's deals. He breathed out loudly through his nose. "Alright, deal."

And with that Johnny broke into a grin and backed off toward the door. "Alright, man, I'll check you out some other time." He pivoted and then walked out. Gabriel waited at the door, watching a small bit of his unwanted past walking down the hall. At the end Johnny stopped and hunched forward for a moment, then he arched back exhaling a cloud of thick Marlboro into the waiting room, before exiting into the parking lot.

The roar of a Harley Davidson outside broke through the background hum of the office a few moments later, unsettling the peaceful calm; and then as the motorcycle sped away, the roar gradually diminished, leaving a temporary disrespectful silence in its wake before the hum returned.

Gabriel walked back into the room, closing the door behind him. He picked up the phone and punched in ten digits in quick succession.

"Good morning, Dr. Charles Stein's office, Nancy speaking." The receptionist had the calm educated air of one who was well paid and not too harried, which was usually the case in private offices.

"Yes, Dr. Stein, please."

"Who may I ask is calling?"

"Dr. Gabriel Dayan. I believe he's expecting my call."

"Certainly, doctor, I'll put you right through."

Several seconds later a gruff and somewhat impatient voice answered, "Dr. Stein."

"Chuck, it's me Gabriel-"

"Oh, Gabe. Just a moment." The voice on the other line softened a bit. Gabriel heard some papers shuffling in the background. He imagined Dr. Stein's tall angling body hunched over the havoc of his desk, searching through various uneven piles of paper for his information. "Here, I got it. Let's see." Gabriel waited on the line while the neurologist mumbled through the results. "Right. MRI of the Brain- no mass, bleed, or volume loss. Essentially normal..." Some more papers shuffled in the background. "Neuropsychological evaluation also performed on the same day completely normal. No cognitive impairment. No concerns."

Gabriel sighed. "I guess that's it then. Thanks Chuck."

"This is good news, Gabe," Chuck said reassuringly. "We've ruled out some bad diagnoses here."

"I know, I know. Just confused as to why there are so many gaping holes in my distant memory."

"Yes, but your recent memory and instant recall are completely intact."

Gabriel could imagine Chuck shrugging his shoulders in a "nothing more can be done" pose.

After a short pause, Chuck ventured, "You know Gabe, I'm not a psychiatrist-"

"And I'm not looking for one."

Chuck continued, "But if you visit the place or places from your past where these memory gaps are, it may help you to remember."

"Thanks Chuck, this is good news," he said finally.

"No problem, anytime. Call me if you need anything."

"Okay." Gabriel hung up the phone and stared at it a while expecting more guidance. He shut his eyes, nodding at the logic of his colleague's recommendation. He just wasn't sure why he was suddenly afraid. It had been years since the storm, and the immediate aftermath came rushing back to him.

The destruction caused by the hurricane became legendary, hundreds dead in the northeast alone, along with billions of dollars in damages. The town of Great Hope weathered the storm better than most on the island. Still there were reports of damages to houses, business, as well as a handful of missing persons.

What was left of the shack after the storm was razed later on, the dark ground underneath suddenly exposed once again, blanching under the searing sun. Without their home to orbit around, the four friends scattered like debris. The gravitational bonds that had kept them all together were now severed, and they disappeared from each other.

The change in Gabriel would have been striking to witness, if one had cared to look. He appeared broken. His left wrist felt heavy and inert, a useless wing that grounded him. The turbulence from the storm would continue to follow him as he wove his way through the decisions he came to make, leaving his mother to start college on the west coast with his father, then to medical school. He mostly kept to himself, allowing only loose connections with friends he made along the way, boys who called their parents by first names, who laughed together with them at seemingly inside jokes. Gabriel felt like a foreigner in their homes, a smiling silent observer who recognized how much was lost in translation. He hovered above his academics, studying just enough to get by, staying out of the spotlight, keeping to the periphery. It was unclear if he chose to forget or if his memory was another casualty of the storm. Wide swaths of time from that summer disappeared, yet he remembered general concepts, the plan, the dead body, the four friends involved, and the failure of it all. Daniel's swaying body appeared intermittently throughout the years to remind him of this last fact, to torment him. Ultimately he made his way back to the east coast to escape the connections he'd made in California. He found work in an inner city free clinic, finding kinship with its ex-cons, and ex-IVDAs, all ex's, all has-beens, people who'd tried to soar and fell to earth, their homemade wings undone by the sun, and were now mere reflections of these failures, their histories scribbled hastily in scar tissue for all to see. It was during his years at the clinic that the swaying bodies were finally kept at bay.

4 5

Dr. Gabriel had difficulty maintaining focus during his after-noon panel, and found the complaints increasingly mun-dane. His thoughts kept turning to the body, and his old friends from his childhood, his crew he hadn't seen in decades. Then there were the worrisome gaps from that night. After his last patient. he sat down at his desk and turned on his computer. He had some leads in tracking Jared. He knew of his father, had met him once or twice. He looked up the name and found a number. Hesitating before dialing, he was unsure what to say. How would he convince the father of a childhood friend after so long of his sincere interest in resuming contact?

"Hello, Park Terrace Grill," the receptionist answered in a practiced monotone voice. "How may I direct your call?"

"Yes, with Adam Scharpe." He remembered back to Jared's father, always dressed in a tuxedo, well groomed, polished, and distant.

"Is he expecting your call?"

"No, he's not." He recalled the disdainful way Jared spoke about his father and stepmother, spiked with so much anger and resentment. "I was calling to inquire about his son."

There was a silence on the other line; perhaps the recep-tionist had been prohibited from dispensing any information on family.

Gabriel pressed on. "I'm an old friend of Jared's and I'm just trying to track him down. You can tell Mr. Scharpe that it's Gabriel."

"Just a moment," the receptionist said, in a tone that gave no false hopes.

After several minutes the voice of Mr. Scharpe came on the line, although somewhat more hoarse and gravelly, the impact of age. Gabriel guessed him to be somewhere in his late sixties, early seventies. "Gabriel?" he asked, as if the name carried many questions the old man had not dared ask.

"Mr. Scharpe. Hi it's me. Thank you for taking my call. I know it's been a long time and you're probably wondering why I'm calling."

"To be honest, I haven't thought any of Jared's friends in years. Gabriel, is it? You lived on the south side of town, by Hope Street."

Gabriel found himself nodding, smiling at the recognition. "Correct, sir."

"How are you doing? What are you up to these days?"

"I'm a physician, married, a daughter, live and work over in Brooklyn."

"Is that a fact? Well, that's great news." Gabriel could see the father warming up on the other side of the line. "Do you keep in touch with anyone else?"

"To be honest, life has been so busy these past several years, I don't have time to keep in touch with anyone."

"I understand." There followed a brief pause. "Well Gabriel, I'm not sure now is a good time to see Jared you see-"

"Please sir, I know it must sound so strange after all these years, me calling out of the blue. But it's important to me that I see him and try to reconnect."

A hesitant silence responded at the other end of the line.

"Mr. Scharpe?"

"Yes, Gabriel, I'm here. How about tomorrow afternoon? Does six o'clock sound good?"

"Yes sir." Gabriel felt a wave of relief. It would be good to see his old friend after so long.

"We're at the same address. Do you need directions?"

"No sir, I remember. I'll see you tomorrow." As Gabriel hung up the phone, the house, the neighborhood, the town started returning to him. Of course he knew how to get there.

46

"**D**anny!" Gabriel called out to his brother's receding form. The sun had long set and the driveway was immersed in shadows. Daniel stopped several steps before the house and turned around to face his brother.

Finally, Gabriel thought, fighting back tears. "Danny," he said, catching up to his brother. Daniel's face was hidden in shadow, but Gabriel knew it was him, no one forgets a brother. "I'm sorry, Danny. I'm sorry, I'm sorry, I'm sorry. Forgive me. Let me take the words back, let me make it up to you." His brother looked back at him passively, silently. "We're brothers," he continued, "partners, forgive me- or not- just don't go inside the house, don't go up to your room, don't-"

Danny turned to go.

"Daniel!" Gabriel reached out to his brother.

"Go home, Gabriel," the face in the shadow replied. "It's too late for me."

Gabriel made his way down the empty subway platform up the stairs and out onto the ten-minute walk, through the unkempt, desolate streets of East New York to his clinic, a depressingly dark grey, one story structure of rigid right angles erected forty years before, at a time when function trumped form and beauty, where he'd now been for ten years. It was set on one of the side streets in the middle of the block, ribbons of spray paint decorating the façade. He'd arrived early, before the receptionist and medical assistant. But he knew one person would be there already. Dr. Ian Burke had been there every day five days a week from seven to seven, since before Gabriel had been hired, turning the lights on before everyone got in and locking up long after the last person had left. At seventy, widowed now five years, Dr. Burke showed no signs of slowing down, or changing his hours. He was a machine, loved by all his patients, feared by many.

Gabriel knocked lightly on the door, startling the elderly physician from behind one of the many towers of patient charts teetering on his desk. "Gabriel! Surprised to see you here this early." Dr. Burke squinted suspiciously. "Hey, don't you have a wife and daughter at home who would enjoy your morning company?" he asked as he pushed a stack of charts to one side. Dr. Ian Burke had arrived forty years before, flown in from Brisbane, Australia to attend a conference, had fallen madly in love with another physician at the conference and had torn up his return ticket. With the slow and sure advancement of years, a patchwork of wrinkles had sprouted and made their way around his sharp blue eyes, and his hair brushed to the side now sported streaks of grey. But the forty tumultuous years as physician, husband, father, and widower had done nothing to dampen his Aussie accent, or his energy

"You're right, Ian. For some reason I got up a bit early and didn't feel like waking everyone up so I thought I'd just come in and get a jump on the paperwork."

Ian laughed outwardly. "Well there's no shortage of paperwork around here," he said, spreading his arms wide at his own collection. "Though it'll take more than one early morning to catch up on any of it. But what's got you waking up so early?" Dr. Burke asked, his lips pursed together as he scrutinized his younger colleague, as if for the first time. "Something troubling you? Have a seat." He pointed at one of the chairs opposite the desk. "Just put those charts on the floor. I'll get to them sooner or later."

Gabriel sank down into the chair sighing. "Thanks, Ian. Not sure where to begin."

"Is it the clinic? Sometimes working in this place can get to you. I know I've had my moments over these past few decades."

"No, it's not that. The clinic is fine. Patients are fine. Just-just dealing with issues from my past, a memory from long ago that's popped up but there are holes in it that I'm having difficulty filling."

Ian nodded patiently, bringing his fingertips together in front of him. "Memories can be like that. The mind playing tricks with you, leaving enough unanswered questions to make you keep guessing."

"I spoke with Charles Stein and-"

"That quack!" Ian half rose out of his chair in mock anger. "Why would you want to bother with him?"

Gabriel smiled at the response. "Well, I thought maybe getting some testing done would help me rule out anything neurological."

"Neurological? Son," Dr. Burke said with a slight impatient grimace, "there's nothing wrong with your brain. You wouldn't have been able to stick it out in this pothole of a clinic if there was something neurologically wrong with you. And there's no need for any more imaging or testing." Dr. Burke tapped the side of his head. "It's in your mind, and unfortunately we as doctors are so committed to diagnosing and treating our patients that we don't give ourselves the time to investigate our own issues. And let me tell you something, doctors have issues, lots of them."

"Stein said maybe if I went back to my old neighborhood it my draw out some more memories. Maybe talk with some people from my past."

"True, true, that may help." Dr. Burke nodded, then leaned in, eyes sharp and focused. "But if you want to get to the root of the problem, young doctor, you to have to go home. Home is where it all begins, where one makes his first and his deepest connections. It's where the skeletons are hidden, the clues to one's own mystery."

"I hope you don't mind my waxing philosophical, Gabriel, but after forty years of talking to probably more than a hundred thousand patients I have gotten a theory about human nature. We say we live in a brutal stormy world, young doctor, and so we suffer because we feel we've been brutalized by it. But this notion of the world as brutal results from a misunderstanding of the very essence of the world, and this misunderstanding results from a disconnection from the outer world. The further we separate ourselves from the world around us, the more likely we will misinterpret the essence of the outer world as brutal. But what many of us don't understand as that the essence of the outer world also exists inside us, and so ultimately the brutality we complain about that exists in the world also exists inside us, an inner storm. And it reveals itself in the decisions we make in our lives. But what many don't understand is that just as we cannot separate our lives from our actions, we cannot separate ourselves from our world. And yet we resist the world within and without, and ultimately suffer as a result. The first step we must make is accepting that the world is as much a part of us as we are a part of it. The more we connect ourselves with the world the more likely we are to find that the essence of the outer world is not brutal at all, it is harmonious, and once we come upon that realization, then we begin to find the harmony in ourselves."

"What about the mistakes we make?" asked Gabriel. "Shouldn't we hold ourselves accountable to the mistakes we make in our life?"

"The mistakes are all part and parcel of being imperfect humans living in this perfect world. Hell, I've made plenty of mistakes in my life. Just ask some of my patients. Sure, sure, many of 'em love me, but some have been full witnesses to my blunders, and a couple of 'em have even tried to sue me. But we can't live our lives worrying about the errors we've made. Our errors offer us keen insight into that which connects us to the world. And I'm not saying we won't suffer at all, nor should we not suffer. I think suffering is an integral part of life. But we must not resist it. We should accept it and then move on. In the end, life is just too short to not face every new day with clear-eyed vision."

Ian Burke stood up suddenly, tall and lanky. He loomed over his desk, shuffling some of the lab results into another pile to be sorted with later on. "But enough of my philosophizing," he said, settling his crystal blue eyes on Gabriel. "You need time to explore your home properly. Why don't you take some time off. I'll hold down the fort for you."

"Thanks Ian," Gabriel replied. "But the morning is going to be too hectic for me to take any time off. I think the panel is a bit thin this afternoon. I might take off after lunch."

"Good 'nough." Dr. Burke replied. "Let me know if there is anything I can do to help."

"Thanks."

"Oh, just so that you know." Dr. Burke shuffled a bit uncomfortably. "I thought I ought to tell you personally, and not have you hear it from our dear incompetent director. I'm retiring at the end of the month."

"You!" Gabriel stood stunned. "Wow, I thought you were going to stay here forever."

Dr. Burke laughed. "I thought so too. Truth is, I met this woman- isn't it always because of a woman - well we've been seeing each other for the past few months. She's a little bit younger than me, not by much, and she's planning on retiring and asked me to join her in this next chapter of her life. And I've been reevaluating my role here, and my life. I figure for the past few years I've always had one foot in the clinic- didn't know where to put the other foot. At times I worried the other foot would wind up in the grave. And I think I still have quite a few good years left in me. So I handed in my letter of resignation yesterday evening. I think four weeks is enough time to find a replacement."

"No one can replace you, Ian," Gabriel said.

Ian shook his head. "Sure they can. They'll probably get someone a little green around the gills, just like I was way back when, and just like you were when you started here."

Gabriel laughed. "You're right about that."

"But whoever they hire will soon get the hang of things. Then they can move all the charts and papers all around this desk the way I've been doing for the past forty years. My only hope is that whomever they find has the stamina to stick with this place. As you know the place is in bit of disarray, and our fearless director is hardly ever around to do much directing. There aren't many doctors like us around. Yes, you and I are quite similar. You remind me of myself way back when. I admire you, Gabriel. Must admit." Ian Burke looked down at his desk, as if caught in a memory, before looking back at Gabriel. "I had my doubts at first but I now realize you have the stamina to stick it out all the way to the end. What's more, you're not a scientist- a technical doctor- you're an artist. The profession has too many scientists and not 'nough artists, communicators. Our patients need communicators, not statisticians. Yes, you have the stamina to stick it out. Just don't lose yourself in the process." Dr. Burke stood up now, having given one of his last and perhaps most important diagnoses and therapeutic plans, grabbed the nearest stack of labs results and hammered them into order. "You have four weeks until I leave to get to the bottom of this mystery of yours, so take as much time as you need."

"Thanks, Ian." Gabriel reached forward and shook the elder physician's hand. The two smiled at each other, remembering the shared ten years, recognizing the end of an era, and the beginning of a new one.

"Remember your home and your family," Ian reminded as Gabriel walked out of his office and made his way down the hallway. "There are no substitutes."

47

For the eighteen years of Isabelle's tenure at Cohen & Cohen, she remained in the wings with red marker in hand, pursuing the guilty through personal injury litigation. As the Cohen brothers, their junior partners, and even more junior associates circled around unsuspecting physicians in the courtroom, Isabelle remained in rapt anticipation of the peace she sought through forced justice. Time became measured in depositions, settlements and trials ending in guilty verdicts. The zeal with which she attacked the upcoming cases galvanized the attorneys, young and old alike. But they all failed to fill the void left by Danny's death, to dull the anger she burnished each day (red pen in hand) to a blinding sheen, or anesthetize the ache in her chest. Still, Isabelle pressed on in blind faith, dedicating more and more of her time and her life to the cause, and less for the self and her home. In later years the purposeful energy became tinged with desperation, though she refused to admit it to herself, the red pen marks took on a more urgent tone, the cross outs sharper, digging into the pages, as if searching for the answers. She took a peripheral role in the mounting successes of the firm, not engaging herself in the many victory parties at Cohen & Cohen, not while there was the guilty to indict. Arthur was the only one at the firm to notice the subtle change in her character, and he looked on in dismay the way a priest looks on the radicalized members of this flock.

In the end, peace came at the heels of an unrelenting cough that siphoned off the oxygen from her lungs during the course of several months, one she chalked up to her now pack and a half cigarette habit. A subsequent X-ray revealed the culprit, a five-centimeter spiculated mass blossoming in her right lung that had seeded a constellation of nodules taking up the upper half of her left lung field, pleural effusions lapped at both bases of the lung fields. She sat opposite her internist who frowned as he read the radiology report to her. He'd nagged her for twenty years about her smoking but he was not one to say I told you so and she was grateful for it. Isabelle had worked enough personal injury litigation to know not only what kind of cancer this was (even without a biopsy), but also that her life expectancy would be measured in weeks. She stood, offering her thanks for his splendid care, but informed him that his services, or that of his consultants, would no longer be necessary. Even as the life drained from her body, she kept the diagnosis hidden from her bosses, dismissing their increasingly worried glances with an impatient wave of her hand, until the end when there wasn't enough time to plan a proper retirement party for her. The two brothers felt for the first time impotent and desperate. Samuel, always one to spot a potential profit, offered to sue her primary care doctor; surely he was somehow to blame. But Isabelle smiled politely and shook off the suggestion, recognizing in her diagnosis what she'd been searching for all along.

Gabriel took a week leave from his residency program on the west coast. He flew in on a red eye and took a yellow cab to the hospital to catch her in her final hours as she drifted off in a morphine induced pre-death slumber. Gabriel walked down the hall of the inpatient ward, which felt at once foreign and familiar. He reached his mother's room (the Cohen brothers had been able to secure a private room). Isabelle was able to recognize him and he sat on the bed and let his mother hold his hand, comforting him as she lay dying in a way she never had when she lived. He tried to will himself to cry but could not; there hadn't been any tears shed between the two of them since Danny. She removed her mask at the end, recognizing the need to breathe the same air as her son. "I'm sorry. I spent too much time trying to avenge Daniel's death, and in the end I failed."

Gabriel leaned in. "I did too."

"It's okay," she said, as if she understood what he felt, or what he couldn't feel. Or perhaps she meant her leaving would be okay as if, in the end, death had been her ultimate goal.

Leon sat in a chair quietly observing. He stood up when his sister had exhaled her final breath, and walked over to Gabriel.

At the funeral, after the Rabbi's prayer, it seemed only fitting that the older Cohen brother should stand and say a few words. Trembling with the emotion of one who knew he'd been the only one to find a meaningful connection with Isabelle, and the only other person who recognized the failure of her endeavor, Arthur spoke about the remarkable woman she was, a tireless and faithful worker, and a true friend. Gabriel looked on as Isabelle's casket sank into the ground's cool embrace, several feet from the remains of her eldest son, where their comingled dust would help to feed the earth's flora together. Gabriel looked on as a spectator at his mother's burial, feeling so little of what he thought he would have felt or should have felt, but recognized himself to be one of very few people to know that Isabelle had finally achieved in death what she had failed to in life.

On the way out of the cemetery both Cohen brothers approached Gabriel and Leon with their condolences. It was a rare occasion for the two brothers together. Their sharply divergent philosophies had become more pronounced within the past few years, and they each took a dismal view of the other's paradigm of justice. Art, now "out" and more honest with himself, had become increasingly disillusioned with personal injury litigation. There were no winners in the end, the plaintiffs were not made whole again, their paychecks did not replace their true losses, and the defendants, whose lives he'd ruined, were guilty of only being human; and he had begun to look towards retirement. Samuel, forever rolling his eyes at his older brother's crisis of conscience, had never changed his focus from the early days. In the end it really was all about dollars and cents, the more the better, and he was more than ready to buy his older brother out. Out of love for his mother he'd keep the name Cohen & Cohen, it would be too much to change the brand anyway. Art shook hands solemnly with Gabriel and Leon, and turned to leave. Samuel, ever the bolder of the two (and less tactful, especially out of the courtroom), as befitting of the thousand dollar suit, cut to minimize his shortcomings, reached a soft fleshy hand on Gabriel's shoulder and ventured further with commentary on Isabelle's litigious prowess, suggesting that perhaps personal litigation would have been a better career choice for him as well.

Gabriel looked down at the younger Cohen brother (who came up to his shoulder on a good day), grabbed his hand in a vice like grip and shrugged his arm off in one motion. "I would never choose to profit off the misfortunes of others."

Leon wrapped a protective arm around Gabriel and guided him away from the lawyer, left to massage his bruised hand.

They walked to a plot on the other side of the cemetery. Gabriel knelt down before a small headstone and read the name and date. "I'm sorry my friend," he said, his voice barely above a whisper. "So very sorry."

48

"Doc, I wouldn't trade you for all the tea in China," Phyllis Thomas replied, her Georgia accent soft and silky. She smiled and nodded her head in agreement even now at her own original summation, one she made years before after her first visit at the free clinic, back when she was like so many other black women there, broken but still with some fight in her. Sixty two years and she'd seen a lot, lived through a lot: HIV, Hepatitis, hypertension, three willful daughters, one of whom the lord had taken from her, the dirty needle still in the poor girl's arm. She knew Dr. G was a keeper. Amen to that.

Dr. G was the reason why she came religiously every four months for her blood pressure and her lab tests, applying a fresh coat of her favorite lipstick and wearing her Sunday best. She would even go to the beauty parlor the day before.

This was the answer she gave the other sisters at the church every Sunday, and what she replied to Dr. G when he asked her why she kept coming even now that she had health insurance (having gotten her life together and all), and could go to a large health center.

He was the only man, sixty-two years and counting, who'd ever put in the effort for her- not even her daddy (that no-good drunk), nor her husband (that no-good lech)- Dr. G was the only man who ever showed up. Not that he was a saint. In her estimation, all men were sinners. Saints were only found in the bible. But at least Dr. G was a sinner seeking redemption.

Gabriel smiled at his patient. Phyllis Thomas was large but not necessarily fat, solid and strong, built for the life he suspected she'd led. He'd had his doubts about her on her first visit, but she turned out to be one of his best patients. The transformation had been remarkable. "Thanks Phyllis."

"What makes you so good, Dr. G? How come I can walk in and say anything I want and not feel judged by you? How come there's no bottle of Dr. G in the store for me to buy?" she asked playfully. She liked teasing her doctors, Dr. Samuels from the ID clinic, Dr. Cacci from hepatology.

"Fear," Gabriel replied.

"Excuse me, chile?"

"Fear," Gabriel repeated, sitting down, suddenly exhausted. "I'm afraid Phyllis, always afraid of failing my patients. I get home every night afraid that I'd let my patients down, that I'd missed something, forgotten a test or just gotten the diagnosis wrong altogether." Gabriel didn't know from where this need to confess came from. He cradled his head in his hand, feeling overwhelmed. "I stay up most nights with this fear, that I'll fail and be exposed as a fraud. My biggest fear is that my patients will recognize this and leave me."

"Excuse me, did you say something Dr. G?" Phyllis asked smiling, breaking the daydream.

"Just that I'll see you in another four months. Stay away from the fast food."

Phyllis laughed, deep and full, as if she'd stored it for the past four months, as if she'd had so few of these. "I'll try, Dr. G, you get home and take some rest. You look tired."

49

As Gabriel pulled the car to the curb he caught site of Mr. Scharpe's figure at the front gate. Gone was the three-piece suit or tuxedo, the executive air, the professionally styled coif Gabriel remembered. The man had aged more than the twenty-five years that had passed. Mr. Scharpe's jeans and polo shirt hung in a way to suggest a shrunken frame. He appeared more stooped and beaten, and he walked with stiff, painful steps to the car. But the voice was the same, purposeful and strong as he approached the car. "Good afternoon, Gabriel. Let's take a drive for a few minutes."

"Good afternoon, sir. Of course." Gabriel shifted into gear and pulled out onto the street. The wealthy neighborhood appeared idle and untended, the street empty of cars, the sidewalk barren of people.

Mr. Scharpe looked straight ahead as if lost in thought. Once they made the turn onto the cross street, he turned to Gabriel and spoke almost mechanically. "To be honest, I was surprised to hear your voice yesterday. None of Jared's school friends have called in years. I'm not sure what your reason is for getting in touch, or what you expect out of meeting with Jared." Mr. Scharpe turned back to the road ahead. "Jared's not the same. I feel it's only fair to warn you."

Gabriel took a roundabout route along Great Hope park, the playground, revamped and expanded, was filled with children and nannies. He rolled down the window, allowing in the voices outside, bright and wild.

Mr. Scharpe continued, recounting a story he seemed to know by heart, having told it countless times, "It was the year after high school, I think you were gone by then, Jared got heavily into drugs. I'm not sure which, his doctor believed there were multiple abuses going on at the time. We- his mother and I- tried an intervention. A bit late, I'm afraid." He paused with a long-withered sigh. "It didn't work. Then we had him committed to an inpatient drug rehab upstate. He seemed to respond at first, but once he was out he was back at it. Then he and a couple of kids- younger than him, young enough- were picked up by the police with a large enough bag of cocaine and he, being the oldest- the only adult at the time, was forced to serve time." Mr. Scharpe shook his head at the memory. "He was transferred to a psychiatric hospital before his time served. The doctor said it was a psychotic break. Whether it was the drugs or not, they couldn't say. When he was finally discharged to us, I knew I had lost him." Mr. Scharpe looked out the window, blind to the passing scenery. "Jared's not the same," he repeated. "If you don't want to see him I will understand. I didn't tell him you were coming."

Gabriel rounded the corner and pulled up to the house again. "Thank you for warning me, I still want to see him."

As Gabriel turned to exit, Mr. Scharpe laid a hand on his arm and met his eyes. "Please, don't bring up too much of the past. It does no one any good."

Gabriel nodded. "I won't."

"Good, let's go around to the side. We don't use the front door much these days."

The late afternoon light followed Gabriel and Mr. Scharpe into the kitchen. Gabriel was shocked at how very little had changed, and yet it seemed so different now, entering this house again, to remember how terribly empty it was back then for Jared, and recognize how empty it had become for Jared's father. "Where's Maria?"

The old man had already started down the hallway to Jared's room. He stopped and looked back at him, genuinely surprised. "You remember Maria?" But then nodded at the obvious. "Of course you would. She passed away several years ago. A very devoted housekeeper," he said, quickly adding, "She loved Jared like her own son." The two paused outside Jared's bedroom. An old Pink Floyd song played on the other side of the door. Mr. Scharpe fished out a key from his front pocket. "I keep the door locked for his own safety. He's wandered off in the past and it was a devil trying to find him and bring him back."

The lock clicked open and the two stepped inside. In front of a large television blasting the harsh hiss of snowy chatter, Jared sat on the floor, legs crossed, his thin lanky frame bent into a question mark, listening with an ear to the screen, his eyes screwed shut in concentration. He had a roll's worth of aluminum foil helmeted to his head. He'd lost weight, his cheeks were hollow, and his eyed were sunken in.

"Hi Jared," Mr. Scharpe yelled above the television, in a tone one reserved for preschool children, or for the hard of hearing. "Look who I have here with me, it's Gabriel. Do you remember Gabriel?"

Jared unscrewed his eyes, turning the volume down, and disengaged himself from the television for a moment. Recognition flickered briefly as the two friends' eyes met. But Jared retreated to his position and said with a tone of impatience, "I thought I told you not to interrupt me when I'm working."

Mr. Scharpe tried a new tack. "Wouldn't you like to change the channel to one that works?"

Jared replied with a tight scowl, "I know which channels you'd rather have me see."

Mr. Scharpe clapped his hands with finality and backed away to the door. "Okay, I guess I'll leave you two to reminisce." He turned to Gabriel. "I'll be in the kitchen when you're done."

Gabriel turned to the departing father with apprehension, but he knew the reasons for being here were important, and he had to see this mission through. Outside the bedroom window the top branches of a maple tree swung to the early evening breeze. He cast his gaze around the room, trying to find something to anchor him to a shared past.

Jared had already turned back to the TV, but had left the volume down.

Gabriel walked over to the bookcase. He remembered many of the books from decades before, but they were scattered, stacked chaotically, some with the covers torn off, some with half the pages missing. He found an old chess set underneath one of the piles of books and pulled it out. "Remember our chess games, Jared?" Gabriel said, shaking his head at the memory. "They would go on for hours. I thought I was pretty good. But after I met you I realized how little I knew. You would win most of them. And even when you lost I had the feeling you were in control of the game all the way to the end."

Jared turned from the television, watching Gabriel sit down on the couch, unfold the board on the coffee table and set up the pieces. He crawled to the coffee table and kneeled on the other side of the chess set.

Gabriel eyed him closely, getting a fuller look. Multiple scabs at varying stages of healing populated Jared's forehead and cheeks. A light beard smudged the lower half of his face, his red-tinged corneas haloed dilated pupils, and small crescents of sleeplessness hung from his eyes. "Up for a game?" Gabriel cupped two pawns with his right hand and hid them from view behind his back for a brief moment, then held his fist up to Jared, his thumb and pinkie pointing out

Jared eyed Gabriel with suspicion, eyed the fist for several moments, then pointed a bony finger at Gabriel's thumb. Gabriel turned his fist over and opened is hand; the white pawn was closest to the thumb.

Gabriel smiled. "Looks like you go first."

Jared looked down at the chess set, as if for the first time. He inspected his pieces, moving from the eight pawns up front to the larger pieces in the back. He studied their every detail, as if he would find a purpose to their being through the intricately carved design. He finally pressed his queen's pawn forward two boxes.

"Do you remember me, Jared?"

"I remember you." Jared replied, not looking up.

Gabriel mirrored Jared's move with his own. "Do you remember our chess games way back when?"

Jared appeared lost in thought, studying the game. His voice, when he finally responded, sounded mechanical. "I remember lots of things from way back when." He pressed the same pawn forward another box, then looked up briefly before retreating to the game in front of him. "I remember lots of games we played, some of them dangerous."

"How've you been?" asked Gabriel, refusing to take the bait. He took Jared's pawn with one of his own.

Jared, scratching at a scab on his chin, seemed not to notice. "I've been okay. These new meds this doctor has me on, they get me confused at times." He pushed another pawn forward. "But I don't take all of them, just the ones that are safe. The other ones I destroy."

Gabriel eyed Jared above the pieces. "How do you know which ones are safe?"

"The shape of the pill. If it's oval or round it's safe. The ones with five sides are bad- five sides, pentagon, pentagram, sign of the devil- even my father's hooked."

"Do you remember my name, Jared?"

"I remember you." Jared looked up to meet his gaze. "You're the angel Gabriel. You're my protector."

Gabriel looked down at the chessboard. He'd taken a few of Jared's pieces; another two moves and he'd have him in checkmate. "Whom do you need protection from?"

Jared looked out the window at a black raven weighing down the top most branches of the maple tree, its small black eyes piercing the window.

Gabriel followed Jared's gaze. "Has anyone come by lately?"

Jared kept staring out the window as more ravens landed on the swaying branches, stretching their wings out wide. The conspiracy now turned their piercing eyes at Jared. "People come and go, no one stays. Sometimes they come in through the door, sometimes they come in through the TV- certain channels- their voices. I block them out with this." Jared tipped his helmet. "They think I'll talk. But I won't talk." He turned back to Gabriel. "A secret is a secret. A pact is a pact."

"Who else, Jared?"

Jared turned to the window, a flash of fear in his eyes. "I hear him coming around the corner sometimes. Like a thunder clap, a loud thunder clap."

"Is it a motorcycle? Is it Johnny?"

Jared put his hands to his ears, his voice raised. "Loud, loud, loud-- I can hear him outside. I know he wants to get me."

"Who, Jared?"

"The devil." Jared looks down at the chessboard. Then looks up expectantly. "Who won?"

Gabriel forced a smile. "Looks like you did again." He leaned in close, his voice shrinking to just above a whisper. "Don't worry about the devil, Jared. He can't touch you, I won't let him."

Jared shook his head earnestly, childlike tears forming at the base of his eyelids. "I won't tell, I won't ever tell."

"I know you won't." Gabriel slowly put the chess pieces in the box and folded up the chessboard. "I have to go now." He stood up and walked the chess set back to the bookcase. "If you want, maybe I can come back sometime soon and we can play chess again." When he turned back, Jared had already repositioned himself in front of the television. "Good bye, Jared." But Jared was no longer listening.

Gabriel closed the door behind him and walked quietly

back to the kitchen where Mr. Scharpe sat hunched over the kitchen table, watching as night advanced on the backyard beyond the glass doors. "Thank you for letting me spend time with Jared."

Mr. Scharpe turned around distractedly. "Oh sure, Gabriel, anytime. I'll walk you out."

Gabriel was halfway down the front stairs when he turned around. "You know he's not taking the medication." Mr. Scharpe flinched slightly. "It's okay to crush it and mix it into his drink. Just get double the number of pills and keep giving him a pill so he doesn't suspect anything has changed."

"Thank you, Gabriel." Mr. Scharpe held on to the door, firmly steadying himself as he slowly shut it.

Gabriel sat behind the wheel, staring at the street in front. After a heavy sigh, he turned the ignition and began the long drive home.

5 0

A silent night descended, starless and black, as Gabriel climbed the stoop to his brownstone home and opened the front door, loosened his tie and walked in.

"Daddy!" a girl's voice half beckoned half ordered from the second floor.

"She was waiting to say good night to you," a woman's voice called out from the lit kitchen in the back.

He removed his shoes and set them by the radiator and slowly made his way up the stairs. His tall form paused at the entrance to his daughter's room and allowed the weight of the day to dissipate. The bedside lamp cast a dim light on a small princess bedframe. A little form squiggled and giggled impatiently under the covers. Small fingers clasped at the edge of her comforter, pulling it high so only a small lock of black hair peeked out.

Gabriel kneeled beside the small bed and reached his hand under the covers, stirring up a round of giggles. "Hi sweetie. Did you have a good day?"

Payal, at four years of age, was sensitive to the many tones her father's voice took. She stopped giggling and sat up quickly. The comforter and sheet slid down, revealing her round, cinnamon-colored face and her compact little body. The large brown eyes of her mother peered out below softly knitted eyebrows. "Are you okay, Daddy?" She laid a hand on his.

Gabriel leaned in, pressing his lips against her forehead, brushing away the small wrinkles of concern. "I'm okay, sweetheart."

Payal reached out a hand to his face. "Why are you crying,

Daddy? Do you have a boo boo?"

Gabriel nodded, smiling.

Payal tapped a delicate finger against his temple. "Do you have a boo boo in your head again?"

Gabriel kissed her forehead again. "Yes, but just a little one, and now that I came here I feel all better."

Payal leaned in against her father's chest, seeking the reward of his warm embrace. "Good," she said, yawning.

Gabriel tucked Payal in as she lay down, drifting into a deep sleep known only to innocent children.

In the bathroom he washed his face and fended off another memory.

51

Gabriel approached, his footfalls barely audible on the hardwood floors of the living room. Priti reclined on the couch, an arm draped over her forehead, covering her eyes, entertained an early evening drain from work and motherhood. Despite the somewhat rumpled ecru blouse and brown slacks she still retained the enchanting aura that had drawn Gabriel to her so many years before. Two empty glasses and a recently opened bottle of ruby red wine stood at attention on the coffee table. She heard, or perhaps sensed him (at times it was hard to know which), and reached out her free hand to him. He sank into his wife's embrace, and they lay breathing in each other's scent as the wear and tear of the day receded into the shadows.

"Long day?" he asked.

"Mmm- let's not talk about my day. Let's enjoy a nice glass of wine."

"Good idea." Gabriel withdrew somewhat reluctantly from his wife's arms. "I was remembering the summer we met." Gabriel spoke as he poured the wine and placed a glass between her curved fingers.

"The second time, you mean." She eyed the wine casually, her mind anticipating the first sip.

"The first," he answered, gazing at her as if for the first time.

Priti sat up startled. "You're remembering."

She knew all about the wide gaps in her husband's memory since they'd reconnected six years before. It was one of those things she'd come to accept in the man she'd waited for

for nineteen years since he'd disappeared, one of the many casualties of the 'great storm' as it had come to be known. That he remembered her was no small consolation. The way he had walked up to her at the Annual Internal Medicine Conference six summers before- his prowl-like walk, from so long ago- she had recognized him immediately, and her heart was racing before he had even reached her. He had been incapable of small talk, even then, and had spoken to her as if picking up an unbroken thread that had been simply misplaced and rediscovered. No, he was not married. No, he was not seeing anyone. Yes, he was in practice. A free clinic at the edge of the city. Even as he had answered her questions, another conversation had been taking place with their eyes, one of remembering. They'd left the conference after the first lecture, unable to focus on anything else but the feel of each other's fingers as their hands met.

They had taken their time undressing each other in his hotel room, each article of clothing a small piece of gold to be appraised and savored. They had allowed themselves this luxury of the moment, which after nineteen years of waiting was something they had learned to appreciate. And the nineteen years had slipped away unnoticed, as their bodies had reestablished their severed ties. But much of that summer had been forgotten, lost within the ocean of time. Lost, save for small pearls of memory that he shared with her, and she had been happy to be one of those pearls. As the sweat of their lovemaking had cooled on their intertwined bodies, she had recounted dry-eyed the tear-soaked hell of those days following the storm as she waited for him. The initial terror had given way to low-level anxiety, which in turn had given way to pain. The pain of his absence had filled her days and nights, for weeks, until the heat of it had cooled and had scarred; and she had been used to scars. But this was the one she would turn to throughout the years, periodically caressing it, tormenting herself with it. She had exorcised these demons into his arms, and he accepted them, and both knew in this embrace that there would be no new scars.

Gabriel clinked his glass against hers. "Here's to us."

Priti kept her eyes trained on Gabriel as she drank. "So what do you remember about that summer?"

Gabriel frowned pensively, swirling the wine in his glass. "'Got a visit from an old friend, although looking back I'm not sure I would have called him that at the time and I certainly wouldn't call him that now." He took another drink before setting his glass down next to Priti's. "Do you remember Johnny?"

Priti nodded, grimacing at the name. "I remember all of your friends. What did Johnny want?"

"Nothing but trouble," Gabriel replied, shaking his head.

"As I remember it, they were all nothing but trouble."

Gabriel closed his eyes as distant images etched themselves on the backs of his lids, nodding. "I think the four of us together were only good for causing trouble. Well, after he left the office-"

"He went to your office?" Priti asked, a look of concern crossing her face.

"He did, but I made it clear he was no longer invited back. But anyway, I went over to visit Jared. Drove to his old house. He has paranoid schizophrenia, and not very well treated."

"Oh Gabriel, I'm so sorry." Priti rubbed his back.

Gabriel stared into his glass, watching the wine swirl inside, lapping the sides. "It was hard to see Jared that way. Poor guy. Definitely misunderstood. I think that's what we all were, misunderstood. But perhaps back then we didn't care who understood us. I went to him to find out more of that summer. You see, Priti, there's something I never told you..."

Later that night in bed, wrapped in each other's arms, Priti held Gabriel tightly to her as he wept.

"What do you intend to do?" she asked finally.

"I don't know, Priti," Gabriel said, drying his eyes. "I first need to find out what exactly happened that night. "Johnny won't say and Jared can't say."

"Was Mr. Winter a pedophile?"

"Yes," Gabriel nodded, "that's one thing I'm sure of."

"Do you feel guilty for his death?"

Gabriel looked up into his wife's eyes, finding the soft sliver of moonlight reflecting off them, and shook his head. "No, but I feel like it accomplished nothing."

"Is that why Johnny was at your office?"

Gabriel nodded. "That, and probably to show off the Harley Davidson he finally got. That thing's as loud as he is."

"What?" Priti sat up suddenly.

"The 'hog' he bought finally. Honey are you okay? You look like you've seen-"

"Him- I saw him," Priti replied, turning to Gabriel, a look of worry in her eyes. "At the playground, I saw him- Johnny. My god, why didn't I think of it sooner?" Priti massaged the tension in her forehead.

"What do you mean you saw him?

"This man on his motorcycle," Priti continued, "he kept riding around and around the playground revving his engine, making so much noise, frightening the children. He was looking right at us." Priti turned to Gabriel again. "He knew it was me and Payal in the playground," she said fearfully. "He knew it was us."

Gabriel narrowed his eyes, the muscles tight on his face. "Why that son of a..." He ground his left wrist into his right hand. His eyes flashed angrily into space, to a distant memory, as an inner demon surfaced. But just as quickly that flash was gone and the demon inside sank back. He turned to Priti and took her into his arms. "I'm so sorry, my darling, my love," he whispered to her. "I never meant to get you involved in any of this."

"What are we going to do?" Priti whispered back.

"I want you to trust me with this. You and Payal will not

see him again. I promise."

"What are you going to do, Gabriel?" Priti began to cry. "Please don't do anything crazy. I lost you once, I don't want to lose you again."

Gabriel caressed Priti's face. "I will not risk losing you. I will take care of this, you have to trust me."

"What are you going to do?" Priti asked again, wiping the tears from her face.

Gabriel kissed her softly on her lips. "Give me a few minutes. I'm just going to make a phone call."

"Who are you going to call?"

"Someone else from that summer," Gabriel replied getting up. "Someone I trust." He stared hard at the phone trying to focus on the phone number his uncle had given him years before. As Gabriel punched in the numbers, the details of that night came rushing back.

The Storm

5 2

August 1983

*A*nd now for the weather. Phil, what's the update on that *pesky Hurricane Frederick? Well, Sandy, it looks like Frederick is going to make landfall this evening. All predictions of it moving outward to the Atlantic have proven dead wrong as an unseasonably cold front to the north is due to push Frederick westward. Forecasters are calling Frederick the storm of the century. North and South Carolina are still reeling from the battering on Thursday, with hundreds dead or missing, tens of thousands of homes destroyed... Governors in all Atlantic states have called a state of emergency. And Frederick has only strengthened, gathering speed with winds upwards of one hundred and fifty miles per hour. Currently a level 4 hurricane, Frederick is getting stronger as it pounds the Atlantic coast. Our own governor called a press conference yesterday evening calling for a mass evacuation off the southern coast line, and asked for all citizens in other areas to stay indoors after eight pm. Better get your umbrella out, Phil. You said it, Sandy.*

Leon awoke to the primal sounds of moaning and wailing, drenched in sweat, and yet when he sat up, eyes open, all was silent. Had he dreamt it? He wasn't sure.

He quickly dressed and tapped on Gabriel's door. No answer. He pushed the door quietly and walked to the edge of the bed. "Gabriel." He gently shook his nephew's shoulder.

Gabriel murmured incomprehensibly in his sleep, grasped his blanket, covering himself, and turned over in bed.

Leon tapped Gabriel's shoulder in assent and walked out.

The sky was a light, cloudless early morning blue. He inhaled sharply through his nose and smelled the briny scent of the Atlantic, arousing his instincts, like the hairs on the back of his neck. There was a storm coming, large and destructive. He picked up his pace that morning; his mind swarmed with plans, plans to protect his sister's house and Sarah's restaurant: plywood for the windows and doors, hurricane straps for the roof, anchors, screws, batteries, flashlight, extra food and water... He made the turn off the service road onto Middle Hope Road. The streets were empty of cars and people. He checked his watch, seven o'clock, too late for this desolation.

A pulsing sound surfaced to the street and rose as a whisper in his ear. At first he thought it was the wind heralding the oncoming storm and looked up. There was a faint rustling of leaves but no sign of the storm. Yet the sound grew louder and more distinct, a wailing, a moaning. He looked around and found nothing. He sped up, looking down every side street for the source of it. Out of the corner of his eye he detected a shadow on the curb. It was a faint gossamer thin silhouette of black, a shrouded faceless figure. He looked to the other side of the street and found a similar figure paused on the curb. He kept running but the figure appeared along every foot of curb he passed, each successive figure slightly more distinct than the previous one, until they were as real as he, countless wailing, faceless women dressed in black with head scarves, their screeching, howling, moaning echoed in his head, their hands up to their faces in agonized mourning.

And as the wailing grew the first drops of rain heralded the approaching storm. The rain grew heavy quickly, falling like a pall. Leon flung forward through sheets of rain, through the gauntlet of wailing women, their siren calls flooding his mind, shutting out all other thoughts.

"No, no!" he cried out. He ran panting to the boulevard, but with every step the boulevard receded into the distance. "No, no!"

And the low, deep chorus of mourners called out to him, beckoning, "Leon."

"Leon."

Leon sat up with a start and opened his eyes. He was drenched with sweat. Gabriel was crouched next to him, his hand on Leon's shoulder. "Are you okay?"

Leon looked around his late nephew's room, anchoring his mind to the moment, forgetting everything but the smell of rain. He met Gabriel's gaze. "Yes, yes, Gabriel," he said, tapping Gabriel's hand. "I'm okay. But we have work to do this morning. There is a storm coming."

"I know," Gabriel replied, standing up. "They're calling it the storm of the century."

"Did they say when it is supposed to arrive?"

"Sometime this evening."

Leon swung his legs off the bed, his strength returned. "We will go to the hardware store after breakfast."

The two worked throughout the morning, securing the roof and garage, shuttering the windows, as well as the front door. Afterward, Leon went around testing the stability and strength of the barricades. Isabelle went shopping with a list drawn up by her brother. The sky rested blue and calm, except for an intermittent breeze that rustled the leaves on the trees. The sun shone bright and eternal, like an indifferent god. The storm was not due to touch down until evening. The three ate lunch in silence, each lost in thought. As Isabelle cleared the table, Leon turned to Gabriel. "I am going to help out at the restaurant. If you can come for an hour or two it would help."

Gabriel leaned in, his right hand covering his left wrist. "Okay, but afterward I'm going to the hospital to visit Achilles and then his mother to see if she needs anything."

Leon nodded in approval. "Of course, just make sure you

are home by eight before the storm hits."

Sarah's Mediterranean was shuttered and secured by three that afternoon, when a steady breeze set in, shuffling the fallen leaves and small detritus outside. The three sisters had planned to stay the night at Sarah's home, which was already protected and on safer ground.

"You are more than welcome to stay with us." Sarah held Leon's hand. "You can bring Isabelle."

Leon smiled back at the show of generosity. "You are too kind, but my sister insists on staying in her own home. But I will be back to check on the restaurant."

"Don't take any unnecessary risks," Ruth chimed in nervously. "Wait until after the storm."

Leon smiled again. "Do not worry, I won't."

He turned back to Sarah. "Your daughter is coming now with the car to pick you all up, right?"

"Yes," Sarah nodded. "She should be here within twenty minutes."

Leon and Gabriel left the restaurant and parted ways on the corner. "See you by eight o'clock." Leon lightly gripped his nephew's shoulder then quickly crossed the street.

5 3

Gabriel watched Leon cross the street then disappear around the corner before making his way to the shack. He climbed the steep slope in long, determined strides. The air was stifling and silent of the usual cacophony of grackles, starlings, sparrows and other birds, but he made no note of this. Jared and Johnny were puffing away on their cigarettes, deep in discussion when he walked up.

"Everything all set," he said, high-fiving both of them.

"Gun is stashed in a very accessible spot in my garage and the bullets are in a box next to it," Johnny offered, his words spilling out, pressured with excitement, his body twitchy with anticipation, withdrawal or both.

"I have the bag inside." Jared nodded to the shack, his lids heavy with the recent adjustment of his mood stabilizer. "I got everything you asked for."

Gabriel nodded in response to his friends' updates. "Good. So the storm is going to hit us at eight, and it'll max out starting at midnight. I'll need both of you here by eleven. I'm supposed to be back at my mom's by eight but I'm planning on sneaking out sometime between ten and ten thirty." He looked from Jared to Johnny to see if he still had their attention. "I'll drive Achilles's car to the hospital and pick him up-"

"How're you planning on getting him past security?" Johnny interrupted.

Gabriel fished out his pack of cigarettes from under his rolled-up shirtsleeve and flicked out the last of the pack. "There's a cafeteria in the basement of the hospital. I took him down there a couple times this past month. I spotted an exit door off to the side next to the restrooms. Leads out to the parking lot. Once we're in the car we go get the perp and bring him back here." Gabriel paused a moment, looking at the cigarette, and made a silent promise to himself and his brother Daniel that, whatever happened tonight, this would be his last. He quickly lit his cigarette, huddling against the scattered gusts of wind. He looked back up at his friends. "Once the perp's here, I kill him, then I dispose of the body in the back of Hope Country Day School." He stopped suddenly as a large drop of rain hit the ground between them. All three looked down at the dark brown spot that had just formed then looked up quizzically at the cloudless sky above them before Gabriel picked up the thread of the plan. He pointed his cigarette end at Johnny. "When I leave to bury the body, you take Achilles back to the hospital. Make sure gets inside before you go home with the gun and bullets. Jared, you clean up the home until I get back to take you to your dad's." Gabriel took a final drag before grinding the cigarette butt under his Puma, exhaling a hot burst of smoke into the sky. "If all goes according to plan we should be back in our beds by four in the morning at the latest."

54

The clouds coalesced overhead, swirling around like an angry mob, blotting out the remaining sunlight. Gabriel pulled over to the curb as Priti ran out to meet him. She opened the passenger door and rushed in, pressing her shivering frame into the harbor of his embrace. The increasing anxieties which she'd tried so unsuccessfully to corral began spilling out. "I'm so happy you came- I'm so worried about this storm- I've never seen my mother and father so anxious- they've spent the last day boarding up all the windows- so many people have died already-"

Gabriel lost himself in her caresses. "Don't worry, we're safe. We're far from the coast," he whispered into her black hair cascading over his shoulder. He looked toward her house and caught sight of an old arching oak tree to the side. "Just keep way from the side of the house where that oak tree sits. Stay inside with your parents and I'll reach out to you after the storm."

"Please be careful." Priti's lips trembled as she spoke, her eyes wet with tears. Never had she been so afraid of losing anyone, never had she calculated so much value to life. The next twenty-four hours opened up as a wide threatening chiasm on the other side of which she feared she would not find him. "You're the one," she whispered softly into the deep reassurance of his embrace. "You're the one." And he was the one, she had been sure of it when he'd approached her the night of the party which now seemed a life time ago. Up until then there had been no one, and she had dreaded the years passing by her, like a prisoner chalking the days on a dark cement wall. Of living her life as confirmation of her mother's fearful predictions years before.

1976

Priti had approached the concealment of her scars with a vigilance that was beyond her ten years. She had chosen shirts and dresses of thick material that revealed nothing. She'd made sure to wake up before her mother had entered her bedroom in the morning, to wait until after her mother had left the bedroom at night, to bathe alone. How long had she expected to keep her physical scars from her parents, her mother in particular? Fathers were expected to be oblivious of their daughter's bodies and minds, of abdicating responsibility for a domain they chose not to own. But mothers were different. They were, or were supposed to be, in tune to the wild rhythms of their daughter's many changes, always on the lookout for them, as additional threads to weave into the bond between them. But again, how long can a child keep scars hidden from a parent? It was several months after she had arrived in the United States that she and her mother went shopping for summer clothes. Her mother, fed up with having to wait outside the changing room, had barged in while Priti was trying on her bathing suit (one she knew she could never wear), and caught site of the scarred back. She coughed to hide the gasp lodged in her throat and turned away, resisting the urge to hug her daughter and weep. Priti caught her mother's expression and clutched at her clothes to cover up her body, blushing wildly. The ensuing silence had been familiar to them, the vacuum of a tacit agreement on what to pursue and what to leave behind in the past that had demarcated the boundaries of their relationship. But now the silence had become deafening as they had driven home, and each struggled to find the words to share with the other, recognizing the impotence of language in defining what one had kept hidden and the other had discovered. It had continued into the evening, so much so that even Professor Patel had paused in his booming dinnertime monologue to make note of it. "Cat got your tongue?" he had asked Priti playfully.

Priti had looked up from her untouched dinner plate and forced a brittle smile in response, grateful for his cluelessness.

Through the shared wall that evening she had heard her mother's horrifying account to her father, feeling more of a stranger in their house than at any time before. She could picture her father's brows knit in confusion and consternation. Conspicuously absent, even for a child, had been the mention of her aunt, her father's sister. There had been no blame cast, only a grim prognosis. "And who will marry her," her mother had asked, "with her back like that?"

Priti had hugged her knees tight to her chest, missing her grandmother and finding herself alone once more.

"I love you," she whispered silently, afraid for Gabriel to hear just yet.

And Gabriel had not heard. "Don't worry, I will," he smiled, brushing his lips across hers. "You'll see, things will be better tomorrow. I promise."

She peered into the wilderness in his eyes and recognized the power of his faith, how unafraid of the storm that he seemed now to be a part of.

He waited until she closed the front door before heading to the hospital.

The roads had quieted down by now, with only a few service vehicles out, and Gabriel reached the hospital quickly.

He made it to Achilles's bedside by six thirty. Achilles lay sleeping, an IV bag draining saline into the veins of his left hand. His eyes had sunk deep in his skull and his lips pursed with every breath. Fear flashed through Gabriel's mind for a brief moment that Achilles would not be able to make it out. He crouched next to the side of the bed. "Hey man," he said, gently squeezing Achilles's shoulder.

"Hey." Achilles's eyes blinked open and he reached his tubed hand across, covering Gabriel's. "They say there's a bad storm coming."

"So it seems," Gabriel replied, searching in his friend's eyes for clues of his strength and will.

"There's not going to be much staff to monitor all the ins and outs of everyone here."

"Even the cafeteria?" Gabriel smiled, knowingly.

"Even the cafeteria," Achilles confirmed, his words coming out haltingly, his voice hushed to a whisper. "I'll probably make it down for a snack, have to stretch my legs and all. It's been my routine for the past week. No one'll suspect, they'll even disconnect me from the IV bag so I can go."

Gabriel nodded. "Good. You want me to check on your mom? See how she's doing?"

Achilles shook his head. "Thanks. No need, she's at her sister's place upstate for the night."

Gabriel caught Achilles's withering gaze. "Are you sure you're up to this?"

Achilles fought hard not to cry. "It's the only thing I'm ready for at this point. Let's do this."

"Ten thirty then." Gabriel grabbed his friend's hand and pulled him in for a hug.

"Ten thirty," Achilles whispered back.

On the way out of the hospital, Gabriel nodded to the hulking security guard, making a mental note once more of the cafeteria exit door to the side of the parking lot.

55

The streets were already dark with rain, and drops began form small pools as he parked his car midway down the block from his house. Staccato gusts of winds pierced the receding calm. He turned off the ignition and gripped the steering wheel with his right hand. Having held his breath for so many years, waiting for this day and this evening to arrive, Gabriel got down to the business of breathing, yet he found himself gasping for air. He forced two slow and deep breaths, in and out, as the stormy night came into focus, then unclenched the steering wheel and exited the car. Many of the neighborhood cars had been already been parked in their garages, and the houses shuttered and boarded up, lending the street the air of a town forgotten and abandoned. He quietly climbed the outside of his house to the gambrel roof and crawled to his window. As he braced himself against the wind, Gabriel pried loose the nails on one side of the plywood and tested his means of escape. He took two more slow, deep breaths and walked in through the kitchen door. He was met with the spicy aroma of his uncle's cooking.

Leon turned from the stove as Gabriel closed the door and he walked to his nephew and embraced him warmly. "Great. Now we are all home safe. Your mother is upstairs resting." They both turned their heads to the sudden howl of wind outside. Leon wrapped a protective arm around Gabriel's shoulder. "Do not worry, Gabriel, this house is secure, remember? And I am cooking a tasty Chicken Sofrito for us."

Gabriel relaxed within the grip of his uncle's embrace. He leaned over to admire the appetizing chicken, potato and spices simmering in the pan. "Mmm, smells delicious. Thank you, Leon. All this running around and working has made me hungry."

Leon frowned. "All your friends are safe, I pray."

Gabriel nodded. "They are, uncle."

Leon smiled and returned to his position by the stove. "Good, good. Go wash up and I will have dinner ready in ten minutes."

Gabriel tiptoed up the stairs, careful not to awaken his mother. He hoped to avoid another confrontation with her, especially tonight. He looked at himself in the mirror; his face betrayed none of the manic pounding in his chest and head. He quickly showered, scrubbing away at the anxiety of the moment, and dressed for dinner. He stuffed two flashlights, a change of clothes for himself and Achilles, and two towels into a backpack and tucked it deep into his closet. He tiptoed past his mother's room and down the stairs to the kitchen.

His uncle had set the kitchen table for the three of them and had already started serving dinner.

"Should I get my mother?" Gabriel asked reluctantly.

Leon shook his head. "No. Let her sleep. I can always heat up her dinner later."

Isabelle's absence from their dinners was a topic neither wished to bring up. It was a tacit understanding that there are victims of life who view the limited paths left to choose before them, and must be allowed to do so.

"What would you like to drink?" Leon set two glasses down on the table. "Water, beer, wine?"

"Water is fine for me."

"For me too. We will celebrate with a bottle of wine tomorrow after the storm," Leon said, pouring the water. "Gabriel, are you okay? You seem lost."

Gabriel looked up, a strained smile on his face. "I was thinking the same thing, uncle. Tomorrow we can celebrate. Tonight we're going to have a great storm, but I guess sometimes we need a great storm to clean up the earth."

Leon stood silent for a moment, looking at his nephew, trying to read his intent or perhaps find solace for his own internal storm. "Perhaps you are right, Gabriel. There's a common saying in Israel, 'the sun shines brightest after a storm'."

But no words could calm their minds as the storm waxed and raged, howling and shrieking and shaking the cornerstones of the community outside. They ate their meal in silence. Words have no meaning when the veil is lifted, exposing reality's chaotic incomprehensible power, because a mere glimpse at the horror of reality is enough to shatter the glass menagerie of our existence. All in Great Hope clung to their meals and prayed to whatever god or gods would listen tonight.

Shortly before ten, Gabriel stood up. "I'm tired, uncle, I'm heading to bed."

"Try to get some sleep," Leon counseled him, patting him on the back as Gabriel made for the stairs. "I will keep watch down here tonight in case there are any problems."

Gabriel stepped into his bedroom and shut the door. He crouched by the closet and grabbed his backpack, then reached for the window but stopped just short. He took several deep breaths to cleanse his mind and steady his heart before opening the window. He slid through the opening under the loosened plywood and out onto the roof and lowered the window, leaving it an inch open then pressed the nails back through the plywood, securing it against the window frame. The wind and rain drenched him within minutes. Tightening the straps of the backpack, he quickly climbed down the side of the house and ran to the car. He fumbled for the keys before finding the right one. He gunned the engine and the car ripped away from the curb and was soon lost in the storm. He kept his headlights off to avoid attracting attention. He'd been over the route enough times and could do it blindfolded which, given the storm that had descended on the island, was how he felt he was driving now. The Chevelle dodged past fallen trees and large unrecognizable detritus on the road. A large glow of lights in the distance suggested he was close to the hospital. He pulled into the parking lot without being spotted by the security guard who'd barricaded himself into the small booth at the entrance as large streams of water began rising on either side.

56

Johnny sat at his kitchen table, sweating through his T shirt and jeans under a heavy black raincoat. He chain-smoked his panic up to the ceiling while the hurricane raged outside, staring intermittently at the hands on the wall clock as the time fast approached ten o'clock. He was alone tonight, his family scattered throughout the town. His father sat geared up and waiting at the firehouse for the night with the rest of the volunteer firemen, waiting for the many frantic emergency calls expected. His mother kneeled on a church pew with Johnny's brothers, praying to God for her salvation along with the other church wives. Some vague promises to both parents had led each to assume he would be safe with the other parent, giving him the freedom to take part in the killing tonight. His absence would be missed and forgotten in the aftermath of the storm.

The clock struck ten and he lifted his helmet off the table and took a deep breath. He'd ridden in storms before, but never a hurricane. And part of the way he'd have Jared on board. He knew this would be a test for him. If he could keep from crashing tonight he would have earned the right to ride a Harley; if he crashed and failed at his task, a Honda.

He burst out of the side door and disappeared into sheets of rain as he ran down to the garage. His backpack lay hidden in a corner. He ran his hand through the contents inside, shaking the box of bullets, fingering the gun, each in their own zip lock bag. Zipping up his backpack, he opened the door to the garage. Finally able to kick start his motorbike on the third try, he rode it out into the yawning maw of the storm.

His helmet offered some protection from the rain, but visibility was limited to several yards in front of him and he was forced to ride at half speed. He passed several police cars on his way to Jared's, but the sound of his engine was lost within Frederick's roar and he rode unnoticed. The one unit that did spot him didn't even bother to give chase, so frightened were the police of moving from their spot.

He made it to Jared's, exhilarated at passing the first leg of his test of will and courage. He rapped hard against Jared's kitchen door until it opened. Jared appeared slightly shocked at Johnny's dark wet outline in the mad rush of the storm. Johnny pushed past him, dripping a puddle on the kitchen floor. He fished into his front pocket for a cigarette but found the pack drenched and gave up the idea. He turned to Jared, impatiently. "Come on, asshole, time to get moving."

Jared startled, looked at his half-eaten leftovers from his father's restaurant. "Uh, okay." He grabbed his plate and went to place it in the sink, but paused a moment, turning to Johnny. "Are you hungry? It's chateaubriand."

"No, I don't want your faggoty ass meat. Get your shit on and let's get the fuck outta here!"

Jared grabbed a black, full length raincoat out of the closet and turned to Johnny.

"Get a couple packs of cigarettes and a lighter and put them in a zip lock bag for when we get there."

"Okay." Jared did as he was told, and brought the baggie to Johnny.

Johnny unshouldered his backpack and unzipped the side. "Put them in here. You're gonna need to put this on." Johnny passed the backpack to Jared. "And be careful, the gun's inside. Alright, let's go."

Cursing into his helmet, Johnny rode slowly along the side streets with Jared holding on tightly as the wind whipped rain against them, thrashing the bike, causing it to swerve more than once. Johnny clenched hard on the handles, his muscles tensed in order to keep his bike upright. They made it to the street next to the hill without incident. Both dismounted, and Johnny ran the bike into the woods with Jared trailing behind. The hill had come alive, with streams of mud running down on either side of them. Halfway up the hill Jared lost his footing and fell against Johnny, sending them both crashing down against several yards of brambles. Johnny hurled a torrent of insults and curses- all lost to the storm- into Jared's dazed face before lifting the backpack off of Jared's body and restarting the climb. Jared got his bearings and scrambled up behind, his movements painful and awkward.

The two sat caked in leaves and mud, dripping water onto the floorboards. They leaned hard against the shaking walls of the shack, which was threatening to collapse on top of them. Johnny took off his backpack and placed it between his legs. He unzipped the side and pulled out the baggie, flicked the lighter on and the inside of the shack came to life for a brief moment. He walked stiffly to the coffee table with the large candle in the center, brought the lighter to the candle and the room lit up again. He looked around and spotted an old issue of the local newspaper in the corner. Walking to the corner and taking off his raincoat and soaked T shirt, he did his best with the newspapers to clean up. He went back to Jared with a handful of pages. Jared lay sprawled against the shack, still wearing his raincoat. He appeared to be sleeping but both his eyes were open. "Here, clean yourself up," he yelled above the din of the storm.

As Jared wiped the debris from his face and scalp, Johnny dished out a pack of cigarettes from the baggie and took out two. He lit both and handed one to Jared.

"Thanks," Jared motioned soundlessly with his lips.

The two sat smoking a celebratory cigarette. The first step of the plan had been completed successfully. They had but to await Gabriel's arrival.

After his cigarette Johnny went to his backpack again

to pull out another plastic bag that had a change of clothes. Feeling the bag a little light, he looked inside. The box of bullets was there, but no gun. "Fuck me!" he exclaimed. Turning to Jared, he gave him a hard kick in the side. "Motherfucker, you dropped the gun! You dropped the gun!"

"What." Jared rubbed his side, appearing dazed.

"The gun, you idiot! When you fell! The gun must have fallen out!" He was yelling now, angry at this rich, entitled waste of a human breath. "You gotta go out there and get it before Gabriel brings that old man in or this plan is done for!"

Jared looked reluctantly at the door to the shack. He turned back at Johnny with a look that suggested there was no way he could find it.

"Jesus H Christ, man! What are you on?"

Jared looked at Johnny then down at the wet floorboard between his legs; what was he on? What wasn't he on? He remembered taking all his psychotropic meds earlier in the night. Then there were some blue pills he'd found from god knows when. He'd popped those too. Then the evening became a bit blurry.

Johnny paced in front of him, another cigarette waving frantically in his hand. "Well, I'm not going out there again. If Gabriel wants this guy popped he's going to have to go out there and get it himself."

57

A chilles rose from his hospital bed despite the fever consuming him. He had begun feeling feverish earlier in the day. His temperature had subsided by the time of Gabriel's visit but had spiked since. Too afraid of the nurses disallowing his walking around, Achilles declined to ask for the antipyretics that would have helped him. Feigning a casual salute to the night nurse by the nurses' station, he headed down to the cafeteria. He slumped slightly against the side of the elevator going down, and limped his way down the hall to the cafeteria. It was empty, thankfully, and he pushed through the exit door and pressed forward into the loud roar of the storm, against the rain and wind to the Chevelle waiting outside.

"Hey man," he yelled as he got into the car.

"Hey, what's up? Glad you made it." Gabriel high-fived him then pulled away from the curb and onto the street. "Change of clothes is in the bag on the backseat."

Achilles shivered with deep rigors as he peeled off his wet patient gown and put on Gabriel's dry shirt and pants. Pulling on his friend's raincoat, he felt no relief from the chill. "Everything all set?" he asked through chattering teeth, trying to keep from shivering too noticeably.

But Gabriel wasn't noticing at all. He kept his eyes trained on the road ahead, swerving away from the debris and rising flood waters. "So far, so good. Shouldn't take us more than ten minutes to get to the perp's place. Jared and Johnny should be at home by the time we arrive.

"Good," Achilles said, hoping ten minutes rest would allow him the strength he would need to carry out the next part of the mission. He closed his eyes and prayed silently for it. A sudden jerk of the car brought his head to the passenger window and he felt a jolt of pain to the side of his head. He brought his hand to his scalp and saw a small amount of blood. It was a minor laceration, he reasoned, and would heal eventually.

"Put your seat belt on," Gabriel yelled as he swerved the car away from an overturned car. "You okay?"

Achilles clicked the belt in and gave Gabriel the thumbs up sign.

They parked in front of the house and walked to the front. By now the storm was the only force present tonight - the neighborhood, the town, the island all ceased to exist. No one would notice or bother with their car in front of Mr. Winter's house. Despite the fever burning inside him he made a half dozen attempts alongside Gabriel to kick the door down. Once inside Achilles felt a second wind of energy and had no problems carrying the old man down the hallway to the car. For a brief moment, he thought he would make it tonight.

They parked the car along the side street next to the steep slope. Achilles clenched and unclenched his fists summoning the will to climb the hill, if only for tonight. Luckily the old man was light and for the first half the struggle was minimal, despite the wet ground, the rivulets of mud and debris. But midway he felt something inside him snap and his strength gave way. He fell with the old man, but Gabriel stood firm and helped him back on his feet.

"Come on," Gabriel yelled at Achilles. "Don't give up, not now."

The second half was a long struggle with Gabriel tugging both him and the old man up the hill. At the top he was back on firm footing and limped forward to the shack, holding the old man's right arm. Inside he slumped against the wall, red cheeked, a puddle of rainwater forming underneath him, and his vision blurred. "I'm okay, I'm okay," he said to no one in particular before passing out.

Gabriel closed the door shut and let the old man drop to the floor. "Okay," he said finally, catching his breath. Standing straight and tall inside the shack he loomed above everyone. "Let's finish this," he pointed to Johnny. "Give me the gun."

5 8

Gabriel burst through the door of the cabin into the violence of the raging storm outside and ran to the edge of the hill that was now dissolving into a river of thick mud flowing down to the street below. A jagged crack of lightning illuminated the sky and earth, briefly outlining Gabriel's form struggling against the gusts of wind and rain outside. He brushed the rain from his face as he scanned the hill for reflective traces of the missing gun. The ground below him gave way to a mudslide and he slid through broken bushes and felled trees to the street. He rose, cloaked in mud, and began running, searching frantically all around the base of the hill. During another burst of lightning he spotted Johnny's motorbike and ran to it. He hunted blindly all around, grasping at the sodden earth.

Inside the shack- their home for the past several years, soon to be demolished and taken away from them and the land converted into god knows what- Johnny pulled the door shut, muffling the storm's roar, walked over to the half-conscious form of Mr. Winter and gave his ribs a solid kick. The old man reflexively contracted and groaned. Johnny turned to Jared, yelling to be heard, "Hey asshole, help me with this fucking slime ball!"

Jared and Johnny hooked their arms under Mr. Winter's armpits and hoisted him onto the chair. The old man's head slumped forward, his chin against his chest. Johnny pushed him back against the chair. "Yo, get me some of that rope you brought," he said, turning to Jared.

Jared walked over and unzipped his duffel bag, rummaged a few moments before producing the rope.

"Here, hold him against the chair while I tie this fuck up."

Jared took over Johnny's position, pushing Mr. Winter's chest against the back of the seat as Johnny tied the old man's arms together and then anchored them to the frame of the chair. "Alright," Johnny announced, hands on hips. "Time we had ourselves a little fun with this fucking pervert, soften him up a bit."

A howling gust of wind crashed the door open and Jared ran to close it. When he turned around, Johnny landed his first punch, sending the man's face awkwardly to the side. "How's that feel, ya damn pervert?" When the man didn't answer Johnny punched him a second time, connecting with the mouth. "Ya like that, huh? I bet you do, ya damn pervert." Johnny turned around to Jared, rabid excitement in his eyes. "Come on, man, here's your chance."

Jared looked at the man's swollen bloody lip. He shook his head tentatively against Johnny's insistence.

"Come on, this guy's a fucking pervert! Gabriel said so himself. For all we know this perv molested him!"

Jared uncrossed his arms and walked slowly up to the slumped form on the chair. He tried to think back in his life. In all of the fights his friends had gotten into, he was always the one who hung back, raising his arm only in defense. Fighting, hitting, it never entered his consciousness. For all his anger he entertained for his father, Jared never once connected it to violence. And the old man sitting in the chair- half beaten already- did not appear to be any sort of monster. But the thought that he may have somehow hurt Gabriel...he raised his hand and curled it into a fist. The psychotropic chemical mix circulating in his brain distorted his sense of time and space and he hoped he'd be able to complete the task. When he looked down, both fists were bruised and bleeding. He looked up to find fresh blood oozing from the old man's nose and mouth.

"Here, let me get a shot at this fucking freak," Johnny said, stepping forward, pushing Jared aside. He took a deep drag off his cigarette. "So you like little kids, huh?" he said through a smoke-filled exhale, the cigarette affixed between his teeth. The old man sat slumped forward, unmoving. Johnny cocked his right fist back and shot through the old man's jaw, jolting his head to the side. Johnny brought his left fist around and punched the face back to center. He repeatedly punched the old man's face using both fists until he grew tired. He pulled up a chair square in front of the old man and leaned forward, admiring his handy work; ecchymotic swellings disfigured the old man's face, blood oozed from his nose and mouth. His cigarette end crackled an orange red as Johnny took another drag; he pulled out the cigarette and looked at its end in a momentary, noise-cancelling trance as the storm waxed outside, shaking the walls and roof, urging collapse onto all inside. Then, as if inspired, he pressed the cigarette end against the old man's cheek. The old man shuddered, his eyes shut tight as the cigarette seared an ashy circle into his flesh. The cigarette glowed an angry red as Johnny took another deep drag, his eyes fixed on his prisoner. He pressed the end forcibly against one of the old man's eyelids. The old man winced and turned feebly away. A low moan escaped his lips. Jared watched in horror as Johnny went to work with his cigarette over the man's face until he'd extinguished it into the man's left ear.

Johnny turned around, smiling gleefully. "Hey, Achilles, look at this fucking pervert, why don't you give him one of your special-"

Achilles lay collapsed on his side, his eyes half open and glazed, his face flushed.

Johnny stood up from his chair and walked over to his friend's form and crouched down. "Hey man," he said shaking Achilles's shoulder. "You okay?" he asked in a tone that suggested more curiosity than concern.

"I'm alright," Achilles mumbled through closed, chapped

lips, his voice weak and hushed to a whisper. "Looks like you're doing fine without me. Just finish the job so we can all get outta here."

Johnny stood straight up. "Suit yourself, but I don't want to be the one hogging up all the fun," he said, turning to Jared. "Why don't you join in?"

Jared stood several feet away from the old man. He opened his eyes wide to the shadowy forms rising from the dark recesses of the room. He shook his head, frightened.

Johnny scowled. "You're in this just like the rest of us," he said grabbing Jared by the arm and shoving him forward. He pulled the chair to the side. "Hold on," he said and walked over to the duffel bag. He came back holding up a flashlight. "Here, give him a few good whacks with this."

Jared took the flashlight loosely in his right hand. He turned around to the bruised form of Mr. Winter and raised his hand. He brought the flashlight down in a glancing blow to the old man's head.

"Harder," yelled Johnny above the storm.

Jared raised the flashlight again, gripping the flashlight a little bit stronger, and brought it down more forcefully. The head dropped with the blow before popping up from the momentum. This time the eyes of the old man were wide open, less in fear than in full anticipation of meeting his destiny.

His lips trembled as he began to murmur out loud, "I- I- I"

Jared backed away, but Johnny pushed him forward from behind. "Come on ya faggot, give it to him harder."

Jared raised the flashlight again, conscious of the man's eyes on him.

He continued to stammer, "I'm, s- s-s-. I'm so- so- so-"

Jared brought down the flashlight harder than the previous two times, feeling the sharp crack of the impact in his wrist.

"That's it!" Johnny said, stepping forward and grabbing the flashlight. "Let me give this thing a whirl."

"I'm so- so- so-"

"You're what?" Johnny mocked, leaning in with a hand to his ear. "You're so, so, so?"

"I'm sorry, I'm so- so- sorry," the old man pleaded.

"You know what, old man? I'm so- so- sorry too." In the next minute he'd bashed the flashlight over Mr. Winter's face, chest, and legs. He felt the rush of the storm as he raised his right arm above his head.

"Stop!"

Johnny turned around just as Gabriel's left bludgeoning wrist shot forward, connecting with his face. Johnny dropped to the ground in a daze, massaging his face.

"What are you doing?" Gabriel shouted as he hovered menacingly over Johnny, dark piercing eyes glared through wet strands of hair matted over his face, his large half naked body slick wet with mud, tensed with fury, as if he had become part of the storm that had burst into their home. "What the hell are you doing!" he repeated. He cocked his left wrist back, ready to pound Johnny again. Johnny cowered underneath raised arms. Gabriel pivoted sharply and walked to Jared, shoving him against the wall. "We are not savages," he yelled into his face. "We are human beings! Do you understand?"

Jared closed his eyes shamefaced, nodding.

"Now untie him."

His head hung low, Jared walked to the semiconscious form draped back against the chair and unraveled the rope; the man's arms dropped limp by his side. Gabriel struggled to open the ziplock bag, finally tearing it, and took the gun out. "Get me the bullets," he ordered. Jared ran to the duffel bag and took out the box and ran back to Gabriel, bullets rattling inside. Gabriel wiped the wet strands of hair from his face with his left arm and swung out the cylinder, exposing six empty chambers. He filled up the chambers and clicked the cylinder closed, before turning around to face the old man. The unrelenting wind gusts hammered at the shack's walls, the wallboards shook with the clatter of an unruly courtroom mob, the loud chorus to a tragic play's inevitable final act. "Jack Winter-" The name caught in his throat. This was the first time he was face to face with the old man and he paused, so much of the last ten years returned to him, so much of that night when he lost his brother, so much pain. He looked up to his brother's swinging, swaying form in front of him. "Jack Winter," he called out again, his voice loud and hoarse. He wiped at his face with his left forearm, whether raindrops or tears it was hard to say. He continued as if he were listing charges to a defendant in a court of law. "You have been found guilty of pedophilia and the ultimate suicide of a young man. You have lost the right for any say here. You have been sentenced to death."

"I'm so- so- sorry," the man spoke through trembling lips. "I'm so- so- sorry."

Gabriel cocked the hammer back and raised the gun, pointing it at the old man's head. Yet the gun shook in his hand and tears began to blur his vision as the man stuttered on. "This is for my brother Daniel, who had no one to trust in this world, not my mother, not my father," Gabriel paused to wipe the tears from his eyes. "And not me. And he found you, but you betrayed that trust, Jack Winter. This is for the betrayal of that trust."

The other boys in the room stared silently at their leader; Gabriel had led them here years before to a home they had created for themselves, and he led them here tonight. Tonight was the culmination of their years together. To each, it seemed as if every act, every word, every decision made had ultimately been for this one night, and each wished for him to shoot the old man. The storm waged war outside the open door, an impassioned observer to the scene inside, almost urging the violence. Gabriel's index finger pressed against the trigger.

59

Leon placed the last dish on the rack and laid the folded towel next to the sink. He let his mind stray to the restaurant, then the three sisters, then Erma. He wondered how they were faring in the storm.

Another rumble of thunder shook his focus through the ceiling, to his sister and nephew upstairs. They seemed like such a broken family, a puzzle missing too many pieces. How similar to his own childhood, growing up without his parents, yet also how different. It was an unconscious reflex, comparing the homes of others to the one he had as a child. All the people in the kibbutz had stepped in to fill the sudden vacuum to raise his sister and him. They were never alone, and they were never without love or guidance. He was not yet two when his parents died. Their heroic deaths were recorded among the many others in the battles that the young Israeli nation fought as it took its own first steps. But his sister was older, old enough to have recorded her parents' presence in their lives; it was much later that Leon recognized how much more the loss had been for her, how she had hid the scar and stoically faced her remaining childhood and young adulthood.

And then she'd experienced loss again, first that of her husband and then of her first-born son. Some people were meant to live their lives with loss. She and Gabriel lived as casualties of wars that had no victors.

He shook his head sadly at the memory of Daniel's funeral, at Gabriel's sad, fretful eyes that day.

Leon was overcome by the desperate need to check in on his sister and nephew upstairs, to make sure they were fine- to do something. He knocked lightly on Isabelle's door but heard no response. Pushing the door in gently, he found his sister asleep on her bed. Quiet and immobile, she seemed more dead than alive. Perhaps this was why she slept so much, to cross the gossamer thin line separating life from death to be with Daniel. The loud hum of the air conditioner mingled with the storm's insistent howling roar outside.

Leon closed the door and walked down the hall to Gabriel's room. He knocked gently but heard no response. He pushed the door ajar and noted Gabriel's empty bed. Stepping inside, he spotted the slightly raised window.

Leon raced down the street as the sky fell apart around him, feeling the small shards of rain against his face, his raincoat doing little to protect him from the storm. He'd paused at the side door, struggling with the inclination to tell Isabelle-then again, what use would there be in worrying her about her remaining son; she would only want to go out herself. He prayed she would stay asleep until he came back with Gabriel. He panicked at the thought of not finding his nephew in time. His mind cycled through the few places he thought Gabriel would be, cursing himself for not having learned his friends' addresses. As he turned the corner a gust of wind almost knocked him to the ground and he was forced to trudge slowly against it, an arm shielding the windswept rain from his eyes. He reached the boulevard and cast frantic glances to either side. All the houses and stores were boarded, the roads branching off were deserted of cars. He was close to giving up and the idea brought him to tears. Upon instinct, he began running to the one place he prayed Gabriel would be. A familiar howl filled him with dread as he reached Great Hope Road. The women from his nightmares began lining up along side the street, their mournful ululations pressing up against his chest and his breathing began to falter.

Sabra refugee camp, September 1982

Leon's grip on the receiver remained iron tight even as the rest of his muscles began aching with fatigue. "I need to talk with someone now."

He strained to hear the response, his jaw clenched. He'd had been standing outside the camp in the same position since ten o'clock the previous evening. He could see nothing behind the wall of darkness, but what he could not see he imagined with what he heard. The cries and pleas were not those of young militant fighters, but of women and children. Disconcerting reports on indiscriminate killings within the camps had been circulating around the various IDF positions around the perimeter.

"I have reason to believe that innocent civilians are being killed." Leon spoke into the 2-way radio, a note of urgency in his voice. He looked through binoculars as the activity in the camp began to take shape in the early morning light. His orders had been to stay along the perimeter and to not enter. The Phalanges, little more than thugs in his estimation, would be in charge of the mop up operation to rid the camp of militant extremists. That they'd taken little to no part in the war up until now, that they'd suffered no casualties, had not been lost on him or his fellow soldiers. But Bashir's recent assassination had fired up passions among their ranks; it had been a clarion call for revenge and there had been misgivings among the high-ranking IDF officers about giving any role to the Phalanges in the operation to clear out the Palestinian refugee camps in West Beirut. Still the orders from above had been to stay put and let the Lebanese in and clean up. But the initial reports about the atrocities began to multiply in the early morning hours. Leon had spotted militiamen leading a group of women and children into a building before a series of shots rang out. "Sir," he spoke into the 2-way radio, more loudly than before

A string of white noise crackled in response.

"Sir," he yelled.

"Hold your position, Lieutenant."

"Women and children," he yelled back.

"That's an order."

He looked helplessly at his fellow soldiers, all of them sons, grandsons, brothers, or fathers, all of them human beings. All aware now of the unspeakable atrocities occurring less than a hundred yards away inside the camps, all gripping their guns, ready for the word to go in and stop the slaughter inside. Leon paced like a caged animal, one hand gripping the binoculars, the other the radio. Both useless in stopping the chorus of wails and shrieks coupled with small bursts of gunfire.

It would be hours before he and the others were allowed in, to bear witness to the carnage. Women, children, the elderly and infirmed, all of them lay in heaps, blood dripping from fresh bullet wounds.

The Israeli soldiers walked numbly by, registering the dead as well as those that had stayed alive- by some miracle- now draped over their dead or dying loved ones, their piercing wails filing up the sky, filling up the Israeli soldier's brains, haunting their minds.

Leon burst through the gauntlet of his memories and onto the steep slope. But the hill had become alive, monstrous, liquid flowing, resistant to trespass. He groped blindly through the wind and rain, grasping at wayward roots to scramble up, his feet struggling to gain traction. After an interminable period of time, Leon pulled himself to the top of the hill; he lay on his back for a brief moment to catch his breath before he rose to his feet and ran to the shack with windows that glimmered dimly from the light within.

He pulled the door and ran inside. Seconds later the gunshot blast from inside escaped into the howling storm outside.

60

Four figures made their way down the hill under the cover of Frederick's rage. Leon carried the body over his left shoulder, leading the way down the hill. Despite the added weight, he kept his footing down the treacherous hill of mud. Johnny and Gabriel helped Achilles down the hill. Achilles leaned onto Gabriel much of the way, his arm wrapped around Gabriel's neck. Johnny carried two shovels with his free hand. Towards the bottom of the hill Achilles's legs gave way and Gabriel had to carry him to the car. Leon opened the trunk and dumped the body in as Gabriel helped Achilles into the backseat and put on his seatbelt. He sat next to him and put an arm around his ailing friend. Achilles felt hot to the touch.

Johnny got into the driver seat and Leon sat up front in the passenger seat. No one spoke as they made their way to the school. All eyes fixed on the road in front of them as Johnny weaved in and out of fallen trees upturned cars, dead animals and other victims of the storm. Many of the roads had been flooded and Johnny was forced to turn around several times. They finally made it to the back fence of the school.

Leon gave final instructions to Johnny. "I want you to drop off Achilles and return here. Then Gabriel will take you to the cabin and you can take Jared home. Make sure you leave nothing behind."

Johnny nodded, not looking back at Leon, so fearful was he of the soldier's eyes, eyes that saw through everything.

Gabriel turned to Achilles. "Okay man, take care of yourself. I'll try to swing by after the storm."

Achilles shook his head and put a hand on Gabriel's neck.

"Forget about me. Live your life. Do something with it."

Gabriel looked back at him as if slapped awake. "What do you mean forget about you? You're going to be some hotshot doctor and-"

Achilles smiled sadly, his voice starting to slur with fever. "I'm not going to make it; I already know. But you have a chance. How about you become a doctor and help someone like me when you get there."

Gabriel looked into the fading light of Achilles's eyes and felt suddenly fearful. He and Leon hurriedly carried Achilles to the front passenger seat. Gabriel clicked the seatbelt for him and turned to his friend once more but found no words to offer. He looked over at Johnny behind the wheel. "Get him to the hospital quickly," he pleaded. He closed the door and turned to Leon, who had already taken out the body and was making his way to the fence. As the car drove off the two hoisted the body over the fence and then climbed over.

Achilles dozed in and out of his febrile delirium, shaking with rigors. Johnny searched his jacket for his pack of Winstons and found them miraculously dry. He lit two and poked one in Achilles's mouth. "Take it," he said, grabbing the wheel firmly with both hands and dodging a fallen tree in the road.

Achilles pawed at the cigarette with a trembling hand. He resisted the initial urge to throw it to the ground, and took a slow sputtering drag. The hot tobacco burned a white path into his lungs and he felt his chest all seize up. He coughed violently, lurching against his seatbelt, but he kept his fingers clutched to the cigarette. He looked over at Johnny and recalled the time years before when his father had told him about his name, and about the river Styx, how it separated earth from the underworld, how all the ancient gods had to swear oaths upon it. And he remembered his father telling him about Charon, the ferryman who would ferry all the new souls across the river.

"I don't have any gold coin to give you," he said, smiling at Johnny.

"Man, I gotta get you to the hospital," Johnny said.

Achilles smiled, shaking his head.

The car weaved its way along the small streets and onto the main road. The gusts of winds continued unabated, whipping sheets of rain against the Chevelle's windshield as the wipers worked frantically to clear the view forward.

"Just leave me at the corner by the hospital," Achilles warned, his voice slurred. "You don't want to risk getting caught."

"No man, I got my orders to take you to the door," Johnny replied, though inwardly doubting the logic behind those orders, and the unnecessary risks.

Achilles, through half closed eyes, saw the workings of his friend's mind and, for once, agreed. "You may get caught taking me all the way to the front. They'll ask questions."

The car made the turn onto Communal Drive, half a mile from the hospital entrance.

"Come on, man!" Achilles summoned the reserves of energy to yell above the howling wind. "You're going to get caught. Even if you drove away, they may get the license plate."

"I have my orders," Johnny repeated, but he felt his resolve beginning to waver.

The car pulled onto the entrance ramp leading to the emergency room.

"If you get caught, they'll stick you in jail," Achilles yelled, laughing now, "and you'll have a whole bunch of Mars bars shoved up your-"

Johnny slammed on the breaks fifty yards from the emergency room entrance. He ran around the back of the Chevelle and ripped open Achilles passenger side door. Achilles by now had undone his seatbelt, still laughing. Johnny pulled Achilles out of the car and pushed him forward to the emergency room doorway and ran back to the driver seat. As he pulled away he saw the outline of Achilles form, blurred by the whipping rain, fall to the ground. "Shit, shit, shit," he muttered under his breath, resisting the urge to drive back and help his friend. He cursed Gabriel the whole ride back to the school.

Judith had chosen to work the overnight shift, to do a "double" in the skeleton crew that was left to weather the storm. Many of the overnight nurses had families, and she knew Achilles had begun to have a fever and wanted to stay with him, even though she'd been assigned to the other side of the floor. The charge nurse allowed her brief excursions from her routine duties, to the different corners of the hospital to search for him. She walked down to the emergency room, moving her large bulk with a speed even she hadn't known possible, every half hour, asking if anyone had brought in a tall teenage boy. A sixth sense brought her down again several minutes after four in the morning. She peered through the large glass emergency room doors to the wrathful storm outside, saw the faint glow of headlights stop at the entrance to the emergency room, pause and then turn around. "It's him," she said. Without waiting to ponder the risks of rushing out into the storm, she pounded the flat square button, and the double doors opened.

A security guard off to the side was caught by surprise. "Hey wait-"

But his words were swallowed up as Judith rushed out into the storm to the familiar form lying on the ground. "I know it's him, I know it's him," she repeated like a mantra to give her the strength to run the fifty yards to Achilles. "Oh blesses, lord," she cried out as she lifted him in her arms and ran back to the emergency room, past the stunned security guard, and barked out a barrage of orders, whipping all the doctors into a mad frenzy to "save my boy!"

It was all they could do, as well as the ICU team, to keep him alive for another twelve hours so that his mother would be able to hold his hand before the infection wrested him away and gifted him to Charon.

61

Jared dropped onto his hands and knees and dragged the first of several towels from his duffel bag across the blood that had begun to seep through the floorboards. He picked up pieces of skull and brain from the pool of blood and deposited them into a large garbage bag then closed his eyes and retched as the contents of his stomach began to rise into his chest.

The storm surged outside the cabin, shaking the rafters and clattering the wall panels, and the clanging rose louder and louder, becoming a hammering in his ears, merging with the roar of the storm outside and a faint but definitive sound of wings fluttering about him. He looked up and he prayed Johnny would return quickly.

Jared returned to the task at hand and looked back down at the floor, finding the old man's blood had only spread further about the floor. He lifted the towel, heavy with blood. Stuffing the towel into the garbage bag, he grabbed more. He scrubbed with renewed vigor, sweat dripping from his face, and after ten minutes he'd only managed to spread the blood even more. He looked on in horror as the blood pooled higher and higher as if a well of it beneath the foundation had been tapped. He hurriedly stuffed the last towel and his rubber gloves into the garbage bag and sat drained, catching his breath. He glanced down at his hands and found the blood had seeped through the glove, staining them. Frightened at his bloody hands, he looked around for something to clean them with. He grabbed a browned copy of the Great Hope Gazette and worked the pages around each finger. But the stain clung stubbornly to them. He wiped them on his shirt and jeans, only to spread the blood onto his clothes. He cried in fright. The wind outside kicked up anew and the cabin shook uncontrollably. Shingles from the roof began peeling off and the storm started to spill inside. He ran about the cabin, packing as much as he could into his duffel bag as more bits of the roof began to separate from the wall, the clattering and fluttering grew louder, and parts of the wall began to fly away. And as the remains of the cabin succumbed to the storm and caved inward, Jared ran out, screaming into the black of the storm. There would be no trace of Jared when Johnny climbed the hill later on that night.

62

2008

Johnny stumbled out the front door of the roadhouse, reaching for the zipper tab of his half-zipped jeans, tipsy off the bourbon shots and Jackie's intoxicating charms in the backroom. The heavy wooden door creaked shut behind him, muffling the bacchanalia inside, leaving him with the silence of the dusty parking lot. He dug his hands into his leather jacket, searching for the keys as he walked the long stretch of motorcycles to his Harley at the far end of the lot. Several yards from his motorcycle he noticed a black van with tinted windows parked uncomfortably close to it. He squinted warily as he reached for his pack of smokes. He walked around his bike looking for any scratch marks; noting none he relaxed his gaze and lit up his cigarette, the first smoky breath of it dissipating into the cool evening air. His thoughts turned to the five-minute drive home and his comfortable bed. He would crash hard tonight; then again Johnny was a man who always crashed hard, and slept, long restful sleeps. He could never wrap his mind around other folks and their problems getting to sleep or waking up in the middle of the night or early morning. Johnny turned to his motorcycle. Tomorrow he would ride back across the waters, terrorize Jared (that nut job) again, then sneak over to Gabriel's place, stick it to him hard. Might be able to get a few thou' out of each of them. Johnny's fingers fumbled with the keys and they fell to the ground. Shit, he was probably drunker than he expected. He got down on his hands and knees and searched around in the dark until he fingered them. When he stood back up a number of things happened in such rapid succession that it gave Johnny the impression of them happening all at once (later on he would still have difficulty being able to chronicle the events in any logical order). The earth began to spin rapidly to one side, a pall descended over the stars and roadhouse lights, leaving the world in darkness, an arm reached around his neck, another gripped his mouth shut, he rose several feet in the air and was sucked back into the airless van behind him.

63

Johnny awoke with, or from, pain all throughout his body, he was unsure which. His eyes opened to absolute darkness. Despite his relative blindness he was sure of several things: one, he was seated in a chair; two, he was immobile, his arms bound behind him, and his legs strapped to the legs of the chair; three, he also couldn't talk, when he tried to open his mouth to call out he found his lips were sealed shut. He began to sink into panic as last night's bar meal soured in his chest. Calm down, calm down. Vomiting would do him no good with his mouth sealed. Time to think. He took a tight breath in through his nose. He was unsure how long he was out for or what had happened in the intervening period- he was jonesing for a cigarette (which doesn't normally occur until soon after waking up in the morning)- he guessed six or seven hours. Who could have drugged him? He scanned through his mental rolodex of people he'd had run-ins with in the previous ten years, people he'd conned or tried to con, people he had threatened or had threatened him, and to his discomfort found the list quite long. It was here that a strange sound surfaced in his consciousness...zip, zip, zip...had it been there before? He wasn't sure; it could have possibly been present the whole time, yet imperceptible until now...zip...zip... zip... It was a subtle, rhythmic singsong scraping sound- hard to place. But he realized now there was someone else in the room, making this sound, and this fact made his heart pound harder. He called out into the darkness but his words came out indecipherably muffled against his gag. The bright flash of a match light blinded him and he shut his eyes for several seconds. When he opened them, he cried out in agonizing fright, his screams muffled by the tape. It was the commando. He stood several feet away, older certainly, but the years had not softened him, some grays in his close-cropped hair were all that betrayed the passage of time. Leon had blown out the match and placed it on the plate with a large white candle next to him, a wisp of smoke curled upwards. He resumed scraping his straight razor along a leather strop that was strapped to the post of another chair, slow purposeful strokes under the slow dance of candlelight.

Johnny shook his head, screaming again into his gag.

Leon stopped stropping and looked up, questioningly. "What?" he asked (his Israeli accent too had not softened with time), and walked over to Johnny.

Johnny arched back in his chair away from Leon's reaching hand.

Leon grabbed the end to the duct tape and ripped it off in one painful tug.

Johnny screamed in pain, then called out to anyone who could or would listen, "Help! Help! Help!"

Leon stood back, his arms behind him, waiting respectfully. "No one can hear you," he finally told him.

"I'm sorry, I'm sorry," Johnny cried out.

Leon nodded sympathetically, then reached over and reapplied the duct tape to Johnny's mouth. "Of course you are sorry. I'm sorry too." He went back to stropping his razor, a large one-inch thick dark metal blade that sang- zip, zip, zip, zip- in rhythmic, meditative strokes.

"Good and evil," Leon began, finally. "Many people see these as two completely separate entities, each in its own world, like heaven and hell. But I think this is somewhat simplistic, don't you?" He smiled at Johnny before resuming. "I see good and evil as being two sides of the same coin. Both are necessary in life and are necessary for each other; one cannot exist without the other. They serve as a dynamic roadmap in our lives, in the choices that we make that define who we are. You see, Johnny, the same act can be seen as good or as evil depending on the circumstances surrounding the act, or the intent behind the act. Take the killing of another human being for instance. The Bible says 'thou shall not kill'. Killing is bad. In fact, many religions see the taking of life as bad or evil. But what if the person we are killing is evil, someone who may harm or kill others. Killing him may not necessarily be bad; perhaps letting him live would be bad."

Johnny went wild in his chair, tugging at the restraints to his arms and legs, shaking his head from side to side. His face turned red and tears began to fall from his eyes.

Leon continued as if he had not noticed. "But what about two people who set about to kill this same evil man? One may have good intentions in killing this man, ridding the world of this vermin," Leon spat out the final word in disgust, "protecting other innocent people, children. But the other man may not have such good intentions. He may want to kill for the sole pleasure of killing, or for the prestige of being a killer." Leon stopped and eyed Johnny warily. "It becomes confusing, doesn't it? You see, the act is the same, the evil victim is the same, but the intentions are critically different. Good and evil, sometimes so difficult to tell apart, the divide is so fine." Leon lifted the straight razor, blade side up, to the light focusing on the integrity of the edge. "Like the edge of a razor." Leon resumed stropping.

Johnny continued to scream against the tape.

"What?" Leon paused, blade in mid-strop. Letting go of the strop, he walked over to Johnny, ripping the tape off his face.

Johnny blubbered tearfully, "I'm sorry, I'm sorry. I donwanna die, I donwanna die. I'll leave. I'll get outa here, I'll never come back here, I'll-"

Leon replaced the tape, stifling Johnny's pleas, and walked back to his position by the chair and resumed stropping. "We all have to die sometime, Johnny. I am sorry to tell you this.

Death is an important aspect of life. Many of my fellow soldiers died in war, many of them younger than you, maybe half your age." Leon pointed the blade towards Johnny. "Innocent lives." Leon looked up at the space in front of him, as if to a memory. "But then again what soldier is innocent, right? There is an unwritten contract we agree to at the start of our training, and at the start of war, that everything we will be asked to do, or everything that will be done to us, is beyond good and evil. We must do what we must do. It is only afterwards that we reflect on the moral conflicts inherent in this contract." Leon resumed stropping. "Some of us are able to accept them and move on, others don't. And in this soldiers and civilians are alike. Most travel through life tossing the same coin in every action, always hoping to see the face of good rather than evil. The key is to always question the face that we see, so that we do not repeat the evil we are capable of." Leon raised his razor and nodded approvingly at the blade. He looked up at Johnny, narrowing his eyes. "Now I know you will leave this area and never come back, right Johnny?"

Johnny nodded emphatically.

"Gabriel and Jared will never hear from you again?"

Johnny mumbled an assent into the tape he hoped Leon would accept.

"Unfortunately," Leon said sighing and dropped the end of the strop, letting it swing and clang against the chair once more, "there is one thing I have to do to you, something I have been wanting to do for a long time." He approached Johnny, blade held out, as Johnny shook his head wildly, his screams tensing the thick tape around his mouth, his thrashing body stretching and straining the restraints about his wrists and ankles.

64

"Alright, ante up boys," John Sr. called out with authority as he mixed the cards, expertly despite the arthritis in his fingers. Of all the damage the passage of time had wrought on his body it was the rheumatism in the joints of his hands and fingers that had impacted his life most profoundly.

"Alright, place your bets." John Sr. dealt the cards deftly to three others at the table, all of them from his squad in Nam, Freddie (his squad commander), Joe (the thumper) and little Stevie. They were all in their mid to late sixties now, their faces and arms were tanned to a leathery finish under the Florida sun, their pale veiny legs planted into dark dress socks and sandals. They'd kept their crew cuts, but they'd traded in their army fatigues for muted pastel polos and khaki shorts. The poker games themselves were more for the company- very little money was won or lost.

Freddie chewed on his unlit cigar. He squinted hard at the cards in front of him, accentuating the fine web of wrinkles around his eyes. "Alright I'll bet a dime," he said, his voice thick and coarse from years of smoking. "Hey John, when's your boy coming down?"

John shifted uncomfortably in his seat at the reminder of his eldest son's threat of an impromptu visit the week before. "Should be any day now," he replied finally.

"What's the boy up to now?" Joe called out loudly above the tinnitus.

John frowned at his cards. "Last I heard he was working for a construction crew up in the Northeast."

Freddie grunted approvingly.

Joe and Stevie called, throwing in their dimes.

"Still got the long hair?" Freddie pressed on.

"Alright, who wants new cards," John Sr. asked somewhat impatiently. "God, I hope not," he said finally. "Otherwise I'll have to take some shears to his head myself."

Freddie shook his head slowly, pulling the chewed cigar out of his mouth, preparing to expound, a subtle smile at his own hand. "It's that new generation, long hair, earrings, hard to know who is who and what is what these days."

The loud roar of a Harley Davidson tore through the peace of the apartment complex, drawing the attentions of all four at the table to the parking lot off to the side.

"Speak of the devil," John Sr. muttered as he dropped his cards on the table. He paused for a moment, his hands pressing against the armrests, as if steeling himself for moment. John Sr. pushed himself up from his patio chair. "I'm out for this one boys. Freddie, you can take over."

"We can wait for you, John," Freddie replied, his smile wide. "We want to see your boy."

John scowled again and turned to face the helmeted figure making his way toward him.

A few feet away, after some pause, Johnny removed his helmet a look of anticipated embarrassment frozen on his face.

John Sr.'s scowl melted into a smile, then a laugh, and before long the father was bent over clutching at his chest unable to control his laughter. "Looks like someone beat me to it," he said in between gasps of laughter. John Sr. finally stood up straight, his smile bright and wide.

Johnny stood shamefaced before his father; his shoulders weighed down by all the possessions he felt it necessary to escape with, his bald scalp turning a bright, angry red under the hot Florida sun. Subtle hints of fuzz had grown in the seven days it took to get his few possessions together and ride down (frequently looking over his shoulder to make sure he wasn't being followed).

"Come on, son." His father put an arm around Johnny's shoulder, his mouth still quivering at the verge of laughter. "Come meet my friends."

6 5

Nine months later.

They pulled up to the curb alongside the park- what had once been home- the edge of so many memories and secrets. Gabriel exhaled sharply, his right hand white-knuckle gripping the steering wheel. He cast an anxious glance at the wooded area awaiting him, ready to enfold him in its wild embrace.

Leon reached over from the passenger seat, gripping Gabriel's shoulder gently. "Come, Gabriel."

Gabriel looked back at Leon, his own heart pounding wildly in his chest, as he tried to recall his uncle's words from the night before. Leon had arrived earlier in the day, after so many years, with his own story to tell. Priti and Payal had already gone to bed, and it was just the two of them huddled around the kitchen table. A dog had barked outside, the bass beat to a popular song had flowed then ebbed down the street, noises of Brooklyn reminding them of the world around them. Leon had explained the purchase Gabriel's father and he had made of the abandoned shack and lot, "an investment" as Raul had propositioned, the one and only business venture Leon had agreed to. Then the marriage between Isabelle and Raul had dissolved the way it did and the land had sat idle. It was after the summer of '83 that Leon had convinced Raul to sell his share. He had decided to convert the land into a park and bird sanctuary that he would open to the public.

Gabriel closed his eyes as he absorbed the alternate reality to the small, rundown shack that had been his home. "What happened that night?" Gabriel had asked, opening his eyes finally.

Leon paused before answering, wanting to recall the moment in his mind to give as clear an account as his nephew deserved so as to reduce the burden of at least this one demon.

"Gabriel, don't!" Leon yelled out from the open doorway, drenched from the storm.

Gabriel kept the gun aimed at Mr. Winter's head, unmoving.

Leon closed the door behind him and took two tentative steps forward. "Don't do it, Gabriel," he called out again, his voice a little softer, gentler. "Don't do it," he repeated. "Don't let this man make you what you do not wish to be. You are not a murderer, Gabriel. Killing him won't stop your pain. It won't bring Daniel back." By now Leon was at Gabriel's side. Had he wanted to, he could have easily disarmed Gabriel; but he spoke softly to his nephew his hand stretched out, he spoke to the small boy suffering inside. "Look at him, Gabriel, he suffers more alive than dead. And you are not a murderer." Leon spread his arms out, pointing to the earth below as if it were sacred ground. "Not here, Gabriel, not now."

Gabriel wiped his eyes against his left forearm then looked up again at the old man. He loosened his grip on the gun and let it fall onto the chair next to him, and walked into Leon's embrace. The storm within Gabriel had broken. He felt his energy give way and fell to sobbing.

"Come on Gabriel, let's go home." Leon hugged him tightly.

No one else moved or spoke; all eyes were on Gabriel. The unifying plan, their individual hopes, their sought after reward; it had all ended. All felt something tear within them, and they all became unmoored from their home and disconnected from each other. Their moment as a band of friends, a gang of rebels was over. So focused were they on Gabriel, that no one saw the old man's right arm move, no one saw him grab the gun off the chair and jam the barrel into his mouth.

The loud explosion drowned out the storm, filling up the confined space of the shack, distorting basic sense of time, so that the second afterward stretched immeasurably for those inside. Within the second of the gunshot Leon pushed Gabriel to the floor and fell on top shielding him, Jared dropped low against the wall, and Johnny reflexively covered his head. Leon looked up quickly and scanned the direction of the gunshot. The old man lay on the floor, his arms and legs at awkward angles, a ragdoll tossed to the floor and forgotten. The gun lay by his hand. The back of his head was gone, an arc of blood splatter on the back wall.

Leon stood up and walked to the lifeless body. He carefully lifted up the gun and emptied the chambers. He took one last look at the body before turning to the others. Instructions had to be given, cleaning the cabin. Disposing the body. Returning the sick friend back to the hospital. And all this had to be done before daybreak. The boys moved mechanically, capable of only following instruction, their inner will broken.

Uncle and nephew had stayed up late into the night talking about the past, about Gabriel's childhood, about Daniel. "Daniel used to go to the lot on the hill. He said it was his favorite place to go to." Leon looked off into space as if remembering the exchange. Leon had told him of a letter that Daniel had written to Gabriel the night of the suicide. "I found it between the pages of a book I had picked up from his bookcase, just by accident. I saw the date on the letter and-" Leon had pressed the letter into Gabriel's hand, recognizing how cheap words were at that moment. Gabriel had looked down at the letter, being struck by the idea that he was seeing his brother's handwriting for the first time in years. It had seemed so similar to his, sharp, crisp, unadorned.

Gabriel caught Priti's sympathetic frown in the rearview mirror and winked unconvincingly. She reached forward and squeezed Gabriel's other shoulder. He turned to look back and found Payal's encouraging smile.

"Are we here yet?" she asked again.

Her innocent impatience comforted him and Gabriel smiled despite the mounting anxiety. "Yes, we're here," he replied. It was their old joke, her same question and his same response throughout any trip they took.

He stepped out of the car and onto the curb. He looked back as two doors slammed shut from the car behind them. Jared and another man stepped out. Clean-shaven and dressed in a button-down shirt and slacks, Jared was a different man from months before. The medications had had a dramatic effect on his symptoms and his father, inspired, had decided to double his efforts at giving his son the best chance at a new life. He had found a different psychiatrist who had reviewed Jared's medical charts, several tomes of data, and had prescribed a more appropriate psychotropic regimen, along with group counseling. It was there that Jared had met Joshua, a 'friend' whom Mr. Scharpe had welcomed, unquestioningly, as he had done all the newfound glimmers of hope in his son's life. Joshua put an arm around Jared's shoulder and they both made their way to Gabriel.

"Are you ready, Gabriel?" Jared asked somewhat worriedly.

Gabriel took a deep breath and nodded. Leon lifted Payal onto his shoulders, eliciting little squeals of delight as he galloped towards the entrance, and Priti looped an arm through Gabriel's as they all followed. The green sign at the foot of a bluestone path read "Daniel's Park and Bird Sanctuary" in white block letters. Gabriel stood in front of the sign reading and rereading the simple message. Both the sign and the path of bluestones that switchbacked up the hill were new to Gabriel, who only knew of treacherous climbs from another life. Leon and Payal led the way, Jared and Joshua followed close behind. Somewhat disoriented, Gabriel was forced to stop several times to catch his breath, and he and Priti were the last to reach the top of the hill. The cabin was gone. Bushes and small trees now populated the plateau at the top. The anxious cacophony of chirps, clicks, and whistles punctured the air by the host of sparrows that flittered from tree to tree and the flight of swallows twisting in the sky high above. Payal, now off Leon's shoulders, was running around chasing the birds while Leon was pointing at something on the ground to Jared and Joshua. The leaves and flowers on the branches fluttered softly in the breath of a young spring breeze. Gabriel approached the group and spotted a plaque embedded in the grass.

He had memorized the words from his brother's letter from the night before. They came back to him now.

Dear Gabriel,

I'm not sure how old you are, reading my letter now for the first time.

I am putting it between the pages of my book, hoping at some point you will be the one to pick it up and be able to understand. I'm sorry. I'm sorry that I'm not strong enough to be there to protect you. I'm sorry I'm leaving you alone.

Please believe me that since I could remember, you've been the one person I wanted to be strong for. It's really been just the two of us. Mom and Dad are too busy hurting each other to know they are hurting us. But there were others who hurt me and wanted to hurt you, and I didn't know how to protect you. I hope you will forgive me one day. Remember always that I love you.

Your brother,

Daniel

66

"Let's go for a run," Raul said as he shook the saltwater from his black curls, directing the invitation to Gabriel. He disregarded his girlfriend at the time, one of the first of many, prone on her towel, the straps of her bikini undone, her skin bronzing under the Caribbean sun that blazed white in the pale sky. Gabriel looked up from his towel, cupping his hand to shade his eyes, and caught Raul's head of curly hair silhouetted by the sun. It had been a year since Danny's death, he'd already started to feel the void left by his father's abandonment in his mother's house, and Raul had called, spur of the moment, a day before the weeklong vacation down in Cancun. It had been almost a year since they'd seen each other, since the only words from Raul were those scribbled on the monthly checks for alimony and child support.

"Of course, Gabe would love to come," Isabelle had replied finally into the receiver, before stuffing several pairs of everything into a suitcase.

Gabriel stood up and ran to catch up to his father who had begun jogging along the beach; two sets of footprints in the wet sand, dotting a serpentine path along the strand. Despite the heat of the early afternoon sun, and his father's brisk pace, Gabriel kept up with Raul that afternoon, running past the resort hotels that clotted the shoreline.

If one were to have asked Gabriel why he ran with his father, he may not have known the answer. He was tired, thirsty, and a little hungry; there was nothing joyful in running, there was no interaction, no talk. One obvious answer was so that he could be with his father, or to get away from the bored, irritated thirty-something tanning herself at his father's expense. Or maybe it was because it was what his father had chosen to do, and there was something good in it, some useful purpose that would be discovered at the journey's end. And this was not an age to distrust one's father.

Or maybe it was time, time as a limited commodity, evanescent, and he ran to chase time, catch the fleeting moments before they passed him by. Or maybe he ran to escape time, to outrun it or the notion of it, because perhaps he had begun to suspect that time, along with other constructs, love, family, all woven together into the delicate meaningful fabric that he had once taken comfort in, was hollow and meaningless, and the fabric had begun to fray.

CPSIA information can be obtained
at www.ICGtesting.com
Printed in the USA
JSHW021051240423
40732JS00001B/24